MW01006671

River Of No Return

JOHNNY CARREY & CORT CONLEY

BACKEDDY BOOKS
P.O. Box 301
Cambridge, Idaho 83610

By John Carrey and Cort Conley
The Middle Fork and the Sheepeater War (Backeddy Books, 1977)

Hells Canyon

Library of Congress Cataloging in Publication Data

Carrey, John, 1914-
 River of no return.

  Bibliography: p.
  Includes index.
   1. Salmon River, Idaho — Description and travel — Guide-books.
2. Salmon River, Idaho — History. 3. Salmon Valley, Idaho — Description and travel — Guide-books. 4. Salmon Valley, Idaho —
History. 5. Boats and boating — Idaho — Salmon River. I. Conley,
Jim Cort, 1944-   Joint author. II. Title.
F752.S35C37   917.96'82   78-52373

Copyright © 1978 by Backeddy Books. All rights reserved. No part of
this book may be reproduced or transmitted in any form or by any
means, electronic or mechanical, including photocopying, recording,
or by any information storage and retrieval system, without written
permission of Backeddy Books.

"Read no history, read only biography, for it is life without theory."
Benjamin Disraeli

"… we must respect the past, remembering that once it was all that was humanly possible."
George Santayana

"There are two diametrically opposed forces forever at war in the heart of man: one is memory; the other is forgetfulness."
Loren Eiseley

This book is dedicated to the Salmon River people whose biographies braided the history of the River of No Return; people like: Sam James, Frank Lantz, Pete Klinkhammer, Bill Jackson, Doc Foskett, and Elmer Taylor — all true to their code as a circle to its center.

Contents

Acknowledgements

Considerable time has gone into the writing of this book. Every effort has been made to check names and facts. But as anyone who has listened to witnesses under oath in a court of law knows, nothing is so fallible as human memory. In many cases we were forced to choose between conflicting stories, taking that which seemed most plausible or cross-checked reliably.

We did this without intending any disrespect for our sources, realizing that at times we may have accepted half truths without hearing the proper half. Such are the limitations of oral history.

If a reader recognizes error or has additional information, we would be grateful for communication; it may someday be possible to print a revised edition.

Obviously even so modest a work as this could only have been accomplished with invaluable help from many people. We wish to express gratitude and sincere thanks to:

Pearl Carrey, Betty Smith, Jim Campbell, Anita Douglas, Paul and Marybelle Filer, Earl and Sharon Perry, Bob and Jill Smith, Norm and Joyce Close, Frank and Hazel Rood, Jerry Hughes and Carole Finley, Don and Marian Smith, Herb and Madge St. Clair, Maisie and Jay Shuck, Babe Marie Brinkley, John and June Cook, Fred and Edna Shiefer, Duane, Marney, and Carole Garrett (of Garrett Photography, Boise, for invaluable help in copying historic photographs), Sister Alfreda Elsensohn, Ethel Kimball, George Mancini and Karen Hopfenbeck, Boyd Norton, Homer and Mary Rhett, Dr. Merle Wells, Harold and Alice Hanson, Adele Armstrong, Gay and Ralph Robie, Lois Geumlek, Bob and Jan Sevy, Lum Turner, Ace Barton, Bill Lassiter, Phil Remaklus, Rex Coppernoll, Sylvan Hart, Everett Van Arsdale, Loy Hollenbeak, Bill Olson, Hugh Eminger, Derl Hollenbeak, Ed and Mabel Altman, Lucile Howard-Kelly, Alice Rickman, Alice and Ronnie Mahurin, Don Nitz, Josephine Patterson, Gladys McLaughlin, Elmer and Eva Taylor, Walt Dailey,

Catherine Wildt, Ben Large, Frank Sotin, Laura Clark, Emma Patterson, Rheo Wolfe, Joe L. Roberts, Afton Rogers, Eva Lancaster, Dave Sumner, Glen Wooldridge, Robert Conley, Allen Say, Betty Dopf, Ray Holes, Frank Elder, Verne Shreve, Jim Moorhead, Kathy Cramer, Al Deffler, Gary and Laurii Gadwa, Selway Mulkey, Leo and Opal Fallon, Anna McHan, Stella Critchfield, Bob Johnson, Dave Giles, Joyce Rovetto, Cyril Neecer, Mike Wilkins, Hank and Sharon Miller, Don Hatch, Glen Hegsted, Frank Butschke, Burt Bunch, Kathy Jones, Bill Sullivan, Elmer Keith, Marge Williams, Don Taylor, Roger Sliker, Idaho County Free Press, Salmon Recorder-Herald, Idaho State Historical Society, Montana Historical Society, U.S. Forest Service, Smithsonian Institution, Intermountain State Bank.

Introduction

This book is intended as a historical guide for persons traveling on, or alongside, the waters of the Salmon River. It is the first attempt to gather a fairly comprehensive history of events on this major American waterway. The authors hope that this work will add a dimension to trips made down the river, a dimension which until now, has been largely neglected.

The *River of No Return* opens with a survey of piloting exploits on the river, beginning with William Clark's appraisal in 1805. Extensive quotations convey a sense of the Salmon as observed through the eyes of early passengers with the first boatmen in wooden boats. Railroad surveys are included as well. The section concludes with motorized trips returning upstream.

The guide portions of the text begin at the base of Galena Summit, on the headwaters of the Salmon, and continue in a general, descriptive manner to North Fork. Events which occurred within easy reach of the road are discussed. There are capsule histories of towns encountered in route.

At North Fork, north of the city of Salmon, the writing becomes considerably more specific: drainages on both sides of the river are treated on a mileage basis, name derivations are given where possible, and history of the sites is related. Locations are given in miles-distant from the headwaters, and in terms of right or left, facing downstream, since most people prefer such directions over compass points.

Readers may notice that the names of women relevant to the text often go unmentioned. Such undeserved obscurity is an unfortunate adjunct to oral history; their names can no longer be recalled. Men are more prominent in the narrative simply because they outnumbered women — according to census figures, by fifty to one. That women appear in the boating section only as writers and passengers again reflects the period's social structure. Though still disproportionately represented, enough women now row the river that their competence as guides is unquestioned.

At the time this book was completed, U.S. Geological Survey maps did not exist for major portions of the canyon. While the mileages on the maps drawn for this history are approximate, they are more accurate than those of the Forest Service map or the Columbia Basin Inter-Agency Committee's river-mile index.

Events concerning several ranches along the river are detailed. Travelers should keep in mind that these ranches are private property and that anyone who enters without invitation is committing a trespass.

There are objects and locations within the river corridor whose vulnerability outweighs disclosure. In the same light, we ask that you conscientiously refrain from removing any article from sites in the canyon. What may be only a souvenir to you might be of great interest to the next party. Please leave it where you found it. Thoughtless people, even on guided trips, have already caused much irreparable damage.

The book is published at a time when the sons and daughters of Salmon River pioneers are being supplanted by their grandchildren, and when Idaho is experiencing an influx of newcomers unlike any since the gold rush. The authors recognized that the sources of early river history were disappearing faster than quarters in a poker game. The pages that follow are a result of that concern. Of necessity, the scope of the undertaking was limited to riparian lands and tributary streams.

Information was gathered over a period of years and miles of travel: in interviews, libraries, bars, resthomes, cemeteries, newspaper files, county records, scrapbooks, photo albums — As Johnny Carrey says, "It wasn't written sitting down."

Samuel Johnson once remarked that there were only two reasons for one to write: "... in order to make man better able to enjoy life, or better able to endure it." If any journey is made more pleasant by the knowledge here conveyed, then the task was well worthwhile.

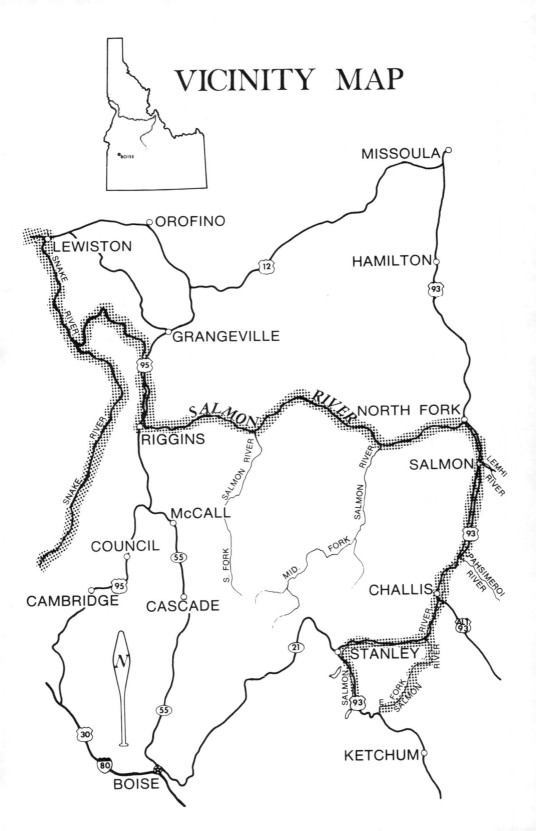

VICINITY MAP

Boatmen on the Salmon

It has been remarked that history is the bed carved by the river of life. That being true, few western canyons can claim a river-bed so deeply incised as that of the Salmon: River of No Return. Recent archaeological excavations indicate prehistoric ancestors of the Nez Perce and Northern Shoshoni lived in the Salmon River Canyon nearly 8500 years ago. Their Nez Perce descendants named the river Natsoh Koos: Chinook-Salmon-Water, and the Shoshoni came to call it Agaimpaa: Big-Fish-Water. These Indians apparently found the river too turbulent for canoes; their trails down tributary streams gave them access to the canyon.

The first white men acquainted with the river were members of the Lewis and Clark Expedition in the summer of 1805. While Captain Lewis negotiated with the Shoshoni for horses, William Clark scouted north-westward from the Lemhi Valley, hoping to discover a river route that would prove easier than arduous land travel. Clark had been informed by Indians that the waters would not yield to canoes, but being an explorer, he had to see for himself.

On August 22, 1805, his journal entry reads:

> The men who passed by the forks informed me that the SW. fork was double the Size of the one I cam down, and I observed that it was a handsom river at my camp. I shall in justice to Capt. Lewis who was the first white man ever on this fork of the Columbia Call this Louis's river.

Clark and his 11 men were camped at the lower point of an island, about three miles down-river from the site now occupied by the community of North Fork. The next day's entry states:

> ...proceed on with great dificuelty as the rocks were So sharp large and unsettled and the hill sides Steep that the horses could with the greatest risque and dificulty get on, at 4 miles we came to a place the horses Could not pass

1

without going into the river, we passed one mile to a very bad riffle the water confined in a narrow Channel & beeting against the left Shore, as we have no parth further and the Mounts. jut So close as to prevent the possibility of horses proceeding down, I Deturmined to delay the party here and with my guide and three men proceed on down to examine if the river continued bad or was practicable, I set out with three men directing those left to hunt and fish untill my return. I proceeded on. Sometimes in a Small wolf parth & at other times Climing over the rocks for 12 miles to a large Creek on the right Side above the mouth of this Creek for a Short distance is a narrow bottom & the first, below the place I left my party. The River from the place I left my party to this Creek is almost one continued rapid, five verry considerable rapids the passage of either with Canoes is entirely impossible, as the water is Confined between huge Rocks & the Current beeting from one against another for Some distance below &c. &c. at one of those rapids the mountains close so Clost as to prevent a possibility of a portage with (out) great labour in cutting down the Side of the hill removeing large rocks &c. &c. all the others may be passed by takeing every thing over slipery rocks, and the Smaller ones Passed by letting down the Canoes empty with Cords, as running them would certainly be productive of the loss of Some Canoes, those dificulties and necessary precautions would delay us an emence time in which provisions would be necessary.

below this Creek the lofty Pine is thick in the bottom hill Sides on the mountains & up the runs. The river has much the resemblance of that above bends Shorter and no passing after a few miles between the river & the mountains & the Current so Strong that (it) is dangerous crossing the river, and to proceed down it would rend. it necessary to Cross almost at every bend. this river is about 100 yards wide and can be forded but in a few places. below my guide and maney other Indians tell me that the Mountains Close and is a perpendicular Clift on each Side, and Continues for a great distance and that the water runs with great violence from one rock to the other on each Side foaming & roreing thro rocks in every direction, So as to

2

render the passage of any thing impossible. those rapids which I had Seen he said was Small & trifleing in comparrison to the rocks & rapids below, at no great distance & The Hills or mountains were not like those I had Seen but like the Side of a tree Streight up. we proceeded on a well beeten Indian parth up this creak (Berry Creek) about 6 miles and passed over a ridge 1 mile to the river in a Small vally through which we passed and assended a Spur of the Mountain from which place my guide Shewed me the river for about 20 miles lower & pointed out the dificulties.

The following day, Captain Clark sent a man on horseback with a letter for Lewis, outlining two plans for proceeding toward the Columbia. That evening he wrote in his journal:

... every man appeared disheartened from the prospects of the river, and nothing to eate, I Set out late and Camped 2 miles above, nothing to eate but Choke Cherries & red haws, which act in different ways So as to make us Sick, dew verr heavy, my beding wet in passing around a rock the horses were obliged to go deep into the water.

The plan I stated to Capt Lewis if he agrees with me we shall adopt it. to procure as many horses (one for each man) if possible and to hire my present guide who I sent on to him to interigate thro' the Intptr. and proceed on by land to Some navagable part of the Columbia River, or to the Ocean, depending on what provisions we can procure by the gun aded to the Small Stock we have on hand depending on our horses as the last resort.

a second plan to divide the party one part to attempt this deficuelte river with what provisions we had, and the remainder to pass by Land on horse back Depending on our gun &c. for Provisions &c. and come together occasionally on the river. the 1st of which I would be most pleased with &c.

Meriwether Lewis agreed with Clark's first suggestion and the expedition left the Salmon, moving north over the Lost Trail Pass. The "justice" or memorial William Clark left his friend Lewis proved ephemeral. Maps made in 1810, though confused about the direction of its flow, were already calling this river "The Salmon."

A curious inscription on a rock at Barth Hot Springs, about 30 miles below the mouth of the Middle Fork, is the source of a story about an 1827 trapper considered the first man to float the Salmon — presumably in a bull boat. Those who repeated the story neglected to carefully examine the inscription itself. The rock is exposed during low flows in late summer and early fall and the engraving on it reads: "THE FLAPPER OCT 18-27." Clearly there is a hyphen cut between the 18 and the 27. Monroe Hancock, an early boatman noticed and publicized the inscription in 1935.

Because of the hyphen, and because 1927 fell within the era of the "flapper" it seemed reasonable to conclude the graffito was the work of a woman passenger on a Salmon scow in the fall of 1927. Passengers on earlier trips left their names on boulders around the spring: E V Reynolds NY 10-1918, S W Harris AD 1919.

The mystery arises from mention of the inscription by George Shoup in a manuscript he wrote, probably about 1940 — even his 10 page holograph can't be dated with certainty.

Shoup was an old-timer, a careful observer and thoughtful historian. He and his party were navigating the river in an 8x16 foot scow and stopped at Guleke Hot Springs, as they were then called. He wrote, "We observed this carving, and others, and our own before we left." He continued, "Though we had well versed historians of the NW the only conclusion was to attribute this being an event of a scout (and of companion) during the thorough exploring by the Hudson's Bay Co. & large personnel of the entire regions of Idaho..." Shoup's name at the hot springs is last in a column of six and is dated 10-3-1919.

If he observed the Flapper inscription in 1919, then the puzzle is far from solved.

The first men to travel the river *were* trappers, but they belonged to John Work's Snake River Expedition and the year was 1832. Work was a Hudson Bay Company factor and brought a trapping brigade into the Lemhi Valley that year. From his camp on the river, a few miles south of the present townsite of Salmon, he recorded in his journal:

> "Sunday, March 25 (1832). Did not raise camp. Four men are preparing to descend the river in a canoe to hunt this evening to the fort (Walla Walla). It is expected they will make a good hunt. Several more Indians visited us."

"Monday, March 26. Fine weather. Raised camp and proceeded eight miles up the river. Four men, L. Boisdnt, A. Dumaris, H. Plante and J. Laurin, left in a small skin canoe to descend the river and hunt their way down. It is expected they will make a good hunt as this part of the river is not known to have ever been hunted by whites.

John Work's men continued to trap and explore Central Idaho. His men on the Salmon, however, experienced hardships. There may have been ice bridges across the river; certainly the water would have been deathly cold. The next reference to the men and canoes reads:

"July 19. The report we have among the Snakes regarding our men who descended the Salmon River being drowned, unfortunately turns out to be true. M. Plante and A. Dumaris were drowned. L. Biosdnt and I. J. Baptise were walking ashore their turn, and escaped and reached the fort (Nez Perce) quite naked. Everything they had, being in the canoe, was lost. The unfortunate accident happened when they were just getting out of the bad road. How it happened the survivors could not tell as they did not see it but found the paddles. The canoe it seems was too small to carry all their baggage and themselves and they walked along their turn about. They had been descending the river more than 30 days and notwithstanding the account we had of beaver they found none. Some of the Nez Perce Indians whom they fell in with after their misfortune, treated the survivors with the utmost kindness."

The most enigmatic figure among the early Salmon River boatmen is John McKay. He was a native of Scotland and a skilled millwright by trade. The taciturn Scotsman once confided the reason for his arrival in the Salmon canyon to Herb St. Clair, of Salmon, Idaho. McKay had constructed a large mill for a company and proudly invited his young wife to inspect it. During her visit her skirt was caught by a flywheel and she was dragged to her death before the machinery could be halted. Broken-hearted, Johnny McKay turned placer miner and recluse along the River of No Return.

Each spring in Salmon City he built a small wooden scow, with sweep blades at each end. Carrying months of supplies which could be adequately supplemented with fish and game, he worked his way down river, placering for gold at sandbars and side streams. McKay would build a little hut, sometimes with the lumber from his boat,

Johnny McKay on the Salmon River in 1912.

McKay's scow upstream, and Guleke's scow below. Cap had stopped to visit the old miner.

and winter in the canyon. Often he would travel down river as far as Lewiston.

By spring he would be back in Salmon, trading his gold for supplies and preparing for the next trip. In this manner he is known to have descended the river at least 20 times.

Lee Miller floated the River of No Return as a passenger in a sweep boat in August of 1920. He had a brief encounter with Johnny McKay. The article he wrote a year later provides a remarkable glimpse of this solitary miner:

"And I gie them the sign," said John McKay, "I gie them the sign — and they knew me."

Under the gray brows, the keen eyes of the Scotchman, the veteran of the Salmon River, flashed. His voice took on a vibrant tone.

"Wild mountain sheep they were," said John McKay, "wild yoes. Two years had slipped awa'," said he dramatically, "two years! And I gie them the sign. And they knew me!"

We sat about the little flat boat of the old miner, Walter; Alethea, whom we dubbed Main Marion; Henry Harty, whom we called The Jersey Lily; My Lady Brown Eyes, who had been promptly nicknamed Precious, and I, of whom they had irreverently spoken as The Bishop. Captain Harry Guleke, who had guided our boat through the treacherous waters of the Salmon River, lingered near, and Percy Anderson, mate, guide and naturalist, sat beside John McKay, while in the rear, and making a substantial background, stood Charley Dodge, our three-hundred-pound cook.

These three made up the ship's crew of the good boat "Precious" and we the passengers. And all the way down the Salmon River, bisecting the great State of Idaho, we had heard of John McKay, the veteran miner of the Salmon River canyon and of his forty-eight years of struggle and adventing on that lonely and dangerous stream.

For weeks we had adventured down The Forbidden River, had successfully negotiated without shipwreck Skookemchuck Rapids, had gone over Salmon Falls unscathed, had shot unharmed past the deadly whirlpools of The Whiplash, had dodged the menacing rocks of Big Mallard, and dozens of unnamed falls and rapids, and now, at the lower end of the canyon we had come upon the most romantic figure of that remote country, John McKay, and sat on and about his little boat, listening with eager ears.

7

"It was a mony a-year agone," said John McKay, swinging his old California gold rocker or cradle rhythmically. "I was minin' on Lone Pine Bar near the Middle Fork. I had struck a fine pay streak and the gold in my little buckskin bag was pilin' up. Spring had come and the flowers were bloomin'. It was a day in June, when out upon the canyon wall a thousand feet above me came the three mountain sheep. And I gie them the sign."

Always when he said these words he straightened up and his eyes glowed.

"And I said to mysel', I'll nae feed them, I'll nae gie them salt. Only will I use the sign to make them know me."

Each of us was wondering what the sign might be; none dared speak, fearing to break the thread of the narrative.

"All summer long they came and looked down upon me," said he, "and every day when they came out upon the cliff I'd gie them the sign. And the gold kept pilin' up in the buckskin bag."

The far-away look in his eye betokened a mental picture of that distant summer.

"And fall came and winter," said John McKay, "and I built a little cabin and laid by the rocker for awhile. And the three yoes which had been comin' down lower upon the cliff came no more.

"Winter passed," said he, "and spring came and with the flowers came the three mountain sheep. And the three yoes had three little lammies wi' them. And I gie them the sign. Summer passed. The pay streak held, the buckskin bag grew heavy. And the three yoes came near, and the three lammies played around my cabin door. And always I would gie them the sign.

"And winter came again, and spring," said John McKay, "and when the yoes returned there were three more lammies. Now there were nine; and I gie them the sign and they knew me."

As we watched him we thought of the years of adventure and patient toil behind him, of the long forgotten hopes of wealth that had been his. We remembered the story of the Scotchman coming from the land of heather a youngster, first to New Brunswick, then Vermont, then Nevada. Here a faint rumor hints of a young wife, of fortune smiling upon him, of a big future looming, then of the tragic death of the bride and of John McKay lost to the world in the remote and lonely Salmon River canyon.

It was hard to realize that this erect, vigorous Scotchman, leading his active, lonely life cheerfully, unafraid, always with the Great Reward just around the bend, had been there forty-eight years. More than twenty complete trips through the canyon he has made in the forty-eight years of placer mining, always returning to enter the canyon again at Salmon City to begin another two- or three-year voyage down The Forbidden River, seeking gold.

"And that summer the surveyors came," said he, "and I told them of my mountain sheep and asked them not to harm them. The chief engineer promised — and he kept his promise. But one day a young mon o' the party, a bad mon, whispered to the cook: 'I can kill a lamb, and it will be fine eating.' And the cook looked at him wi' scorn in his eye and said, 'Kill a lamb and you'll cook it yoursel'. I'll nae cook it for ye. And I'll nae cook ye anither bite in this canyon.' So said the cook, who was a gude mon. And the young man was ashamed. And so no harm came to my sheep.

"Winter came," said John McKay, "and my pay streak ended; and I drifted on down the Salmon River. And two years later I was back again on Lone Pine Bar, and it was summer. And out on the cliffs came three mountain sheep. The lammies were gone, but I recognized my old yoes. And I gie them the sign and they knew me."

Tears of pride were in his voice as he told of these wild mountain friends. And our eyes were misty.

"And ye'll be wondering about the sign," said John McKay. Indeed we were wondering — but feared to ask. "It was but this," said he simply, "I held my arm high above my head, my right arm, and waived my hand gently to and fro, but they knew it for my sign an' they knew me."

And in his story John McKay had painted a picture of his own kind, wandering life among the mountains and the wild things that know him there.

McKay was last seen along the Salmon below Riggins, trundling his possessions in a wheelbarrow. Herb St. Clair said that McKay finally went to San Diego, California, and was never heard from again.

In any event, the Scotsman left his name in the canyon of the Salmon. There is a J. N. McK 1872 inscription on a rock facing the river near McKay Creek, a similar mark dated 1907, at Cove Creek, by the grave next to the road, and a third engraving: J. N. McKay 1872 + 1905 + 1911, on a rock at Barth Hot Springs. The letters are chiseled with the skill of a man deft at dressing stone. They are mute testimony to the life and legend of Johnny McKay.

By curious coincidence, other eyes focused with interest on the Salmon River canyon the year John McKay chose to begin his half-century of riparian residence. The Northern Pacific Railroad Company (now the Burlington Northern) was looking for a route from Montana, across Idaho to Washington. The proposed new route was to enter Washington by way of Lake Pend d'Oreille, in northern Idaho. The board of directors of the Northern Pacific had decided that a route might be found through the Rocky Mountains that was enough shorter to warrant its adoption over that of Pend d'Oreille. With this in mind, they ordered extensive surveys of the Clearwater and Salmon River canyons.

In 1872, survey parties were organized under the direction of Northern Pacific's chief engineer, A. Milnor Roberts. He selected Col. W. W. DeLacy, C. E., as the most competent man to conduct the Salmon River survey.

The Colonel assembled a party of 25 men and built four boats in Salmon. They left on June 15. The story is best told by the newspaper accounts of the time:

"Idaho Signal," Lewiston, July 20, 1872

In another column we publish an account of some of the North Pacific railroad surveys which are being progressed this summer. Among these is the service being performed by Col. DeLacy down Salmon river to Lewiston. The Idaho *Standard* mentions the presence of the Col. at Salmon City on June 6, with his engineer, preparing boats in which he was to start down the river in 2 or 3 days.

(This indicates that the N.P. has not yet decided which is the best route, or they would not be going to the expense

McKay's inscription on a rock at Barth
Hot Springs.

Johnny McKay in 1920, rocking for gold
on the river. A full day's work might put
three yards of gravel through the rocker.

of these several surveys: Salmon river, Clearwater river
and Pend d'Oreille.)

... Again, the survey of a line along down Salmon river,
almost parallel with other surveys north of it, cannot be
reasonably considered for the purpose of a tributary
branch of the main trunk, for after leaving the Lemhi
valley it would traverse a distance of from 350 to 400 miles
in a canyon of the river, where no strips of bottom or table
land are found suited to habitation for any large number of
population, and where the abrupt mountains on either side
are continuously from two to 5000 feet above the water of
the river, and the country receding back from their summits for many miles on either side is broken and abrupt,
and ill-suited to settlement, and hence incapable of fur-
nishing business for a railroad, and the lands of little value
to the company. Hence the only object that company can
reasonably be supposed to have in making this survey is to
determine the practicability of the Salmon river low pass
through these mountains as the route of their main trunk.
"Idaho Signal," Lewiston, August 3, 1872

Colonel Walter W. DeLacy in 1886, age 66 years. He learned civil engineering and topography at West Point, and before undertaking the Northern Pacific survey down Salmon River, he had done topographical work on the staked plains of Texas, the Isthmus of Tehuantepec, the thirty-second parallel of latitude from San Antonio to San Diego, and at Puget Sound. DeLacy served with the Texas Rangers, fought in the Yakima Indian War, and laid out the townsite of Fort Benton, Montana.

"Northern Pacific Railroad." The Boise *Statesman* of the 27th ult., contains the following:

This week we publish a letter from Col. Shoup stating that Co. DeLacy had built 4 boats at Salmon City, and was actually surveying a route down the Salmon, and that another corps of engineers were surveying from the east side of the mountains into Lemhi valley. Col. Shoup calls this a branch road. Either this is a mistake, or the N.P. co. have conceived the idea of diverging at or a little east of the Rocky mountains and running the main line by Pend d'Oreille lake and a branch through Lemhi valley and down Salmon river, and either follow down Snake river to the mouth, or cross as soon as they get below the Blue Mountains, somewhere near the mouth of the Sonton, and keep directly west to Walla Walla and thence to Pendleton, through the Umatilla valley and on down to the Dalles. There are many reasons for believing this is a matured plan of the company, if the country is practicable for building the road. It is a gradual plain from Salmon up the Lemhi to the summit of the Rocky mountains. There are no obstacles to encounter except in descending the Salmon river. In distance it would be a great saving. No route could be found so short by 100 or 200 miles. There are very many small valleys along the Salmon, of great value when the road is built, and a large amount of good timber, but the general character of the country is as rugged and broken as any on the coast. This route would open up the quartz mines in the central portion of our Territory, and the country though so rugged and barren, would be rich in the production of gold and silver. There is much hope that this route will be adopted, and we congratulate our Lemhi, Warren's, Camas Prairie and Salmon river friends on the probable chances of a railroad. We shall not feel envious of our neighbors if they get a road first, but wish them all the success imaginable.

"Idaho Signal," Lewiston, 14 Sept. 1872 p3

"Col. DeLacy at Warrens." From our regular correspondent at Warrens we learn that Col. DeLacy of the N.P.R.R. surveying party, coming down Salmon river, arrived in Warrens on the 11th inst. He reports the distance from Salmon City to the junction of the south fork with the main Salmon to be 120 miles, and the difficulties of the route not by any means insurmountable.

Idaho Signal, 28 Sept. 1872 p1

"Letter from Warrens" From our regular Correspondent. Warrens, I.T., Sept. 18, 1872 Editor I.S.: As I mentioned in my last, Col. DeLacy and Col. Long, of the N.P.R.R. engineers, were in town last week. They came in for supplies, mail matter & etc., and returned last Friday. The balance of the party, 23 in number, were camped at the mouth of the South Fork. The party left Salmon City June 15 and arrived at the forks Sept. 8, averaging, as near as may be, a mile and a half a day — working time. They ran this line of survey on the south side of the river, crossing to the north side 7 miles above the forks. They speak rather encouragingly of it as a route for a railroad. They say it is rough, which all who are acquainted with this river are aware of, of course, but think the grading ought not to cost more than the average of the line elsewhere. It will be a slow route Col. DeLacy says, on account of the continual curves one way and the other, there not being so much as a half mile of straight line in a piece on the part yet surveyed; but the difficulties of curve and grading will be in a measure offsetted by the fact that it is 100 miles shorter, and may reach 200, than any other proposed route, and the further advantage that it is wholly free from snow in the Winter. They expect to reach the wire bridge in about 2 weeks. They have several boats and 12 boatmen.

I gather the following statistics: The distance from Salmon City to the mouth of the South Fork is 120 miles and a fraction; from Napias creek to South Fork, 75 miles. The altitude of the mouth of the South Fork is a little over 2300 feet. Warrens is 6120 feet high. The ridge at the head of Slaughter creek, on the trail between here and the forks, is 8160 feet high. I didn't learn the average grade of the part of the river surveyed.

With you in Lewiston a railroad surveying party is probably not much of a novelty, but all our citizens agree that this one is a matter of some consequence to us.

"Idaho Signal," Lewiston, Oct. 19, 1872 p2

"Salmon River Survey." Henry Elfers, Esq. of John Day creek, arrived in town on Friday eve. From him we learn the following facts in relation to the survey of the Salmon river route by Col. DeLacy of the N.P. engineers. When Elfers left John Day's the survey had been completed as far as the canyon just above the mouth of Slate creek, and would be completed to a point below the mouth of Slate creek today. The distance from Salmon City to the forks of Salmon is 120 miles; thence to the wire bridge about 20 miles; thence to the mouth of Slate creek about 36 miles, making the entire distance from Salmon City to Slate creek about 176 miles. Elfers says that Col. DeLacy expresses himself as highly pleased with the route; that he has found it entirely practicable; that he has found but 2 places where there would be any danger from slides, and these could be easily guarded against; that the blasting for the grade would be nothing in comparison with what he anticipated when he commenced the survey; that there would be some short curves, though none to impose a barrier which could not be overcome by skillful engineering. The sides and summits of the mountains on either side of the river for the whole distance contain an abundance of good timber for railroad construction, and not a single mile of the entire road would ever be liable to obstruction from snows in the Winter.

The Col. says if the measured distance from his present point to Lewiston via the mouth of Salmon river and down Snake river be proportionately less with that from Salmon City to Slate creek, from former estimates, he will be able to reach Lewiston inside of 80 miles, thus making the entire distance from Salmon City to Lewiston along the Salmon and Snake rivers 250 miles.

The Bozeman Pass, through which the road is to be constructed from the head of the Yellowstone, is in the same latitude with Salmon City, and the distance only about 150 miles, so that by the Salmon River route the whole distance from Lewiston to the point where the road first touches the Yellowstone will be about 400 miles. From the Bozeman Pass to the head of the Pend d'Oreille Lake by

15

the northern route is about 450 miles. Thence to the mouth of the Snake 225 miles. Thus the Salmon River route saves a distance of 135 miles.

Colonel DeLacy must have been guarding his opinions when he expressed himself to Henry Elfers. His true evaluation of the route was contained in the telegram he sent Milnor Roberts, which Roberts quoted in his report to the president of Northern Pacific a week later:

Portland, Oct. 25th, 1872

Gen. Geo. W. Cass

President,

Dear Sir:

My latest advices from DeLacy's party are dated at Slate Creek on Salmon River expressed to Walla Walla and telegraphed to me at Kalama: Answer to my telegraph, expressed.

"Telegram received — Reached John Days river yesterday with survey, one hundred eighty miles from Salmon City. Get here tomorrow with survey. Estimated distance from John Day's River to mouth of Salmon fifty-five miles: thence to Lewiston forty miles, (called) (It is certainly more, if Maps are of any value there.) Calling it as here assumed 55 to the mouth of Salmon, and 40 to the mouth of Clear Fork at Lewiston, it gives a total from the head of the Missouri River (common point) via the Salmon River route to Olympia 994 miles.

Via Lake Pend d'Oreille and Columbia River 986 miles — Difference 8 miles.

Still, in favor of Clark's Fork of Columbia River route, via Lake Pend d'Oreille.

Col. DeLacy reports general features of Salmon River. From Salmon City to Napias Creek 46 miles, rock slopes one to one, some rock points requiring tunnels, a few flats, three or four bridges, cuts and fills, light curves, not sharp. From Napias Creek to Shessler's old ferry, 104 miles, all rock; one third loose, two thirds solid rock, with many rocky points to be tunneled, very difficult country. Line run on South side of river North side clearly impracticable. Average grade about 18 feet per mile, all rock work: but line can be much improved on location.

16

From Shessler's Ferry to State Creek, 36 miles. Country much more open, with many flats and bars; rock soft and easily worked; sharp bends in river, many require short tunnels. Farming carried on.

General result; line practicable with large amount of rough and expensive work. Very little soil any where on river. Some slides occur on South side; are rare. River, with many bends, runs nearly west from Salmon City to Little Salmon, then turns north, nearly. Curves on line not generally sharp or long, but short tangents everywhere. Slopes generally steep.

Col. DeLacy expects to reach Lewiston by end of November.

Very respectfully yours,

(Sgnd) A. Milnor Roberts,

Chief engineer

The newspaper accounts, however, continued to carry a sanguine tone.

"Idaho Signal," Lewiston, North Idaho, November 2, 1872, p2

"Salmon River Survey By the Northern Pacific Railroad"

We have before made brief mention of the progress of the railroad survey down Salmon River. By the numerous routes which the Northern Pacific Company are causing to be surveyed through the high ranges of mountains between the extremes of their contemplated road (before they commence construction through any one of them) they are evincing a prudent foresight far different from that of the Union Pacific, and one which promises the construction of a road where nature has provided the best route. Should a road be built over this route the Upper Salmon Valley, the Bitter Root Valley, the Beaver Head, the Payette, and little Salmon Valleys, and even the Wallowa and Grand Ronde Valleys, all of which are good agricultural valleys, would be immediately tributaries to it, while at the same time it would be in close proximity to the rich quartz districts which have been partially developed at various points in the Salmon range of mountains. If it be true that the engineers on the northern route have already exceeded

17

their limit of grade per mile, and are unable to proceed without extending that limit further, and the Salmon River route proves not only about *one-fourth* of the limit given, there is the best of reason for supposing that the sagacity, as well as economy of the Company, will dictate the construction of their road over the Salmon River route.

DeLacy's survey arrived in Lewiston on November 16. Theirs was a remarkable accomplishment. A list of the members of the crew appeared in the city's paper:

"Idaho Signal," Lewiston, November 23, 1872 (Saturday) p3

"The Surveying Party"

The following comprises the members of the party under Col. DeLacy, which arrived here last Sunday Morning (Nov. 16):

Chief Engineer, Col. W. W. DeLacy;

Compassman, Christopher Billop;

leveler, Wm. Gibson;

Topographer, Leslie Wilkie;

commissary, Col. Thos. Long;

chainmen, John Irwin and H. Twogood;

rodmen, W. Llewellan and Edward Gibson;

cooks, J. Howland and H. Fisk;

axmen, U. G. Everist and J. M. Kirkendall;

boatmen, Charles Scoffin 1, Henry Burnham 2, Jerry Stinson 3, Morris Smith 4, Pratt Stedman, T. Rossmussen, Thos Williams, C. Julholland, Chas. Rich, Frank House, John Hays and R. White.

The above company have been upwards of 5 months on the survey of the Salmon River route, a very difficult work and heretofore considered a dangerous one, and have not had a quarrel nor an accident during the whole trip. The only loss suffered was having a pet dog die. Great credit is due Col. DeLacy and his skill as chief, and to all their subordinates for their fidelity and obediance to orders.

The press was quick to laud the achievement and equally eager to push the advantages of the Salmon River route:

"Idaho Signal," Nov. 23, 1872, p2
"The Salmon River Survey"

Col. DeLacy's survey of Salmon River has de-
monstrated the fact, that the construction of a railroad
down that river is not an impossibility, nor even a work
impracticable. The character of the route is so much better
than has heretofore been supposed, that even the most
difficult portions of it may be considered trifling compared
with our previous conceptions. We learn that the party
have not at any point been obliged to drop the line of
survey, but have been enabled to survey a continuous line
of levels for distances from Salmon City to within two
miles of Snake River, a distance of 248 miles, the average
grade of the river for this entire distance being only 12.22
feet per mile. That portion below White Bird Creek, a point
197 miles below Salmon City, being the most difficult.

The greatest barrier to the construction of this road is
about 20 miles of the distance just above the mouth on
Salmon River, and just below the mouth on Snake River.
We learn that this would require almost a continuous
tunneling to keep the uniformity of the grade. The point at
the mouth of White Bird is about 63 miles distant from this
place via Camas Prairie while the mouth of Salmon is 53
miles distant from White Bird, and 45 from this point; so
that in case the road could leave the Salmon River and
cross direct to this point, there would be a saving of 35
miles distance.

The obstacle in the way of coming direct is in getting a
railroad grade out of the canyon of the river to Camas
Prairie. We have the opinion of several connected with this
survey, and of those who have made observation of the
place, that the ascent can be made by leaving Salmon
River at the mouth of Slate Creek and entering the prairie
from Rocky Canyon, and that this ascent can be more
easily made, and at less cost, than the construction via
mouth of Salmon.

We learn that a pass in the mountains to Salmon River
from the east, reaching the river a few miles below Salmon
City (N. Fork?), has been found, whose elevation is only a
little above 5000 feet above sea level, and the distance

through this pass comparatively short. If this be so, the advantages which this route presents over all others yet surveyed, are not to be despised by that Company. All claim that it saves 150 miles of distance as compared with the Pend d'Oreille or Coeur d'Alene routes; that it will always be below the snow line; that it will have a permanent and dry road-bed when once constructed; that its grade will be less and more uniform than any other; that it will be more on a latitude with the Bozeman Pass and draw some support from sources which otherwise would flow into the Union and Central Pacific or Dalles and Salt Lake road, would it be constructed, and that it will open up a mineral country which no other road can ever do, which will add greatly to its support.

It has some disadvantages, such as it will require more time to construct it, and the cost per mile will be much greater, and for 200 miles of the distance the lands adjacent will not be so valuable for agricultural settlers. The more eastern part has, however, large quantities of excellent timber which would be of great value to the Company in case the road should be built. But everybody wants to know whether this road will ever be built. Those must be asked who know and are willing to give the information. These engineers don't assume to know. They make their observations and surveys and report the data to the Company who alone can determine. What of these data we get hold of and contrast with such as we receive from other surveys, may enable us to approximate to a conclusion, which may be as near correct as that of most of the engineers in the field.

We have reason to believe that this road will ultimately be built by that Company, but not before a road over the northern route. When built, however, it will be the greatest transcontinental route of the Company, and will not be excelled by any in speed and permanence, and freedom from obstruction occasioned by winters in this north latitude.

But the survey had proved that the Salmon and Clearwater routes were impractical and slightly longer than the Clark's Fork-Pend d'Oreille track. More importantly, there were economic advantages to the northern route: access to the rich ores of the Coeur d'Alene region, immense stands of timber on both sides of the lake, and more potential towns and markets requiring railroad services.

A. Milnor Roberts wrote a summary of the survey which might be considered covert tribute to the men and the canyon:

This survey down the Salmon river may I think be regarded as the most difficult instrumental survey ever made in the United States. The route on the eastern side of the mountain to connect with the Salmon river, which was admirably surveyed by M. T. Burgess, C.E., presented no extraordinary difficulties other than heavy grades and some costly work; but the survey through the Salmon River Valley — if Valley it can be styled, was a series of extraordinary and ingenious labors in overcoming great natural obstacles. And when this remarkable and hazardous survey was finished and connected at the common point near the mouth of Snake River, instead of being many miles shorter, as some had anticipated, it proved to be 12 miles longer than the route via Helena, and vastly inferior in every element of a railroad with a much higher summit, heavier grades, more curvature, much greater cost, and running through a region so utterly forbidding as to afford no hope of any local business, with the name. In every reasonable sense it is an impracticable route.

A search of the Burlington Northern and Minnesota State Historical Society archives failed to turn up a single photograph from the survey. It is possible none were taken.

Placer mining gave way to hard rock mining in Idaho by the 1880's. Mining interests began to develop at Shoup on the Salmon River about 1882. Lacking roads, machinery and supplies arrived by trail on pack strings which hauled from Carmen, near Salmon. It wasn't long before men were studying the river road, wondering whether it might not offer easier and quicker transport than horse and mule.

Men like Jim Compton, Josiah Chase, and Tom Savage built scows to haul stamp mill equipment to the Kentuck mine. John Parody built a flat-bottomed scow in the fall of 1883 and made a successful freight run from the mouth of Fourth of July Creek to Shoup. He sold the boat for its lumber and returned to Salmon on horseback. A pattern had been established.

In the years that followed the Salmon newspaper, the *Idaho Recorder,* frequently listed departures for Shoup, Mintzerville, and Thomasville:

> September 10, 1887. Steamer "Idaho" left on Wednesday for Shoup. Mr. Ritter and family (3) of Kansas City boarded here, en route for Pine Creek to reside there. Capt. Eli Suydam, Pilot Sanderland, other passengers: Jas. Fudge, Henry Breenan, Jack Hennesey, J. H. Duray, J. E. Booth, Miss Elma Edwards. Total 11.

Interviews with old-timers indicate that the term "steamer" was facetious. There were a few attempts at combination stern-wheel rowboat rigs, like those of John and Sandy Barracks, but wooden scows with sweeps were the "steamers" successfully adapted to the River of No Return.

These boats, which could be built in three days, were roughly eight feet in width and 32 feet in length, angled up at the ends. The double hull was made of longitudinal green lumber planks, with interior planks running athwart the barge, while elevated floor boards prevented wave-water from wetting supplies. The gunwales were generally three feet high, double walled to facilitate grocery storage. The seams were calked with pitch or tar.

The steering devices were two 28 foot poles fitted with 14 foot blades which rested in the water, one at the bow and the other at the stern. These "sweeps" were pinned at a pivot point. A sweep exerts and experiences considerable leverage in white water. For that

reason they were sometimes counter-balanced with green wood or stones near the handles and it took two men to run a large boat. Boatmen stood on an elevated deck, usually with hobnail boots for traction, and operated the sweeps above the passengers. The captain took the front sweep, reading the water and calling his decisions to the rear pilot. Sweeps allowed the scow to travel on the fastest current and to use the momentum gained for maneuvering on slower currents. They required more skill, but less effort, than an oar-powered boat. The sweep boat was an efficient craft, often carrying tons of freight to the mines, while drawing only 14 inches of water. Its only shortcoming became apparent when docking: it was necessary to bump along the bank until someone could get a bowline around a boulder.

Some have mistakenly considered sweep boats an Idaho invention. But flatboats or broadhorns, as they were called, were in use on the Mississippi a hundred years before they were seen on the Salmon and their wood walled many a house in New Orleans.

The boatman whose personality brought the Salmon scow and the River of No Return to national prominence was Harry Guleke. He arrived in Salmon several years after others had been using the river as an avenue for freight as far as Shoup. Yet it wasn't long before he became the most magnetic and knowledgeable boatman on the river.

Harry Guleke was a strapping, muscular, handsome and friendly person. According to Don Smith, of North Fork, Idaho, Guleke always greeted acquaintances on the street with a booming but mellow,

Loading scows at Salmon, Idaho.

Boat at the Salmon bridge about ready to cast-off for Riggins.

"Well, well, well, well." He was outgoing, as McKay was withdrawn.

Harry was born in New York in 1862. He came to the Lemhi Valley from the Henry's Fork country of the Snake River where he had been working as a government trapper.

He started learning the river as a bailer and swamper for George Sandiland. Sandiland had worked under Elias Suydam and later with C. V. Gilmer. When Gilmer quit the business, Sandiland brought his younger brother Dave aboard. Beginning in early April, and operating through October, they would haul five to eight tons of machinery and supplies on each trip to Shoup. Eventually the Sandilands quit floating in order to work at the Monoleth mine in Shoup and that left Guleke king of the river. It wasn't long before he was affectionately known as "Captain Guleke."

Elizabeth Reed, of Salmon, recalled that Guleke's first trip all the way to Riggins was made in October of 1896. Dave Sandiland, the younger of the brothers, had come back to work with Cap as his first mate.

Harry "Cap" Guleke, front sweep on the right with Percy Anderson on the left, handling the rear sweep (1917).

Cap Guleke's presence so dominated the navigational history of the River of No Return over the next 40 years that it seems worthwhile to include three first-hand accounts of trips he made.

The first is an early trip run from Salmon to Lewiston for R. F. Dwyer, a mining engineer, and his younger brother J. V. Dwyer, both from Omaha. Photographs were taken on the journey, but queries of the Dwyers now living in Omaha failed to discover any pictures. The narrative was written by J. V. Dwyer in 1903, a year after the trip:

"My brother and myself left Salmon City on the 8th of November on a hunt for big horn sheep, and descending the Salmon river thirty-five miles to the mouth of Indian creek, outfitted at the store of the Kittie Burton Gold Mining Company, which is located about five miles up Indian creek from the mouth. We there bought a flat boat, 36x10 feet in size, and loading our possessions on this boat, started down the stream for Big creek, where we camped for a number of days, hunting the mountain sheep and deer in the high mountains. We had arranged for Captain Guleke to join us at Big creek before the winter ice had formed, but on Thanksgiving day the storm began in an unmistakable way and we then knew that if we were to make the river trip it would have to be made at once.

"November 29 we started down the stream without waiting for Captain Guleke, and reaching Poverty flat about the middle of the afternoon, fifty-five miles below Salmon City, found that the river for a quarter of a mile was blocked with slush ice. It was right then that trouble began and we surely had enough of it within the next week. Going to the foot of the slush ice gorge we started to clear out a channel through which the boat could be floated, and by the time night had come on, we had cleared the channel with the exception of the last three hundred feet. This we expected to finish within half an hour the next morning, but were disappointed in this, as the next morning we found that the ice flow of the previous night had again choked the channel worse than ever before. Three days we struggled with this ice flow, when we were joined by Captain Guleke and another day was spent in a last effort to remove the obstruction. The Captain then advised that a smaller boat be made, which could be portaged over the gorge on a toboggan. The building of this boat occupied two days, the tools in use being a dull saw and hand ax, and the material planks from our larger boat and from the remains of a smaller boat we found stranded at Poverty flats. A large portion of the supplies were left in the large boat.

"Once started down the river in the smaller craft, our troubles may be said to have been over, as there was never the least doubt about reaching the mouth of the river, although on several occasions there seemed to be considerable doubt about our making the trip alive. The first day after leaving Poverty flats and before we reached the mouth of the middle fork of Salmon river, we struck another ice gorge, over which we portaged with little difficulty. The next day from this we entered the Black canyon, which has a length of something over ten miles, and which took three days to traverse. During these days the hours were filled with excitement and risk. Seven ice gorges were met and surmounted. In no case was the ice solid, the solid ice reaching out from the shore on each side and leaving in the middle of the stream a channel, which was filled up with slush ice, and enormous snow balls, this slush ice and snow sometimes reaching below the surface to a depth of ten or fifteen feet. In this stretch of the river there would be a quiet reach of water, its surface mirroring the enfolding hills, while below this would come a rapid or fall, where the water, a sea green color, would rush down a rocky gorge, on a twenty per cent grade, or perhaps fall almost perpendicularly for ten or fifteen feet. The channel in these swift places would be plentifully besprinkled with huge red and green granite and sand stone boulders, and the waters would be lashed into foam. At the foot of each of these falls would be a combing wave, apparently rushing back up stream, and on several occasions these waves almost swamped the boat. But it was not the rushing waters, alternating with pools of quiet depth, that formed the greatest charm in the scenery.

"The name Black canyon is no misnomer. It was and is a black canyon in very truth. Floating on the quieter stretches of the river and looking toward the heavens, it seemed as though the scene told its own history of the great mountains of granite which had been reft by the giant hand of the Almighty, raised in anger against an unworthy world, leaving here a gash in many places five thousand feet in depth, and which in many places even the erosion of the ages has not more than gently scarred, while in others the evidences of the great convulsion which had split the rocks asunder were apparently as fresh as on the day when the cleft was formed. On either side there would be nothing but the bare rock walls, red and green and blue and brown, with never a blade of grass or shrub, while far above, forming a fringe for the clear blue of the sky, which showed in a thin slit like a silver thread, was the dark blue of the forest, intensified by the dazzling whiteness of the snow that sparkled with all the shades of light that would be given out by a cluster of diamonds. The memory of the three days spent in traversing this Black canyon will be with me through the years to come.

"After we had traversed the Black canyon, no other dangers that the river might have in store for us could produce more than a pleasurable excitement, and each rapid and fall was met and conquered without the quickening of a single pulse beat. Beautiful scenery, sublime in its loftiness, did not end with the Black canyon, and in many ways the stretch of river between White Bird and the junction of the Salmon with the Snake rivers furnished as beautiful scenery as can be found anywhere on the American continent. After leaving White Bird, the river, although wild in its flow, gave evidence along its banks that man had come here and made this his home. There were a number of little homes, with vineclad porches and orchards back of the house. Occasionally there were long stretches where the river ran in deep gorges and where the sun does not strike the water during eight months of the year. The walls of the canyon here are a chocolate colored basalt, and in many places the columnar basalt stretches from the water's edge for a thousand feet or more into the air, the columns rising like cathedral spires. In other places these cliffs of columnar basalt have been faulted and the columns, in place of soaring skyward, are placed at almost every imaginable angle.

"We reached the mouth of the Salmon river December 17th, and two days were occupied in reaching Lewiston. After leaving White Bird we had been constantly warned to beware of the Wild Goose rapids, and so much had been told us of the dangers of the passage there that we had

27

almost decided to line over the rapids, something we had not done in our whole trip. All during the forenoon we had been keeping a careful watch for the Wild Goose, and finally about noon, unable to stand the suspense any longer, the boat was pulled ashore near a house, and a farmer asked how far it was to the Wild Goose. We were much surprised when told that we had passed the rapids about six miles."

In the years that followed, Guleke provided reliable freight service for the canyon, training other boatmen in order that he could take two or three boats each trip. In Riggins or Lewiston they would sell their boats for five dollars and return overland to Salmon.

Tragedy struck one of Cap's trips in 1897 for the first and only time. In Pine Creek Rapids, George Sandiland caught a rock with his rear sweep and was catapulted overboard. He washed underneath the boat and drowned.

The early 1900's were a period of renewed interest in railroad routes. Scouting parties and surveyors visited the canyon by boat in 1906, '08, and '09. Guleke and Dave Sandiland took them through to Lewiston. In 1909 the Gilmore and Pittsburg Railroad survey was made down the river to Lewiston. This was the railroad which eventually reached Salmon from Armstead, Montana, and was taken over by the Northern Pacific. Priceless photographs from this survey were given to Jim Chapman on the Snake River by a member of the crew. His daughter, Doris Babcock, collected them.

The survey crew and a school teacher on the lower Salmon. One of the surveyors later returned to marry a Salmon River girl and raised a family in Lemhi County.

The G & P crew constructed a smaller
boat from one of their larger scows. Note
the bottle on top of the boat.

The survey boats covered against early
winter weather. When the G & P reached
Salmon it was referred to as the "Get off
& Push." In 1939 the rails were sold as
scrap metal to Japan.

The Gilmore-Pittsburg survey in late
fall, on the Lower Salmon. Guleke
contracted to keep the crew provisioned
through the canyon.

Guleke and Dave Sandiland were busy floating heavy mining equipment at this time, as well. John R. Painter had started to develop his Salmon River Mining Company at Five Mile Creek above the South Fork of the Salmon.

Caroline Lockhart, a novelist of the period, who was infatuated with John Painter, made a trip down the river in 1911 and published an informative account the following year:

> If by any chance there is a person who would like to experience the sensations of a man about to be hanged I can tell him exactly how to get them.
>
> Cowards die many deaths before their time, it has been said and I died so frequently shooting the rapids of the Salmon River between Salmon City, Idaho, and the placer diggings of the Salmon River Mining Company, one hundred and fifty miles below, that the grave no longer holds any terrors for me. Even the distinction of being one of the first two women ever to attempt this hazardous trip was no solace to me at times when I was less than a foot from my Everlasting Punishment, and at such moments glory seemed a puny thing indeed.
>
> Those who know the West from the Mexican border to the Canadian line consider the Salmon River the wickedest water, next to certain portions of the Snake, between these boundaries. It rises in the Saw-tooth Range and flows some three hundred miles through the longest canyon in the United States, finally emptying into the Snake on the line between Oregon and Idaho. The country it drains is the wildest part of the mountainous State and between Salmon City and Whitebird, a distance of nearly two hundred miles, it is practically uninhabited. The game is primitively tame and the deer and mountain sheep peer over the cliffs or stand staring at the water's edge, curious and unalarmed.
>
> The boatmen who have successfully pitted their skill and strength against the sinister power of the Salmon River can be counted on fewer than the fingers of one hand. There are now but two in Salmon City who can be considered pilots, and so great is the fear of the rapids that those who have made the trip either as boatmen or passengers are a comparative handful.

Therefore, when John R. Painter, general manager of the Salmon River Mining Company, sent over ninety thousand pounds of machinery through the rapids with the loss of but one boat, it was an achievement which marked an epoch in the history of the fearsome and ill-famed river.

Nine barges were built to convey the unwieldy machinery, each barge being thirty-seven feet long, five feet high, eight feet wide, and braced at intervals with two-by-sixes. The steering gear, called "sweeps," was handled by two men standing on a high platform. It consisted of two young fir trees over six inches in diameter, twenty-five feet in length, with a twelve-foot plank bolted obliquely to one end and balanced on a pin in either end of the boat.

It was a clumsy affair, this flat-bottomed barge, with trees and planks for steering, but it was the only type of craft that could ride the rough water and skim the rocks that lie so menacingly close to the surface. The barges were sent in fleets of three, piloted by Captain Harry Guleke, Captain David Sandilands, and a man named Cummings.

In the uneasy days of waiting for the men to return from the first trip by the roundabout railroad route, while the water was creeping up as the snows far back in the mountains melted under the hot May sun and while the fate of the boats was in doubt, I heard much of the river and its rapids. The Pine Creek Rapids were the ones over which the natives seemed particularly to wag their heads.

In confidence I asked an Old Timer: "Honest, now, is it really so bad?"

"I'll tell you about me, mum. I have fit Injuns and I ain't afraid of a gun, er a knife, er pizen, er grub in the Bismark Restauraw but you couldn't git me down that river 'thout tyin' and gaggin' me."

"And the Pine Creek Rapids — you go through them —"

"Like a bat out of hell, mum."

At last the news ran through the isolated mountain town. "They're home! Cummings wrecked his boat! Sandilands came through without a scratch! The Philadelphia dude who went along to bail is sick in bed with fright!

31

Guleke's boat filled to within six inches of the top! He hung on a rock till after midnight!"

The return of two North Pole heroes never caused more excitement. In detail we learned how Cummings deserted his boat, he and his hind sweepman and bailer, as soon as she struck, and crawled to safety on a rock though the boat floated a mile and wrecked herself by filling from the side, taking with her machinery which meant a loss of many thousands of dollars to the company.

A portion of the day following the boatmen's return was spent by them in making and balancing the sweeps on their pins and it was three in the afternoon before they were adjusted to their satisfaction.

And the men themselves — the heroes of the people — Guleke and Sandilands — whose fame is nearly as wide as that of the river itself? Well, they had the characteristics one likes to find in men who do brave things — namely, gentleness and modesty.

There was Guleke, big as a bear and as strong, and with a bear's surprising agility as I afterwards learned — low-voiced, deliberate, with a slow, pleasant smile and a droll fashion of shaking his head and saying: "Well, well, I declare!"

Many are the tales they tell of his strength — how, in an emergency, he broke a sweep in two, a tough green fir tree, to save a girl's life, and they chuckle over the story of how, upon an occasion, when attacked because he would not drink, he knocked the belligerent down three times and then said plaintively: "What's the matter with you? I don't want to fight," not being conscious that the fight had started.

Sandilands, the Scotchman, was of a different type; slender, wiry, more nervous of temperament and imaginative, gentle of speech as a woman, yet with the same reserve force which characterized the other riverman.

In contrast to them both there was Cummings, swaggering, self-assertive, ever mindful of the grandstand, and who, when again entrusted with a boat, at the last moment took advantage of his employer's necessity to make fresh demands, knowing that the boat must go then or perhaps not for weeks owing to the rapidly rising river. I began to understand something of the reason for the feeling of distrust and dislike entertained for him by his neighbors.

At the hind sweep with Captain Guleke, in whose boat I was to go, there was George Preece, big, blond, with a humorous, dare-devil look in his wide, blue eyes — a giant, too, in his strength.

Finally Captain Guleke and Preece took their places on the platform and I scrambled over the boxes and machinery to the stern where the bailer also stowed himself. The ropes were cast off and the boatmen gripped their sweeps. The bridge was black with people shouting lugubrious farewells as we swung into the current. Mr. and Mrs. Frank Symes, of Salmon City, were passengers in the second boat with Captain Sandilands, and saying good-by to their friends as though they never expected to see them again this side of the grave.

A tiny Chinese woman peered at us through the brush as we floated past, and her brown hand fluttered in delighted recognition of our friendly good-by. It was obvious that the rural telephone line had been busy, as entire families roosted on the top rail of the fences at the various ranches for twenty miles below, patiently waiting our appearance.

The remainder of that day and the next forenoon, while we were drifting the sixty miles between Salmon City and the little settlement of Shoup, was comparatively uneventful. The battle with the river, the result of which no good boatmen ever prophesies, but merely hopes and fights, did not begin until we reached the Pine Creek Rapids, three miles below Shoup.

We camped for luncheon a half-mile from the rapids.

"We don't want to start through there feeling weak," explained the Captain.

The gravity of the boatmen throughout the meal was contagious. Something uncommonly like nervousness destroyed my usual interest in food and put a damper upon my chipper spirits, nor was there anything calculated to reassure me in the suggestive preparations which began when our luncheon was done.

Life-preservers were dug up from beneath the cargo, boxes readjusted to give the baler room to work, heavy-soled shoes replaced by canvas ties, coats and hats were thrown off, shirts unbuttoned at the throat, and every nail and splinter removed from the platform. It is perhaps needless to remark that I did not keep on superfluous clothing myself, and I made a mental arrangement with my subconscious mind to see that I froze to my life-preserver if anything happened.

The river valley had narrowed until the mountains rose from the water's edge, and the natives of Shoup were perched among the rocks like eagles to watch the boatloads of imbeciles sink or swim in the notorious Pine Creek Rapids.

"Throw off the lines," said Guleke in his quiet voice, but I noticed that there was a different look in his mild face now, a steady shine in his level gray eyes.

Into the eyes of Preece, who faced me at the sweep, there came a kind of reckless glitter, which before the trip was done I came to recognize as a sure signal of danger ahead.

There was something creepy, ominous, in the very quietness with which we glided from the stiller water of the eddy into the channel. Nobody spoke; it was silent as a graveyard, save for the occasional lap of a ripple against the boat. The big pilot, half-crouching over his sweep, made me think of a huge cat, a cougar waiting to grapple with an enemy as wily and as formidable as himself, and, for a space, we crept forward with something of a cougar's stealth.

Then the current caught us like some live thing. Faster and faster we moved. The rocks and bushes at the water's edge began to fly by. I thought I heard something. It sounded like the rumble of thunder far back in the hills. It grew louder with every beat of my heart. Preece, at the sweep, dropped his eyes for an instant and grinned.

"Hear 'em roar?"

Hear 'em roar? Oh, mother! Did I hear 'em roar! It sounded like a cloud-burst in a canyon — like the avalanche of water dropping over Niagara.

I stood up and stretched my neck to look ahead. What I saw made my heart miss four beats. I took a fresh grip on my life-preserver and wondered how long it would take me to shuck myself out of my khaki skirt.

As far as I could see there was a stretch of spray and foam, short intervals of wild, racing water, then more spray and foam where it churned itself to whiteness against a mass of rocks. And from it all came a steady boom! boom!

The bailer craned his neck.

"Gee! That looks fierce!" He began hastily to roll up his sleeves and trouser legs.

We were racing toward it now as though drawn by the invisible force of some great suction pump. I caught just a glimpse of a man lying out on a projecting boulder with a camera focused upon a spot ahead of us. Then I saw Preece grip the sweep handle until his knuckles went white.

For an instant it seemed as though the boat poised on the edge of a precipice with half her length in midair before she dropped into a curve of water that was like the hollow of a great green shell. The roar was deafening. When the sheet of water that drenched us broke over the boat it seemed to shut out the sun. The barge came up like a clumsy Newfoundland, with the water streaming from the platform and swishing through the machinery in the bottom. Guleke was there at his sweep, unshaken by the shock, throwing his great strength upon it first this way then that, to keep it in the center of the current — the tortuous channel through which we were tearing like mad.

There was an occasional low-voiced command from the Captain, and the man at the hind sweep responded before the words had left his lips, and responded with all the muscle of his arms and shoulders and weight of his body. It was quick and tremendous action, or none. There were places where a single instant's tardiness meant our finish. There was no time to rectify mistakes. A false move, a stroke of the sweep too much or too little with that terrifying force behind us, and our boat would crash and splinter on a rock like a flimsy strawberry box.

35

Sometimes the water shot over the top of partially-submerged granite boulders, again it struck them with a force which made it boil and seethe. We sat, the bailer and I, in tense, strained silence and during that seven miles Guleke never lifted his eyes or relaxed the muscles of his set jaw, but steered with the grim sureness of knowledge and determination. The praises I had heard no longer seemed extravagant. A novice would have lasted in that water about one minute, or only so long as it would have taken him to drown.

Finally the boat ceased to leap, the booming white water grew fainter and ahead of us lay a little stretch of peace. Guleke straightened himself, and there was satisfaction in his voice as he looked at the lolling white tongues behind him and said:

"Well, well, I declare, they didn't get us that time!"

"That's the worst, isn't it?" I hoped that he would not notice the quaver in my voice.

"Oh, no; it gets worse as you go further down."

I stopped wringing my skirt.

"Worse!"

"Yes, there's the Growler, the Big Mallard, and the Whiplash that I mind more than the Pine Creek Rapids. I especially dread the Growler and Dave hates the Big Mallard. His brother was drowned in the Pine Creek Rapids, too. We both breathe easier when we're around the Whiplash."

I felt the goose-flesh going in and the prickly heat coming out. If he did not particularly mind the Pine Creek Rapids but dreaded the places that were ahead, what might they be like, I asked myself.

"One of the reasons that this river is so bad," he continued, "is because the current changes with every stage of the water. A place that we can get through in safety one time will wreck us the next. The water is a whole lot worse than it was the other trip down. It's higher, so we can't see the rocks, and can do less against it. We never attempt to run below Shoup in high water."

This was all comforting.

36

"Look! See that slab of rock sticking up? That's where they buried a fellow they fished out of the river."

The lonely grave among the boulders and the pines was not calculated to cheer me.

The breathing spells were brief after this. There was the Dutch Oven — a quick turn, with rocks around the corner — and the Ebenezer Rapids where, on the third trip down, Captain Sandilands struck a rock and saved his boat by sheer dogged courage, working for more than two days in swift and icecold water in a pouring rain. Then came the Long Tom Rapids, a rough, splashy piece of water where the waves curled back and struck the bottom of the boat until the lumber creaked. The Captain referred to it pleasantly as a "nice ride," and perhaps it was. Any one of the rapids, where I could not actually see the whites of Old Man Death's eyes, was beginning to seem comparatively nice.

Proctor's Falls came next, which was a reef of solid bedrock, so named for one Proctor who was better known as "Death-on-the-trail," owing to his propensity for killing Indians. Death-on-the-trail, who was wrecked among the rocks and lost his outfit, thereafter took the land route when he traveled.

Horse Creek Rapids, Little Squaw Rapids, the Devil's Teeth followed, each dangerous in its own way.

The scenery had been growing wilder, the mountains higher, now rising straight from the water's edge to sawtooth peaks against the sky. The river was narrowing to half its width and boiling as it piled up inside the narrow, gloomy walls. The boat began to rush forward with fresh impetus, and there was a quizzical expression on the hind sweepman's face as he said:

"We're coming to the Black Canyon."

There was no need to tell me that we were coming to something, for again I heard the boom of water dropping from a height — a sound with which I had become familiar at the Pine Creek Rapids and which I was not likely to forget.

"Hang on!" advised the bailer whose eyes, I observed, seemed mostly whites.

The warning was quite unnecessary for my fingers were already making dents in a two-by-six.

We slid into the air. The front end of the boat seemed to drop straight down and the stern rose. I remarked mentally that we appeared to be going over a waterfall. Foam, hissing like carbonated water, shut out the light. When we came up gasping and I looked behind us, I observed that I was entirely correct in my surmise. It was a waterfall with a drop of seven feet!

Cap Guleke running Carey Falls.

The boat shot through the chill dusk of the canyon with its solid walls of black granite rising to a height of one thousand five hundred and two thousand feet and worn as smooth by the action of the water through countless ages as though it had been polished, at the rate of fourteen miles an hour. We went through the five miles of box canyon in less than thirty minutes.

The Bailey Rapids and the rapids at the head of the Mitt Haney bar followed, then Captain Guleke watched his chance and swung the boat from the fast current into an eddy until she was close enough to shore for Preece to jump with the rope.

"The Big Mallard is around the point," explained the Captain and there was a furrow of anxiety between his eyes. "We always go ahead here and look out a trail."

"I think I'll go along. It must be interesting to see from the shore."

The Scotch boatman, Sandilands, who also had landed, replied grimly:

"Oh, yes, you'll find it interesting."

Interesting? It was terrifying. I looked in a horror I made no effort to conceal. It is no disgrace to be scared at the Big Mallard. In fact I wish to say that the person who is not afraid at certain places in the Salmon River has not sense enough to be afraid. I have met rapids before — shot them and poled over them — but never anything like the rapids of this river, and he who makes the trip can assert with truth that he has taken the wildest boat ride in America.

Words seem inadequate and colorless when I think of describing the Big Mallard. As we stood among the boulders, looking up at it in nothing less than awe, I could well understand the dread it inspired even in such men as Captains Sandilands and Guleke.

The river, running like a mill race, came straight but comparatively smooth until it reached a high, sharp ledge of rock where the river made a turn. Then it made a close swirl and the current gave a sudden rush and piled up between two great rocks, one of which it covered thinly. Behind this latter rock the water dropped into a hollow that was like a well and when it rose it struck another rock immediately below that churned it into fury.

It was Cummings, the third boatman, no longer swaggering, loud-mouthed, and boastful, but white as paper to his ears, who finally said in a strained, subdued voice:

"It's a whole lot worse than the first trip."

Captain Sandilands and Guleke continued to regard it with grave faces.

Guleke shook his head.

"We can't make the other side of the rock; we've got to come through here."

I could not believe he was in earnest. I had not thought they had even considered this narrow passage-way. The space was not wider than twice the width of the boat and the masses of the rock so close to the surface on one side, that yawning hole on the other, the turn around the ledge giving so little time to act and get results in the tremendous current that it looked like deliberate suicide to attempt it. It seemed sure and utter destruction.

No one spoke as we returned to the boats. My feet dragged and I had a curious goneness in the region of my belt buckle. I even considered howling until they let me walk, although it was not possible to make a landing for several miles below. I lost faith in my life-preserver, past achievements in the water were no consolation; we were all going to drown then and there and I knew it! It was in this frame of mind that I crawled limply into the boat.

Nothing could exceed the caution with which the pilot worked the boat into the current that it might catch it in the proper way and place. He watched the landmarks on either shore, measuring distances and calculating the result of each stroke like a good billiard player placing his ball. He knew and we all knew that the error of a single stroke too much or too little in such close quarters meant death to one or all of us.

We were full in the current now. The turn was just ahead. Was it possible that Guleke with all his great strength and marvelous skill could place the boat so that in the final rush between the rocks it would cut the current diagonally? Too far to the left meant the submerged rocks, too far to the right meant the yawning green hole, which looked to be bottomless from the shore. It did not seem within the range of human possibilities to do so.

As we whipped around the point I forgot something of my fear in looking at the pilot. The wind blew his hair straight back and the joy of battle was gleaming in his eyes as he laid down on the sweep. His face was alight with exultation; he looked a monument of courage, the personification of human daring. Fearlessness is contagious, and a spirit of reckless indifference to consequences filled me as we took the final rush. It lasted only a second or two,

40

but the sensations of many years were crowded into the tense moment when on that toboggan slide of water the boat shot past the rocks on the left and cut the hole on the right so close that half the stern hung over it and the bailer stared into its dark depths with bulging eyes.

The boat leaped in the spray but our nerves relaxed, for we knew that we were safely through.

Sandilands' boat was not far behind, and, as soon as we could see, we turned in quick anxiety to watch its fate.

"They're too close!" exclaimed Preece in consternation.

Our hearts rose in our throats while they took the shoot. It looked to us as though they were headed straight for the hole. We could see the bow dip and then the mass of spray hid her. Had she cleared the hole sufficiently to get over? From our position it did not look as though she had.

We glanced inquiringly into each other's faces and the seconds seemed minutes long before we saw her plunging in the center of the spray as though she were being tossed up by a geyser. The sweep had been torn from the hind sweepman's hand and we could see him and the bailer fighting desperately to regain it. The boat was whirling like an egg-shell. We turned a bend that lost her to our view and our suspense was great until the river straightened some miles below and we saw both boats coming.

At the Growler I remember only a rushing between rocks and a roaring and the Captain's triumphant chuckle:

"Well, well, I declare! They didn't get us either."

The Whiplash was the last place regarded by the boatman as really "bad water." The Whiplash, they said, differed from them all, although no two were exactly alike and each required different tactics.

When the men threw off their hats and twitched at their belts I knew that the Whiplash was close. We shot from the extreme left of the river to the extreme right and faced a high, perpendicular wall of rock which the current had worn to a half-circle at the base. The current swirled around this half-circle until the full force of it struck the end of the wall and leaped into the air and curled back, making a cavern that was like entering the dusk of a windowless cabin.

The strength of the boatman was concentrated upon placing the boat in the outer edge of the current and taking the swirl in that position. It looked to me as though we were going as straight and hard for the wall of rock as the full force of the current could send us. The circling swing of the boat was like the motion of a merry-go-round and the accompanying music was the thud of water against the wall which resembled the dull boom of a muffled cannon. We were swinging sickeningly close to the point, which formed the end of the half circle and the water was rising against it to twice a tall man's height.

I would not have wagered a cent on the result one way or the other. Even Preece turned his head and was staring hard at the narrowing space between us and the point. I clenched my hands tight and waited for the shock that it now seemed surely must come. But before we plunged into that cavern I caught a glimpse of the Captain's face. There was a smile upon it like the sun breaking through the clouds and I knew that his trained eye had gauged the distance and all was well.

"A few more nervous strains like that --!"

"Say, what are those things in your eyes?" inquired the bailer impudently.

"They might be tears," I admitted, "but you're not looking so rosy yourself."

"Most people change a few shades at the Whiplash," replied the Captain. "The whitest man I ever saw was a prize fighter and he said he felt as though he had been in the ring."

"But we are safe now? There is no more danger?"

Captain Guleke shook his head.

"You are never safe on this river until the boat is tied up."

A cry from Preece startled us.

"They've struck a rock! My God! There goes Mackey's sweep!"

The bow of Sandilands' boat was reared high on a rock at the head of the Lemhi bar. The stern was settling low in the water. We could see the commotion while they were pulling the front sweep from its pin and tying the woman to it. Guleke and Preece were working with the strength of half a dozen men to make a quick landing. But the river was too swift and we ran a mile before they could get close to shore.

Wrecked scow on a Guleke trip.

We jumped for the rocks and tore our way through the thick underbrush back up the river. A sweep went by, and some wreckage. Coming out upon a point, I saw that the rock where they had hung was clear. The boat was nowhere in sight! I felt curiously quiet all at once, and stopped running.

"It's all over with the Symes family," I thought, and went on reluctantly, dreading what I might see.

A shout of joy came from some one ahead. "They're ashore! They got in!"

They were safe on a rock although the water was flowing over all but the bow of the boat.

A change in the current was responsible for the accident. When the Captain saw the danger it was too late to stop and the boat struck with a splintering crash and was only saved from sinking instantly by a big fly-wheel in the bottom. When it had seemed that they must take to the water a wave had lifted them. They tried to get the sweep back on the pin and failed. Mackey then threw his body over the sweep and held it down while the Captain swung the boat into the only landing place on that side of the river for miles. Symes, the passenger, who was no antelope, broke the world's record for a standing jump when he leaped with the rope and none too soon for the boat could not have gone fifty feet farther.

It was twenty-four hours before the machinery was unloaded and replaced in the repaired boat.

"Your 'sand' is all right," said the boatman flatteringly when we parted. "You rode through rapids that the survey outfit of the Pittsburgh and Gilmore Railroad walked around."

I felt that it was something for which to be thankful that my cowardice was not of the conspicuous kind.

Harry Guleke with passengers on the upper Salmon. He charged a thousand dollars a trip at the turn of the century.

Another Guleke trip run in 1921 received national publicity in the pages of *Field and Stream* magazine a couple of years later. That boat carried three women, one of whom was Eleanor "Cissy" Patterson, also known as the Countess Gizycka. She was a notable Washington society figure, a fine horsewoman, marksman, hunter, swimmer, distance walker, and party-giver. Cissy had a career in the publishing industry, including editorship of the *Washington Herald*, chairman of the *New York Daily News,* and part-owner of the *Chicago Tribune*. She died in 1948; her daughter married Drew Pearson.

The Countess was 36 years old when she came down the Salmon. Percy Anderson ran the rear sweep, Ben Ludwig accompanied them as cook and guide.

The trip covered 14 days in mid-July. An amusing excerpt from her diary follows:

Wednesday, July 20

Terrific heat, devouring sun. R. E. and I are both beginning to give way as to temper and general morale. Disorder, discomfort. Impossible to find anything in the dufflebags kicked about the bottom of the boat. Poor and monotonous food, restricted company. Boat smells of bilge water, and many more equally unpleasant things. Today, I sat at the bottom of the boat for an hour, listless, dejected, a broken comb on one side and a forgotten sock floating in the sump at the other.

In the afternoon we drop down to the Proctor Ranch and land before supper. Mrs. P., twice a widow, very slight, between fifty and sixty; still pretty, though sunburnt and wrinkled. She has beautiful eyes, one greeny-brown, the other browny-green.

We climb up to her cabin just as she and her three beaux — two old bachelors and the inevitable hired man — are sitting down to the most delightful looking supper. A large, three-layer chocolate cake is prominent in the middle of a white-spread, "homey" looking table. The captain introduces us.

"Won't you come in and eat supper?" she asks, simply.

But R. E. and I hesitate, politely, as we were taught to do when children.

45

"Oh --, thank you so much, -- but I think perhaps we might disturb you. Hadn't we better wait outside till you've finished."

Mrs. Proctor, being a Westerner, took us at our word.

"Alright. Just make yourselves comfortable on the porch. We won't be long."

R. E. and I shamble forth and sit down on the step, completely unnerved — almost in tears. Fried chicken, fresh peas, light bread, coffee and chocolate cake--!

We debate whether to walk right in and say we've changed our minds and act as if we didn't know better. After all, lots of people do just such things and get away with it. But neither of us are sufficiently bold of spirit. The blow had been so very unexpected.

Presently, weary of waiting like jackals at the gate, we get up and wander dispiritedly through the lovely orchard, seeking consolation in an occasional currant or bite of green apple — ears cocked, still hoping against hope.

But Mrs. Proctor finally joins us. She tells us how her first husband was drowned in the river, and of the wild night she spent trying to save him. He had an iron hook for one hand and couldn't swim very well, she said. Mr. Proctor and the third man in the party were saved. And after it was all over she told Proctor he would have to come home to the ranch with her, for she couldn't manage the place alone. In a year they were married, and very happily, it would seem, though not for long. For Mr. Proctor, returning from town, where he had gone to buy some teeth, fell off in a snowbank, got pneumonia and died.

She accompanied us on our way back. When we reached the bank she spied a mammoth rattlesnake, as big around as my arm; and having screamed twice she then rushed about gathering up rocks with which to kill it. Then, like a little fury, she closed in nearer than I care to and pelted the snake, wounding it severely.

"Oh! Get the men," she cried. "Get the men. Kill it. Just feel how my heart beats," and she took my hand, pressed it to her side, and fell half-fainting in my arms.

The plank from the shore to the boat seemed to both embarrass and frighten her. She gathered up her skirts and laughed and cried and all of us took turns in coaxing her across.

On leaving, she called to her hired man — I forget his name — a handsome, lazy-looking individual of French descent, and he tenderly, indulgently conducted her, little step by little step, over to the shore.

She is a perfectly charming lady, Mrs. Proctor. And I feel sure that, after a decent interval of mourning, the wedding bells will ring for her once more.

Thursday, July 21

Late last night we confided to the captain our sorrowful experience of the earlier evening. "My, my," he condoled, gravely concerned. "That's too bad. If you'd only — Well — I'll go — I'll go and see what I--" and he ambled off along the gangplank in the dark. In less than an hour he returned, carrying a complete chocolate cake on a platter and a jar of currant wine tucked under one arm.

Like any good boatman, Cap made his share of mistakes. He lost a boatload of machinery destined for the Painter Mine. On another occasion he had to walk a party out from Salmon Falls when an error by his rear sweepman wrecked the boat and all supplies.

While hauling groceries from Salmon on an early trip, Guleke forgot to deliver a sack of flour to Mr. Layton at the mouth of Indian Creek, just below North Fork. When Cap discovered his lapse, he decided to leave the sack at Shoup. On his next trip Cap was met at the Shoup landing by an irate Mr. Layton. He forced Guleke to carry the flour all the way back to Indian Creek, prodding the boatman with a rifle barrel whenever his pace slackened.

Harry Guleke ran several trips below Lewiston. He once contracted to haul some salvaged machinery from Painter Mine near the South Fork to Lewiston. The buyer lived in Portland and Guleke decided to take it all the way down. He tied up at the Portland docks and located the buyer running a haberdashery two blocks from the dock. The buyer was so pleased that he outfitted Cap with new clothes from bootheel to hatband.

Late in life, Guleke married a widow not long after her husband drowned in the river. This event produced some unfair rumors which claimed Cap was responsible for the man's death. The victim's name was Matt; he was regarded as a town soak. Matt paid a visit to Ace's still on an island in the river a couple of miles below Salmon. On his way back to shore, Matt fell off the swinging bridge. It was December and his body was found near Diamond Creek in the spring.

Cap Guleke never had any children of his own but children liked him and watched for his boat. He made a point of carrying oranges and candy which he would toss to kids on the riverbank if he didn't have time or place to stop.

By 1930 Guleke was nearly seventy years old and floated the river less frequently. Elmer Keith, of Salmon, ran some summer and fall hunting and fishing trips with him. Cap swallowed the anchor after his last trip in 1939. He died at his home in Salmon in 1944 and is buried in the town cemetery. His grave stone carries the simple and appropriate inscription: "River of No Return."

Members of the 1929 Salmon River crew. Their Air Cruiser rafts are stacked in the truck, beneath the elk, which was killed on the trip. Left to right: Vance McHan, Virgil McHan, Joseph Gulick, and Jay Redfield.

The first inflatable boat trip, and quite possibly the earliest trip run solely for the pleasure of floating the river, was made October 16, 1929 by four Idahoans: Virgil and Vance McHan, Joseph Gulick, and Jay Redfield. They looked on the journey as simply a "sporting adventure." The group was prepared for at least one eventuality because Joseph was a minister and Virgil was an undertaker.

The McHan-Gulick party bought two rubber boats, of the type used by Admiral Byrd, from Clifton, New Jersey, for $90 each. They were 9½ feet long, 3½ feet wide, with 14-inch tubes, separated by three diaphrams.

The men started from Shoup, using paddles and taking turns towing a third rubber boat which held their food and duffle. They soon learned to kick the supply boat loose at the head of a rapid.

Each boat capsized frequently; patching and portaging were sometimes required. Their kapok lifejackets didn't last long. But the men enjoyed their trip and arrived in Riggins after 13 days.

The National Geographic Society sponsored a Salmon River expedition in 1935 which brought the canyon increased notoriety when an article appeared in the magazine the following year. The boatmen for that expedition were Monroe Hancock and John Cunningham.

Hancock's was a name that became associated with Salmon River boating for many years. He had been raised on the Snake River, near

Group photograph of the 1935 National Geographic Society expedition. John Cunningham in the rear, second from *the left, and Monroe Hancock on the far right.*

Huntington, Oregon. His father was a commercial sturgeon fisherman. Hancock learned sweeps and the Salmon from Harry Guleke.

John Cunningham, on the other hand, lived at Butts Creek and was described by Mrs. Hancock as "fit only for a rear sweep, since he could never make up his mind which way to go."

With low water, in early October of 1935, Hancock and his cook took the scow from Salmon to Ebenezer Bar, below Shoup. There Cunningham and the passengers embarked.

Howard R. Flint, Regional Forest Inspector of the U.S. Forest Service, began the trip with a cold, got soaked during a rainy night at Barth Hot Springs, and had to be evacuated by air from Mackay Bar to Missoula, Montana. He died there.

The party reached Lewiston October 28. Hancock donated the boat to Lewiston State Normal School — now Lewis and Clark College. No one there knows what happened to the scow, though the expedition's banner is displayed in the campus museum.

Bus Hatch, Frank Swain, Royce Mowrey, and Alton Hatch, together with four passengers, ran the Middle Fork of the Salmon in July of 1936, and continued down the Main river to Riggins, upsetting their boats for the first time in Big Mallard Rapid when they became distracted by the antics of a bear. They were using 14-foot wooden boats with oars — a new sight on the Salmon.

A respected, fascinating figure in western river lore ran the river from Salmon to Riggins in August of the same year. He had been a placer miner along the San Juan River in southern Utah in the early 1900's, lived as a recluse along the Colorado, in Glen Canyon, and was selected as the head boatman for the U.S. Geological Survey of the San Juan and Green River in 1921-22. His name: Albert "Bert" Loper.

Two letters which he wrote to Lois Guemlek, a reporter for the *Salmon Recorder,* are published here for the first time:

———————————————◆•◗•◆———————————————

Mouth Horse Creek, Idaho

Mrs. Guemlek:

On leaving Salmon we had our little troubles, encountering many shoals, and in one place there a tree had fallen entirely across the river, and I only missed having a mixup by inches, and in another place someone had a boom across the river and we had to drag the boat bodily over it.

After passing North Fork we came to our first real rapid at the mouth of Dump Creek, and while it was not so awful bad it slapped us around a bit at that and when we passed it by we had a good supply of water in our open compartment. We had several nice "White Water Rapids" between there and Shoup. On leaving Shoup we encountered some real water — first was Pine Creek Rapid and the next just below was Big Sheep Eater and in running the two it required about all the river skill at my command and if the builders of rapids had put in one more rock they would have had to put it on top of one that was already there. We encountered "White Water" around every bend of the river but the next real one was Ebenezer Rapid at the 3-C-Camp but then we had an audience of about 100 of the boys — it being Sunday — We had been hearing of the awful Long Tom Rapid so we approached it with a little apprehension, but out side of about three very big rocks to miss we had some wonderful water it being nice and rough but no rocks.

It was only about one half mile to the mouth of Middle Fork so we ran down below the mouth and camped and it was while we were in this camp that we encountered our first cloud burst and the Middle Fork sure messed things up and the river of no return was not the beautiful river that we had been having and we could not look down and see the bottom of the river any more, so the river beautiful was more like the Colorado river.

On leaving the camp below Middle Fork the first rapid to be encountered was Cramer rapid and as we had looked it over before the big rain we paid no more attention to it and as there was two feet more water there was also a change in the rapid and you may have heard of step children getting slapped around — well that was us but it was an exhilerating ride at that and was hugely enjoyed by us, but we took more water in the open compartment than at any other place. We came next to Proctor Falls and out-side of having to dodge about four very big rocks we had our usual wild ride at the bottom of this one too.

We are now at the mouth of Horse Creek with the big rapid to run the first thing when we start out again, but we may lay over here a day or two for I want to go to the top to a Ranger Look Out Station and look at the country from the

top down instead of from the bottom up — I will try and let you hear from me some time after I have (?) run Salmon Falls — if I get a chance to send out
                                        BERT LOPER.
We have come a distance of 132½ miles and have made a drop of 2155 feet we are just loafing along and trying to see every thing that there is to see.
                            Riggins, Idaho.
                            Sept-17-36.

———————————————◆●◆●◆———————————————

Mrs. Lois Guemlek,
    Salmon City,
        Idaho.

Dear Mrs. Guemlek:
    I believe that I left you at the mouth of Horse Creek so I will try and pick up from there and, to the best of my ability, try and give you a little idea of some of the things we have done and also some of the things that has happened to us. The first thing on leaving Horse Creek was the running of the big rapid just below and it was sure a beauty with lots of big high and foamy waves but no rocks so we had our wild ride and it was some sport when there is no rocks to bother — I suppose we are a little conceited about our boat but it could not do better for it is sure made for rough water. We continued on our way and met the customary rapids and, I suppose, got a little "cocky" and when we came to Little Squaw we had some time keeping Old Betsy (The Boat) from going head on into a cliff where all the water was trying to pile up in one place, and the worst of it was that we had an audience of Mr. & Mrs. Lantz but we made it all right and it acted as a check up on us for a day or two but we soon got careless again.
    The next was the Devils Teeth Rapid and for looks it was a humdinger but was not near so bad as it looked. The River is changing some for above the fall per mile was more

52

evenly distributed over the entire mile but now it is more dead water between the rapids and that makes all the fall come in the rapids so the increased size of the rapids.

We continued on our way and with the customary number of rapids, and bad ones, until we came to Big Squaw, and having got slapped around in Little Squaw, and having been told that the female of the species is more deadly than the male we were more careful but it proved that it was not bad at all. We met a couple of miners at this place and learned that we were just two miles above Salmon Falls so we knew that we had some thing to do but on reaching the bad one we stopped and took a look and after that we returned to the boat and in 30 seconds we were over and tieing up below with a wild ride behind us. We continued on down and soon reached Barths hot springs where two of the victims of Salmon Falls are buried and from there on to Mr. Hancocks where we layed over for about three days and it was sure a pleasure to visit with Mr. Hancock and his wife.

Mrs. Guemlek I find that if I get this off on this mail I will have to cut out a lot that I would like to tell you. But to make a long story short it was a wonderful trip of 233 miles with a fall of three thousand two hundred ninty five feet. We had many side trips and climbed the mountains in several places and I never ate so many trout in my life in so short a time.

We made our arrival in Riggins at 3-30 P.M. Sept. 16 and I only wish that I could tell it to you instead of writeing it, so wont you write me and tell me what you think of the trip.

Sincerely yours,
BERT LOPER
73- SO. 2ND EAST,
SALT LAKE CITY, UTAH.

———————————•◆•———————————

Bert Loper drowned on the Colorado River, July 8, 1949, at 80 years of age, when his boat capsized in Mile 24½ Rapid.

If any name can be said to have supplanted that of Guleke on the Salmon River, it could only be Smith's. Clyde Smith and his son Don, who was 15 at the time, came down the Main Salmon in 1930 on a wooden scow they constructed in North Fork. Not being made of green lumber, the boat was too rigid to absorb repeated impacts, and they wrecked it on a rock in Long Tom Rapid. Undismayed, the family settled at the mouth of the Middle Fork, building a cabin which still occupies the bar on the downstream side of the confluence. They headquartered there for eight years.

Clyde Smith was from Kansas and had spent time in British Columbia and Montana before coming to Idaho. He made a sweepboat run on the Snake River in Wyoming from Jenny Lake to a point 40 miles down river, shortly before arriving in Salmon.

Don Smith on the left and Clyde Smith, right, with steelhead on the Main Salmon.

The family placered for gold, gardened, hunted, and fished in order to survive. When America became involved in the second World War, the Smiths left the river to work in war-related industry. They returned in 1944 to guide the Army Corps of Engineers down the river on a power-site inspection. Again in 1945, they boated the Corps' survey party through to Lewiston in wooden scows, taking two and a half months.

When placering played out around the Middle Fork, the Smiths began working their way down river in wooden boats provided with removable canvas roofs. When they found a likely spot, with lots of driftwood for fuel, they would beach for the winter and go back for a last boat load of supplies before the river iced over.

They also began outfitting for tourists, hunters, and fishermen. In 1943 they took the Fredric Christian motion-picture party down from Salmon and carrier pigeons were used to send messages back to town. In 1948 they floated the Wolff party to Lewiston in the first welded aluminum scow used on the river. It was lighter fully-loaded than were the wooden boats when empty.

Robert, born in 1941, was the first of three sons raised by Don and Marian Smith. If any person can be said to have earned the mantle of the most skillful boatman on the river, it is this man.

Bob Smith moved to the river when he was six years old. About that time his father took him on his first float trip. He studied water in general and the Salmon River in particular. He learned oars, sweeps, and eventually motors. By the time he was 14, Bob was taking the Forest Service down the river in a rubber sweepboat.

Bob Smith as a child, with the first boat he ever built.

In 1960 he attempted to run a power boat up the Colorado from Lake Mead through Grand Canyon. The craft had two 80-hp. Mercury outboards but the water was high and they were unable to overcome Lava Falls.

Hell's Canyon of the Snake presented another challenge. Bob, along with Paul Filer, attempted to run it in 1962 with an open 20-foot aluminum boat powered by twin 50-hp. Mercs. At that time there were awesome rapids above Granite and Wild Sheep: Squaw, Buck, and Kinney Creek — since inundated by an Idaho Power dam. As Bob remarked, if an engine failed "you might as well throw your hat in and go after it." He ran all the rapids — up and back — in one day.

Bob has handled a variety of boats, and cargoes improbable as jeeps and bulldozers. He is a fishing guide, pilot, and builder of aluminum jet boats.

He is also the only man who can actually run the river in the dark. With an aluminum hull and exposed jet pumps a single mistake represents nothing less than expensive repairs. Yet he has managed this phenomenal feat on several occasions. It means that he has memorized the location of every rock that can come within inches of the river's surface at any waterflow. It requires a muscular effort of the imagination to even conceive of such an accomplishment. Only the steamboat pilots who ran the Mississippi at night in the 1800's displayed similar ability. Bob Smith has no betters and no peers among this country's jet-set.

Bob Smith constructing his first power boat. Left to right, the Smiths: Jack, Kenney, Don and Bob.

The River of No Return experienced a new phase of river traffic in 1947. Glen Wooldridge of Grants Pass, Oregon, arrived in Riggins, Idaho, the first week of July. While he had never run the Salmon before, he was a veteran Rogue River boatman who had helped pioneer motor trips from Grants Pass to the ocean. Wooldridge had decided to challenge the famous River of No Return.

To this end, he had designed a 22-foot plywood boat, with a high bow and a forward sheer. The boat was powered by a 33-hp. Evinrude outboard motor.

Glen brought two men with him: Reuel Hawkins of Gold Beach, Oregon, to handle the oars in an emergency, and Thomas Staley, a photographer.

In addition to duffle and groceries, they started out with 400 pounds of gasoline and oil, and a spare 22-hp. motor.

A crowd of curious on-lookers gathered in Riggins that morning. Few believed the men could be so foolish as to attempt the up-river passage. Those who did believe made no effort to conceal their skepticism. But Wooldridge and his friends set off.

They worked their way up-river, running about five hours a day. When a rapid failed to yield on the first attempt, they would retreat, lighten the load, and let Glen run through alone. At Ruby Rapid they had to resort to a line.

Wooldridge stood in the back of the boat operating the motor with an extension handle. By the end of the third day they were at the mouth of Panther Creek above the Middle Fork. They hadn't intended to go farther, but the *Recorder Herald* of Salmon wanted to publish a story saying they were coming up to Salmon so they decided to continue.

After laying over for a day, the men pushed up through Pine Creek Rapid and had an uneventful run to the town. A large crowd greeted them at the bridge. The last day's run took five and a half hours.

Glen Wooldridge sold his boat to Paul Keep who lived a little way above Riggins. Wooldridge later made a second trip up the river. The boat rested near the road by Carey Creek for years, until high water wrecked it in 1974.

The Wooldridge trip was much publicized because it was the boating venture that filched some of the magic from the name "River of No Return." Yet two earlier "return" trips went largely unremarked.

Glen Wooldridge motoring up the River of No Return in 1947. His oarsman, Reuel Hawkins is seated in front.

When Don and Clyde Smith brought the Army Corps of Engineers down from Salmon in two wooden scows to survey the river in 1945, they were accompanied by a 17-foot boat with a 22-hp. engine. The Corps provided the boat and three spare engines.

To facilitate the survey, Don would drop off a rod man, motor down as far as could be seen, drop the instrument man, and motor the second rod man down as far as he could be viewed. When calculations were completed, Don would motor back up to the first rod man, pick him up, then the instrument man, and repeat the process.

On days when they moved the camp boats, Ed Wilson would row the motor boat four or five miles down to the first scow, Don and Clyde would motor back to the second scow and run it down while Ed rowed the motor boat a second time.

They dumped the boat a few times, but in this manner they returned in stages several times over every stretch of the river from Lewiston to Salmon.

Even more intriguing is the information carried in the *Salmon Recorder-Herald* in 1937. At that time Phil Rand wrote a series of articles on the history of the North Fork country. In one piece he cites Allen C. Merritt, a reliable old-timer, as authority for the statement that in the winter of 1866-67, George Thomas, Jim M. Nighswander, William Smith, and Bud Martin camped at the mouth of the North Fork, having come up the Salmon from Lewiston by boat, starting in 1865. Thomas and Nighswander were the first men to clear ranches up the North Fork.

George E. Shoup recalled the same incident in his history of Lemhi County, which was serialized in the Salmon paper in 1940. Shoup spelled Nighswander "Neicewander," and said his partner, Thomas, was a fearless, powerful sailor.

If their story is true, it means the second trip of record on the Salmon was a reverse passage. Perhaps "River of No Return" was a misnomer all along.

UPPER SALMON

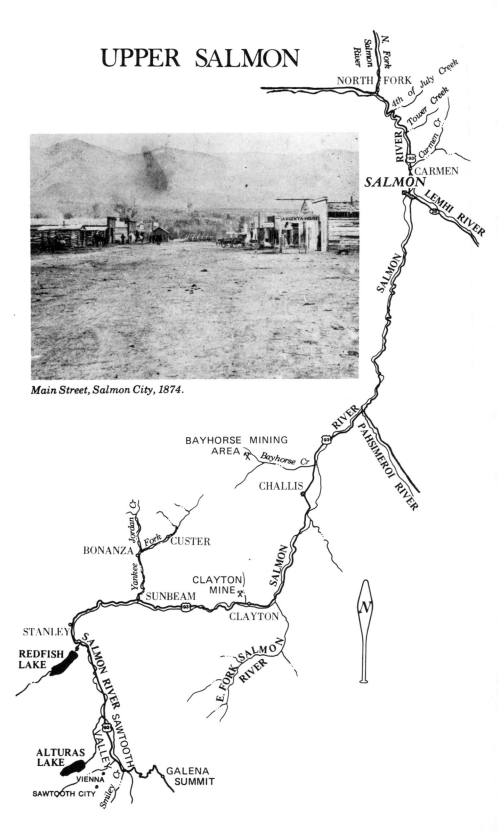

Main Street, Salmon City, 1874.

N. Fork
Salmon
River

N. Fork

NORTH FORK

4th of July Creek

Tower Creek

Tower Cr

Carmen Creek

CARMEN

SALMON

RIVER

LEMHI RIVER

SALMON

RIVER

PAHSIMEROI RIVER

BAYHORSE MINING
AREA

Bayhorse Cr

CHALLIS

Jordan Cr

Fork

CUSTER

BONANZA

Yankee

SALMON

CLAYTON
MINE

SUNBEAM

CLAYTON

STANLEY

E. FORK SALMON

RIVER

REDFISH
LAKE

SALMON RIVER SAWTOOTH VALLEY

N

ALTURAS
LAKE

VIENNA

Smiley Cr

GALENA
SUMMIT

SAWTOOTH CITY

Along the Road:
Galena Summit to North Fork

The River of No Return draws its headwaters from the Sawtooth Valley, just below Galena Summit on U. S. Highway 93. The source of the river is about 75 air miles northeast of Boise and 25 miles northwest of Sun Valley. Tributary streams like Pole, Smiley, Fisher, and Fourth of July Creeks join the overflow from Redfish Lake and the Sawtooth Wilderness to make the Salmon a respectable river by the time it reaches Stanley. From this point, the waters flow almost 400 miles to their confluence with the Snake, making the Salmon the longest river contained within one state — Alaska excepted.

For 170 miles, from the foot of Galena Summit near Alturas Lake, to the town of North Fork, Highway 93 flows like a flume, its every curve dictated by the river. But at North Fork, the River of No Return crooks abruptly westward, while the highway continues north toward Montana.

Galena Summit was crossed in mid-September, 1824 by a brigade of 40 Hudson Bay Company trappers and Iroquois Indian trappers under the command of Alexander Ross. Ross had been in charge of Fort Nez Perce; his party came up Big Wood River and went down the Salmon past Challis.

Ross' men rendezvoused at the Three Tetons in the fall and traveled to Flathead Post where Ross was replaced by Peter Skene Ogden. Ross is remembered as a censorious Calvinist who "seemed possessed of every virtue except charity."

Driving north on U.S. 93 through the Sawtooth Valley toward Stanley, the Sawtooth Range can be seen on the left, or western side of the highway, and the White Cloud Peaks can be observed off to the right, or eastern side of the road.

Two mining camps, Sawtooth City (1879) and Vienna (1880), were located west of the highway between Smiley Creek and Beaver Creek. Ore was freighted on a wagon toll-road over 8700-foot Galena Summit to the Philadelphia Smelter at Ketchum until mills could be

Aerial photograph looking southeast over U.S. Highway 93 toward Galena Summit. Headwaters of the Salmon and Smiley Creek airstrip in the center of the *picture, Pole Creek on the left, Beaver Creek and the road to Sawtooth City on the right.*

built at the mines. Both camps approached ghost town status by the time the first settlers took their homesteads in the valley.

❖

Stanley Basin and the town of Stanley are named to honor Captain John Stanley, oldest member of a prospecting party which entered the area in the summer of 1863.

Upper Stanley, along the banks of Valley Creek on State Highway 21, just off U.S. 93, was first occupied by Arthur and Della McGown and their two children in 1890. They built a log cabin, ran a

Aerial view across the southwest end of Big Redfish Lake. This view is looking directly up Redfish Lake Creek Canyon *into the Sawtooth Range. All the area beyond the upper end of the lake is in the Sawtooth Wilderness.*

View across Highway 93 and the Salmon River to Big Redfish Lake and *the Sawtooth Range in the background.*

store selling beef to miners and packers, and operated a saloon and post office until 1895.

The site was not considered a town until November, 1919, when Bartlett Falls surveyed and recorded lots and streets. The place was often referred to as "Dogtown" because the Niece family kept so many hounds. At present, Harrah's Reno and Lake Tahoe is the major corporate land holder in the community.

Lower Stanley, on Highway 93, began as a four-room log hotel, in 1902, at the mouth of Nip and Tuck Gulch on the Salmon. It was next to the road that was constructed up-river from the mouth of Yankee Fork.

A large log store was built in 1907. The lower townsite was the first to use Stanley's name, but its post office and school were lost to upper Stanley, and consequently it never quite prospered like the higher location. Lower Stanley was frequently called "Squawtown" because it was said that the women there did all the work. Today, Stanley is the focus of a considerable summer tourist trade. One-day float trips on the Salmon River embark from the lower townsite.

The town of upper Stanley as it looked in the early Thirties.

Yankee Fork enters the Salmon River from the north at Sunbeam, 12 miles below Stanley. This stream has a fascinating mining history.

Prospectors from Loon Creek, a tributary of the Middle Fork of the Salmon, moved onto the Fork in the early 1870's, when their Middle Fork claims played out. Yankee Fork mines got off to a slow start, until the summer of 1875, when William A. Norton discovered a high grade vein with an exceptionally rich three inch seam. It proved to be the answer to a prospector's prayer. He was able to pound out in a hand mortar $11,500 worth of gold in 30 days. He called his mine the Charles Dickens.

The following summer, Jim Baxter, E. M. Dodge, and Morgan McKeim discovered the General Custer. It too was a prospector's dream. Most of the vein was exposed on the surface and so the miners could avoid expensive developmental work. The low cost of getting the ore out greatly enhanced its value. They packed their rock to a Salt Lake City mill and realized $60,000 the first year. Subsequently, they sold their claims for $285,000. In the meantime, D. B. Varney discovered the Montana mine on Estes Mountain.

Doubts were overcome in 1879 as thousands of miners began a belated rush to the Yankee Fork. The mining towns of Bonanza City and Custer were established and began to grow. Freighters used Challis as a supply center, and a toll-road stage service from there to Bonanza opened in October of 1879.

Milling machinery was hauled to the General Custer and a 30-stamp mill was in operation by 1880. With competent engineers, backed by San Francisco capital, the mill ran for a decade and produced eight million dollars from the lode.

Norton took half a million in gold out of the Dickens before his death in 1884. The Charles Dickens and the Custer mine and mill were eventually acquired and capitalized by a British concern. They used the mill to process ore from both mines. Fraudulent manipulation of Dickens-Custer stock forced the company to close in 1892.

A new company used the Custer mill to work the Lucky Boy vein parallel to that of the Custer. They halted operations in 1904, after about a million dollars worth of production.

Boating on the Sunbeam Reservoir.

Diversion tunnel and primitive fish ladder at Sunbeam Dam.

Sunbeam Dam today. It is uncertain at this time who is entitled to an accolade for dynamiting the south abutment. However, there is no limit to what can be accomplished if no one cares who gets the credit.

The Golden Sunbeam Company brought in a new mill near the Montana the year the Lucky Boy shut down. Obtaining significant production in 1907-'08, the company decided to expand their mill and installed a dam on the Salmon River for hydroelectric power in 1910. Sunbeam hoped to process enormous reserves of low-grade ore but had to abandon their plans the next year.

The evils of the dam outlived the company. A poorly designed fish ladder allowed some passage of steelhead trout and chinook salmon at certain water stages. However, sockeye salmon, which had been plentiful in the Salmon River headwaters, were virtually wiped out. Dynamite was used to remove part of the rock adjacent to the dam in 1934. The section which remains can be viewed from the highway.

Custer and Bonanza were ghost towns by 1912, but low-grade placers were dredged successfully from 1939 to 1942 and from 1946 through 1951. Almost two million dollars was realized from these efforts. Driving up Yankee Fork today one can see the wasteland of tailing drifts that is the legacy of a dredge operation. The land seems to hold these marks like a grudge. The dredge itself is drydocked at the mouth of Jordan Creek, between Bonanza and Custer.

The old school house in Custer contains the McGown museum, now run by the U.S. Forest Service.

———————————•—●—●—•———————————

Clayton, 19 miles north of Yankee Fork on Highway 93, was founded in 1881 when the Salmon River Mining and Smelting Company began operating a smelter there for the mines up Kinnikinic and Slate Creeks. The smelter operated sporadically until 1904. A large slag pile on the south end of town, by the river, serves as a reminder of those times. Clayton still has a number of active silver mines; the Clayton Silver Mine two miles up Kinnikinic has operated since 1929 and employs about 35 people.

An early photograph of Clayton, with the Salmon River smelter at the lower right.

Charcoal wagons hauling fuel for the smelter at Clayton.

Three miles below Clayton, the East Fork of the Salmon enters the Main river. About a mile and a half up that fork was the site of Wagontown, known as Crystal City by 1880. Because Challis received a handful more votes, Crystal lost its chance to be the seat of Custer County in 1881.

The town was the terminus of the wagon road that came from Ketchum over Trail Creek to Big Lost River and down Road Creek to the East Fork. The road was gradually extended to Clayton. Crystal City's business was supplying freight to the nearby mines. Only evidence of foundations remains.

———————————————◆●◆———————————————

Bayhorse Creek enters the Salmon a dozen miles down river from Clayton, on the left. Though a claim was filed as early as 1872, rich ore wasn't discovered on the creek until 1877. A town, originally known as Aetna, then as Bay Horse, was located about two and a half miles up the creek from the present highway. Bayhorse served as a center for silver and lead mines like the Ramshorn, Skylark, and Excelsior.

The mining town of Bayhorse, two and a half miles up Bayhorse Creek from the river.

A water-powered five-stamp mill and a 25-ton smelter were built. The smelter required large amounts of charcoal to produce the high temperatures necessary to melt out silver and lead, so a flume was constructed to bring quantities of wood to the six charcoal kilns. The kilns still stand, as do a number of buildings in the town, which is fenced to protect the owner from liability suits by trespassers.

The valley between Bayhorse Creek and Challis was explored by Michael Bourdon, Hudson Bay Company trapper, and a party of free trappers who had been outfitted by the Company in 1822. The brigade took 2200 beaver that season.

Michael Bourdon, who was one of the most prominent French-Canadian trappers in the Pacific Northwest, lost his life in a battle with the Blackfeet the following year — possibly on the Lemhi River south of Salmon, more likely on Henry's Fork of the Snake River.

The mile-high town of Challis lies two miles north of the junction of Highway 93 and Alternate 93. The first settlement, Garden City, was at the mouth of Garden Creek but the townsite was relocated four miles up the creek in 1878. It was named after Alvah P. Challis, who helped lay out the lots.

The main street of Challis, Idaho. Date unknown.

A. P. Challis, a member of John Stanley's party, had been in the California gold rush, along the Fraser in British Columbia, and in Boise Basin. Summers he placered in Stanley Basin with his partner, Henry Sturkey, winters were spent at their Salmon River cattle ranch. Challis was an honest, generous and well-loved man.

The town became a trading center to the nearby mines and was connected by toll road to Custer. Challis valley was a good wintering ground for pack stock and teams used by the freighters.

Northeast of Challis can be seen the brightly colored bluffs of the Lemhi Range.

The Pahsimeroi River enters the Salmon from the east, about 20 miles north of Challis. The snowy slopes of Borah Peak, at 12,655 feet the highest point in Idaho, serve as the source for this river. Its name is a Shoshoni word: Pah, "water," sima, "one" and roi, "grove," so in English the word means grove of trees by water.

Warren Ferris and his men from the American Fur Company camped in the Pahsimeroi Valley during the winter of 1831-32 and killed over a hundred buffalo there. They called the river the Little Salmon.

Thomas "Broken Hand" Fitzpatrick and Kit Carson, with a party from Santa Fe, New Mexico, arrived on the Salmon River in 1832 and wintered 40 miles north of the Pahsimeroi, near what was to become the site of Salmon City. When winter was over they resumed trapping toward the North Platte.

In July of 1866, gold was discovered in the Leesburg Basin west of later Salmon. Travel to the mining district converged at the mouth of the Lemhi River, and Salmon City began to form on the west side of Salmon River. It originated as a collection of tents with merchants, peddlers, tradesmen, saloons, and eating places.

Early photograph of Salmon 1870's.

Small boats ferried men and supplies across the river for a fee. Charles Chamberlain and Chris Darnutzer built the first pack bridge across the river in 1867. They charged a 25-cent toll.

The same year, logs were cut for buildings which would develop the town on the east side of the river. Most of the construction was up on the higher bench east of the river; the lower land was primarily occupied by Chinese.

Salmon in the 1900's.

First car in Salmon, 1905. Note child with hat looking through bridge railing behind rear fender.

George L. Shoup, who had the community's major mercantile business, helped lay out a main street and two cross streets. Two blocks of Main Street soon represented the "business district."

All of the lots were simply held by squatters rights until Judge Beattie obtained a patent for the townsite of Salmon in 1882. The town was incorporated 10 years later.

Ranches were established to raise range cattle, vegetables and grain were grown. A log cabin school was opened. In 1889 George Shoup received a Presidential appointment as the last territorial governor of Idaho. The following year, he was elected the first governor of the state.

Life in Salmon at present reflects the town's origins; it is still largely based on cattle ranching, crops, dairying, timber, and recreation such as river-running, hunting, and fishing. Set on the banks of the River of No Return, against the impressive backdrop of the Beaverhead Mountains, Salmon remains a historic and colorful city.

About half a mile north of the town of Salmon, the Lemhi River flows into the River of No Return from the southeast.

Bands of northern Shoshoni under Chief Cameahwait occupied the Lemhi Valley, southeast of later Salmon, at the time of Lewis and Clark's visit. Cameahwait was a brother to Sacagawea and died in a skirmish with the Blackfeet.

In 1855 a party of about 30 Mormons left Bear River, Utah, and arrived on the Lemhi River after 22 days. They established a fort, intending to do missionary work among the Indians whom they considered Lamanites. Since their journey required the same number of days as did that of King Limhi leading the Nephites to Zarahemla in the *Book of Mormon,* they named their stockade Limhi. The word was corrupted to Lemhi and was eventually affixed to the Indians, the river, and the mountain range.

Fur trappers referred to the junction of the Lemhi and Salmon as "the forks of the Salmon." The forks were busier than an anthill during the winter of 1831-1832. Milton Sublette and Jim Bridger led a Rocky Mountain Fur Company brigade up from Bear River to winter on the Salmon with the Nez Perce. Warren Ferris' men of the American Fur Company had already arrived in October. In November, Henry Fraeb showed up with supplies for the Rocky Mountain Fur Co. With him was the famous "merry mountain man" Joe Meek. Then John Work and Francois Payette appeared with 56 Hudson Bay trappers. A whole cavallada of mountain men was camped at the forks that winter. There must have been "smart doin's," cheerwater, squaws, and many a windy spun before the green-grass moon arrived.

Salmon City about 1890. The river flows across the middle of the picture, with the Darnutzer-Chamberlain bridge in the center, crossing at Price Island.

Aerial view of present day Salmon.

Carmen is on Highway 93, four miles north of Salmon. It is named after Benjamin Carmen who had a sawmill on the creek there, while he ran a log carpentry business in Salmon.

The Nez Perce buffalo trail crossed the lower section of the stream, which was called Salmon Creek by Lewis and Clark.

East of this point the Beaverhead Mountains, part of the Bitterroot Range, form the Continental Divide.

Just outside Carmen is a sign commemorating the winter camp of Captain Benjamin L. E. Bonneville. Bonneville's was a brief and curious presence during the height of the fur trade. Born in France, a West Point graduate, the Captain persuaded the commanding general of the Army to give him a leave of absence to "examine the locations, habits, and trading practices of the Indian tribes, visit the American and British establishments, and study the best means of making the country available to American citizens." One clause in his instructions ordered him to collect "any information which may be useful to the Government," permitting him wide interpretive latitude.

Bonneville left St. Louis May 1, 1832, with 110 men and 20 wagons of trade goods and supplies. He left some of his men on the Green River to trap down to the Bear River and into Crow country. He then proceeded toward Salmon River since it had been represented as a more eligible place to winter.

The Captain came by way of Jackson Hole, Teton Pass, Pierre's Hole, and down the Lemhi River. He arrived about five miles below the confluence of the Lemhi with the Salmon on September 26, 1832. With him was the notable trailbreaker, already an experienced mountain man, Joseph Reddeford Walker. For nearly half a century, Walker was to roam the west, discovering among other things, Yosemite, the Giant Sequoias and Walker Pass.

The men with Bonneville and Walker began building their winter quarters across from present-day Carmen. Warren Ferris and two trappers visited Bonneville's fort early in November. Ferris described it as being in a cottonwood grove on the west side of the Salmon River: "This miserable establishment consisted entirely of several log cabins, low, badly constructed, and admirably situated for besiegers only, who would be sheltered on every side, by timber, brush, etc." The men also constructed a secure pen into which the horses could be driven at night.

(Samuel Parker, a Presbyterian missionary, visited the site of Bonneville's camp three years later, and his description has caused some historians to believe the cantonment was on the east side of the river, near the mouth of Carmen Creek.)

Because of the large number of Nez Perce and Flathead Indians and their inevitable horse herds, grass and game began to grow scarce around the fort. Bonneville had to alter his arrangements. He sent Walker with 50 men to the Snake River, planning a rendezvous in July. Retaining a handful of free trappers, the Captain cached his supplies and established a second winter camp on the North Fork until Dec. 9.

Some historians argue that Bonneville spent Christmas up the Lemhi near Swan Basin, others say up the North Fork. In any event, after Christmas the men apparently went up the Pahsimeroi and over to the Snake, returning to their Salmon River caches in March, 1833.

Captain Bonneville overstayed his military leave of absence by nearly two years. When he returned to Washington, D.C. in 1835, he was astonished to learn that he had been dropped from Army rolls. President Jackson sent a recommendation for his reappointment to the Senate and a few months later the ex-trapper was reinstated to his former rank in the Seventh Infantry.

The mystery that shrouds Bonneville's private undertaking concerns its real purpose and the manner in which it was financed. On returning from the frontier in 1835, Bonneville went directly to John Jacob Astor in New York, even before reporting to authorities in Washington. Was he doing reconnaissance for the Government or was he trying to recover the trade lost by Astor at Astoria? Since Bonneville sold the narrative of his travels to Washington Irving, who rewrote it and then burned the original manuscript, the answer to this intriguing question may never be known.

Driving north on U.S. Highway 93 from Salmon to North Fork, the road closely parallels the route of William Clark in 1805.

Just below Bird Creek on the eastern side of the road beneath some streaked, conglomerate bluffs is a sign which reads:

On August 21, 1805 Captain Clark and his party camped near this spot. Clark wrote: "Crossed the River and went over a point of high land and struck it again near a Bluff on the right Side ... those two men joined me at my camp on the right Side below the first Clift ... This Clift is of a redish brown Colour, the rocks which fall from it is a dark flint tinged with that Colour. Some Gullies of white Sand Stone and Sand fine and white as Snow."

The reddish streaks can still be seen from the road.

About half a mile farther north at Tower Creek, (once known as Cherry Creek, and then as Boyle Creek) is another sign:

Captain Clark after viewing the continental divide on August 22, 1805, remarked: "We set out early passed a Small Creek on the Right one mile and the points of four mountains verry Steup high and rockey, the assent of three was So steup that it is incrediable to describe."

The first road along Salmon River in 1903, near Tower Creek.

On August 31, 1805, after returning to this locale from his trip down the Salmon River, Clark joined Lewis and the party turned from the Salmon River and traveled up Tower Creek. Clark wrote, "we proceeded on the road on which I had decended as far as the first rim below and left the road and Encamped in Some old lodges at the place the road leaves the creek and assends the high country ... passed remarkable rock resembling pirimids on the left side."

77

The expedition bypassed the river bluffs, climbed over a saddle, dropped down to the North Fork of the Salmon (which they called Fish Creek), went up this stream and camped about six miles north of present-day North Fork at the mouth of Hull Creek. On September 4, the party ascended a "high Snow mountain," which was probably Saddle Mountain and crossed the Bitterroots between the East and West Forks of Camp Creek. They journeyed down the Bitterroot Valley, re-entered present-day Idaho, and went west by way of the Lolo Trail and Clearwater River.

Wagonhammer Spring, creek, and commercial campground can be seen on the west side of Highway 93, about two miles south of North Fork. The camp and creek take their name from the discovery of a wagon wheel wrench on the site in the 1860's, probably left by a party of prospectors from Utah who were unable to get their three wagons north from this point.

In the early 1900's there was a sawmill on the creek run by William Hoffman and his family. Trees were bought at a fixed price from the Forest Service, cut with two-man saws and hauled on wooden-wheeled, single-axled carts. The carts were pulled from the woods by a team of horses; one end of the logs was allowed to drag on the ground, acting as a brake. Before the logs could be sawed at the mill, the rocks which had become embedded during the hauling operation had to be picked out with a hand axe.

Hoffman's mill was steam powered; in addition to lumber, he manufactured apple boxes, ship-lap siding, tongue-and-groove flooring, and shingles. He hauled his products to Salmon, taking 13 hours for a trip.

On the slope along the east side of the highway, north of Fourth of July Creek, are the remains of a wooden flume weathering on the skirt of the hills. This flume was cut and built by William Hoffman. The boards were an inch and a half thick and carried water for two miles — from Fourth of July Creek to his ranch at Wagonhammer.

Along the River:
North Fork to Corn Creek

U.S. Highway 93 leaves the River of No Return at the settlement of North Fork. The river swings west and the Salmon River Road goes with it for 46 miles. By the time it reaches this bend, the Salmon has traveled about 180 miles from its source in the Sawtooth Valley.

It is interesting to view the river from North Fork to Shoup as seen by a passenger on a scow in November, 1887. John Booth was floating with freight on a scow run by Captain Eli Suydan and Pilot George Sandiland.

Booth wrote: "From North Fork the river runs smoothly through a wide canyon for three miles when the lake is reached, which is three miles long and a half a mile wide. At this time of the year large white swans are plentiful here. These swans are very tame and swim close to the boat. There are also plenty of ducks, which the hunters kill very easily.

"Fish and other game abound in and around the lake. While passing through all is stillness; only the songs of the birds and the crack of the hunter's rifle can be heard. After an hour's ride we find ourselves nearing the outlet of the Salmon lake at Dump Creek."

A few miles down-river from Dump Creek was Pilliner Bluff, a high and dangerous cliff with a precipitous trail. Plymouth Rock, right in the center of the river, was the next landmark. Then came Tourist Bluff, near the Spayds' ranch, where deer, bear, and antelope could frequently be seen.

Farther down, near Merritts' ranch, was a 500-foot-high landmark called Pulpit Rock. Black-snake Rapids were then traversed, and just below this the scow passed between two huge rocks, known as the Golden Gate.

Ending the story of his float, Booth wrote: "Then we enter Shoup, an engineer blows the whistle, the boat sails up to the wharf, the gang plank is thrown out and our journey is ended."

Mile 181.5: **Donnelly Gulch** is the drainage to the right, or north of the river and the road. It is named after James Donnelly, an early settler.

George Shoup wrote that in 1872, a ferry boat built and run by Frank Shoto operated below North Fork at what would later be called Rose Ranch. Shoto accommodated traffic on a much used trail that went through Moose and Napias Creek Basins to Leesburg.

Fred and Charlie Rose bought this ranch from a man named Brown who was the original homesteader on the site. Fred and Charlie were brothers and naturally enough the place became known as the Rose Ranch. They were running the ranch in about 1900, raising hay, vegetables, and berries. They sold their produce in Leesburg, Ulysses, Gibtown — wherever there was a market. In October, 1910, they patented the flat across the river, now known as Rose Gulch, as part of their ranch.

After the Roses were gone, the ranch was taken over by Mr. Hovey, who raised cattle there. He drove about 20 head of cattle up across the East Fork of Sage Creek and encountered Stonewall Bollinger who had just taken up a ranch there. Stonewall told Hovey he could run the cattle around his place, but if they went through his garden he'd kill him. Hovey began pulling down Bollinger's fence bars and told his brother to push the cows on through. Stonewall pulled his pistol, shot Hovey in the head, and took to the hills.

For 20 years Bollinger was a wanted man, but his family saw to it that he got necessary supplies and the sheriff couldn't catch him. At the age of 40, Stonewall surrendered. The jury found he had acted in self-defense and pronounced him "not guilty."

The Forest Service has purchased the Rose Ranch.

Mile 182: **Rose Gulch** on the left across the river.

Mile 182.7: **Camel Gulch** across the river. Named for the John Camel family that lived at the mouth of the arroyo in early days.

Mile 183.8: **Deadwater Gulch,** a right-side drainage going to the river. A natural rock ledge extends across the Salmon and serves as a dike retarding the river's flow, thus creating a body of slackwater known as "the lake."

A rare, single box elder tree can be found growing on the riverbank just above the gulch.

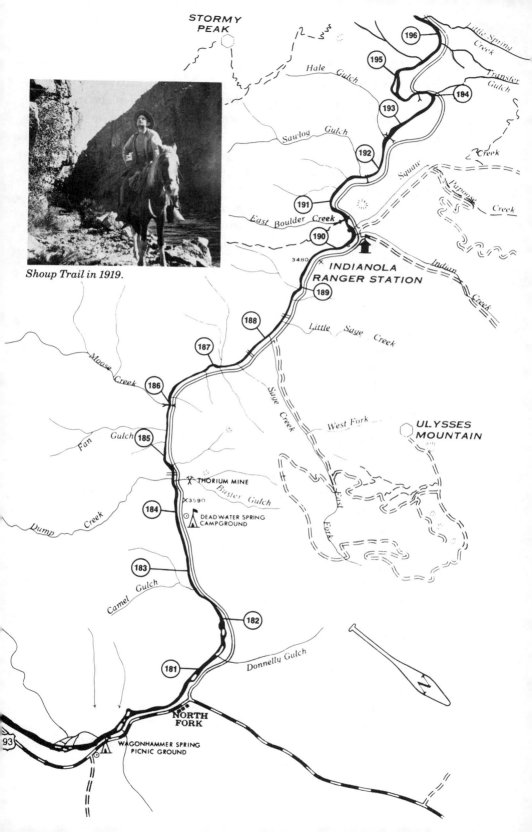

STORMY
PEAK

Little Spring
Creek

196

195

Hale Gulch

Transfer
Gulch

193

184

Sawlog Gulch

192

Creek

Squaw

191

Papoose
Creek

East Boulder Creek

190

Indian

3480

INDIANOLA
RANGER STATION

Creek

189

188

Little Sage Creek

187

Moose Creek

186

ULYSSES
MOUNTAIN

West Fork

Fan Gulch

185

THORIUM MINE

Buster Gulch

X3590

East Fork

184

DEAD WATER SPRING
CAMPGROUND

Dump Creek

183

Camel Gulch

182

Donnelly Gulch

181

N

NORTH
FORK

93

WAGONHAMMER SPRING
PICNIC GROUND

Shoup Trail in 1919.

Mile 184.4: **Buster Gulch** on the right. Guy Buster had a cabin here. He would go up to Donnelly Gulch and visit with a young woman who was cooking for Mr. Brown, who was then about 70 years old. Brown disliked Buster and occasionally told him to get off his property.

Brown had a few hundred dollars and Buster decided to kill him. He conspired with the cook to lure Brown down to Buster Gulch on the pretense she was having problems with Guy. When Brown arrived, he struck Buster with his cane and Guy shot him. Then the couple went up to Donnelly and got Brown's money.

At the trial, Buster displayed some bruises and claimed self-defense. He got off. But other men's lives don't make a soft pillow at night. Years later, the woman finally told the truth about the incident.

Mile 184.5: **Dump Creek** enters on the left side of the river. Dump Creek Jones was an old placer miner who lived by the creek where it empties into the river.

The enormous gravel outwash at the mouth of the creek is evidence of a troubled ecosystem. McNutt had placer claims around 1884 at the head of Moose Creek, the next drainage downstream. He had a reservoir at the head of the creek and cut a hole through to Dump Creek to dispose of his tailings. When his reservoir broke, Moose Creek began to drain into Dump Creek. The canyon walls at the head of Dump Creek are so sheer that erosion quickly became a severe problem. Rock from the creek can be seen on bars for miles downriver. There are Forest Service plans to restore Moose Creek to its rightful drainage.

Mile 185.4: **Fan Gulch,** so called for the shape of the alluvial deposit at its mouth.

Mile 186: **Moose Creek** on the left. Early miners in this section reported seeing many moose.

Mile 187.3: **Sage Creek** comes in on the right. A Frenchman and his Indian wife lived on this site from 1887-90.

John Moore bought William Hoffman's sawmill at Wagonhammer Creek in 1929 and moved it to Sage Creek where it operated for several years.

Mile 190.3: **Indian Creek** flows in on the right. It heads 12 miles above, on the Idaho-Montana border. Captain William Clark was on this creek August 23, 1805, as he reconnoitered the River of No Return. He left most of his party up-river on a flat just across from

Moose Creek while he and his guide came down to get a better view of the river.

Mr. Layton had a saloon at the mouth of Indian Creek in 1886, with a couple of girls hustling for him. The trio managed to get some of the miners' claims and much of their gold.

A good-natured miner, nicknamed "Wild Bill," was persuaded to jump some of Layton's quartz claims up Indian Creek. When Layton caught him, he marched him at rifle point back up the creek and forced him to remove the new claim markers. Then he murdered Wild Bill. Layton next compelled a teen-age boy, Fred Bevan, who lived nearby, to swear Bill had been killed in self-defense. Layton only got about a year in jail for his deed.

A rough road was pushed up Indian Creek in 1901 by the county and subscription. It was used to haul equipment from the river to the gold-quartz-mines which had been located in 1895.

The important mines were the Kittie Burton and the Ulysses, six miles up the creek. The Burton was on a ridge to the west and the Ulysses was high on the eastern side of the valley. Several houses, a large boarding house, and a 30-stamp mill were constructed. A sizeable community gathered, with 45 men working at the Kittie Burton alone.

The mill burned in 1904 and was rebuilt as a 15-stamp mill. Cable tramways with 22 buckets connected both mines. The tram was almost a mile long. Water power ran the mill in the spring; cordwood fuel produced steam power during the rest of the year. The mines were steady producers for several years. Today only a few houses still stand.

The Forest Service has maintained a ranger station at Indian Creek for many years. Indianola is a coined name used in Texas, Iowa, and Mississippi.

Mile 190.5: **Squaw Creek** on the right. William Clark, with his Indian guide Tobe and three other men, ascended this creek six miles on August 23, 1805. Their provisions were exhausted, so they ate fish, serviceberries, and haws by the stream. Clark named it Berry Creek. He wrote that there was "a well beeten Indian parth up this creak."

Clark and his men crossed a ridge, descended again to the river (perhaps by Spring Creek) then climbed a high point about three miles upstream from Shoup. From this vantage, Captain Clark could see Pine Creek Rapid and about 20 miles down-river. The view was enough to convince him of the utter impracticability of that route.

They spent the night back on Squaw Creek, near the mouth of Papoose Creek.

Clark's journal says that the next morning he carved his name on a pine tree at the mouth of Squaw Creek. Returning to the men he'd left up-river at Little Moose Creek, he sent a message to Lewis with John Colter. The note outlined the difficulties presented by the river, while suggesting the land route that Lewis decided to follow. (Colter would be the only man permitted to leave the expedition on its return journey, and gained lasting recognition for his discovery of Yellowstone.)

Around the turn of the century, the Niece family, a widow and three children, lived at the mouth of Squaw Creek.

The mouth of the creek was the scene of considerable activity in 1933, when Camp 92 was established for the Civilian Conservation Corps. The bar along the river was more extensive at that time.

Civilian Conservation Camp No. 92, at the mouth of Squaw Creek. Much of the bar next to the river has been washed away.

The Corps was here to extend the road down-river and meet crews which were working east from Riggins. One of the rare, fortunate consequences of the second World War was that it interrupted this effort long enough for it to become permanently obstructed.

A sizeable stone fireplace on the edge of Squaw Creek Road, about a hundred feet off the Salmon River Road, is the only visible reminder of Camp 92's location.

Mile 190.7: **East Boulder Creek** enters on the left shore. Jim Hall built the cabin here. It was once known as Park Creek, after an old prospector who lived here.

At one time Bob and Kate Moore lived at the mouth of this creek. When Will Rogers said he "never met a man he didn't like" he apparently had not cut trails with Bob. Moore beat his wife with considerable frequency. They moved from East Boulder to Clear Creek, up Panther Creek. When they sold out there, Kate moved to Bannock, Montana. Bob followed her and beat her again. Enough was enough — one night while he was sleeping she removed his head with an axe. No more Moore.

Mile 191.7: **Sawlog Gulch** across the river on the left. Trees cut here were floated to Shoup for timbering the mines. Elmer Purcell, who is buried on the Middle Fork, had a hardrock mine somewhere up Sawlog — he never revealed the location.

Mile 192.5: **Hale Gulch** on the left side of the river.

The Jim Hales lived here in 1920 and were able to feed their children with the help of revenue from moonshine made on the place.

Mile 193: **Spayd and Winn Ranch.** This is the 280-acre flat on the left side of the road, but on the right hand side of the river.

Charley Spayd and Thomas Winn were the original locaters on this piece of ground. Spayd was here at least as early as 1887; Winn had joined him by 1896. They worked together.

In 1906 Tom took a pack string loaded with vegetables and meat to the Ulysses mine. When he returned, he saw Spayd lying in the field by a pond. Thinking Charley was sunning himself, Tom went to the house where he noticed Spayd's gun was missing. He went back to the field and found his partner, who had been in poor health, had killed himself. Winn took his body to the Ulysses cemetery and buried him.

Tom found packing beef to the Ulysses-Burton mines such a chore that he tried driving them up there on foot, luring them along with a load of hay. At a certain point, the cows decided they'd gone far enough and humped for home. Tom shot some and went on to the mines with the meat. The miners complained about the toughness of the beef. Winn told them the meat was tough, but the next load would be a lot tougher.

Winn also raised sizeable watermelons which he hauled by the wagonload to Big Hole, Montana. He could never raise enough, as the farmers, in the heat of haying season, would buy all he could produce.

In 1920, Tom Winn contracted to build the road from Transfer Gulch to Shoup for $1500. It took him six months and cost $500 more than he bid, but he didn't regret it, feeling he had done a good turn for the folks in Shoup.

The ranch was sold by Tom in 1916 for a good sum. He married at age 72 and he and his wife lived out their days in Salmon.

The place changed hands frequently. Washington Elliott got it from Winn to raise cattle, hogs, and hay. Elliott had a family with three children. He sold to Hyrum Marsing, who raised seven children, horses, cattle, and hay there. Jack Smoot lost the ranch to the bank in 1934; Guy and Horace Roberts leased it in '35. Then it was owned and sold in succession by Leo Iverson, Earl Poynor, Emmett Reese, and finally Carl Kriley in 1968. Shortly it was subdivided into 32 five-acre parcels.

Tom Winn in the watermelon field on his ranch.

Waterwheel at Tom Winn's place in 1925, used to lift irrigation water onto his desert entry homestead at the mouth of Transfer Gulch.

Mile 193.5: On the point across the river from the road, about a mile below Hale Gulch, is the two-story log house built by Frank Hall and his three boys about 1915. Bill Hall, one of the sons, is buried in a marked grave on the property.

Mile 194: **Transfer Gulch** on the right. The name recalls the time when this point was the end of the wagon road. Supplies going farther down-river had to be transferred to pack stock or scows.

Mile 194.5: The 60-acre clearing across the river, just below the gulch, was homesteaded in 1914 by Charley Twining. He sold the place in 1921 to Magnus Bevan, who had seen it while working with Tom Winn on the road to Shoup.

Magnus' father brought him from Helena, Montana to Gilmore where for two years he went to school in a tent. The family moved to Ulysses in 1908.

Bevan bought Twining's place for $200 and a 1916 Dodge. It was known as the "Poor Farm." He set about clearing the brush and trees. Magnus felled 13 large cottonwood trees with an axe in one day — while he was sick with the chicken pox. He fenced the farm, planted hay, raised cattle, and worked summers for the Forest Service.

He married Hazel Swett (Rood), from Vernal, Utah, in March of 1933. They lived on the place for 10 years and had two children: Hilliard Bevan of Creede, Colorado, and Verda Broadbent of Challis, Idaho.

The Bevan family sold their farm to Ed Hagel and moved to Panther Creek, where Magnus died in 1975. The place on the river was eventually subdivided, like the old Spayd-Winn Ranch.

The Bevans, who worked the "Poor Farm" across the river below Transfer Gulch. Left to right: Verda, Magnus, Hilliard, and Hazel.

87

Mile 197: **Spring Creek** comes in on the right. Up-river from the stream and just below the road is a small cyclone-fenced graveyard. The four foot white marble tombstone is that of Henry Clay Merritt, born June 4, 1843, died November 2, 1884.

Merritt was a boatman and the superintendent of the Kentuck mine at Shoup. While bringing supplies down in a boat with Jack Gilmer, he was knocked overboard near Indianola and drowned. His body was recovered near Spring Creek and so he was buried there.

The crumbling wooden grave marker is that of Baby Pinckard, son of Eva M. and William P. Pinckard. The child's headstone adds that he died July 14, 1941.

William Pinckard was a CCC worker. The Card family, up on Pine Creek, moved down to Shoup so their children could go to school. William became interested in Miss Eva Card and they were soon married. They moved up Boulder Creek behind Shoup.

When Eva's time arrived, her husband neglected to get her to a doctor and the child was breach born; the baby died, the mother almost died. The Pinckards left the area a short time after the burial.

Spring Creek was homesteaded in 1900 by James Hibbs. He came to Salmon from Missouri in 1895; went on to Shoup to work in the mines and did some boating with Guleke and Sandiland.

Mr. Hibbs and his wife, Mamie, raised nine children on this site. They had a garden that must have looked like a small farm, grew fruit, kept pigs, chickens — anything that would provide a meal. Mrs. Hibbs must have been a prodigious worker: in addition to all the other chores, she washed clothes for the miners at Shoup.

Jim was no slacker either. He had a water-powered sawmill, boated lumber to Shoup, and packed some of it to the mines. After the road was completed to Shoup, he was the first person to buy a car and he established the Salmon River taxi service, taking people to Salmon and back at $15 a head. In the winter he would haul the Model T on a sled with a team of horses to North Fork and back, using the car for the run between North Fork and Salmon.

Hibbs also operated a hunting outfit from Spring Creek in the fall, charging $25-a-day per person — the price included food, stock, and packer.

As the children grew, they helped with the chores. They walked to the Shoup school and back each day.

One of the daughters, Della, married Charley Twining and moved across the river.

An older son, Clarence, decided to get married in June, 1924. Father, mother, bride, and bridegroom drove the Model T to Salmon for the ceremony. While they were gone, the younger children left at home decided to play a joke. The river was on flood stage. They all went down to the sand beach and made obvious tracks going into the water. Offshore they wrapped their feet with gunny sacks and wore them until they had waded down to and across the Pine Creek bridge.

When the bridal party returned — no kids! The tracks were discovered and drowning was feared, until footprints were found on the other side of the bridge.

Older brother Jimmy followed the trail for 16 miles, and discovered them all swimming in Panther Creek with the Rood kids, whose ranch they'd gone to visit. Understandably puckered, he cut a club and sailed into them. Jimmy switched them all the way home, but it was nothing compared to the greeting they got from mother and father, who were mad enough to paw sod.

(At the time of this writing, all of the Hibbs children, except Fannie, have died.)

Spring Creek was sold in 1930 to Bonner Bevan, brother of Magnus. Norma Costello bought it in 1935. In 1945, Howard Wilson sold it to the Forest Service and it became a public campground.

Mile 197.6: **McKay Creek,** an indistinct drainage on the right side of the road. The creek and flat are named for Johnny McKay, early Salmon River boatman. This camp should have been named Sam James Flat to perpetuate the memory of that remarkable man.

Sam James, said to be a cousin of Frank and Jesse James, discovered the Kentuck mine at Shoup and some mines at Pine Creek, and sold his claims for considerable money. He continued to prospect, but he was generous to a fault with his good fortune. Sam would ride to Shoup on a big white horse called Blucher. At the outskirts of the town, he would stop to pull out his fiddle, then gallop in while playing 'Arkansas Traveler' — when they heard him coming, men would throw the saloon doors open so he could ride on in. James would order drinks for everyone, dismount, and let someone take his horse to the stable. He would continue to buy drinks for everyone until he was drunk as a wheelbarrow, then his friends would carry him over to a rooming house for the night.

Sam James had a log hotel with a fireplace at McKay Flat and he would round up 25 or 30 miners in Shoup and have them come up to the flat where he would house, feed, and liquor them for the whole winter without charge — just because he enjoyed their company.

After a lengthy prospecting foray, he sometimes came into Salmon and always set up drinks for the boys in Al Smith's saloon. One evening they decided to have some fun with James so they got him drunk, called in a prostitute and had a justice of the peace marry them. Then they marched the couple off to a hotel room.

In the morning Sam woke, turned to the lady and said, "And who are you?" "I'm your wife, don't you remember getting married?" she replied. "The hell!" exclaimed Sam, and out the door he went.

Early photo of Shoup, with bridge which gave access to Middle Fork trail.

The curious twist to this story is that Sam James died not long after the joke had been played. The lady kept track of him and claimed his bank account after his death. There were plenty of witnesses to her marriage. She inherited almost $70,000.

Sam James Flat (McKay Creek) is a Forest Service campground now.

Mile 198.2: **China Gulch** across on the left. According to Herb St. Clair, a Chinese fellow built a hut here, but never did any mining.

Mile 198.4: **Shoup and Boulder Creek.** Prior to 1881 the only mining done in this area was placer mining along the river. Then Sam James discovered the Kentuck and Pat O'Hara located the Grunter mine. These were the first quartz gold discoveries in what was to become known as the Mineral Hill district. Others followed:

Lost Miner, Big Lead, True Fissure, Spring Lode, Humming Bird, Monolith. By 1890 there were more than 300 claims.

The original town was called Boulder City and petitioners for a post office wanted to call it that, but the postal department in Washington D.C. chose the name Shoup to honor the governor who was in the Capitol that week.

The town was located around the buildings of the Grunter mine, which is the first collection of wooden buildings below present day Shoup. Lacking a road, all supplies and equipment arrived by pack train or barge. It was two days by trail to Salmon.

Shoup from Graveyard Point, after the road was pushed down from Transfer Gulch. According to Herb St. Clair, 14 people lie in unmarked graves in the cemetery.

Mining and milling machinery were floated down. Saloons and a school were established. In the 1880's, Shoup had a population of almost 200.

The Grunter mill was powered with an overshot wooden waterwheel. By the 1900's, it was often shut down. The mine operated for the last time in 1938-1939.

The Kentuck had a 10-stamp mill at the mine, and a later mill at the mouth of Pine Creek where the foundation can still be observed at the south end of the bridge. An aerial tramway brought the ore down to the mill. With quiescent periods, the mine was still operative in 1918. The CCC boys removed the cables and portions of the mill when they put the road through. The rest of the mill was salvaged for iron as part of the war effort in 1941.

The Gold Hill mine and mill occupy the site just below the Grunter, where the three-story shed-roof metal building stands next to the road. About $125,000 was spent to develop this mine during the Depression. One week after it began operations, the ore was all gone.

The mine which can be seen across the river, just below Shoup, is the Clipper Bullion. The mine belonged to Eli Suydam and had a five-stamp water-powered mill. Water was brought out of Boulder Creek and across the river in a 10-inch pipe supported by cables and wood. The pipe went up the side of the hill and into a ditch, which then carried it to the mill. The ditch line can still be seen from the road.

A newspaper clipping from the Salmon paper in 1895 gives some idea of how rich the Bullion ore was:

E. S. Suydam came from Shoup Saturday bringing with him 13 pounds of retorted gold estimated to be worth $2900, which was obtained from 65 tons of ore from his mine, the Clipper-Bullion.

While the mines may be quiet, with no one to use them, Shoup is still an active town serving boaters, hunters, fishermen, and other vacationers.

Mile 200.1: **Pine Creek, Pine Bridge, and Pine Creek Rapid.** In 1881 Sam James and Pat O'Hara arrived from Big Creek (now Panther Creek) and spread their blankets under a large pine tree. At that time the area was heavily timbered with Ponderosa pines but many were used for fuel, stulls, and lumber.

The cabin a quarter mile up-river from Pine Creek, opposite the Gold Hill mine, belongs to Glenn Hegsted, a retired pharmacist from Blackfoot, Idaho, who has lived on the river for 30 years. Hegsted was Senator Dworshak's campaign manager.

Glenn lives on the site once occupied by a German miller named Julius Weimer. Weimer left his country to avoid being drafted into the German army in 1879.

Once in America, he came west and worked for a Missoula miller until he got his employer's daughter pregnant. The people of the town were going to hang him, but he broke jail at night with another prisoner and crossed the state line above Gibbonsville. The year was 1887.

Weimer went to Fourth of July Creek from Gibtown and bought a farm with a partner. It wasn't long before he was in trouble with his partner over that man's wife, so he left his place to the partner and moved to Pine Creek. He began another farm where he raised vegetables which he sold to the mines. He kept 30-40 head of horses which could carry produce, and snowfall was mild enough that he never had to feed them.

Julius sold his Pine Creek place in 1906 and moved down to the Hegsted location on Salmon River. He lived there until he was 90 and then moved to Salmon where he expired at age 95.

Julius Weimer with Edma Barton.

About two miles up Pine Creek, just below Sawmill Gulch, are the graves of Mrs. Scotty Stewart and her son, Tommy Hardy. The boy died of the flu in the epidemic of 1918. The mother died as the result of injuries sustained when she was thrown from a burro that had been spooked by a contentious dog.

Pine Creek Rapid, the thrash of whitewater seen below the bridge, is where George Sandiland drowned in August, 1897. He was boating with Cap Guleke and was knocked overboard by the rear sweep handle. They were hauling freight to Mike Cohen at Cohen Gulch.

Joe Lockland also drowned in the rapid and was packed in a coffin from Shoup to Salmon, where he was buried.

Mile 201.6: **Cohen Gulch** on the right side of the river. Michael Cohen (probably spelled Coan, possibly Cohan) was an Irishman who came to the Salmon River from Gilmore and Leadore.

He had a hard rock mine up the gulch behind his cabin. Mike drove almost 2000 feet of tunnel all by hand, with a singlejack, between 1907 and 1955. He had some rich ore but he never processed any of it or tried to pack it out.

Clyde and Don Smith running a sweepboat through Pine Creek Rapid in 1945.

Cohen would work for the Forest Service until he had a grub-stake, then work on his mine. Once he was sick enough to hear the harps of heaven, so he left $8000 to the Catholic Church. When he recovered, the doctor told him he ought to live a good while, so he went to see about getting his money back. Father told him it had been given to a worthy cause and there were no provisions for a refund.

Mike liked to play poker in Salmon, but he got carried away once and lost his train ticket to the Gilmore mine. He had to walk back almost 50 miles. Cohen said, "After that you'll never see Mike broke again." The rest of his life he always managed to have some money in his pocket.

Mile 202.6: **Big Sheepeater Creek** on the right. Obviously, a vestigal name.

Just below the mouth of Sheepeater Creek, across the river from the road, was Johnny Rowe's residence from 1918-1932. He had a cable and cage for access to his mining claims across the river. Johnny and his partners, Percy Anderson and Eli Roberts, wanted to sell their claims to Ed Bills, of Salmon. The three of them tried to cross over the river by cable when the water was high. The weight was too much for the cable anchor, which gave way, dropping them all in the river. Eli caught the line, and with Percy holding onto his legs, made it hand over hand to shore. Bills drowned. Ray Mahoney recovered his body

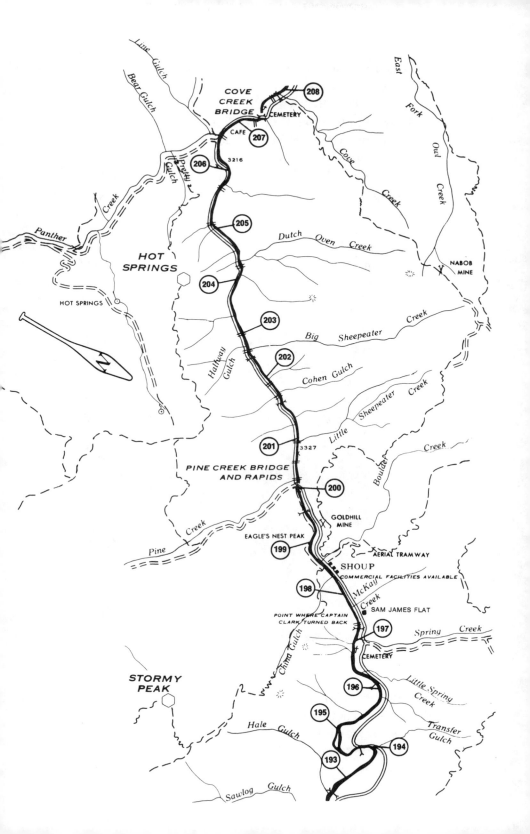

at Long Tom and packed him to Shoup by way of Owl Creek, because the river had washed out the trail.

Mile 203.7: **Halfway Gulch** on the left. This drainage is the midway point between Pine Creek and Panther Creek.

Mile 204.3: **Dutch Oven Creek** on the right. Named for a stone formation at the head of the two mile drainage.

Mile 206.7: **Panther Creek** flows in from the left side canyon. For years this stream, particularly the portion below Musgrove Creek, was known as Big Creek. It was often confused with the Big Creek on the Middle Fork.

Frank Rood, his brother Willard, and their father, took more than 300 mountain lions out of the drainage during the 1900's. Frank was known as the "King of the Kitties." His cougar kills account for the derivation of the present name, a change that was made in 1935.

Frank Rood on the left, with Hacksaw Tom in 1935, holding a mountain lion taken on Panther Creek.

Mr. Shenon patented some mining claims at the mouth of Panther Creek. There are also some graves there, but at this date it does not appear possible to identify the dead.

Three miles up Panther Creek, at the mouth of Clear Creek, was a community known as Camp Dynamo. A hydro-generator had been installed there in 1886, and lights lit up the country all the way to the sawmill on Beaver Creek. That mill had a sash saw run by water power.

Frank and Hazel (Swett) Rood had a ranch on Beaver Creek for years. As a boy in 1918, Frank had gone to school in Shoup. Their recollections concerning sites along the river from Owl Creek to North Fork provided valuable historical reference.

There was a CCC camp in the 1930's on the flat just below Panther Creek on the same side of the river as the road.

Mile 207.4: **Cove Creek bridge.** The grave which can be seen next to the road at the north end of the bridge is that of John Burr, who died at the age of 30. Billy Taylor, of Salmon, said that his father and John Burr were passengers on a Shoup-bound scow in 1897. John was a good swimmer and had been in and out of the river all during the trip. When the boat reached Shoup, Burr dived off to help get the bowline ashore. He never came up, and his body was recovered at Cove Creek.

On the large benchmark rock between roadbed and grave is one of John McKay's inscriptions that tells us he passed that way in 1907.

Mile 207.8: **Cove Creek,** named for the small inlet just above its mouth, enters on the right.

Mile 208.3: **Frank Butschke's** house to the right of the road. Oldest of seven children, Butschke bought the cabin in 1931 from Harry Harrelson for $800. Frank improved the building and lived on the place until he was 90 years old, when he moved to a Salmon resthome. Interviewed there at the age of 96, he still missed living down along the river.

Mile 209.2: **Owl Creek** flows in on the right. This creek is reported to have acquired its name from a number of owls that roosted in a pine grove up the stream.

Mining was done where the east fork meets the main creek.

A Mr. Walton took up the Owl Creek property around 1900. Chris and Charlie Stauffenberg, uncle and nephew, had Owl Creek in the Twenties. Ray Mahoney acquired it in 1928 and kept it through the C.C.C. era. The road arrived at Owl Creek in 1935. Mahoney had a drinking place where the cabins now stand, and Sam Popejoy sold beer and whiskey to the C.C.C. boys. They were so eager for the taste of alcohol that they would get shoes, shirts, coats, etcetera from the commissary and trade them for liquor. Popejoy could sell shirts, coats, and boots for a reasonable price to river people and everybody was happy.

After Ray died, Mr. Plosser got the land; he later sold it to Fred Porter, who owns it now.

Mile 210.3: **Skull Gulch** on the right. Name attributed to the skeleton found by CCC workers. It was that of a Sheepeater Indian killed and left by early miners Reynolds, Jones, and Dan Hurley. Hurley is buried on the Rood Ranch, up Panther Creek. Dan gave the story to Frank Rood, before the former died in 1932, aged 96 years.

Mile 211: **Cherry Flat** named for Mr. Cherry who lived by skim-digging along the river.

Mile 211.4: **Ramshead Lodge.** Joe Groff patented a 40-acre mining claim here which he worked around 1900. The open area is known as Poverty Flat, supposedly because nothing would grow in the poor soil.

About half a mile down the road from Poverty Flat, on a rock face, on the right-hand side of the road and chest high, are some typical Salmon River pictographs — not nearly as imaginative or depictive as those found along the Middle Fork.

Across the river from Poverty Flat can be seen two sets of buildings made of weathered boards; the last residence of Hacksaw Tom.

He was born Thomas Morris Christensen, March 5, 1875, in Norway. His parents brought him to America a couple of years later and they settled on a piece of land near Racine, Wisconsin.

When Tom was grown he married a Danish girl named Annie. Together they worked a farm at North Cape; their first son was born in 1903.

Christensen began to itch with a wanderlust he would scratch all his life. He moved his family by train to Salt Lake City. There he worked as a carpenter until an injury to his foot and the death of his second son made him feel moving might change his luck for the better.

They stopped near Ogden, Utah, and took up residency in an abandoned house which turned out to be overrun by rattlesnakes. Tom began learning their ways. He spent time trying to tame the older snakes, but the younger ones, he stated, "can't be trusted to do anything right." His wife, who had a difficult time coping with rattlers in the washroom, bedroom, and chicken house, was pleased when Tom decided to move to Idaho in the spring of 1907.

The family traveled to Soda Springs in southeast Idaho and spent the winter in a log cabin at nearby Wayan. Game was plentiful and

Tom ran a successful trapline in the marshland and foothills. A large part of their diet was curlews, curlew eggs, and prairie chickens.

In the spring, the Christensens moved again by canvas-covered wagon to a deserted ranch; fall found them at Gray's Lake living largely on ducks. (The lake is now a National Wildlife Refuge.) With winter coming on, they returned to Salt Lake City.

Tom worked in Salt Lake for a while and then decided to take the family back to Wisconsin. In the spring of 1913, they settled on a farm there, just south of the Canadian border. Christensen found an abundance of fur-bearing animals to trap, guided summer fishermen, and did some maintainance work for resorts nearby.

Spring brought the usual bout of wanderlust. By now there were four children and Annie didn't trail with the idea of moving again. Tom began drinking and lost his temper frequently. His wife did washing at the resorts to have food for the family. The following spring, Tom walked off to the train station at Eagle River.

He went to Gardiner, Montana and set up a harness and saddle repair shop, while running a trapline around the outskirts of town. In Montana he got in trouble with the law and sawed his way out of jail, earning the nickname "Hacksaw."

Tom was back in Idaho working for the Cattlemen's Association from 1915-1920, near Ashton. Then he moved to the Salmon River.

He still couldn't settle down. He had two different houses at Shoup, lived in a house by the walnut tree at Spring Creek for a while, then moved to a cabin at the mouth of Ebenezer Creek, before landing across the river from Poverty Flat.

Hacksaw Tom wore a rattlesnake skin hatband and belt. He went to dances at the Shoup schoolhouse, where he liked to play the fiddle, mandolin, and guitar. He got along well enough with people he liked but his habit of carrying live rattlesnakes inside his shirt didn't endear him to many. He loved to pull one out and show it off; if it frightened someone, so much the better. Undoubtedly he had problems getting a dancing partner.

The rattlesnake man made a living trapping, guiding hunters, and doing odd jobs around North Fork. His trips to town were infrequent, but he always carried some snakes in his shirt when he went. Tom was known to have no trouble getting a drink in a saloon when he pulled out a *Crotalus atrox* and set it on the bar. Usually there was no one else left to serve.

It is interesting that the snakes Hacksaw kept around his cabin and carried in his clothes were not raised in captivity — several reliable witnesses observed him at times when he would pick up a large snake on the trail and then tuck it gently under his shirt.

Hacksaw was also an expert taxidermist. His sense of humor meant that most of his creation were abnormal: jackalopes, steelhead with squawfish mouths, fur-bearing trout, and other tourist shucks.

"Hacksaw Tom" Christensen with a rattlesnake.

In later years, Wes Low, of Salmon, wanted to buy Hacksaw's place as a fishing retreat but was sure he couldn't pay what Tom wanted for it. Herb St. Clair had Wes draw $1500 in small bills out of the bank. The two of them went down the river and spread the money out on the shore across from Tom's cabin. Then they called him over. "Will you take $1500 for your place?" asked Herb. Hacksaw looked at all the bills for a moment, then said, "You bet I will," and began gathering up the money.

Hacksaw Tom Christensen left Salmon River in the fall of 1955; he was 80 years old. He went to Salmon to get a bus for Phoenix, where he wanted to visit his brother. He showed up for the bus dressed only in his underpants. The driver told him to go get some clothes on if he wanted a ride. He did so, without protest. Maybe he just wanted his fellow passengers to know he wasn't carrying any reptiles.

Phoenix proved to be merely a short stop on the way to Tortilla Flats where he could look for the Lost Dutchman mine in the Superstition Mountains. After a spell, he returned to Phoenix and lived in a home-made trailer while making the rounds of garbage cans for food. Other campers called the police and he was taken to the hospital.

When he had recovered sufficiently, he caught a bus for Salmon, but near Idaho Falls he went completely crazy. The police came for him at the depot and committed him to the asylum at Blackfoot, Idaho. He died there in February of 1956.

A mountain in the Salmon River Range wears his name, his fiddle rests in the Lemhi County Museum, and his legend still lives along the River of No Return.

The cable crossing at Hacksaw's place was the scene of a tragic drowning in May of 1947. A man and his two sons were crossing to visit Tom. High water caught the basket and in the ensuing struggle, John and Guy Davis perished.

Charles Warren Puckett, who lived in a dugout across the river and placer mined there before Hacksaw arrived, also drowned when the cable failed in 1935.

Mile 213: **Lake Creek** on the left. This stream comes down three miles from Dome Lake. Pat Leonard and Charlie Putt homesteaded a ranch at the mouth of this creek. Charlie drowned in 1926 while trying to wade across the Middle Fork above its mouth, in order to get down to his placer claim. Leonard kept the place until 1930, when he sold it to Ed Gwyther. Ed was a Civil War veteran and had lived in the canyon for 18 years. Guleke found him dead in the cabin in 1934, apparently of heart failure. His brother, Jack, held it until his own death.

Mile 213.2: **Ebenezer Creek and Bar.** This campground is divided by the road. The bar takes its name from an early resident, Ebenezer Snell. He mined with a rocker.

This was the site of Civilian Conservation Corps Camp 401 during the Thirties. While the area is now a Forest Service campground, extensive CCC rock wall and cement slab work is still evident.

A rare, introduced Russian olive tree is growing on the site.

C.C.C. Camp No. 401 at Ebenezer Bar.

Mile 213.8: **Colson Creek** enters on the left. The Colson brothers were packers and miners.

Mr. Pope lived at Colson Creek in the early 1900's. He wrote a match-making service and they sent him a "heart in hand" woman from back east. She arrived in Shoup, only to discover there was no way to get down-river to Colson Creek. So she had to go up Boulder Creek, around Owl Creek, over mountains, and rope down cliffs to meet Mr. Pope. He was taller than a wagon tongue, raw-boned, and wore glasses. She was about 5 feet 2 inches, an ample woman. They were married.

In time they had four children: two boys and two girls. Guleke would bring them supplies on his boat. During the summer, the family didn't wear enough clothes to patch a bullet. A big piece of iron hung on a wire by the trail where the boat landed. There a sign read: Ring the bell so we can get our clothes on.

By 1918, some of the children were getting old enough to go to school so they would stay in Shoup for the winter and come back to Colson Creek in the spring. Most of the children were in their late teens before they ever got to Salmon. In all that time they never saw a doctor.

Mile 214.3: **Shell Creek** on the left. Named for Ebenezer Snell, the early day settler at Ebenezer Bar. The spelling has been altered.

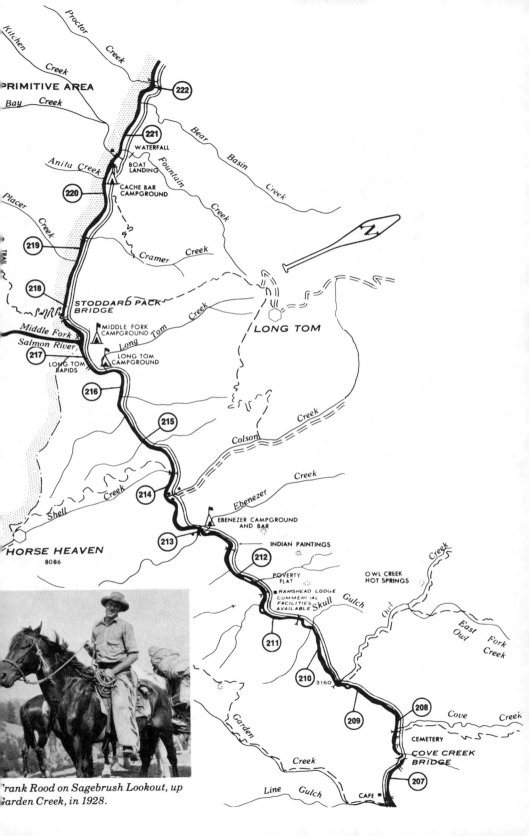

PRIMITIVE AREA

Kitchen Creek

Proctor Creek

Bay Creek

(222)

(221) WATERFALL
BOAT LANDING
Anita Creek

(220) CACHE BAR CAMPGROUND

Placer Creek

(219)

Cramer Creek

Fountain Creek

Bear Basin Creek

LONG TOM

TRAIL

(218)
STODDARD PACK BRIDGE

MIDDLE FORK CAMPGROUND

Long Tom Creek

Middle Fork

Salmon River.

(217)
LONG TOM RAPIDS

LONG TOM CAMPGROUND

(216)

(215)

Colson Creek

Shell Creek

(214)

Ebenezer Creek

HORSE HEAVEN
8086

EBENEZER CAMPGROUND AND BAR

(213)

INDIAN PAINTINGS

(212)

POVERTY FLAT

OWL CREEK HOT SPRINGS

RAMSHEAD LODGE
COMMERCIAL FACILITIES AVAILABLE

Skull Gulch

Owl Creek

East Fork Owl Creek

(211)

(210) 3160

(209)

Garden Creek

(208)

Cove Creek

CEMETERY

COVE CREEK BRIDGE

(207)

Line Gulch

CAFE

Frank Rood on Sagebrush Lookout, up
Garden Creek, in 1928.

C.C.C. men grading the Salmon River road in 1934.

Conservation crew mixing concrete on the road.

Mile 216.5: **Long Tom Creek** and campground on the right. Considerable placer mining was done at this site; Elmer Purcell, among others, was working this bar in the 1930's. (A long tom combines aspects of a sluice box and a rocker.)

Road crew floating an air compressor for drilling powder holes in rock along the edge of the road.

Mile 217.2: **Middle Fork** of the Salmon flows out of the canyon on the left side of the river to join the main stem at this point. The Middle Fork heads in Bear Valley about 125 miles up-stream, not far from Stanley Basin.

Clyde and Don Smith's cabin, built in 1930, occupies the bench on the downstream side of the confluence.

The Smiths on the porch of their cabin at the confluence with the Middle Fork.

Mile 217.8: **Stoddard Creek** pack bridge. This bridge was built from materials brought down from Cove Creek. The Stoddard Trail, which begins on the far, or south end of the bridge, goes back to Big Creek in the Idaho Primitive Area.

Mile 219.2: **Cramer Creek** comes in on the right. Jack Cramer was an early prospector who wintered his horses on this spot.

Mile 220.3: **Cache Bar Campground** just below the road and across the river from Anita Creek. This has been an alternate site for terminating Middle Fork trips and the Forest Service has developed it as a launch site. There are three versions accounting for the name's origin: 1) Cap Guleke kept a cache here (Oliver Williams), 2) A river-rat prospector by the name of Cache lived here (Neale Poynor), 3) The man operating a rocker here did so well he called it Cash Bar (Herb St. Clair).

Mile 220.6: **Kitchen Creek** runs out on the left. The rough country at the head of the creek was known as Hell's Kitchen. Kitchen Creek is an old placer mining claim. The foundation for a cabin, which must have existed about the time of the Leesburg rush, can be seen a hundred yards up the creek. Charley Potsky was on the claim in 1920. Oakie Grogg built a cabin there with split vertical logs and a skylight in 1929. Cyril Neeser had the place from 1950 until the early Sixties when the Forest Service burned his house and hauled his hydro-generator out.

Mile 220.8: **Fountain Creek** falls in on the right. Named for the lovely waterfall that drops down the canyon just back from the road.

Mile 221.7: **Bear Basin Creek** on the right.

Mile 222.1: **Proctor Creek** comes in on the left, across the river. The Proctor Ranch was a significant stop for early boating parties. It is mentioned often in trip accounts; but the derivation of the name is unknown at this time.

Monroe Hancock may have done some prospecting on the place, Colin Smith had it in the 1940's, and it is owned at present by ex-river outfitter Cliff Cummings. In 1961, Cummings experimented with a 16-foot airboat on the Salmon below North Fork, propelled by a 185 h.p. airplane engine with twin rudders mounted in the slipstream.

Mile 224.3: **Salmon River Lodge** on the left side of the river. Dave and Phyllis Giles operate a floatboat-jetboat and pack operation from their guest ranch on Butts Bar. They can house up to 20 people on the place. Horse trips which leave from the lodge go up to Butts, Kitchen, and Cottonwood Creek drainages. The Giles bought the

Cunningham's cabin at Butts Bar — he didn't build the structure, but did expand it.

lodge from Austin Smothers in 1967.

John Cunningham built his second house on this flat and worked a placer claim across the river at Corn Creek. Only a foundation wall remains.

In the Thirties, this spot was the river crossing for parties attempting to go farther down the canyon on foot. There was a cable and basket.

Dave and Phyllis Giles' Salmon River Inn.

John Cunningham fishing on the river.

Mile 224.6: **Butts Creek** enters on the left. The flat below Butts Creek is known as Cunningham Bar after John Cunningham, who boated with Monroe Hancock. Cunningham had a good-sized cabin there; he kept cows and chickens, had an orchard with apples, peaches and apricots, and raised a garden which had everything from corn to watermelons. He made some homemade wine, ate venison, and for cash worked on a sweepboat or ran his hydraulic placer mine just below the orchard. Jack was from the southeast.

Mile 224.6: **Corn Creek** and campground. There are two explanations for the name — take your choice. One informant claims corn sprouted on the site after a packer spilled some seed. Another source claims it is named for the type of placer gold recovered from the bar.

Corn Creek Campground is the end of the road and the starting point for most float trips and jet-boat excursions on the River of No Return. The Forest Service maintains a checkpoint trailer office at the campground. A permit is required in order to float the river. Elevation at the put-in is 2,929 feet.

A trail parallels the river on the right bank from Corn Creek Campground to Dwyer Creek, 12.3 miles downstream. Its origin is discussed in the section concerning Lantz Bar.

If experience is indicative, then anyone going on a trip down the Salmon needs to be reminded: I) Wear a lifejacket. II) Leave no litter — particularly cigarette butts. III) Be careful with fire; use existing fire rings. (A carelessly tended campfire at Corn Creek in the summer of 1961 started a contagion of flame that charred 17,000 acres.)

On the River:

Corn Creek to Chittam Rapid

Mile 224.8: **Wheat Creek** on the right — named for its proximity to Corn Creek.

Mile 225.2: **Killum Point.** The point takes its name from the Jack Killum family that lived on the left bank, in the small open area about 400 yards above Gunbarrel Creek.

Jack Killum was a lawyer who had a nervous breakdown and came to Salmon with his wife and five children in 1935.

They drove down to Deadwater and camped. There Mike Wilkins, the game warden, had to give Jack a ticket for fishing without a license. Killum was a gentleman about the citation. He wrote the governor a letter praising Wilkins for doing his job, and explained that he had been fishing without a license, not because he disliked the law, but because he simply couldn't afford the fee. The governor, C. Ben Ross (Democrat), bought a license for Jack and sent it to him.

Killum sold his old car at Deadwater, gathered his family's belongings in a boat, and headed down the river. He wrecked on a rock in Pine Creek Rapid, lost most of the supplies and had to be rescued by rope.

He managed to get down-river to Killum Point and built a cabin right on the trail. Jack called himself "a friend to mankind" and placed a door on each side of the cabin so that anyone coming down the trail had to come through his house and be properly welcomed.

Killum had published a book of poetry and was certain he could be a literary success if he had the time and solitude to write. There is no evidence he ever found time to write after reaching the river.

The family went bare as new-born birds most of the summer. They had a garden and did some placer mining. John Cunningham would often bring vegetables down the trail from his place for the Killums. Jack also notarized papers and trapped in the winter.

The two oldest boys and the girl, Daisy, eventually moved to Salmon. One boy's habit of carrying pistols got him the nickname "Two-Gun" Killum.

The younger boys, Hugh and Marvin, were well-taught at home by their father. They went to public school for one day in Salmon and didn't like it because they felt the children "played too much in class."

For three years, about three times a year, the boys would walk most of the way to Salmon. On their spring trip, they carried calypso orchids (also known as fairy slippers) with the bulbs wrapped in moss. They sold the flowers for eight cents each and usually collected about ten dollars which they used to buy a Mother's Day present.

Hugh and Marvin Killum in Salmon with calypso orchids for sale.

Their father, ex-attorney Killum, wearing a fur hat, came to town even less often. But with his ready wit, he was a sought-after speaker at the Rotary Club when he did come.

Mrs. Killum died of cancer in 1941. Jack went to Salmon in 1942 to teach at the defense training school. Hugh and Marvin remained in the canyon alone — they were 15 and 13. For a while they worked on a lookout tower. Finally all three moved to Alaska.

Mile 226. 5: **Gunbarrel Creek** comes in on the right. The creek is believed to have gotten its name from a rifle left in the crotch of a tree near the rapid.

Mile 226.6: **Gunbarrel Rapid.** On a high stage of water (60,000 c.f.s.) this rapid presents a major problem for river-runners. It is necessary to be on the right-hand side of the river as one comes around the bend above the rapid, since under such conditions there isn't time to ferry across.

Mile 227.8: **Horse Creek** is the substantial stream flowing in on the right.

Howard Sims' oral history of Horse Creek, as recorded by Gene Powers, is fascinating. During the boom days of mining, prior to about 1890, the Horse Creek drainage was known as Big Sheep Creek. A man named Jess Reynolds, who had the store at Shoup, and a trapper named Allen, went up to Big Sheep Creek to trap. They packed their supplies and traps to the big meadow at the main forks of the creek, built a cabin and prepared to spend the winter trapping, primarily for marten. They turned their large herd of horses out on the south slopes of Big Sheep Creek.

In early spring they got "cabin fever" and decided to visit civilization. On their way to the Bitterroot Valley on snowshoes, they stopped for lunch by a campfire and Reynolds fell asleep. Allen saw his chance to own all the furs and terminated the partnership by shooting Reynolds while he slept. Allen took the pelts but was caught and hanged before he got out of the country. This left the horses on Big Sheep Creek without any owners. They roamed the hillsides for several years until they were captured by local people or winter-killed.

Because of this horse herd, people began calling the stream Horse Creek. Later almost all the side creeks and forks received names associated with horses: Pinto, Colt, Bronco, Roan, Filly, Cayuse, Stud, Mustang, Broomtail, Fantail, etc. The exception was Reynolds Creek, a branch of Horse Creek, on which Jess Reynolds and Allen built their cabin in the winter of 1891.

There was a pack bridge from Horse Creek to the Stub Creek trail until 1970. The Forest Service condemned it and Dave Giles reluctantly took it down. The Horse Creek trail can be followed across the Bitterroots into Montana or down Idaho's Selway River.

Neal Allen had a cabin at the left end of the Horse Creek bridge for about 10 years. Allen was big enough to hunt bears with a switch; double tough. He had worked as a Royal Canadian Mountie in British Columbia. On one occasion he was given an award for killing a lion that escaped from the circus. He carried a rifle and traveled with two

112

big dogs that wore pack sacks, like mules. He mined on the head of Moose Creek. Most men went around Neal like he was a swamp, and he feuded with Frank Lantz. There were a few people who respected him, like Mike Wilkins.

Allen apparently committed suicide in his mining cabin on the head of Moose Creek. The Forest Service burned Allen's cabin by the bridge.

Mile 228.4: **Stub Creek** comes down from the left. Joe Scoble used the site as an outfitting base for years. It is now a use-permit held by Hank and Sharon Miller, of Salmon.

The trail from Stub Creek climbs 5000 feet to Butts Creek Point and eventually connects with the Stoddard Creek trail in the Primitive Area.

Typical Salmon River pictographs, located below Devil's Toe Creek.

Mile 229: **Legend Creek** is the drainage on the left; it seldom contains water. The creek may take its name from the red pictographs on the bluff just above the high water mark. The paint was obtained from mineral oxides mixed with grease and water. The designs are not standardized and cannot be translated because in every case the meaning attached to the painting was so individual it could be explained only by the person who put it there. The location of some pictographs might suggest the purpose was magical, but more often it appears the work was simply an enjoyable means of self-expression.

No pictographs in Idaho have been dated by the radiocarbon method and rarely can their age be determined. The Legend Creek pictographs, however, have figures on horseback which means it is probably safe to say that they are later than 1750.

Legend Creek is the first drainage on the river within the Bitterroot National Forest and the Salmon River Breaks Primitive Area. Breaks and Forest extend down-river on the right side, until the Bitterroot halts at Sabe Creek. The Breaks Area continues to Jersey Creek.

Mile 229.8: **Bow Creek** on the right.

Mile 230.3: **Fern Creek** spills down the left bank.

Mile 230.4: **Spindle Creek** on the right. The name means "thin shanked." Colin Lovelock was here in the early Fifties — the stone terraces are his doing.

Mile 230.8: **Lucky Creek** on the right. Probably given its name by a pleased placer miner.

Mile 231.5: **Cottonwood Creek** is the substantial stream flowing in on the left. The creek represents the western boundary of Salmon National Forest, the eastern limit of the Payette, and the beginning of the Idaho Primitive Area. This primitive area encompasses the left bank all the way to Five Mile Creek.

Mile 232.2: **Phantom Creek** on the left.

Mile 232.3: **Rainier Rapids.** The rapid has an interesting hole at the top-right in lower stages of water.

Mile 232.4: **Rainier Creek,** insignificant, on the right.

Mile 232.9: **Alder Creek** on the left. River alder and white alder grow along the Salmon, mostly above Riggins.

Mile 233.8: **Otter Creek** on the left and Eagle Creek on the right. George Lear came to the river in the early Thirties and built a cabin at Otter Creek. He was 20 years old at the time. He used a row boat to cross the river where he placered and hydraulicked. He tunneled in the winter and worked a ground sluice with a box in the summer. He had a gas-driven 2-inch pump with a foot valve in the river as his water source. Lear left for four years and when he returned he went to Disappointment Creek.

114

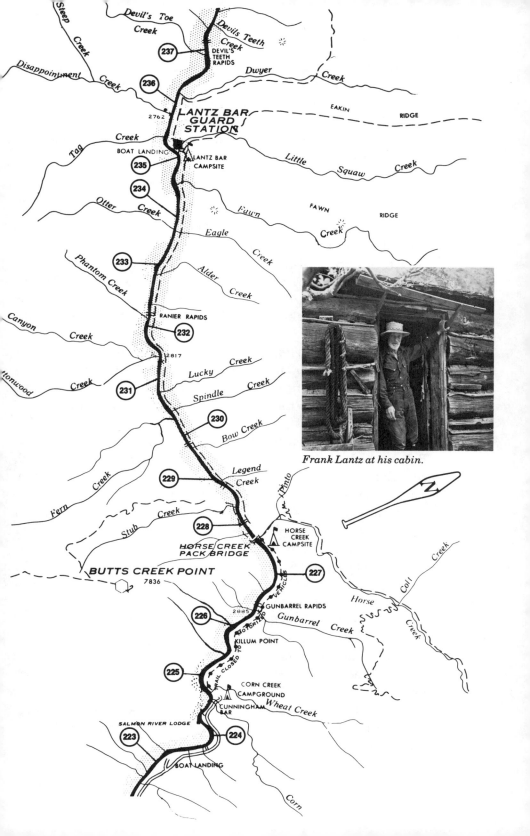

Steep Creek

Devil's Toe Creek

Devils Teeth Creek

237

DEVIL'S TEETH RAPIDS

Disappointment Creek

236

Dwyer Creek

EAKIN RIDGE

2762

LANTZ BAR GUARD STATION

Tag Creek

BOAT LANDING

235

LANTZ BAR CAMPSITE

Little Squaw Creek

234

Otter Creek

Fawn Creek

FAWN RIDGE

Phantom Creek

Eagle Creek

233

Alder Creek

Canyon Creek

RANIER RAPIDS

232

2817

Cottonwood Creek

Lucky Creek

231

Spindle Creek

230

Bow Creek

Fern Creek

Legend Creek

229

Pinto

Stub Creek

228

HORSE CREEK CAMPSITE

HORSE CREEK PACK BRIDGE

BUTTS CREEK POINT

7836

227

Horse Creek

Coll Creek

226

2885

GUNBARREL RAPIDS

MOTORIZED VEHICLES

Gunbarrel Creek

KILLUM POINT

TRAIL CLOSED TO

225

CORN CREEK CAMPGROUND

CUNNINGHAM BAR

Wheat Creek

SALMON RIVER LODGE

223

224

BOAT LANDING

Corn

N

Frank Lantz at his cabin.

Mile 234.5: **Fawn Creek** runs in on the right. Johnny Briggs, a cougar hunter with hounds, built a cabin at Fawn Creek, after living at Smith Gulch. When the bounty on lions was dropped, he moved out and went into the logging business, only to be killed by a falling snag.

Dan Lord, who cooked and boated for Don Smith, wintered in the cabin for two years after Briggs left.

———————————————◆•◼•◆———————————————

Mile 235: **Lantz Bar** at Little Squaw Creek, which pours down through the gravel bar on the right.

Occupancy of this bar dates back before 1900. Oscar Eakin lived here prior to 1916, perhaps as early as 1906. His cabin on the flat was situated about 150 yards above the present buildings on the west side of Little Squaw Creek. One of his trapping cabins survives in the mountains to the north.

From 1916 until 1921, Mitt Haynie lived on the site. He was a prospector and packer and is discussed more fully at Five Mile Bar.

John McCoy, along with a brother and sister, bought out Haynie in 1921; they were on the bar until the fall of 1923. The McCoys had over 70 head of horses.

Lantz moved to the bar in 1925. None of his friends — and Frank B. Lantz had more friends than hell has fiddlers, have felt wordsmith enough to suitably characterize Lantz. We who didn't know him then, can only hope to sketch his biography with a qualified adequacy.

Frank Lantz was born February 20, 1890 in Middle Fork, near Buckhannon, West Virginia, the son of Virginia farmers. As a boy, he loved to hunt rabbits and squirrels.

When he was 22, his uncle, Claud Lansbury, offered to take him to Oregon. Frank was "willing to go anyplace," especially if it meant he could hunt lion and bear. On his way to the coast, he got side-tracked by a cousin, and the two of them worked as sheepherders and laborers for several months.

Lantz said his cousin was "quarrelsome, couldn't keep a job, and liked to crook an elbow." However, Frank enjoyed pulling a cork himself.

The pair eventually parted, with Frank shocking grain in Lemhi, Idaho, in the summer of 1913. During the winter, he trapped the high country around Salmon.

116

Walking out of the mountains that winter, Lantz had the misfortune of getting frostbitten feet. Gangrene developed in the toes of one foot. He went into the hospital and the doctor wanted to amputate his foot but Frank wouldn't let him. Nonetheless, they did have to remove three toes.

When he left the hospital, Frank had two dimes in his pocket, so he took a job as a gandydancer, laying track for the Gilmore Railroad. Turnover on the crew was so great that in 30 days he was the senior member of the gang. By then he, too, was ready to quit, with 17 dollars in his pocket.

In 1914, he met a German named Dan; they bought some fishing equipment and a frying pan and tried hooking their way to Montana in order to find work as loggers. When they got to the Big Hole country, they decided the mosquitoes were big enough to skid logs, and retreated to Salmon, where Lantz took a job on a ranch for almost a year.

Frank headed down the Salmon River in 1916 with John Cunningham and another fellow to homestead on Butts Bar, later known as Cunningham Bar. Then Uncle Sam drafted him for World War I. Accepting the bland, unquestioned assumption that national interests override human interests, he went to France for two years as a sniper.

Released from the service, he decided he'd better see Oregon. But he didn't like it there. "When it rains more than 24 hours a day, it's time to move on," he said.

At this point, Lantz returned by train to his native West Virginia. Recalling that visit, he said he couldn't get his mind off Idaho; while sowing oats, the drill would seem to hum "Salmon River, Salmon River."

Thinking a change of pasture might make the calf fatter, he quit one day in 1922, telling his father he was going back out west. It may have been during the next couple of years that he "cut timber in every timber-producing state in the west except Arizona." At some point he also worked on a ship, because his nephew could recall his descriptions of the muddy Amazon.

In any event, mid-May of 1925 found him back on the Salmon River loading all his possessions, and a year's supplies, on a scow to go down to Little Squaw Creek. (There had been some falling out with Cunningham at Butts Bar and Frank had decided to move farther down stream.)

The spring runoff must have already been underway, because Lantz wrecked his boat in Gunbarrel Rapid and was knocked unconscious in the turn-over. He regained his senses in a backeddy, among some willows. Everything was gone except a sack of wet flour. There was "damp powder an nothin' to dry it"; another man might have given up, but Frank was from West Virginia, tough as boot leather. He made his way back to Salmon, found a fellow who owed him money and collected on his loan, gathered up some more supplies, plus three horses, and packed in by trail. Likely lies in the mire when unlikely gets over — this time he made it. On his way in, he found his dog, which he thought had drowned; it had gone back to Cunningham's on the other side of the river.

He used the boards from his boats to start his first cabin. He planted an orchard of 80 trees: apples, peaches, plums, pears, and apricots. He panned for gold, averaging $6 a day. Frank Lantz became grafted to the canyon.

Frank Lantz, with his dog, Ring, in front of his blacksmith shop.

He fought a lightning fire on a mountain behind the bar and the Forest Service offered him a job. Frank took it — for 27 years. He began building trails. At that time to get to Shoup it was necessary to go up over Horse Creek, so the river trail had priority with him. After several seasons he had it completed.

During the winter, he would trail clear down on the Selway to keep snow shoveled off the Forest Service cabins at Deep Creek, (now Moose Creek). He ran a trap line there and packed fall hunters for about 12 years.

There is a sentence in Genesis: "It is not good for man to be alone." The bar was like Eden without Eve. Frank made occasional trips to Hamilton, Montana, where he met a lady his age, Jessie Leona Lockwood, cooking in a restaurant there. They were married in Hamilton, October 23, 1935. They went to his canyon home, where she had never been before.

Jessie loved life on the river. She worked for the Forest Service too, handling radio messages from the fire lookouts. She grew a garden, made small batches of beer, kept a diary. Together they built a new two-story cabin. It was just the whisker of August, 1940, when they moved into it.

If, as Mark Twain observed, "civilization is an endless multiplication of unnecessary necessities," then the Lantzes weren't very civilized. They had a gas washing machine and refrigerator in later years. They had a radio so Frank could hear baseball games and listen to the news. There were a couple of steamer trunks full of history books. In the fall they would make a trip to Salmon for winter supplies.

Jess was always busy. "She was busy every single minute," said Frank, "till 15 minutes before she died," — of a blood clot, June 3, 1955. She was buried in Corvallis, Montana. Her loss must have left a terrible emptiness in Lantz, but it is a backcountry adage that no one can long afford grief.

Frank worked for the Forest Service until 1952. He strung telephone lines and fought fires. In 1929 he was on one fire for over a month.

Those efforts were only a staircase to his real monument: the Salmon-Bitterroot trails. He built most of the trails from Horse Creek to Sabe Creek, and to within 10 miles of the Magruder ranger station — almost 200 miles in all. Much of the work he did alone, all of it by hand. Sometimes he had the help of a two-man crew, and in later years, they had drills and dynamite. Frank always laid out trail with a horse in mind — he would consider the grade a horse could climb without difficulty. He worked a full eight hours and expected no less from anyone else. When using black powder on a trail in 1929, he received a severe head injury caused by a flying rock.

Jessie Lockwood Lantz in her younger years.

The Forest retired him in 1952, a move he never appreciated: "They said, 'You're no good anymore, too old,' and retired me." Despite the ranger's objections, Lantz took one of the old government mules into retirement with him. "He was tired," he said.

Frank tended his fruit trees and garden. He kept the place irrigated and green, wearing rubber boots as a concession to rattlesnakes. He raised hay for his horses on the 20 acres.

Frank sold his acreage to the Forest Service in 1958 for $3600, receiving a lifetime special use permit for himself. The North Fork District still uses it as an administrative site.

Lantz was a trump, with a heart as big as a saddle blanket. Everyone agreed he could see through people like an x-ray, judging their character after five minutes — and he was never wrong. If he liked you, he'd go to the end of the trail with you; if he didn't, you'd better move on.

As a person, he loved lemon meringue pies, corn whiskey, baseball, horses, and dogs. He had little use for laziness, politicians, paper work, and of all things, tomatoes. The worst thing he ever called anyone was a "dirty Boxer" — (the Chinese "Boxers" tried to expel foreigners in 1900).

Frank Lantz in 1965.

On the morning of October 14, 1964, Dick Leonard, a Forest Service summer guard on the place, set a large tub of water on the wood stove and built a roaring fire. He planned to put the water in the washing machine. Leonard had put a propane tank behind the stove; the heat may have vented the tank. In a short while, the log house was ablaze.

Lantz and Leonard had little luck saving anything from the flames, since there was no water pressure to fight the fire. (Frank said he did rescue an old hat full of holes.) The fire spread to the first house, a wood shed, and storage shed. A small granary was spared, as was the blacksmith shop.

Joe Scoble was power boating on the river and reported the fire to the Salmon National Forest. They tried to send a helicopter but winds forced it to land at Indianola. Two bentonite planes from Salmon made drops on the fire to prevent it from spreading up the hill.

Scoble went back and took Lantz and Leonard to his Stub Creek headquarters where he outfitted them with utensils and supplies, then returned them to the bar.

Lantz had lost everything: years of work, priceless rifles, photographs, books, crystal ware — items that had been in his family for 200 years. It must have been hard to swallow, especially at age 74. But it was done — nothing he could do would make the crust a bit browner. He sent out one request: "Send me some chewing tobacco."

The response of his friends was a measure of their regard for the man. The supervisor for the Bitterroot National Forest, Harold "Andy" Anderson, immediately put a "stop" on all the districts' lumber. He called the G.S.A. supply center in Spokane, ordered nails and plywood, and sent trucks to pick it up. He levied on the districts for the money to pay the freight. Then he gave his staff a leave of absence, without pay, so they could go down to the bar and help build a new cabin. Winter was coming and there was no time to lose.

The power boaters responded magnificently: Don and Bob Smith, Joe Scoble, Wayne England, George Austin — in the middle of their steelhead season, they dropped their fishermen out along the banks and hauled tons of building materials to the site without charge.

The effort was co-ordinated by one civil service carpenter, who had measured the foundation and then pre-cut the lumber to match the plans he drew in Hamilton. Hammers swung by lantern light. A staff member's wife served meals. Frank watched, muttering and embarrassed. They told him to stay out of the way, so he helped bring materials up from the beach.

In a week they were moving him into a new house. Not as large as the two-story, two-bedroom old house, but comfortable, with all appliances converted to propane. He was tremendously grateful — particularly since he didn't have to move to town. "There'll be no towns for me as long as I've got my health," he said.

The following summer, the Forest Service extended the cabin 12 feet. It is the upper, modern house still on the bar, built over the old storage cellar. The district engineer also installed a 5000-gallon redwood holding tank up the creek so that there would be plenty of pressure in a 1.5-inch pipe line.

Lantz Bar, showing Frank's third house, built with volunteer labor. The second log house was located just in front of this cabin along the row of stones which can be seen in the lower right hand corner.

Harold Anderson received an official reprimand for his personnel file. The reasoning went: if it was a legitimate building, he should have paid the employees; if it was unauthorized, he shouldn't have spent the money. They decided to call it an "equipment shed," since such temporary buildings don't require site-survey, plans, plan modification, Washington review, appropriations, etc. The world needs more Andersons and fewer bureaucrats.

Frank looked after his orchard, read a great deal, and shook down blankets for his frequent visitors. He never carried a watch and refused to operate on a schedule. Anyone coming down from Shoup would gladly bring him his mail in exchange for a cup of coffee and conversation.

One day in 1965, he tumbled over and woke up lying on the ground. He decided he had a heart problem, but never did much about it. He took no medicine, though he eventually gave up whiskey. He wrote a will, and had his friend, Harold Hanson, witness it. That will was never seen again.

Frank spent a week in the hospital at Hamilton in the fall of 1966. He was falling into years. He spent several weeks in the Daly Hospital there in 1971, fighting a bad case of pneumonia and its aftereffects. He recuperated at his nephew, Verne Shreve's, house, but he longed to return to his place by the river, which had been his home for 46 years.

So strongly did he insist on returning to the bar, that Verne took him to Harold Hanson's place, near North Fork, and Harold jet-boated him back to his cabin.

Ten days later, October 12, 1971, after fixing an early morning breakfast, and calling to his friends, Harold Hanson and Craig Cornn, to come and join him, he was found slumped over the table, dead. That afternoon the Forest Service helicoptered his body to Hamilton so that he could be buried alongside his wife, Jessie, in the Corvallis cemetery.

If success is measured by the size of the hole a man leaves after he dies, then Frank B. Lantz's death left a Carlsbad along the River of No Return. He is missed by those who knew him, and we who didn't know him can only wish we had.

There is a grave between two flat stones at the west end of the large meadow at Lantz Bar. At the time of this writing, it has not been marked. Coy Lansbury is buried there. He was the son of Frank's Uncle Claud, and was born Feb. 3, 1910.

Coy came down the river in the fall of 1927 to stay with Frank. In the spring he got Rocky Mountain Spotted Fever from a tick bite. Lantz went out 40 miles to get some medicine, but Coy died May 19, 1928, before Frank could return, and John Cunningham, who happened by, buried him.

Mile 235.3: **Tag Creek** comes in on the left.

Mile 235.8: **Disappointment Creek** flows in from the left. Named by a disillusioned miner. The early history of this stream has apparently been lost.

Jack Avery lived in a cabin on the downstream side of the creek for eight years, 1926-1935. He was a friend of Frank Lantz and worked for the Forest Service from 1937-1941.

George Lear lived at the house for a while, and Charlie Rowes moved there in March, 1944. Wayne England put up a new building on the site. There was an orchard, strawberry patch, and grape vines.

The Forest Service burned all the dwellings some time ago. The flat is used by hunting parties in the fall.

Slim's hexangular cabin. Never finished, it's builder was forced to leave the canyon, and his last name can no longer be recalled.

Mile 236.3: **Dwyer Creek** flows in on the right. This drainage was named for the Dwyer brothers who made a river trip with Guleke in 1903, mentioned in the boating section of this book.

On the bench above the river, on the downstream side of the creek, is an unfinished, harmonious, hexangular cabin. Its design is unique among cabins along the river. Its builder was the cabinet maker and lumber planer for Frank Lantz's second house. His name

125

was Claud "Slim" (unknown) and he started the cabin in 1938.

Slim was a quiet, easy-going fellow who never untied his tongue about his past, but from occasional wistful remarks it had evidently included a woman. He was poor as a whip-poor-will, but a talented craftsman. He tanned hides with wood ashes, fished in the creek, slept in a sleeping bag, and began the cabin. But he couldn't quite make it; he didn't even have enough money for bullets, and he finally had to leave the canyon.

The trail up Dwyer Creek goes along Thirsty Ridge and back down to the river at Big Squaw Creek.

Mile 236.9: **Devil's Toe Creek** on the left.

Mile 237: **Devil's Teeth Rapid.** The name is attributed to the legendary Johnny McKay who met Satan coming up the river and knocked his teeth out with a sweep, creating the rapid. The run is on the left, between the two molars.

The old snag at the camping area on the left has a stain showing the highwater mark for the flood of 1974.

Mile 238.8: **Elkhorn Creek** enters on the right. Austin Smothers had a cabin on this bench, but it was burned by the U.S.F.S.

Mile 239.5: **Chamberlain Creek** rushes in on the left. This considerable stream is named for John Chamberlain, an early beaver trapper who worked its headwaters, about 20 miles from the river, as early as 1895. Lieutenant Catley's soldiers crossed the head of Chamberlain Creek during the Sheepeater Campaign of 1879.

It was on an early trip through Chamberlain Basin that R. G. Bailey discovered a cabin with a skeleton in rags on the bed, and a note charcoaled on the table: "My God I am blind."

The Basin had a moose population at the turn of the century. It's now considered a major elk breeding ground in the Idaho Primitive Area. There is an airstrip, constructed by the Forest Service.

Mile 240.3: **Fortune Creek** on the right.

Mile 240.7: **Thirsty Creek,** right side.

Mile 240.9: **Little Devils Tooth Rapid.** The tooth fairy seems to have taken the teeth.

Mile 241.9: **Big Bear Creek** comes down on the left.

Mile 242: **Big Squaw Creek** flows in from the right.

Norm and Bill Guth's outfitting cabin for hunters, fishermen, and vacationers is about 150 yards below Big Squaw on the right. The Guths have been outfitting for over 20 years and had the Thomas Creek Ranch on the Middle Fork in 1955. In 1967 they got the Squaw

Creek camp from Don Smith.

Their pack stock is brought in from Lantz Bar by way of Thirsty Ridge.

Mile 242.9: **Smith Gulch** on the right. The cabin on the bench was built by Johnny Briggs, who was mentioned at Fawn Creek.

Johnny Brigg's cabin at Smith Gulch.

Mile 243.5: **Cub Creek** on the left.

Corey Bar is across the river, just below Cub Creek. Elmer Purcell had a good-sized log cabin on the bar from 1936-1941. He wintered there, bringing what supplies he needed down from Shoup. He had dogs and would spend his time cat hunting.

Mile 244.5: **Arctic Creek** falls in from the left bluff. This stream marks the top of "Black Canyon" which extends downriver for a couple of miles. The name refers to the somber, exposed granite of the Idaho batholith which can be viewed here. This spot also represents Army Corps of Engineer's Dam site #170.

Arctic Creek is the upper limit of a Grand fir-Douglas fir community that begins about 10 miles downriver at Raven Creek. Grand fir has a clear successional superiority over the Doug fir at the present time. Some Western yew are found, as well. The understory includes plants not encountered elsewhere on the river: trail plant, twinflower, bluebell, beadlily, bedstraw, Texas vetch.

The grand-fir community may be a recessional remnant of a type that in humid times covered a much larger area. The site is unique in that its vegetation doesn't occur elsewhere in the river corridor.

A Forest Service ecological analysis done in 1971-72 concluded that commercial boating at Arctic Creek and Magpie Creek was not compatible with the perpetuation of this unique understory community. Since nothing has been done to protect it, it is probably wise to avoid camping at Magpie Creek.

Mile 244.8: **Salmon Falls.** The falls was a serious obstacle for boats until it was repeatedly dynamited. It was known as the Black Canyon Falls. The rapid is flooded out in high water (over 25,000 c.f.s.), and on lower flows it can be run through any of the three slots, depending on boat size and water stage. The left run is probably preferred.

Cap Guleke scouting the left side of Salmon Falls.

Reloading a scow at Salmon Falls, after lightening it for the run through the rapid.

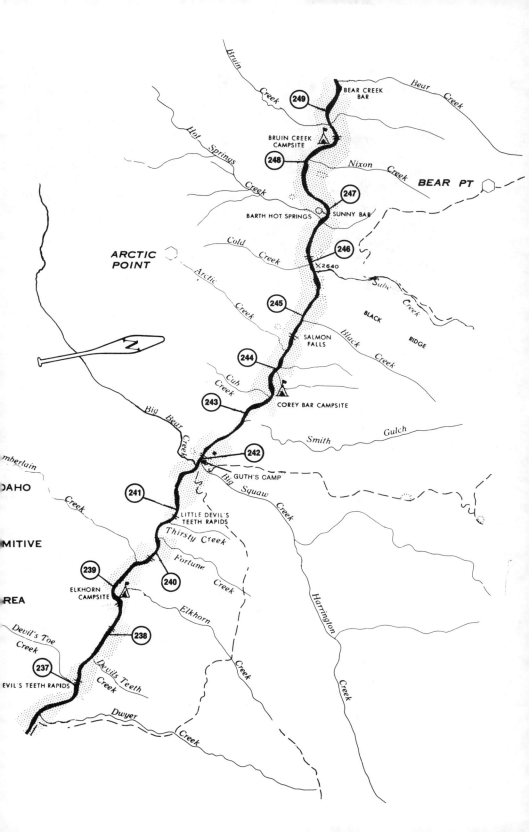

Bob Smith making the center run at Salmon Falls carrying a jeep on a pontoon sweepboat.

Mile 245: **Black Creek** enters on the right.

Mile 245.8: **Sabe Creek** pours in from the right. The word is from the Spanish: "know." This creek comes 10 miles from 8200-foot Sabe Mountain and forms the boundary between the Bitterroot and Nez Perce National Forests.

Mile 245.9: **Cold Creek** on the left.

Mile 246.7: **Sunny Bar** on the right. The tent cabins are one of Bob Smith's fishing camps. The flat below the cabins was cleared by Bill Miller in the early Thirties. The rock wall was the foundation for Ralph Smother's board cabin in the 1950's. The house was burned.

Mile 246.8: **Barth Hot Springs.** Steam rises from the left bank as the 134-degree water splashes down rocks from the spring.

The location was known as Guleke Hot Springs for nearly 30 years. Elmer Keith said Guleke used the cabin on the flat. Don Smith remembers a fellow growing rye for whiskey there. At the turn of the century there was still evidence of extensive placer mining efforts, including a whip-sawed wooden flume carrying water out of the creek for almost a mile. Chinese miners did some of the early placering. R. G. Bailey said large numbers of elk were using the springs as a lick in 1903.

Ralph Smothers built this cabin in the 1950's at Sunny Bar across from Barth. It was burned.

Hard Boil taking a bath at Barth Hot Springs on a Guleke trip.

The names on various boulders are evidence of the spring's popularity with early floaters. McKay's inscription is on a smoothly polished stone below the highwater mark and the Flapper's carving is just to the left of it.

The modern name for the springs is that of Jim Barth, who had the place in the Twenties.

131

There are two men buried at Barth in unmarked graves, who both drowned in separate accidents at Salmon Falls. Hugo Vater was knocked out of a sweepboat at the rapid and his body was found by some men swimming at the springs. Maisie and Monroe Hancock buried him in 1934, right against the cliff by the big yellow pine tree. The little cross they placed has disappeared. Hancock took Vater's partner down to the South Fork so he could fly out.

The following summer Anthony March rafted the river with Bill Miller. They wrecked in the Falls and March dived after his bedroll, but he never needed it again. Cap Guleke found his body by the springs and buried him above the creek on the upper flat.

Mile 248: **Nixon Creek** on the right. It was named for Bert Nixon (the other wasn't worth honoring). Bert worked for the Forest Service as a fire lookout for 35 years, much of that time on Bear Point lookout at the head of Nixon Creek. He had three head of horses which he wintered in Weiser. He took special care of them and quit his lookout job rather than be required to use them for pack stock. Bert anticipated male chauvinism by 30 years: He said, "Women lookouts are all right, but they talk too much. This lookout business is a lonely job made for old fellows like I am. But you take a woman now, she's just got to talk. And so she's on the Forest Service telephone visiting with other lady lookouts a good share of the time. Me, I just do my talking to my five burros and keep my eyes peeled for fires all the time."

Mile 248.8: **Bruin Creek** flows in on the left.

Mile 249.5: **Bear Creek,** on the right. Monroe and Maisie Hancock had a log house on the flat on the upstream side of the creek; the area is rather overgrown now. Hancock built the cabin in the fall of 1932; they spent the previous winter at Lantz Bar. Bert Loper visited them here in 1936. Maisie planted peach and walnut trees. Mountain sheep killed the peaches by eating the bark.

The cabin was later cut up for firewood. Some walnuts survive, along with sweetpeas and iris.

The whitewater which runs down the left side of the boulder bar, just around the curve below Bear Creek, is Hancock Rapid.

Maisie Hancock-Shuck in 1919; lived at Bear Bar for six years.

The Hancock cabin at Bear Creek, which was cut up for firewood.

Mile 250.8: **Dillinger Creek** twists down its steep drainage on the left. Named for Sampson Dillinger. Born in Indiana in 1839, he was the first discoverer of gold on Oregon's Rogue River. He was a miner all his life: California, Oregon, and Idaho — arriving in Elk City in 1865. He placered on Mallard Creek and averaged $30-a-day. Sam built the first arrastre in Dixie and in 1892 was the only inhabitant of that town. He must have been a renowned hiker, as it was said of long or tiring trails in those days, "Sam Dillinger must have stepped it." Dillinger Creek is steeper than a cow's face.

The state record mountain goat was shot on this creek by a hunter guided by Dick Rhett.

Mile 250.8: **Deer Park Creek** on the left.

Mile 250.9: **Army Corps of Engineer's Dillinger Dam** site.

Mile 252.1: **Andy the Russian's** cabin. A faint trail goes up the left bank into the brush. The dilapidated cabin is on the upper end of the clearing which is being reclaimed by second-growth yellow pine.

Andy's surname was Strauss. He lived in this cabin, wasted nothing, grew great quantities of flowers, and went around naked as Adam. Whenever a boat stopped, the guide would go ahead to let Andy know he had visitors, so he could pull on a pair of shorts.

Charlie Ayres accepted a bear steak dinner invitation from Andy one evening. After the main course, the Russian served huckleberry pie. Charlie ate it, then got to wondering where Andy discovered huckleberries, so he asked. "Oh, I found them in the bear's stomach," Andy answered.

Strauss had a daughter, Helen, who visited him regularly. When his eyesight began to fail, she entrusted him to a rest home in Grangeville. Andy ran away, and through a series of rides got on the road down to Whitewater Ranch. Lew and Catherine Wildt, owners of the ranch, met Andy hobbling down the road as they returned in their vehicle from a trip to town. Catherine Wildt had shared lunch with the Russian many times; they stopped to ask him where he was going. "To Mr. Wildt's ranch." "I'm Mr. Wildt," said Lew. Andy didn't recognize them, he was confused. They took him to their home and he asked to stay there.

Andy Strauss stayed for the winter. At times he hallucinated and his health didn't improve. He gave the Wildt's his $39 monthly pension check for board.

Andy the Russian at his cabin, with a passenger from a Don Smith float trip.

One spring morning he told Lew he was going for a walk — something he had often done before. When he failed to return, a general search was initiated. Andy was found by Bob Mott up on Vista Point, dying of exposure. His daughter took him to Grangeville, where he was buried.

Across the river, about halfway between Deer Park Creek and Rattlesnake Creek, just below the highwater mark, is a grave dug in 1935. George Kelsey was camped at Bear Bar one stormy night when an old fellow wandered in and acted like he had only 39 cards in his deck. From remarks that he made, George figured the man was in

Andy "the Russian" Strauss' cabin as it appears today.

Paul Kriley (left) with Andy the Russian (right).

trouble with the law. Suddenly the stranger jumped up screaming, "They're coming! They almost got me!" and dashed off into the darkness.

Kelsey knew he'd get shot if he chased him, so he waited till dawn. He found the man frozen, next to a large rock where he'd built a fire. George got Sam Meyers to help him bury the fellow. Kelsey had gotten the man's last name, so Maisie Hancock took a hammer and spike and etched the name on a stone, which she placed on the grave.

Mile 253.3: **Rattlesnake Creek** drains in from the right. The Crofoot Ranch is about a mile up the creek.

Bruce Crofoot was a small, sandy complected Scotsman who came into Salmon River country in 1910. He built a cabin at the mouth of Sheep Creek. He had a couple of burros and was interested in trapping and mining. Unfortunately he had what had been diagnosed as an advanced case of tuberculosis. He made a habit of eating all the mold he could find, particularly bread mold. It may not have been effective, but before long he recovered completely.

He settled at the mouth of Bargamin Creek for a short time, but was persuaded by the Forest Service to take an area with more agricultural potential up above the river.

Crofoot homesteaded the Ranch by 1912, though he didn't record the deed until 1924. He operated a trap line. Jay Shuck saw him on Plummer Creek in 1912, headed for Rattlesnake Creek with two burros and a burro colt named Porphyry. He trapped some with Ed Harbison and Vic Bargamin. The 1924 earthquake knocked his cabin off its foundation.

In 1926 Crofoot got lip cancer and was advised to see a doctor in Grangeville. On his way back, he got a telegram near Dixie saying his crippled sister was not expected to live. Bruce had given her his inheritance, so he went to check on the situation. He never came back. People heard later that he went to Mariposa, California, but got cancer of the tongue and jaw and experienced an agonizing death.

Jim Smith and Tom Dale got the place in 1951. They lived in the small cabin, but found they were different as chalk and cheese, and split up in the spring.

The Stewarts sold the 50 acres to Frank Santos, a logging contractor from California. He hauled in a sawmill, built a new lodge, and scraped out an airstrip. A road was pushed up from the river with a 7000-pound bulldozer brought down on a scow by the Smiths. The Forest Service was displeased, but as with all bureaucracy, forgiveness is easier to obtain than permission.

There is a grave at Crofoot Ranch. It is that of Tom Newson, who died of blood poisoning after having a tooth extracted.

The trail on the upstream side of Rattlesnake Creek goes to Bear Point and Center Mountain; the trail on the downstream side leads from Crofoot to Sheep Hill and over to Bargamin Creek.

Mile 253.3: **Magpie Creek** streams in from the left.

Mile 253.6: **Raven Creek** on the left. The trail on the upstream side of the creek can be followed to Chamberlain Basin.

Mile 254.2: **Hida Creek** comes in on the left. It is named for Lee Hida who was known as the "King of Sourdough." Hida worked on the Comstock Trail and was watchman for the Comstock mine for many years. Hida Point was named for him while he was still alive.

Mile 255.8: **Bargamin Creek** and campground on the right. Early maps called this stream the "Little Salmon." The name changed in 1920. The name "Bargamin" belonged to a prominent Richmond, Virginia, family. Their son, Vic, went to the state university for two years before deciding, like Thoreau, that "education makes a straight-cut ditch out of a free, meandering stream." Bargamin drifted west in the 1880's, and stopped in Colorado to hunt, trap, and prospect. Feeling crowded there, he headed for Idaho with a bunch of burros and homesteaded on a meadow near the headwaters of Mallard Creek, at a site now called the Cook Ranch.

Vic ran a trapline between the Salmon and the Clearwater. He established a series of nine cabins, each a day apart, furnished with bedding and stove. During the summer, he used his burro train to pack supplies and haul wood to the cabins.

His foresight paid off, when Bargamin had an attack of rheumatism one winter and survived only because he was able to reach one of his cabins on Magruder Mountain.

It was six miles up Bargamin Creek, on tributary Cache Creek, that the saga of Henry "Dynamite" Moore transpired.

Henry was setting mink traps on the creek in November of 1930. He stopped at a cabin, started a fire in the stove and fetched a bucket of water from the stream. Re-entering the cabin, he was stunned by an explosion that shattered the stove. His legs were broken by slabs of stove iron thrown by the blast, but his flesh wasn't torn.

Lying on the floor, Moore tried shooting the phone off its hook as a distress signal, but that didn't work. He than drank a bottle of iodine, hoping it would end his misery. The injured man slipped in and out of consciousness. He managed to build a small fire in a dishpan on the floor and using a broom handle knocked some icicles in through the empty windows to ease his thirst. Night and day blurred in his agony.

Charlie "Toughie" Tuttle, Moore's trapping partner, became concerned when Henry failed to show for Thanksgiving dinner at the Dale Ranch. He went up Bargamin looking for his pard and found him two days after the accident.

Toughie packed Moore almost four miles before going to Allison's for help. They called Dr. Boyd in Elk City, then rigged a stretcher and packed Dynamite toward Red River through the snow. They met Dr. Boyd in route; he gave Moore a shot, then set the bones in his legs.

Dynamite Moore was taken to Lewiston and was out of the canyon for almost two years. One spring he returned, aided by a cane. He settled at Mackay Bar, at the mouth of the South Fork, and began clearing the first airstrip in the canyon. He worked by hand, moving rocks with the help of a wheelbarrow. The strip he made began serving as a means of emergency evacuation for the sick and injured and still does.

The stove explosion proved to be the result of dynamite caps stored by a Forest Service employee. The warning sign which had been left was apparently knocked over by wood rats. When lawyers investigated the situation, they found the cabin belonged to the Forest Service and Moore had been trapping inside a game reserve, so he was never compensated.

The campground is on the downstream side of the creek.

The trail up Bargamin Creek goes to the Red River road and to Three Prong Ridge.

Mile 256.2: **Bailey Creek and Bailey Rapids.**

The creek is named for Robert G. Bailey, an Idaho writer, politician, and printing press operator. He spent considerable time along the River of No Return, making his first trip with Guleke in 1903. Bailey saved much of the canyon's history by publishing the first book on the Salmon River.

Bailey Rapid is about 300 yards downriver from the creek and is usually run a bit right of center.

Mile 257: **Myers Creek** and the Allison Ranch on the right. Sam Myers was a southerner, born in 1837. He fought in the Civil War, with General Sherman in Georgia, and received a government pension.

Myers did some placering at the creek and kept a number of handsome horses. He lived there 40 years. Coming down from Dixie on the Churchill Trail with a load of winter supplies in 1923, he was thrown into a tree by a halter-pulling mare, and it cost him his life. He is buried in the Dixie cemetery.

The spot is now known as the Allison Ranch. Myers cabin, located by the barn, was torn down. Elmer Allison got the place from Myers' heirs by paying off a thousand-dollar mortgage held by Ed Harbison, Vic Bargamin's trapping partner. Sam Myers must have accumulated some gambling debts in Dixie to have owed Harbison that much money.

Everett Van Arsdale (left), June and John Cook at the Allison Ranch. John added the front porch. Photo was taken in 1963.

Allison had been to the ranch in 1922. The next three years he spent working in the Coeur d'Alene mines to pay for the place. Lee Hida stayed as a caretaker, harvesting the calf crop as his wage.

Elmer built a cabin on the site where the upper house is now located, but it was destroyed by fire. He lived in the blacksmith shop across from the barn, while he and George Wolfe built a new house.

Joe and Emma Zaunmiller were persuaded to come down from the Harbison-Bargamin Ranch to help Allison raise cattle. Elmer had taken title and gave Joe a half interest in the ranch. They sold the meat around Elk City. Joe returned to the Harbison place in 1931.

A sawmill was built for Elmer by Bill Jackson. The mill was located just above the present barn and cut all the lumber for that structure. Someone was touchy as a teased snake — Elmer and Jackson had a dispute, and Bill left, but not before the sawmill ground to a mysterious halt.

Four Californians, two doctors and two orchard owners, bought the ranch from Allison in 1946. The lower cabin was built as their quarters by Elmer, Tex Mott and one of his boys. Allison was going to remain as caretaker, but he acquired a "mail-order" bride from Milwaukee. Charlotte was in her sixties and had lived in that city all her life. As Allison's health deteriorated, she persuaded him to move to Lewiston.

It was later discovered that the lower cabin was actually on Forest Service land. Discussions considered trading some deeded land or trail right-of-way for the location, rather than destroying the cabin, as was demanded.

The Californians decided to sell in 1959 and John and June Cook bought it. John had been running a large cattle ranch near Whitebird with Warren Brown. John was suffering from angina and thrombosis; had been warned by a doctor to give up the cattle business. He had to be helped in and out of bed and never left the house without morphine and nitroglycerine tablets in his jacket pocket. But at Allison he did as he wanted: cared for the orchard, put up fences, rode horses, became an authority on Winchester rifles. The small airstrip allowed for a plane in emergencies.

After ten years, the Cooks sold Allison Ranch to Robert Hansberger and moved farther downriver. Harold and Phyllis Thomas bought the 60 acres from Hansberger, modernized it, and made it available to paying guests. With Tom Close looking after the cabins, orchard, flowers and garden, it remains perhaps the most delightful private inholding on the river.

Mile 257.5: **Sapp Creek** on the left; a name of unknown derivation.

Mile 257.6: **Fivemile Creek** on the right, usually called Little Fivemile so that it isn't confused with a creek by the same name only 20 miles downriver. The remains of a small cabin can be detected on the downstream side of the creek, back against the bank. The cabin was occupied in the Twenties by a man who wintered his horses near Deer Park Creek. He had two daughters that he treated like servants. He would kill game but required them to carry his rifle, dress and pack the meat. They split wood, cooked, and did all other manual tasks required to survive in the canyon.

Mile 257.7: **Split Rock Rapid.** The river swings to the right, then straightens for the rapid. The run is down the right-hand side.

Mile 259.2: **Silge Creek** on the left. Fred Silge was a highly educated German musician, who had played in some of the cathedrals of his homeland. In his late teens, he was brought to America by his father so that he would not be drafted by the German army. Fred never spoke about his past, or his reasons for coming to the canyon, but he did play music for his friends in his cabin. He ran Campbell's ferry for several seasons, then drowned in the river when a cable was hooked by a snag on high water.

Mile 259.4: **The Thomas Place-Yellow Pine Bar,** the bluff on the right-hand side of the river.

Any natural hardship is better than an unnatural life, and homage must be paid the people who lived and labored here.

Truman G. Thomas was a railroad engineer in Spokane. His fondness for whiskey cost him his job and his wife.

Truman corresponded with a cousin, Celestia, who ran a rest-home in Rochester, New York. When she developed heart trouble, the doctor advised a change of pace. Truman invited her west, and they were married — each for the second time. Children existed on both sides, but not from this wedding.

Truman and Celeste came down to Yellow Pine Bar in the early 1900's and settled in a cabin across the river below Richardson Creek. After Eugene Churchill drowned in the river, Mrs. Thomas was apprehensive about crossing the water, so they moved over to Yellow Pine Bar and lived in a small cabin built by an earlier occupant. Truman planted an orchard on the bar. A ditch brought water from the spring to the house.

The cabin caught fire one summer and burned to the base. Leslie Powelson and Joe McKnight came down from Dixie and built a new house for the Thomases. They finished it with whipsawed lumber from a mining flume.

Thomas proved up on the 36 acres in 1924. In 1927, at the age of 83, he died. He was buried on the edge of the bar, just southwest of the present house.

Celeste and Truman Thomas at Yellow Pine Bar.

The same year that Truman died, Celeste sold the place to Charley Ayres for $500. She spent the winter in Elk City, and the following winter with Molly Harbison at the Bargamin-Harbison-Cook Ranch, which the Thomases had owned; then she returned to the east, residing with her son until she died.

Charley Ayres' daughter, Maisie, had spent the summer of 1924 with Celeste Thomas on Yellow Pine Bar. Her father first saw the place as cook on a scow with Hancock and Cunningham. He and his wife, Sarah, were born in Missouri, and moved to Idaho as youngsters. Before coming to Salmon River, Charley worked for Woods Livestock Company of Montana.

The old Thomas house, photographed in 1931. The peak of the barn can be seen on the right.

Charley and Sarah went down the river from Salmon in the spring of 1931. They left their daughter, Marie "Babe" Ayres, with Maisie, who was ill, at Cunningham Bar. In the fall, Tex Mott, who had known the Ayres in Montana, arrived at Cunningham's, and he and Babe were married in Salmon. They returned to Jack Cunningham's place and all of them went down-river, dropping Maisie and Monroe Hancock at Lantz Bar where the couple planned to winter. At Yellow Pine Bar, the Motts found Charley and Sarah had a new log cabin up to square. The Ayres' boys, Tom and Gene, trailed down in time to help the Motts and Ayres finish it. Boards from the Ayres' scow and Mott's honeymoon boat were used in the floor and ceiling of the new, two-story house. More wood was cut by Ayres and Elmer Allison at Allison's mill and floated down to complete the project.

Babe and Tex lived in a cabin near the Dale Ranch that year. Their first child, Bill, was born in October, 1932, at Elk City. Then they moved to Yellow Pine Bar.

There was a battery-operated phone system along the river in those days. Portions of it still function, and wire strung from trees can be glimpsed at times above the right bank. The line ran from Red River down into the canyon and over to Big Creek. While it was put in by the Forest Service, it was maintained by the river people. The line from Red River went to Bat Point, then down to Yellow Pine Bar and up to Allison's. A branch line went down to the Dale Ranch. For a while that spur was abondoned, but in 1945 a heavy wire was used to connect Dixie, Jim Moore's place, and Zaunmiller's at Campbells

Ferry with the Dale Ranch and then on up to Yellow Pine Bar, over to Richardson Creek and up to Allison Ranch. It required some effort to keep the line repaired — winter storms, tree limbs, and animals would knock the wire down until spring. But in summer and fall it was a cherished means of communication: everyone would get on the phone for a visit in the morning and in the evening.

Sarah and Charley Ayres, with their children Marie and Tom, in Montana.

The Ayres boys with their father in 1930 on the Pahsimeroi. Left to right: Tom, Gene, and Charley.

145

Charley Ayres had a placer claim called the Bluebell at the mouth of Richardson Creek. The 1924 earthquake cut the spring water on Yellow Pine Bar to half its previous flow — most of the water began running out down by the river, as it does today. So in 1932, Charley was already thinking about developing the bench across the river, where Richardson Creek would nourish a garden and power a sawmill. He worked at clearing that bar over the next two years.

The house the Ayres built on Yellow Pine Bar.

In 1932, a second son, Bob, was born to Babe and Tex Mott at Yellow Pine Bar.

The following fall, Charley and Sarah, with the help of their daughter, began pulling in logs to build the new house across the river. The women helped roll the logs up, while Charley notched and fitted them. The Ayres planted fruit and nut trees and tended a two-acre garden on the side. Game provided a source of meat. Gene, Tom, and Tex worked at outside jobs to provide cash for staples.

When she was seven and a half months pregnant, Babe snowshoed out to Elk City in order to have her third son, Gene, in Grangeville. Then she returned to the canyon.

Charley built a water-powered sawmill and cut boards for the new cabin. He added a barn and chicken house. They grew hay for their stock. Charley and Tom built a ferry to replace the rowboat they used to cross the river, but high water took it out two years later. The boat was reactivated until a second ferry was installed in 1947.

About 1938, Ayres began guiding and packing for hunters. He built a trail up Richardson Creek in order to hunt Dillinger Creek and Harlan Meadows. Making that trail was an impressive feat — the country is steep enough to slide a grasshopper.

Babe had her first daughter, Nancy, in 1938, then almost died in childbirth when she delivered Rosa in 1940.

A difference of opinion makes horse races. Charley Ayres and Elmer Allison had a misunderstanding. The fact that Ayres' stallion, Old Silver, kept going up to Allison's place and bringing Elmer's mares back down across the river, where he'd get them with foal, didn't help matters at all. The Ayres moved out to Ontario, Oregon, in the spring of 1941, to run a beer parlor Tex had acquired. It wasn't long before they decided to return to the banks of Salmon River.

Pretty Sarah Ayres' health deteriorated. She had been through one operation in Grangeville; now she became seriously ill. Babe, who had snowshoed out because of an ulcerated tooth, met Hancock coming up the trail as she returned. He informed her that it was necessary to get Sarah to a hospital. Tex, Gene and Tom got the Dixie mail sled, and Don Ingraham towed it with a Cat. The party left Elk City at seven that evening, but it took until eight the next morning to cover 13 miles to Trapper Creek. All the next day and night they moved toward Yellow Pine Bar, arriving there at three-thirty in the morning.

They placed Sarah in a sleeping bag and Monroe rowed her to the Mallard Creek road. There Floyd Dale took her by car to the sled, and she was carried first to Elk City, and then to Lewiston, where she died of cancer a few weeks later.

Charley Ayres returned to his outfitting business at Richardson. He had half-a-dozen camps, and in 1949, 39 head of stock. The Motts were often there. Babe's last child, Dick, was born in 1943, at Grangeville.

Charley was 72 years old before he decided to quit the outfitting business. He gave his car to his son Tom, Yellow Pine Bar to Gene, and Richardson Bar to Babe. He died in 1949 and was buried in Elk City.

Gene Ayres sold Yellow Pine Bar to Tracy and Doris Watson in 1947. Tracy, a finish carpenter, was troubled by a heart condition. Doris had grown up on the Snake River, and taught school in Orofino and Golden. She had been to Yellow Pine Bar as early as 1942.

Doris and Tracy lived in a platform tent overlooking the river for the winter of 1947 and the summer of '48 while they, and her children by a prior marriage, Gene, Don, and Zoe, and Zoe's husband, Earl Eidemiller, built the two-story log house which now occupies the site, and which can be seen from the river. They used horses to bring in the logs and split roof shakes from yellow pine blocks. When the building was completed, Earl and Zoe moved in, while Tracy and Doris went up to Allison Ranch to live.

The Watson-Eidemiller house built in 1948, which can be seen from the river.

Earl was one of nine children. He had a couple of years of geology at the University of Idaho, and was something of a rockhound, making agate jewelry. The divided drawers which held his mineral collection are still in the cabin. So is the cabinet built to hold their record collection for a hand-cranked Victrola. Eidemiller worked for the Forest Service and did some boating for Don Smith. He and Zoe had four children.

During the winter, Earl and Zoe piled up the stones for a corral back on the bar. It held their stock and sometimes a few pigs for fattening.

Late in the summer of 1948, Doris Watson, her son, Don Sigler, Monroe Hancock, Tex Mott, Oakie Grogg, and Wendell Stout began construction of a one-room log schoolhouse on the bar below the Yellow Pine buildings. It was located close to the trail, back against the rocky bluffs — called "Whispering Cliffs" because they echo the soft sound of the river.

When classes began, there were eight students and Doris was the teacher. Hers was a complicated task but she was admirably suited for it: intelligent, resourceful, imaginative, and firm. There were five Motts who came across from Richardson by ice or boat, depending on the weather: Bob, Gene, Nancy, Rosa, and Dick. Kay Barlow stayed with Doris, Eric Stout boarded with the Motts, and Mark Robins, the son of a family living at the mouth of Mallard Creek, resided with the Motts.

There were two first-graders, a girl who had been in 14 schools in one year, and 13-year-old boys. Doris had to locate a common denominator. One of her questions concerned the difference between county, country, and continent. A little girl piped up, "Well, Salmon River is a country, I know that much anyway."

The school had desks packed in by horse, and blackboards that arrived the same way. There were a few books. "You'd be surprised what you can learn from all sorts of things besides school books," Doris remarked. The Grangeville Free Press sent packages of paper. A Spokane trucking firm donated half-a-dozen atlases which were used, with imagination, for geography, English, civics. Doris observed, "It's amazing how children can learn when something is presented to them." Young Dick Mott could grasp number concepts when they were put in terms of horses and mules. A lot of pack stock rolled off Bat Point while he learned subtraction. They went outside and discovered the differences among pine trees, learned the names of wild flowers, indentified birds. Mornings often revealed cougar tracks in the snow around the schoolhouse.

The children put on a Christmas program. They even had a hot lunch program provided by Babe and Doris. There were report cards, of course. By year's end, everyone tested ahead of his median grade level.

The following year there were not enough children for a school; so they went out, better prepared to learn, and one can guess they found public school more orthodox, but less interesting, less fun. It wasn't long before the Forest Service burned the school house. All that remains to affirm it ever existed are a few charred logs, some unexpended stovewood piles — and knowledge, carried by the students who were conscientiously taught there.

The Yellow Pine schoolhouse with teacher and pupils. The building was burned by the Forest Service.

Classroom session at Yellow Pine: Doris Watson at the blackboard looking at Kay Barlow. The other children are Motts.

Tracy Watson became seriously ill in 1951 and had to fly out of the canyon; Doris left with him. She went to work for the Forest Service. "After you've lived on the Salmon River, it takes a long time to get over being homesick," she said.

Before the Watsons left, they tore down the Ayres' house, which was in sad shape. The Watsons and Eidemillers sold out to Warren and Jane Brown, of McCall, Idaho, in 1956.

At the time of this writing, Terry and Donna Beeler have moved to Yellow Pine Bar and have been engaged by the Browns to restore the house, improve the landing strip, and caretake the property.

Babe Mott-Brinkley was on Richardson Bar for the last time in 1949. She lives in Grangeville. Her children have scattered across four states and Canada, and she now has 30 grandchildren.

The Forest Service disallowed Ayres' mining claim and burned all the buildings there.

Three unmarked graves can be found on Richardson Bar, not far from the former location of Ayres' cabin. Eugene Churchill is buried in one, Mr. Bergman, father of Reho Wolfe, is in another, and the identity of the third person has unfortunately been lost.

———————————— ◆ ● ◆ ● ————————————

Mile 260.1: **Richardson Creek** on the left. The creek and its fork are named for an early-day packer: Harlan Richardson.

Martin Humes had a cabin on the upper bench below Richardson Creek. C. H. Prescott, who had placer diggings across from the mouth of Mallard Creek, lived in it for a time, and so did the Thomases when they first came to Yellow Pine Bar. A 1931 forest fire burned the cabin.

Humes is buried on the bench. He came to Salmon River from Elwha River country in northwestern Washington, where he was a hunting guide. He placer mined along the Salmon.

R. G. Bailey, who knew Martin, said he was a big man, and got sick when he drank copiously at Barth Hot Springs after helping to pull a boat upriver to the springs. He lingered all fall, refusing to see a doctor, and died on Christmas eve. He may have had tick fever. His friends blasted out the grave in order to bury him. His family sent the headstone down with Cap Guleke to mark the site.

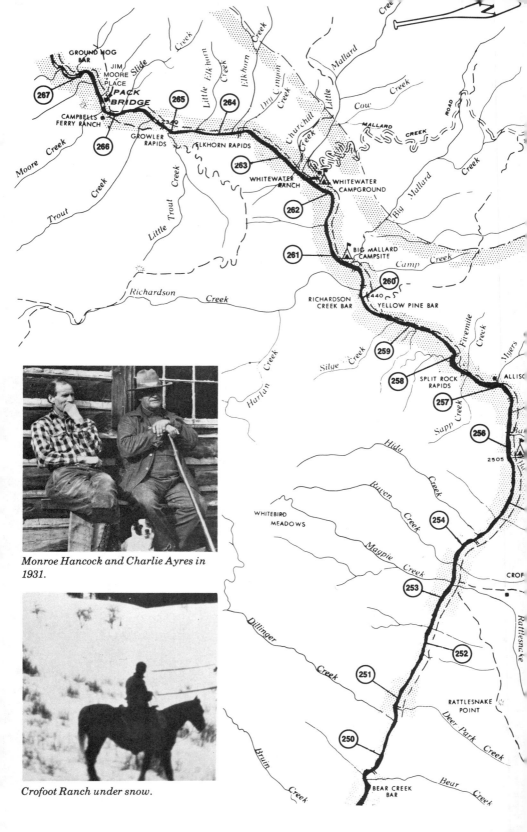

GROUND HOG BAR

JIM MOORE PLACE

SLIDE

PACK BRIDGE

Creek

Little Elkhorn Creek

Elkhorn Creek

Dry Canyon Creek

Little Mallard Creek

Mallard Creek

ROAD

(267)

(265)

(264)

CAMPBELLS FERRY RANCH

2340

Churchill Creek

Cow

MALLARD CREEK

(266)

GROWLER RAPIDS

ELKHORN RAPIDS

(263)

Moore Creek

WHITEWATER RANCH

WHITEWATER CAMPGROUND

Big Mallard Creek

Trout Creek

Little Trout Creek

(262)

(261)

BIG MALLARD CAMPSITE

Camp Creek

(260)

440

Richardson Creek

RICHARDSON CREEK BAR

YELLOW PINE BAR

Fivemile Creek

Myers

(259)

Silge Creek

(258)

SPLIT ROCK RAPIDS

ALLISO

Harlan Creek

(257)

Sapp Creek

(256)

2505

Hida Creek

Raven Creek

(254)

WHITEBIRD MEADOWS

Maypie Creek

CROF

(253)

Rattlesnake

Dillinger Creek

(252)

(251)

RATTLESNAKE POINT

(250)

Deer Park Creek

Bruin Creek

BEAR CREEK BAR

Beur Creek

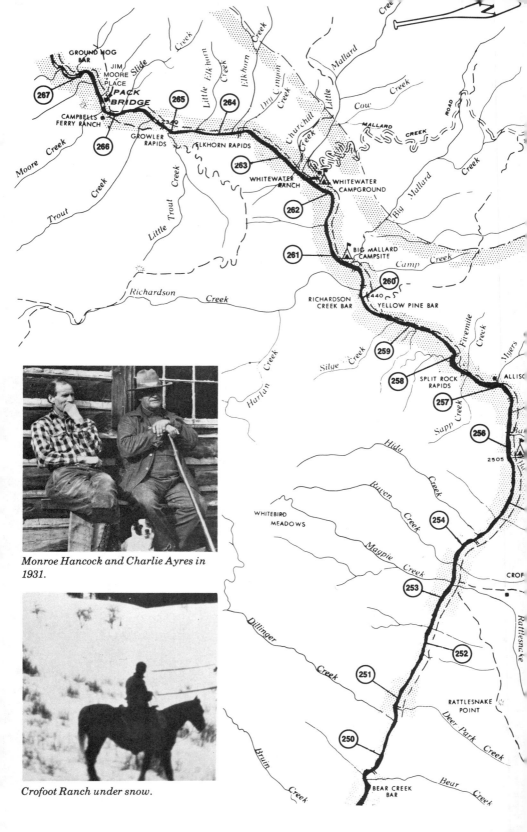

Monroe Hancock and Charlie Ayres in 1931.

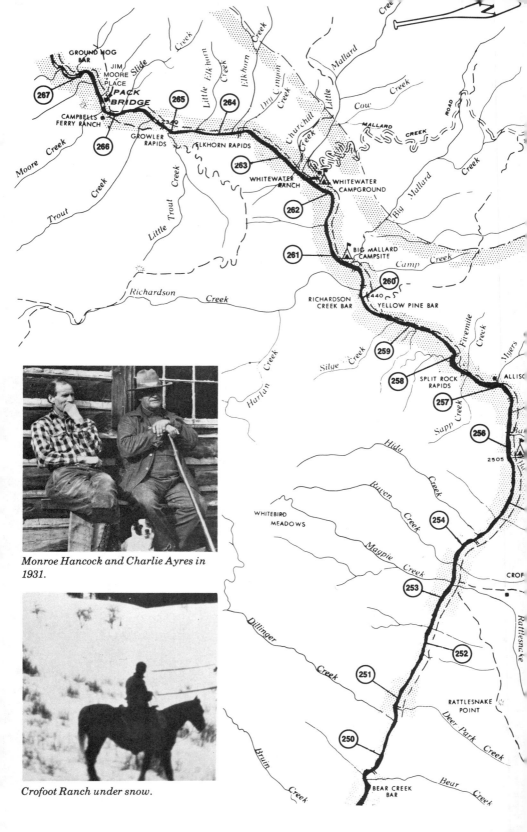

Crofoot Ranch under snow.

Mile 260.5: **Big Mallard Rapid.** Considered a problem rapid by boaters, it is washed out in high water. On lower stages the run is down the left-hand bank, going through the slot to the left of the big boulder.

Guleke had grief with his scow here. So did the Hatch-Swain party in 1936, turning over three of four boats because they were distracted by the antics of a bear and her cub on the bank and didn't notice the rapid until it was too late. Said Frank Swain, after the turnover, "I saw Fahrni's bald head bobbing down the river and I thought: there goes Bill to Riggins — the hard way!"

Jerry Hughes rowed the far right side of Big Mallard on very low water in September of 1974 with a 24-foot pontoon carrying a jeep — a remarkably skillful piece of boating.

Cap Guleke and Elmer Keith running Big Mallard Rapid in 1931.

Mile 260.7: **Big Mallard Creek** on the right. Peter Mallard was an early miner on this stream. The campground is just below the creek.

Evidence of a foundation and iris can be found on the upper flat. Toll Low lived in a log cabin here at one time. He was from Colorado and a friend of Ed Harbison. Toll built the Jack Creek trail up Mallard Creek.

Mile 261.4: **Oakie Grogg's** cabin was located on the left bank and could be seen from the river, before it was burned.

Oakie came to the River of No Return from the Carolinas, running like he'd been shot at and narrowly missed. He had been — by Treasury agents who caught him working a whiskey still; he escaped by snaking his way down the road in some tire ruts. He left a wife and two children behind.

Grogg was on the river in the early Thirties, with a second wife, Vonda, who was crippled by polio. She had a boy and a girl. They moved down the river on a houseboat, staying at places like Kitchen Creek, Corey Bar, and Sheep Creek. Vonda left him in 1941.

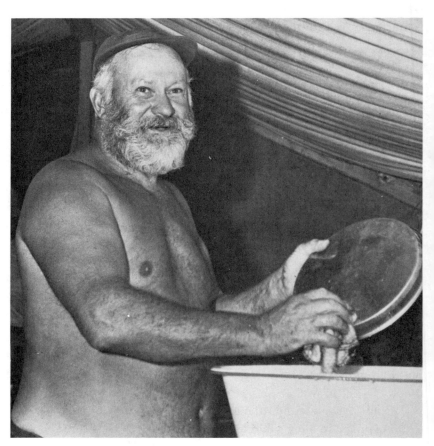

Oakie Grogg cooking in camp for Don Smith.

He did some placering. At times he cooked or boated for Don Smith. Oakie still made moonshine. When Paul Filer received an order of copper tubing at his Elk City store addressed to Oakie Grogg, he thought somebody was playing a joke on him.

While he had never finished grammar school, Oakie was wise as a tree full of owls. He was well educated: loved to read and remembered what he'd learned.

In later years, Oakie looked like a jovial Santa Claus — enough white whiskers to make a hair blanket, and a belly like a hay bale with the middle string busted. He enjoyed teasing and joking.

Grogg had an impromptu cabin, of split red firs covered with dirt, on the bank below Big Mallard. He went down to the Dale Ranch one morning to get a chicken from Mrs. Wildt. He said he wanted to make a broth, because he wasn't feeling well. Some boaters found him in his cabin later. Conjecture has it that he died from a ruptured appendix.

Mile 261.8: **Hank "the Hermit" Kemnitzer** lived on the left bank in a dugout cabin. He was befriended by John and June Cook at the Allison Ranch.

Hank was a will-o'-the-wisp miner, digging his shaft above the bank with a five gallon bucket and a large spoon. He pursued the chimerical bonanza, and often expressed his hard-held dream of sending June on a vacation to Hawaii, while he and John would sit in a castle he built on the bank of the river, sipping wine through the long afternoons. Like an answer to prayer, the bonanza was mighty slow in coming.

Hank had a dog, Queenie, that slept on the end of his bed. He called June one afternoon on the phone, worried that he had gotten lice from the dog. There was a rash on his wrists and ankles. June figured he'd simply gotten some poison ivy, but she couldn't go down to check until John got back. In the meantime, the Hermit became convinced he could feel lice under the itching. He took a box of DDT powder and rubbed it into the broken skin. By the time the Cooks reached him, he was deathly sick. They took him out to Grangeville, but he died. As Dmitri said, "What terrible tragedies real life contrives for people."

Mile 262: A large metal boiler can be found on the right bank, at the top of the eddy, in low water. It was destined for the Painter mine, and was lost by Cap Guleke when he wrecked in Big Mallard Rapid.

Mile 262.1: **Jess Root's** grave on the right, just above the trail.

Jess was born in 1881 and went to school in Meadows Valley. His father took him trapping in Chamberlain Basin, but it was a winter of protracted hardness and they moved nine miles down Chamberlain Creek where they built a cabin and established the first Root Ranch (the second Root Ranch was on Whimstick Creek).

When young Root grew to manhood, he was big enough to grab your legs and make a wish — but he only would have wished you well. He was a generous, easy-going, affable giant.

Fred Shiefer and Jess Root went to Salmon once and bought a mower and rake for the Root Ranch which Guleke hauled to the mouth of Chamberlain Creek for them. Then they packed and dragged it up the creek all the way to the ranch.

Jess owned and operated the store and post office in Warren for many years. He sold it and went to Salmon with the Storrey family to get involved in a mining venture. While alone on a boat at Kitchen Creek in 1936, he was apparently killed for his gold by a man from Seattle. The Storreys, who weren't present at the time, were convinced he was murdered.

A search was made for his body, and he was discovered at the top of the backeddy here two days later, by Maisie Hancock. Root's coat was over his head.

(The year and information on the present Forest Service marker are incorrect.)

The crew that boated down river looking for Jess Root's body: left to right: rear, Alvin Killum, John Storrey, Monroe Hancock, Jim (unknown), and Clyde Smith. Ford Hughes in front.

156

Mile 262.2: **Whitewater Campground,** on the right. The Mallard Creek road access to this campground was pushed in from Elk City with C.C.C. labor and two Cats operated by Lum Turner, in 1938. It was a Forest Service project, but a 1973 Forest Service resource inventory calls the road "an impairment to solitude."

Mile 262.3: **Churchill-Dale-Whitewater Ranch,** on the right, hidden from the river.

This 120-acre ranch has a colorful history reaching back to 1897, when C. Eugene Churchill first settled on it. According to Robert Bailey, Churchill came to Idaho from the Mesabi iron mines in Minnesota. Gene lost his hand in a mining accident there, when rock in a ledge he was working shifted and pinned him. He had no alternative but to apply a tourniquet and amputate his hand at the wrist. He replaced it with a leather harness and a hook.

Churchill homesteaded on Little Mallard Creek, built a substantial house, and did some placer mining. He and his wife, Ella, cleared the land, planted an orchard, put in alfalfa. An extensive irrigation ditch system watered the site.

The Churchills kept pack stock and cattle. They hoped to make a living selling beef, fruit, and vegetables to Dixie, Elk City, and over to Thunder Mountain. Gene was on the trail for a week at a time. He lost much of his market when the Thunder Mountain boom played out, aggravated by the Monumental Creek slide that flooded the town of Roosevelt.

In September, 1915, some fellows from Rattlesnake Creek came down to Churchill's place and arranged to sell him their boat. Gene, C. H. Prescott, and Truman Thomas went up to get it. On their way back down, they wrecked on a rock near Richardson Creek. Stranded in the river, they succeeded in getting Mrs. Thomas to cross the water below them with a small boat and go to the Allison (later) place for help.

Sam Myers was there. It was raining and Mrs. Thomas was chilled, so he put her to bed, and headed down to see what he could do. Mrs. Churchill got Harbison and Bargamin to join the rescue effort at dawn.

With ropes they tried to pull Gene ashore on the north bank. They didn't keep the rope evenly taut, his leather harness broke, and not being able to swim he was pulled under near the bluff on the north side. The men crossed the river and pulled Prescott and Thomas in on the Richardson Creek side.

157

Gene Churchill's body surfaced 25 days later in the eddy above Richardson Creek and his friends buried him there on the bar. He was remembered with affection by the scores of people he fed and lodged without charge.

C. Eugene Churchill in front of his house at Little Mallard Creek.

In a short while, Ella Churchill married C. H. Prescott, who had come to the river after spending most of his life on the cattle ranges of Texas. For Ella it turned out to be a case of new regrets soon crowding out the old.

Prescott went hunting with a friend and they went up separate ridges. When he topped out, Prescott sat down on a grassy slope to eat his lunch, accompanied by his little black dog. His friend across the canyon took him for a bear with cub, and shot him through the hip. By the time Prescott's bleeding was controlled and he was packed off the mountain, he was in a bad way. He never really recovered his health, and died in 1921 from pneumonia contracted on a trip to Elk City. He is buried in Newsome. (It was Prescott and Mrs. Churchill that Cissy Patterson disguised as the Proctors at Proctor Ranch in her 1921 trip, quoted in the boating section of this book.)

Ella Churchill-Prescott, whose health was frail at best, became ill after her second husband's death. Joe Hoover came in to care for her. So did her sister, Bertie Lyons, who arrived on a Guleke scow. Despite their attentions, Ella passed away in the fall of 1922. She was buried behind the barn, with a large uncarved stone set as a marker. Bertie took a piece of chalk and wrote "Dear Sister Ella" across the rock.

Joe and Bertie married, and in 1924 took title to the ranch. But, unaccustomed to such isolation, Bertie began to lose her mind. Her daughter would come visit her all summer, but after she'd leave, Bertie complained that her kids never came to see her. When Maisie Hancock brought Bertie's mail, she would be accused of reading or stealing the children's letters. Finally, Joe had to sent her out to a resthome in Orofino. She died there. Hoover, in 1930, sold out to Floyd and Goldie Dale.

The Dales were from Oklahoma, fine horse people. Goldie was an Osage Indian. They made a go of the place for many years, raised cattle and did some packing. The Dales were good neighbors and well-liked.

The Churchill-Dale ranch in 1945, now known as the Whitewater Ranch.

Before Bill Jackson helped him build his own sawmill on the place, Floyd boated a large load of lumber down from Allison's ranch. He wrecked in Big Mallard Rapid and had trouble getting out of the river when his pants got hung on a nail in the raft.

Lewis and Catherine Wildt took over the place in 1944. They expanded it and ran a few cattle, but Lew worked outside at times. They stayed on their place by the river for 17 years.

In 1966, Edward I. Robertson, of Nampa, Idaho, acquired the ranch. The name was changed to Whitewater Ranch, and it is the center of a guest, hunter, and fisherman operation managed by Zeke and Marlene West. There is a landing strip on a bench above the river.

The old Churchill trail went through the Harbison-Cook Ranch; the new one goes nine miles to Dixie over Churchill Mountain.

Mile 262.5: **Little Mallard Creek** on the right.

Mile 262.6: **Churchill Creek** enters on the right.

Mile 263.7: **Dry Canyon Creek** on the right. Just below this drainage, but above Elkhorn Creek, can be seen the rock remnants of Monroe Hancock's last cabin. He lived here before he left for Grangeville.

Mile 263.7: **Elkhorn Rapid.** The rapid is on the other side of a blind curve to the left and should be approached from the left side. On high water, Elkhorn develops a nasty hole at the lower end caused by a large rock, which is exposed at lower flows. On low flows, Elkhorn requires considerable maneuvering for pontoon rafts, but it's an easy run for small boats.

Mile 264.5: **Little Elkhorn Creek,** on the right.

Mile 265: **Little Trout Creek** enters on the left.

Mile 265.2: **Growler Rapids.** The rapid is supposedly named for an irascible fellow who lived in the stone-walled cabin just downriver at Slide Creek. The name reflects his disposition.

The rapid on low water presents more of a problem to jet-boats than it does to float boats.

Mile 265.4: **Trout Creek** streams in on the left. The burned-over area was scarred in 1931 by the massive Corral Creek fire. It began at Bob Highland's place on Campbells Ferry. Another smoke started just below the South Fork, and the two burned together. It burned up Highland's hay and then turned into an awesome conflagration with an 85-mile front of flames. It jumped the river in places, noticeably at Elkhorn Creek.

When it was over, the Forest Service decided it was started by Bob Highland — probably by his still.

They were preparing to prosecute him, when Everett Van Arsdale came down from his lookout on Sheep Hill, where he watched for fires for 31 years, bringing his records of lightning strikes. He pointed out that he had logged lightning hitting Trout Creek that day, and the case was dropped.

There was so much smoke from the fire that Maisie Hancock said her watermelons at Cunningham Bar never ripened. The Thomases at Yellow Pine had to go to the river with handkerchiefs when the fire skipped past, across from them.

Mile 265.9: **Slide Creek,** on the right. Remains of the "Growler's" cabin on the upstream side.

Mile 266.1: **Campbells Ferry Pack Bridge.** The pieces for this bridge were floated down from the road end at Little Mallard Creek on a bridge pontoon with sweeps by Don Nitz and Tex Mott in 1955. After the parts were unloaded, the men would float to Mackay Bar, roll up the boat, and haul it, via Dixie, back down the road to Whitewater Ranch. A new load would be underway in the morning. They had over 100 tons of materials which required 20 trips. **Campbells Ferry Ranch** is located on the left bluff, at the south end of the bridge.

Don Nitz (left) and Tex Mott (right) boating materials for the Campbell's Ferry bridge from the Mallard Creek road-end.

161

William Campbell was a "likeable Scotsman," a friend of the Stonebrakers who settled Chamberlain Basin in 1898. Campbell located the ranch and built a cabin there.

William Campbell, original locater at Campbell's Ferry — a rare photograph.

In 1900, he contracted, along with Bill Stonebraker, Harry Donohue, and August Hutzel, to build the Three Blaze Trail, allowing a more direct route from Grangeville and Buffalo Hump to the Thunder Mountain boom area on Monumental Creek. The men were paid three thousand dollars by subscription. The trail came down from Dixie to a ferry the men constructed at the river. The Three Blaze then went up Little Trout Creek to Burnt Knob, across Chamberlain Creek to the top of Ramey Ridge, then down Ramey and Big Creeks and up Monumental Creek.

The trail and the ferry were heavily used. People could cross for 50 cents, cows were charged a dollar. Jim Moore, living across from Campbells Ferry, claimed 1800 men came through between 1900 and 1902. In the summer they hauled supplies by backpack and mule; in the winter they dragged provisions on hides behind skiis or snow-shoes.

Bill Campbell mysteriously disappeared the winter after the trail was finished. He snowshoed to the Roosevelt mine where he worked, but refused payment of wages in gold, saying it was too heavy to carry. He took a check instead. He vanished on his way back to the river, — he was never seen again and the check went uncashed.

There are two likely explanations concerning his fate. One is that he froze to death in a snow storm. The other seems more credible: Bill was engaged to Gene Churchill's adopted niece, Stella. He probably decided to stop and visit her. While crossing the ice, he fell through and drowned. (The niece later married Robert Bailey.)

In 1906, Campbell's cabin burned. Warren and Rose Cook, and Rose's brothers, Oscar and Joe Aiken, replaced it with the cabin which stands on the bluff over the river. That winter, Rose Aiken Cook and her baby died in childbirth and are buried on the slope above the garden.

Fred Silge, (discussed earlier at Silge Creek, Mile 259.2) took over the Ferry and ran it for several years. He and Joe Sorrel were killed in 1916 by a freak accident. As they crossed the river by cable basket in high water, a drift tree came by and its upturned limb snagged the carrier and dumped them into the water. Neither man was ever found.

From 1927 to 1935, Bob Highland was on the 80-acre spread. He had placered at Shorts Bar, near Riggins, before moving to the ferry. Bob had an old friend, Oscar Waller, who stayed on the ranch with him, and there is some reason to believe Oscar is buried in an un-marked grave on the place.

A wheat farmer from Walla Walla, Washington, born in 1891, Joe Zaunmiller, came to the Ferry in 1933. He had been on the Harbison Ranch seven years earlier. Highland gave Joe a half interest in the place after a couple of years. Zaunmiller was a packer and guide, and ran the ferry until 1956, when the Forest Service installed the bridge. Three years before he died, Joe sold Campbells Ferry to John Crowe, a hereford rancher from California, who is the present owner.

The grave of five-year-old Norman Wolfe is next to the trail that goes from the bridge to the Cook cabin. He fell while crossing the log over Big Mallard Creek in June, 1945, and his body was recovered at the Ferry.

The airstrip for Campbells Ferry runs up the slope of the clearing beyond the buildings.

Campbell's Ferry Ranch as it appears from the air, with sidehill landing field in center of picture. Photograph taken by Bob Fogg, backcountry pilot for 40 years.

Ray Holes and hunting party using the Campbell ferry on their way to Harlan Meadows.

The Caswell brothers at Thunder
Mountain. It was their gold discovery
that set off the boom necessitating the
Three Blaze Trail through Campbell's
Ferry to Monumental Creek. When the
Caswells sold their claims for $100,000,
they gave half the money to the man who
had given them a $500 grubstake.

Jim Moore's Place: Beyond the north end of the bridge, on the flat above the right bank, is a clearing speckled with log buildings, known as the Moore place.

Jim Moore came to Salmon River from Kentucky, two years before the turn of the century. Gene Churchill stayed the winter and helped him build his house.

After 1897, settlement in the Forest Reserves was restricted to agricultural use by the Forest Homestead Act. Since Moore only held the ground as a mining claim, he couldn't waste the trees there, so he built the profusion of buildings as he cleared the flat. The nine log structures were hewed with a broad axe over a period of about 15 years. Time's disfiguring touch has dealt leniently with Moore's work — the dressed logs remain an impressive tribute to his skill and enterprise.

Moore sold beef, hides, and vegetables to the Thunder Mountain traffic on the Three Blaze Trail. He also made whiskey and peach brandy.

He irrigated his fields and orchard with a hewed log flume that carried water from Slide Creek. He spaded his garden and hauled hay to his barn. He trapped coyotes that came for his chickens.

165

Jim was an unusual man. He had pistols and a .50-caliber rifle in his cabin and undoubtedly would have used them if he thought someone was looking for his still. He kept a stout mare as his watchdog and fed her baked biscuits. He was literate, but read only non-fiction. For almost 30 years he never went farther from the river than Dixie.

Jim Moore as he looked in later life. Drawing by Pat McFarlin.

When Jim Moore died in the spring of 1942, he was at least 70 years old. His date of birth is uncertain because he claimed to be an orphan, who ran away from his foster father's unfair abuse. Jim's grave is on the slope, just above the last building on the up-river end of the flat.

Jack Wenzel put the sink in Moore's cabin after Jim was gone. He ran an underground pipe from the creek for water.

The Forest Service challenged the validity of Moore's 1900 Slide Creek placer claim and had it declared void in 1966. Through a rare lapse in Service policy, the cabins weren't burned. They were recently nominated to the National Register of Historic Places.

Jim Moore's house, right of center, and his root cellar just behind it.

Jim Moore's grave.

Mile 266.7: **Ruff Creek** comes in on the left.

Rex Coppernoll had a cabin on the bench on the upstream side of this creek in 1934. He, his wife Clara, and their two children, and Rex's younger brother, wintered there, living in a tent until they could finish the building. Rex's brother built a six-foot wooden pelton wheel arrangement, with battery storage and phone wire, that gave the cabin the only electric lights on Salmon River at the time.

About every 10 days, Coppernoll would make the 14-mile round trip to Dixie for 75 pounds of groceries. On his way back, he'd let out a whoop from Rabbit Point, his dog by the cabin would bark, and his wife would know he'd be home in an hour and a half.

In 1935, Rex worked in Lewiston. He let a young fellow named Bob Hemminger winter at his place.

Before Bob went in, Rex told him to get a new pair of boots because hobnails were dangerous in the winter, and he advised him not to kill any sheep, unless the deer were too poor in the spring.

No sooner had Hemminger arrived at the Coppernoll cabin, than he went up the creek and shot a ram, ewe, and yearling on a hill where the spring had iced over. The slope was slick as soap, and Bob fell as he tried to retrieve the yearling. It was a month before his body was found, frozen in the ice. He was buried in March, above Coppernoll's cabin. The grave was marked in 1977.

Mile 267: **Groundhog Bar** on the right. Back in the woods a few rotten logs are relics of one of the oldest cabins on the river. Apparently, only Jim Moore knew who once lived here.

On highwater, a rapid called "Whiplash" forms in the curve at Groundhog. At flows over 65,000 c.f.s., it becomes one of the fiercest rapids on the river. In 1974, the eddy line flipped a motor-driven pontoon.

Mile 267.2: **Fall Creek,** on the left.

Mile 278.8: **Lemhi Creek** flows in on the left, draining the Sheepeater Buttes.

Mile 269: **Lemhi Bar** on the left, just below the creek. This 20 acres was called China Bar, because from 1882-1884 it was worked extensively by Oriental miners. They came up the river to the site and were supplied by China Can's pack string from Warren. The diggings must have been fairly rich to have detained them so long.

China Can, Salmon River packer from Warren, who supplied the Chinese miners at Lemhi — China Bar.

The Bar's more prevalent name, Lemhi, is derived from Harry "Lemhi" Serren. Harry lost his way in the Lemhi Mountains in the middle of winter, when even a polar bear would have hunted cover, and managed to survive the experience with nothing worse than a nickname. He also weathered the Rains Massacre in 1879, at the mouth of the South Fork of the Salmon.

After the Chinese left, Serren spent many years placering on the bar. The Eakins helped him construct a hydraulic system to move more gravel.

Edward Oscar Eakin patented the claim in 1925. He sold it to Jack and Maisie McKay in '26, and they wintered there for two years. Then, in 1929, Jack sold to Bill Gaines.

Gaines was from Missouri, and used the bar to grow alfalfa for his cattle on the north side of the river. He hauled hay across on the ice.

When John Gleixner got the place in 1945, he sold off Gaines' cattle, and left it to his son, John Jr.

Since 1961, Lemhi has been owned by Frank Santos, of California, who also owns the Crofoot Ranch at this time (1978).

Santos sold some lots to friends. The three green-roofed cabins constitute Bob Smith's outfitting lodge, used principally for fishing parties.

Mile 269.5: **Rhett Creek** flows in from the right. The clearing with buildings upriver from the creek and a short rifle shot from Lemhi Bar has a history congruent with Lemhi's because it was usually owned by the same people.

William Rhett was born in 1845, a native of Virginia. He was a medical student in New York, and at the request of his professor, exhumed a cadaver with two other students. They were caught, and fled for their lives, since such an action was considered a hanging offense. According to his grandson, Homer, this was the incident that pushed Bill Rhett to Salmon River. He was a pioneer in early Florence and Warren, and loaned the horse to Tolo which she used to warn the settlers in Florence of the Nez Perce outbreak. William was living in Kalispell, Montana, in 1923 and had changed the spelling of his name to Rheiter.

The numerous descendants of William and Mary (Turner) Rhett have a well-known name among Salmon River ranchers. There is another Rhett Creek on the river, below Riggins.

William Rhett (Rhieter) in 1923 at Kalispell, Montana.

170

George Trader planted the orchard at Rhett Creek, expecting to sell fruit at Thunder Mountain. For a while the spot was known as the Eakin place. Oscar Eakin was the river's early equivalent of a real estate agent. He moved around — Pistol Creek, Lantz Bar, Disappointment Creek, buying and selling mining claims for a reasonable price. Rhett Creek was never homesteaded; it was always held as a claim.

Bill Gaines, from Missouri, got the place in 1929, ran cattle there, and had Everett Van Arsdale and Leonard York build him a new cabin when Jack McKay's burned down. Gaines' new house is the log building which faces the river. His barn was built next to the hill so hay could be slid into it. He ran cattle on the spread and the hills behind it.

In 1945, Bill sold the outfit to John Gleixner, and used the proceeds to realize the long-delayed dream of visiting his children in Missouri. Bill Gaines had forked a horse over some of the roughest country in Salmon River for many years. Ironically, in Missouri, he was struck and killed by an automobile.

The Gaines cabin was the center of a significant drama in September, 1958. Reho and George Wolfe moved their seven children from Lewiston, Idaho, to Rhett Creek. The Wolfes had lived in Salmon River country for several years. George had worked for the Forest Service, farmed as a tenant rancher, and instructed students in music.

The Wolfes had decided all but one of their children were doing poorly in school, and that by getting away from the complicated and distracting demands of city life their children could learn basic values and excel in their studies.

Reho filed a mining claim on the Rhett place and she and the children moved in. Monroe Hancock boated their supplies down. George Wolfe returned to his jobs: giving violin instruction during the day, and running a railroad store at night.

The bureaucrats were understandably upset. The county district school supervisor called a special meeting of the school board. A criminal complaint for contributing to the delinquency of minors and causing their habitual truancy was filed against Mrs. Wolfe.

171

The Wolfes had many friends. No one was interested in serving the summons. The county prosecutor refused to take action, saying the object of compulsory education law was to see that children are not left in ignorance, and not to punish parents who provided their children with instruction equal or superior to that obtainable in public schools. Idaho's attorney general was called to Grangeville, where after a conference with the prosecutor, he dismissed the case.

During the furor, Mrs. Wolfe and her children went quietly about their correspondence courses. The letter notifying her of the action was incorrectly addressed, and the post office managed to send it to four different towns before getting it to her — 15 days after the hearing had terminated.

The Wolfe children in front of the Gaine's cabin at Rhett Creek: left to right, Carol, Linda, John, David, Bill, Sharon, Marjorie, and standing behind them, Rheo.

Then the Forest Service decided to take the Wolfes to court in order to test the legality of Reho's mining claim. She walked 27 miles to Red River in order to attend the hearing. It established that Mrs. Wolfe had met all the requirements of the mining laws and that her claim was valid.

The children made substantial progress and learned more than textbooks could offer. At the time of this writing, Reho holds a special-use permit on the Gaines place, and she, her husband, and a number of their children spend portions of their summers at Rhett Creek.

The small cabin back in the woods, on the downstream side of Rhett Creek, was inhabited by Colonel McCrae — alias Montana Frank. In appearance he was an elderly man with white hair and spade beard, resembling Buffalo Bill. The Colonel had an attractive young wife, so all river and trail traffic paused at his cabin — feigning interest in his true tales of life on the Montana frontier.

Mile 270.5: On the right shore, on an overhung rock about 25 feet from the water, are some Indian pictographs. There are similar paintings, on the same side of the river, but closer to the water, about half a mile farther downstream.

On the left side of the river, one can see the remains of a stone cabin, at the water's edge, just above Blowout Creek.

Mile 271.3: **Blowout Creek,** on the right.

Mile 271.5: **Paine Creek,** comes in on the right. Relics of an old cabin can be seen on the upstream side.

Mile 272.5: **Boise Creek** seeps in on the right.

Jack Ranger's grave.

Mile 273.6: **No Mans Creek** on the right. On the downstream side of the creek, at the edge of the trees and visible from the river, is a wooden Forest Service grave marker which reads: Jack Ranger, born about 1903, died under mysterious circumstances about 1928.

Jack Ranger killed a mountain sheep across the river. He should have then gone upstream to Boise Bar, where A. C. Carpenter lived with his children, June and Charlie, and borrowed A. C.'s small boat — called the "Floatin' Coffin." Instead, Ranger decided to swim the river. He didn't make it. The only "mysterious circumstance" surrounding his death was the fact that there was no water in his lungs when he was found. River people figured he had a heart attack. His death occurred in the summer of 1925 according to Maisie Hancock, who was on the river at the time.

Mile 273.8: **Tepee Creek** enters on the right.

Mile 274.1: **Painter Mine-Jersey Creek.**

Edward Oscar Eakin had claimed the Jersey Creek bar in the early 1900's. He had a pigeon-hole post office with a desk there when John R. Painter came down the river in a scow with Cap Guleke.

Painter was an orphan adopted by a wealthy New York family. As a young man, he became a marksman and a trophy hunter. It was his interest in game that caused him to hire Cap. He liked the canyon enough to buy the Jersey claim, about 1908, from Eakin. But unlike anyone else on the river, J. R. was out of his element: too proud to cut hay and not wild enought to eat it.

John R. Painter at his cabin not long before his death.

The transplanted New Yorker built the first hunting house-lodge on the river; he called it "The Bungalow." The bungalow was a large log building, with a stone fireplace, French windows, a trophy room, bar, mirrors, pool table — all floated down on scows. He planted a variety of trees, imported a small herd of Jersey cattle, raised some hogs in pens.

A number of his eastern society friends came to visit and to hunt. Caroline Lockhart, a well-known novelist of the time, spent the winter of 1914 with Painter, and wrote *Man From the Bitterroot,* whose central character is supposed to be modeled on J.R.

Johnny McKay, the boatman-placer miner mentioned earlier in this book, discovered coarse gold concentrated along the left bank of the river near Painter's lodge. Not being a hardrock miner, McKay wasn't interested in the lode, but he informed J.R. of the likely prospect. J.R. asked A.C. Carpenter to attempt locating the source, and when Carpenter succeeded, Painter paid him off with apricots.

J.R. tapped the DuPonts as a source of capital for his mining venture. The tunnel was begun on the left bank, on the slope facing the river. Guleke boated three loads of equipment to Fivemile Bar the first season. A sizeable Edison mill was installed at the mouth of Fivemile Creek, (downriver from the mine). A mile-long ditch carried water from Fivemile Creek to the bluff above the mill where it was dropped through a penstock which ran the generator that powered the mill. Bill Hart packed ore almost a mile from the mine to the mill.

The DuPonts invested $60,000 in the operation, but in 1918 a fire put a halter on it. Painter claimed the Germans had sabotaged his mill, but it's more likely the water pressure was too much for the generator.

J.R. had more than one string in his guitar. He had Guleke bring new materials, and Bill Jackson built a water-powered two-stamp mill at the mouth of Little Fivemile Creek. Bill Hart and Clyde Painter (no relation) packed the ore down and the system worked well. It was rich ore: Hart packed three boxes to a smelter which returned over $1800. Living and cooking quarters were installed next to the mill.

Painter had a housekeeper, from Montana, living at Jersey Creek, named Ellen Galbraith-Jones. She had a daughter, Catherine Jones. Ellen and J.R. eventually married. When Painter died in August of 1936 (contrary to the marker), he was 75 years of age. His grave is on the upstream side of Jersey Creek.

Mrs. Ellen Painter sold the claim to Gordon Prentice and J.S. "Si" Devenny. She then moved to the Foskett ranch, up Skookumchuck Creek, with her daughter, Catherine, who married Clyde Painter. Ellen died of old age; Catherine perished in a snowstorm while working cattle on the ranch.

Ellen Galbraith-Painter in her later years.

Prentice and Devenny spent $30,000 developing a tramway from the mine to a new mill established on the north bank, just downriver across from the tunnel. This was a Chilean ball mill with a flotation system to recover the gold. Most of the machinery was brought down a skid road from Dixie to within a couple of miles of the mill, then Cat sledded to the site. Once again the mine's prosperity proved ephemeral as a bubble.

Since 1971, the property has been owned by Mackay Bar. The headframe over the mine blew down in a storm. The mill burned one August when a fellow from Mackay Bar came up to get some steel with a cutting torch. The bungalow burned in 1922, but a fireplace marks its location. The weathered board house, glimpsed from the river, below Jersey Creek, is J.R. Painter's second home. It was used as a cook shack and boarding house by the miners that worked for Prentice and Devenny.

176

Truck with pump at Painter Bar was rigged by Haywire Wilson for irrigation and fire protection. The chimney which stands by the river is all that remains of the "Bungalow."

Painter's second house, which can be glimpsed from the river. It was later used by the miners working for Prentice and Devenny in the Thirties.

177

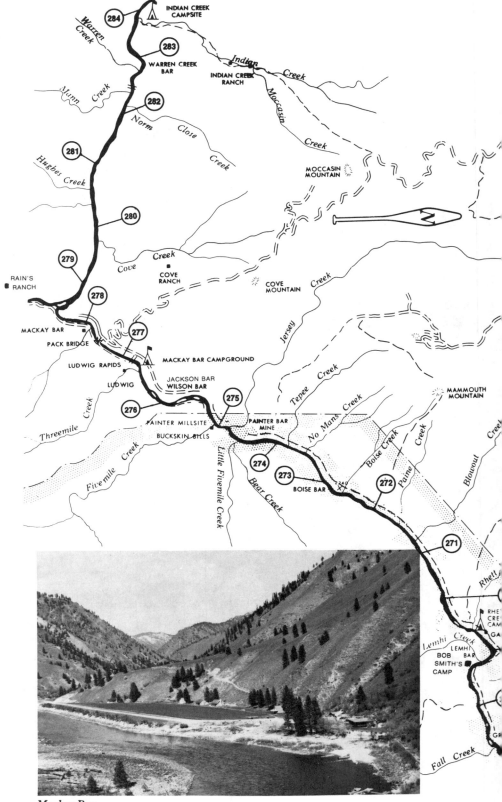

Warren Creek

284

INDIAN CREEK
CAMPSITE

283

WARREN CREEK
BAR

Indian Creek

INDIAN CREEK
RANCH

Munn Creek

282

Norm Close Creek

Moccasin Creek

281

Hughes Creek

MOCCASIN
MOUNTAIN

280

Creek

Cove

RAIN'S
RANCH

COVE
RANCH

COVE
MOUNTAIN

Cove Creek

279

278

MACKAY BAR

277

PACK BRIDGE

Jersey Creek

LUDWIG RAPIDS

MACKAY BAR CAMPGROUND

LUDWIG

JACKSON BAR
WILSON BAR

Tepee Creek

MAMMOUTH
MOUNTAIN

275

Threemile Creek

276

PAINTER MILLSITE

PAINTER BAR
MINE

BUCKSKIN BILLS

No Mans Creek

Boise Creek

Paine Creek

Blowout Creek

Fivemile Creek

Little Fivemile Creek

Bear Creek

274

273

BOISE BAR

272

271

Rhett

RHETT
CREE
CAM

GA

Lemhi Creek

LEMHI
BAR

BOB
SMITH'S
CAMP

GR

Fall Creek

Mackay Bar.

Mile 275.1: **Fivemile Creek and Bar** on the left. Named for its reputed distance from the South Fork. From artifacts and relics found on the site, Fivemile Bar is known to have been used by Indians and by Chinese miners. It was also the first mill site for the Painter Mine. Pieces of machinery from the mill rest in the grass. Lengths of the penstock pipe can be seen on the hill behind the bar.

Of course, Fivemile Bar is best known for its longtime resident, Sylvan Ambrose Hart, alias Buckskin Bill, alias "Last of the Mountain Men." Much has been said and written about him. At the authors' request, he has written his own autobiography in his seventy-first year, for this book.

———————————— •◆•• ————————————

Indian Territory in 1906 was definitely pioneer times. Houses were cedar log or sod. I was born in a dugout May 10, 1906.

The first animals that impressed me were fat toads. I really liked these insect-getters, and when I went to a place that had no toads, I wondered if the people there were clean.

I had a small creek to play in, with cutbanks some 15 feet deep. A twine string, a bent pin, and a piece of salt pork got me many crawfish. I cooked and ate their tails. Mourning doves don't nest very high, and I collected fat squabs about ready to leave the nest. My first hunting was with my bare hands. I got catfish in Eagle Chief Creek in the manner of a varmint. A catfish digs a hole into the bank. You put in your arm and there is likely to be a catfish with sawtooth horns, a snapping turtle, or a water moccasin! I got three and four pound catfish.

Smokeless powder helped me to get game and to deal with my enemies. In those days hawks ate chickens, so I killed a hawk, roasted it and fed it to my chickens. Early day blackbirds destroyed whole fields of grain. The answer seemed to be to make blackbird pie. Great Uncle Ambrose, about 1912, picked 28 blackbirds for a pie. I put eleven yellow-headed blackbirds in a pie.

179

Ducks were a big help in preparing a meal. I killed ducks, picked and cleaned them and cooked them for my parents. I laid in the peanut patch in 106 degree heat, watching gophers pushing out dirt, but I didn't fire till I saw their whiskers.

Canada geese were a little too much for a kid, but adults used whiskey-soaked corn and gas lights to take them. People thought nothing of running down young rabbits. The last few swaths in a wheat field held quite a few cottontails and jackrabbits that you and your dog could easily get.

The first of the big disasters there was communicable disease. Influenza made even me so weak I had to stop and rest. It settled in some part of your body — in my case, it weakened my hearing.

Sylvan Ambrose Hart in 1912, age six years.

I had a very good grade school teacher, Jack Wilcox. His strong point was English and he taught you to diagram sentences. High school and college repeat what you should have learned in grade school. In a one room schoolhouse you could learn all grades at once. In high school if your grades were good you need not take the monthly examination. On those days, I went squirrel hunting or field butchering with my father. You can't have good meat unless you know how to prepare it.

In college it is best to take the most difficult courses offered. When I had to translate English into Greek, I got up at four o'clock. At one time or another I have studied Greek, Latin, German, French, Russian, Portugese, Spanish, Swahili, and Norwegian. Actually, it is words that interest me and I still get up occasionally at four to study Greek words.

Inside his stucco cabin, Sylvan displays some of his handmade copper pots. Many of his utensils and tools reveal Hart's consumate craftsmanship in wood, horn, and metal.

Most students fear hard work, which you certainly got in the Texas oil fields. There was danger, crime, bad air, and poor housing. The fumes make you dizzy and you have to know when to go out and get some air. A gas well can burn you in seconds but you have to work on it. (You can read a newspaper at midnight five miles from a burning well.) I had a year in Petroleum Engineering as a graduate student, which was interesting and difficult.

My reaction to the Depression was to find a place with natural resources to defeat it. I could have found no better place than Salmon River. I spent some $50 a year then for what little I needed to buy. I always had a garden. It was easy to get fruit and I made moccasins and clothing out of animal skins. There were copper plates lying around (at Painter's mine) that I made into cooking utensils. A little later, I made complete guns. I made many prospecting trips in the hills for minerals. The longest walk I made was a hundred miles to Grangeville.

When war came, I left and became a toolmaker at Boeing's factory in Wichita, Kansas. The F.B.I. was looking for me, and they found me in a combat area in the Aleutians. In '42 the Japs were a bit discouraged with Kiska and when they pulled out we came back to the U.S.

The Norden Bombsight was the most secret and difficult course you could get in the Air Force. Toolmaking was easy for me since it wasn't as difficult as what I'd been doing at home. I was up all night studying bombsights, near Denver. I rigged myself a machine shop in a hallway at Peyote, Texas, and I came up with a new invention or idea every month for caring for bombsights or autopilots. Your inventions belonged to the Air Force and ratings were frozen for 18 months. Eventually I became a buck sergeant.

Back in the hills, I took up where I left off. I became a summer lookout for the Forest Service on Quartzite and Oregon Butte. In 1960 I skinned elk for Mackay Bar during hunting season. I also hunted when they used helicopters there.

A trip to Iceland and a trip to North Europe helped me a great deal. I took in the Moscow circus.

Paul Filer examines one of Sylvan Hart's handmade flintlock rifles — a masterpiece.

Where you spend 50 years among wild animals you get to know them, not as the book says, but as they really are. It's been 20 years since a biologist dared mention an eagle carrying off a baby mountain goat. By going to a mountain where lions kill each day, you know how much they eat in a week. The best animals are otters, and other animals clean up their fish scraps.

Finally, does any man's life accomplish anything? In my case, soldiers in desperate straits thought that I could have survived so they were inspired to do so. If you can make a gun, you don't worry about breaking it. Strange food doesn't bother you because you have already tried it. Fear is a formidable enemy; if you don't have it you can concentrate on what you should do. On a trip in the hills, memorize each trail, hill, bush, tree, rock, watercourse, and mountain range. The next time you see them, you meet an old friend.

The cherry blossom pink stucco buildings are Sylvan's. The lemon-colored multi-storied house against the hill was put up by Hart's nephew, Rodney Cox, who lived there with his wife and children for several years in the Seventies. They left after a tragic accident took the life of their oldest boy, while bringing wood down the slope with a vehicle.

The shingled log cabin glimpsed from the river on the bar below Fivemile Creek is that of Mitt Haynie. He came to the river by way of California's Mother Lode, the Buffalo Hump, and Dixie. Mitt was a miner, prospector, packer, and splendid cook. In addition, he was a lovable, kind, helpful kleptomaniac. Nobody on the river was bothered by this habit — they'd go up and ask him if they could borrow a hammer or saw, or whatever article had disappeared, and he would supply a copy of the missing item, which he had taken from someone else.

(Sylvan Hart lived in the Haynie cabin when he first came to the river.)

Mile 275.5: **Jackson Bar** on the right, by the cove which displays evidence of hydraulic mining.

Our syntactic resources seem insufficient to convey the proper impression of Bill Jackson: Genius of the Salmon River. He was a presence: 19 hands high, chest wide as a barn door, dusky complected, dark hair, handlebar moustache, he wore a venerable, peaked black hat and Levis with buttons slotted through a wide belt. When he came to town people noticed him.

Of Bill's past, it is known that he worked as a seaman, a north woods logger, and a Pennsylvania iron miner. No one knew whether he had formal training as an engineer; it's likely he was simply an intuitive mechanical genius, who could make anything from nothing and make it work well. He had a three-dimensional mind and many believe he was the best millwright in the whole northwest. Jackson was a light-year ahead of his time.

He traveled up and down the river, inventing and fixing, irrigating and mining. The ranchers at Mackay Bar saw him arrive in 1916, with supplies, a few hand-made tools, and one heavy quilt. Bill fashioned a raft and floated down the river to spend the winter mining.

As he did all his life, Jackson gouged a hole in the bank, shoved a couple of logs in for support, and slept partially protected. When the nights got cold enough to split a cow's horn, he simply freshened his fire. Becoming absorbed in a mechanical project, Bill would work night and day, oblivious to the weather. Two men looking for him in the spring, found him on Sand Flat, above Warren Creek, a wild apparition with hair that didn't know a comb and eyes that looked like powder pans.

Bill Jackson, the Genius of Salmon River. When killed in 1962, Bill was 87 years-old.

The whole river knew the ashes of his campfires. Water was his bondslave under an open sky. He used it to run sawmills wherever he went. He built one for Elmer Allison and another for Floyd Dale. He made one below the bank at Trout Creek that was a masterpiece — the mangle and blade had the only metal it contained. Without a drill to put a hole in the blade, he shot out its center with his rifle. He built a water-powered stamp mill for J. R. Painter. He constructed a massive dipper-stick wheel to put water on Jackson Bar — its machinations were mysterious to those who saw it, but it worked, floating on the river until high water took it out. Then Bill harnessed a Cat motor and rigged a dragline to a wooden scoop. Nobody knew what he was thinking, and he let high water take it too, without ever saying what he had in mind. He fashioned a hydraulic ram, the likes of which no one had ever seen before.

Jackson would go to town and get drunk as a fiddler's bitch, but on sobering he would return to his projects. He could be stiff-necked at times, but if he liked you, you were solvent with him. Bill was usually calm as a horse trough; distaining commotion or fanfare of any kind. He was frank, even outspoken, and optimistic about everything except human nature. His generosity sometimes left him broke as the Ten Commandments, yet he would not do for money what he wouldn't do for kindness. Few people ever paid for his mills.

In later years, Bill Jackson left his Bluebird placer claim at Jackson Bar for the Foskett Ranch purchased by Ellen Painter. He built her a sawmill and solved the problems of an irrigation pipeline that kept freezing up, — with vents and a pump spliced into the line.

Mrs. Painter bought a new trailer as living quarters for Jackson. He looked it over and decided it wasn't very handy. So he removed all furniture and partitions, stacked them outside, and made his bed on the floor.

It's been said, "Not he who has little, but he who desires much, is poor." The one luxury the genius ever allowed himself was a Ford tractor. It was his undoing. Returning on the Salmon River road from a friend's funeral in Whitebird, Bill Jackson went off into the river, about a mile north of Skookumchuck. He is buried in the Whitebird cemetery. His epitaph could well be Alice Rickman's remark, as she reminisced about him: "Bill Jackson was always doing nice things for people."

Mile 275.6: **Wilson Bar** on the right, above the bluff. Wilson Bar is the latest Forest Service name for Jackson Bar; Bill Jackson was still there when the Wilsons arrived.

Howard Allen "Haywire" Wilson came to the bar in 1937, believing he had purchased the Painter mine property, and discovered he'd been euchred into a claim downstream. He had been running a salvage truck business in Seattle. The union began insisting he hire union drivers, but it was Depression times, and with a family of 12 children, drivers had to work more than eight hours a day just to keep the wolf from whelping her pups on his porch. So he decided to move to Salmon River.

Howard "Haywire" Wilson: 1888-1946.

With six of their children, the Wilsons didn't homestead the bar, so much as colonize it. There were two handsome boys and four girls, pretty as a heart flush.

The first winter was difficult, because arriving in the fall meant the family had no time to build or garden. They ate beans and potatoes and lived in frame tents.

In the spring, Haywire went to work as a trail boss for the Forest Service. He did some placering at a claim above Bill Jackson's. His wife, Nellie, and the children grew an ample garden. They raised mules, kept some horses and cows, three hogs, 13 milk goats, and chickens. They smoked and canned their meat. Two rooms were added to the 10 x 12 foot cabin that was already on the place.

Haywire believed that Sunday was a day of rest, and all the bachelors on Salmon River were invited to Sunday dinner. The Wilson girls might partially explain why the weekly event was so well attended.

The Wilsons on Wilson Bar: left to right, Nellie, Allene, Myrel, Joan, Alice, Johnie.

When the Wilson boys returned from the war, the family built a large two-story house, with bedrooms upstairs and down, a sizeable kitchen and dining room.

The Wilsons hayed the whole bar, broke horses with a buggy, and used a team and bull rake to put hay in the barn. The alfalfa hay was sub-irrigated and usually provided two cuttings.

The girls were good hands with stock; they could ride anything with four legs and a tail. Alice, with her blond hair, doubled for Marilyn Monroe, in the film River of No Return, swimming her horse across the river for take after take. The children got to watch the movie at Mackay Bar, where there was electricity, but all the footage filmed with the kids had been cut.

The first two years, the children went to school in Dixie and boarded there. Then Nellie taught them through the eighth grade, and they got their high school diplomas by taking equivalency tests.

In 1946, tragedy struck the bar when Haywire was killed as his dump truck rolled off the bank toward the river. The girls married, one by one — "and down they forgot as up they grew." Nellie, Robert and Allene moved to town in 1950 so that the youngest girl, Myrel, could go to school.

Some Forest Service employees burned the Wilson house. The shell of the barn remains near the road. A riveted boiler, salvaged from a donkey engine on a logging show in Stites, stands in the flat. The Wilsons would build a small fire under it and in 20 minutes have all the bath water they needed. The old tractor was one Robert brought in to fix, but it never ran. The tiny log enclosure at the edge of the trees was used to fatten hogs before they were butchered.

The years have gone from is to was, but the Wilson children still carry warm memories of the years they spent here.

Mile 276.8: **Threemile Creek** threads its way down on the left. It's three miles from the South Fork, supposedly.

The bench above the river was settled at an early date by an industrious and educated German, Ben Ludwig. The remains of his log cabin have been incorporated into a contemporary, corrugated cabin.

Ben had the customary garden and fruit trees. He had the nickname "A.B.C." Ludwig, because he kept and read an unabridged dictionary; he could spout words that ran eight to the pound.

Ludwig wouldn't speak to the Dixie storekeeper if he met him in hell carrying ice on his head, so he took his pack stock all the way to Clearwater for supplies — a distance six times as far.

He sold his 28 acres in October, 1924, and returned to the east.

The rapid below the creek is named for Ludwig.

Mile 277.5: **Mackay Bar Bridge.** The bridge was built for pack stock in 1935. The cables were looped and strung continuously on a string of mules and brought down from Warren by Fred Badley and Roy Stover.

The road to Dixie, which bootlaces up the hill on the right, was financed by John Oberbillig in 1937-38, and bulldozed by Potato King Joe Marshall. He had been told it would be impossible, but when he finished he said he'd built irrigation ditches that were more difficult. Prentice and Devanny continued the road up to Painter Mine.

189

Mile 278: **Mackay Bar,** on the left bench. Archaeological excavations indicate the stretch of river from Growler Rapid to the South Fork had the highest prehistoric population density in the Salmon River canyon. There is considerable evidence at Mackay Bar, on both sides of the river, and on the west bank of the South Fork, that the Mountain Sheepeater Shoshones used the site for winter camps in the eighteenth and nineteenth centuries.

Mackay Bar as seen from the air. Airstrip is on the right, main lodge in the center, and the South Fork enters the main river from the top of the photograph. Scars from the Salmon River Placer Company's efforts can still be seen on the point.

Cables for the Mackay Bar bridge looped from mule to mule. The packers are about to leave Warren for the river.

The first white settler, about 1900, left his name on the bar. William B. Mackay and his wife built a log house above the bench, on Mackay Creek. They did some placer mining and raised a small herd of cattle. William died in 1916, and is buried on the bar. His estate took title to the land in 1923.

Fred Burgdorf, and his hired hand, Freeman Nethkin, ran quality Durham cattle on the Secesh Meadows — Burgdorf Hot Springs summer range. In the fall, they trailed the cattle over Burgdorf Summit down to Mackay Bar. The calves were weaned at the ranch and then the cows were pushed across the river to winter, recrossing in the spring. Hay was raised and stored in two large barns. There was a house at the time, which has since burned.

Burgdorf sold out his cattle operation in 1910, to Andy Nelson. Nelson consolidated three ranches, just up from the mouth of the South Fork, into one: Tom Copenhaver Flat, Burgdorf's Ranch, and the Rains' Ranch. There had been a good market for meat at the mines in the mountains, and at Thunder Mountain and Warren.

As the boom subsided, Nelson sold his cattle and tried raising sheep. He switched back to cattle. Pat Parks worked for Nelson at the mouth of the South Fork for many years.

Tom Dawson was another resident of the bar. He raised dapper, spotted burros, until one with a colt kicked him. Complications from the injury caused his death in Warren.

191

Perry Nethkin, cousin of Freeman, acquired Mackay Bar and sold it to John Oberbillig in 1937. Oberbillig organized the Salmon River Placer Company to mine gold from the point at the mouth of the South Fork. He financed the building of the road down from Dixie, on the north side of the river.

An electric generator was to be used for power at the mining site. A tunnel was blasted through the rocky point on the right side of the river, where it bends to join the South Fork. Upstream water was to be diverted through the tunnel, driving a turbine as it flowed out at the confluence. The generator was never installed, but the lower end of the tunnel can still be seen from the river.

Immense amounts of equipment were flown in from McCall: 300 tons from 1936-38, in two-ton loads. Another hundred tons arrived in 1939. Machinery too bulky for the airplane was skidded down to Painter Mine and floated to the bar.

This mining venture, like many others, never really reached production. World War II interrupted plans. The gravel scree slope on the left side of the river, immediately before it meets the South Fork, is the result of S. R. Placer Company's efforts.

Al and Mary Tice rented Mackay for the year of 1955 from Mr. Oberbillig. They arrived with their two-week old daughter. The following year the Tices spent at the Badley Ranch, up the South Fork. When John Oberbillig died, the Tices bought Mackay Bar from John's sons.

They worked to make the place a successful sportsman resort. The lodge they built burned on Christmas eve, but they had a new one up by spring. The Tices subdivided the airstrip and sold lots for home sites. They flew, trucked, and boated building materials.

Robert Hansberger bought the 61 acres from Al and Mary in 1969. Al stayed on as manager for Mackay Bar Corporation for several years. It remains an active center for hunting, fishing, and boating vacations.

Diesel generators now provide the bar with electrical power. The two thousand foot airstrip on the bench is the same one Dynamite Moore struggled to clear; it is the best landing field in the canyon.

There are three graves grouped at the east end of Mackay Bar, about 200 yards past the Hansberger house. One holds the remains of William Mackay, another is that of Mr. Whitmore, who lived across the river, and the third is Fred Ipe's, a young miner whose parents lived in Warren, and who committed suicide one spring at the mouth of the South Fork.

The flat across the river from Mackay Bar is known as Hay Bar. Mr. Whitmore had a garden and some horses there. The cabin against the shoulder of the hill has had a succession of miners and packers winter in it: "A. C." Cornelius Carpenter, Carl Garrettson, Jim Bragg.

Mile 278.5: **South Fork Salmon River,** on the left.

A large volume could be written on the history of the South Fork alone. There are two events concerning this tributary which are significant enough to include here.

The Rains Massacre (murder would be a more appropriate description) occurred one and a half miles up the South Fork. James Rains had a small farm on the west side of the stream and was baling hay for Warren with two of his friends. His 18-year-old brother-in-law, Albert Webber, was in the cabin. It was twilight, the evening of August 17, 1879.

Site of the Rain's cabin a few years after it burned.

193

A volley of rifle fire whizzed past the hay press. The men had been warned by Lieutenant Catley's troops a few days earlier that there could be trouble with the Sheepeater Indians. Rains had taken his family to Warren as a precaution, then returned with Lemhi Serren and Jim Edwards to finish gathering the crop.

As the men ran for their rifles in the cabin, James Rains was hit twice and fell. Hearing gunfire from the house, Edwards and Serren decided Webber had been killed, so they retreated to a creek bottom and headed to Warren for help.

Crossing the South Fork before there was a bridge:

Joe Fowler leading a horse which was used in the Sheepeater War.

Bob Deering in his dugout by the Deering Creek Ranch.

Team of horses pulling a wagon across in low water.

Tom Carrey's cable crossing — no baggage and no transfers.

The gunfire the two men had heard was Webber's, as he shot back at the Indians. He tried to defend the cabin and doctor Rains, who had crawled inside. Rains died. The Indians built bonfires so they could watch the cabin. When the fire at the rear of the cabin burned low, Albert dug under the floor-sill and crawled to an irrigation ditch. He succeeded in getting to Warren the next day, though suffering a shoulder wound which troubled him the rest of his life.

A company of 18 armed volunteers returned to the Rains Ranch, where they found only smoky ruins. The bones of Rains were taken to Warren for burial.

Albert Webber's daughter, Mabel Webber Altman, lives in Kooskia, Idaho, at the time of this writing and assisted the authors with this account.

The South Fork was the scene of another catastrophe in more recent times — one that involved the destruction of the most prolific summer chinook salmon run in the Columbia River system.

The South Fork drainage (and much of the Salmon) is part of the Idaho Batholith, 10 million acres of granitic rock characterized by steep slopes and highly erodible soils.

Young salmon begin as eggs deposited under 4-10 inches of gravel. They incubate in a salmon nest, hatch after three months, and remain as fry in the gravel until they have absorbed the food in their yolk sack. The fry emerge, reside in the stream until six inches long, migrate to the sea, and normally return to spawn after two years.

Fine sedimentary particles are not conducive to salmon egg survival. The particles cling like glue to the eggs, causing suffocation, and clog escape passages between gravels used by the fry.

In the Fifties and early Sixties, the Forest Service conducted substantial timber sales in the South Fork watershed. Logging and logging roads caused tremendous erosion of fine-grained soil. Sediment build-up in the South Fork was so disastrous that most of the salmon-steelhead habitat was destroyed. A run once estimated at 10,000 (55% of the Columbia's summer chinook) was reduced to 300 fish.

The Forest Service and the Corps of Engineers discerned a problem. Logging was ended in 1965, and fishing, the most important economic resource of the South Fork, was not permitted. The river

196

was given 10 years to restore itself. Millions of dollars were spent by State, Federal, and private agencies. The stream itself has reduced sediment in many of its pools from 16 feet to seven or eight. But no more than 200-250 nests have been counted in recent years.

The Forest Service proposed resumption of logging in the South Fork unit on the Boise and Payette National Forests. The land use plan and environmental statement were challenged by conservation organizations and the Chief of the Forest Service ordered the Forest Supervisors to revise their plans.

At the time of this writing (1978) the new plan calls for development of almost 59,000 presently roadless acres and an annual cut of 28 million board feet. The trees will be expensive to harvest, but since the timber buyer receives full costs for removal plus 13 per cent for profit and risk, taxpayers will subsidize the logging. If one happened to be both taxpayer *and* fisherman, it might make him mad enough to raise hell and put a chunk under it.

Mile 279.7: **Cove Creek,** on the left. The ranch up on the forks of this creek was settled by George Otterson. (He also held title to Mackay Bar in 1923.) He raised a few horses, and worked on an irrigation system which he got too old to finish. To complete it, he gave a half interest to Fred Badley and Roy Stover. Badley eventually bought their shares. The improvements made over the years were burned by a forest fire; the place hasn't been farmed since the Forties and is used as horse pasture by Mackay Bar.

Mile 280.1: **Henry "Red" Harlan's draw and ridge** on the right. Known as "Salmon River Red," Harlan kept to himself, living in a log-tent-dugout at the forks of Cougar Creek, just down river. In the summer he slept under a tree; deer and mountain sheep moved fearlessly around his camp, and mingled with his horses.

In later years he moved up river to this draw, and the ridge above it. Red spent at least 20 years along the river. He could be frosty as a November night and it was advisable to announce one's presence well ahead of arrival. Toward the end, Harlan was so crippled with rheumatism, he used crutches. He began to jump his head hobbles — had delusions that people were riding his horses at night.

Ivan Gustin and Al Tice finally flew him to Grangeville, where Red sacked his saddle and was buried in Prairie View Cemetery.

197

Mile 282.2: **Mann Creek,** on the left. The name was in use by 1900, derivation unknown. It was across from this creek that Bill Jackson wintered when he floated down from Mackay Bar.

Mile 282.5: **Warren Creek** pours in on the left. James Warren, described in the 1903 *Illustrated History of North Idaho* as "a college man, generally liked, but led astray by bad habits and bad company," is credited with finding paydirt on the headwaters of this stream, where the town of Warren sprouted. Jim Warren, though allowed his pick of the claims, failed to cash in on his discovery, and was last heard of as a "cattle king in Wyoming."

The main street of Warren's Diggings.

Warren Creek comes through Warren Meadows, and then drops 3650 feet in its 10-mile trip to the river.

The Romine Ranch straddles Warren Creek about two and a half miles from the river. Dick Hanley located there in the 1890's with a small herd of cattle, which he summered on Warren Meadows. Hanley was murdered on the outskirts of Warren in a dispute over some mining tools, while the deputy sheriff he had summoned stood and watched.

Frank Jordan took over the ranch in 1900. He was a diabetic, and stayed on the place until his death in February, 1918. He is buried near the house.

The acreage was then worked by Roy and Irene Romine. They built a large house and raised their son and daughter there, until the children were old enough for school in Warren.

The property served as base for hunting and outfitting by Clayton Watson and Bryant Roberts in later years. It is now owned by Doctor Howard Adkins, an eye surgeon in Boise.

The ditches terraced on the bank behind the flat at Warren Creek were put in by Chinese miners in the 1880's.

A Fourth of July drilling contest in Warren, about 1925. The driller is single-jacking on a granite block, while the second man hands him fresh steel. The best distance recorded by a miner in such an event was 28⅝ inches in 15 minutes.

The stone cellar on the bank of the river, just downstream from the creek, is the basement of Slim Davis' cabin. Slim was a school-teacher-turned-miner who salted his sluice box so it passed inspection. He was on the bar for three years during the 1960's.

Cap Guleke and Elmer Keith encountered a horrible rapid in 1931 at Warren Creek, caused by a flash flood which washed enough gravel out to temporarily dam the river.

Such phenomena are uncommon, but not extraordinary on the Salmon. In August, 1864, the *Boise News* carried the following article:

Wooden steam-powered shovel with wooden turntable, operating in Warren meadows in 1904. It pulled itself forward on rails by extending its bucket. A horse drew the two-ton carts. The shovel was burned by some boys trying to drive pack rats out of the turntable.

Steam power drew the carts to the top of the platform where they dumped their contents into a washing plant. Water was diverted from Steamboat, Stratton, and Warren Creeks through a 400 foot flume, which carried away the courser gravel, to the left. As gravel piles grew at the far end, the length of the flume was gradually shortened.

John Keenan, Esq., who has just returned from Florence informs us that during his trip and while on the Salmon, he witnessed a singular freak in the water of that river. The water fell one day very suddenly, receding several feet from its usual standard, when all at once it took a turn and came up again higher than ever, thick with mud, and so warm that it would have been unfit to drink if clear.

The basement of the Slim Davis cabin, just below Warren Creek.

Mile 283.8: **Indian Creek** trails out to the river, on the right. The name was derived from pictographs a mile up the creek, which were covered by a slide in the 1920's, washed down the canyon from a cloudburst.

Andy Nelson lambed his flock in 1914-15 in the basin on the creek, above the river. The next year the Matzke brothers, from Wisconsin, settled on the Indian Creek Ranch. The brothers, Fred and Ed, had worked as entertainers in a circus.

The Matzkes brought a ditch around from Moccasin Creek to water their hayfield. They put up a log house, barns, and corrals. They planted an orchard. The brothers acquired some quality cattle from the Deering Ranch on the South Fork.

Fred had to serve in World War I, while Ed remained to prove up on the homestead. When Fred returned from the war, he decided to farm in Washington. Ed gradually lost his mind, and rode off leaving everything: cattle, horses, chickens, dog. He was committed to the asylum at Blackfoot, Idaho. The cattle were butchered on the range and sold to the mines.

Pat Parks packed in haying equipment, losing all but a handful of his cattle in the icy winter of 1928. Jess Reed bought the ranch for John Carrey in 1936 at a tax sale. Carrey held it for an outfitting headquarters, as long as there was hope the Salmon River road might be extended. It is now owned by Dr. Adkins, of Boise. He hired Eddie Close to restore and caretake the property.

While Eddie was renovating the Matzke cabin in the summer of 1977, he discovered Ed Matzke's will, hidden behind an interior window frame. It read:

July 22 and 1925

I have got $190 in Jesse Roots store, yet Please give it back to Mr. ...izzi... for that $150 note I owe.

Everything else I've got and possess go to my brother Charles B. Matzke, and I give him same there of without bond. This is my last will

Ed H. Matzke

P.S. Or you can go ahead and sign my name to the U.S. pattent paper and go ahead with the same and they will be long to you, Charles.

Ed.

During the second World War, a pair of draft dodgers (or resisters) lived in a foxhole covered with brush on the upstream side of the mouth of Indian Creek. There was a ladder down into the hole. They stole provisions from the James Ranch. The men were never apprehended.

While deer hunting one fall on the ridge above, Norm Close looked down, and seeing light through the rocks below his feet, jumped back. On closer examination, he discovered loose boulders formed the roof of a fort against a stone slab. Inside he found a canteen, and an escape exit down a steep gully. The fugitives could observe the river from their stronghold and flee undetected if approached from above or below. Smoke stains indicated the shelter had been used extensively.

Looking downriver from Indian Creek, the ridge in the distance which appears to cross the river is Bull Creek Ridge.

The Matzke cabin, built in 1916 at the head of Indian Creek.

Mile 284.3: **James Creek - James Ranch,** on the left.

Orson James settled the spot in 1901 and remained for 20 years. Before he arrived, Chinese miners had run a ditch up to Rugged Creek in order to have water to placer the bar. James planted the mandatory orchard and garden. His cabin is the log structure close to the river.

James was a Welshman and a Jack Mormon. He had been a bullwhacker freighting with 12 oxen from Utah to Boise, and along the Snake River.

He lived with a man named Donnelly, a one-armed Civil War veteran, who grubstaked James. But Orson was such a poor manager, that Donnelly had to cache food at what is now known as the Romine Ranch, so that there would be enough to get through the winter. If

James had lots of bacon, it all went in the beans at once. If he had corn, he'd feed it to the chickens. His friends downriver, Shepp and Klinkhammer, would loan him their cat to clean mice out of his cabin.

James obtained homestead title, but his health failed and he sold out to Norman Church, cousin to the Matzkes across the river.

Orson James resting next to his cabin at James Creek.

The ranch went through several owners, among them: Pete Klinkhammer, Walt Miller, Roy Romine. When Bryant Roberts and Clayton Watson acquired the site, they put up the lodge in order to operate it as a hunting and fishing business. They cleared the airstrip with a horse, Fresno, and wheelbarrow. Jim Larkin flew in with dudes and supplies.

Dr. Adkins owned this property for years, and Norm and Joyce Close, with daughters Donna and Heather, moved down from Mackay Bar to manage the place for several years. When the Close family left the James place, they moved to their own ranch on Cow Creek, but Norm continues to boat the river, guiding fishermen.

Mile 284.9: **Rugged Creek** on the left.

Mile 285: **Cougar Creek** on the right. The slopes of Cougar Creek look steeper than a church roof, and all rimrock. But beyond these rims lies good horse country, a bunchgrass basin hidden from the river. A short-cut trail from Warren to Dixie came across the river here. It went up the creek to the top of the mountain, around the head of Indian Creek, hit the Mackay Bar trail on Jersey Mountain, and went on into Dixie.

In the early days, a reliable horse on the breaks of Salmon River country was more important to a cowboy than four-wheel drive is to the modern rancher. If one was mounted on a Cougar Creek cayuse, he was traveling on God-proud horseflesh. There is an interesting story behind this fact, that involves the old trail and Cougar Basin. It was told by Orson James and George Otterson.

A large pack train came through one summer going to the Bitterroot country. They swam the horses, while Orson boated their saddles across. The men had a prize thoroughbred mare and stud colt. After swimming, the colt was lame and exhausted. They had to leave it behind, as they went up Cougar Creek.

The colt recovered and grew to be a fine bay stallion. He was never caught nor handled. After a few years, there were beautiful bay colts on the range which proved to be remarkable saddle horses. Everyone in the Mackay Bar country raised them.

When Norm Church got the James Ranch, he decided to move the old stallion across the river from Cougar Creek with some of the mares. He and Joe Powell roped the horse, but he fought the rope and pulled his neck down. When that happens to a horse, it's usually fatal, as it was in this case. So ended the era of "Cougar Creek saddle stock."

Mile 286.5: **Rabbit Creek** runs in on the left side.

Considerable mining was done on Rabbit Creek. The only permanent settler was Steve Winchester. He built a house, barn, and outbuildings by the mouth of the creek, and grew flowers, fruit, and vegetables. There was a sawmill on the place, as well.

Steve was related to the Winchester firearms family and received a remittance from them at intervals by way of the Warren post office. He was educated and eccentric.

Winchester left the country when he developed a facial cancer. The claim is now held by a Californian. The present cabin was built by Don Sigler from the materials he salvaged from Winchester's barn.

Steve Winchester on his Rabbit Creek sawmill. The water powered mill did everything except saw lumber.

Mile 287.2: **Shepp Ranch and Crooked Creek** on the right.

The dullest diary is better than the sharpest memory. Because journals were kept on a daily basis, Shepp Ranch has a history more intact than any on Salmon River — an unabridged chronicle spanning 75 years. Once deciphered, the story presents a picturesque, if inconvenient, past.

Graves, lodge-rings, and arrowheads indicate the alluvial apron at the mouth of Crooked Creek was used by Nez Perce Indians in the 1800's. The Mallick family were Nez Perce and farmed the bar before 1900. Their diligence was responsible for a system of irrigation ditches and the first orchard.

The Mallicks moved to Grangeville prairie and a string of prospectors took their place: Four-eyed Smith, Tom Copenhaver, Charlie Williams: all worked Crooked Creek claims.

Charlie Shepp, the Ranch's namesake, was born in Iowa. He prospected for a few years out of Seattle, before going to the Klondike in '98 with Rex Beach, his partner.

Shepp came to the Buffalo Hump (north of the ranch) during the boom of 1900. He trailed down the West Fork of Crooked Creek and filed a mining claim called the Blue Jay. Charlie acquired a younger partner in Humptown, Pete Klinkhammer, who helped him build a cabin at the mine, and spent time between it and the Hump.

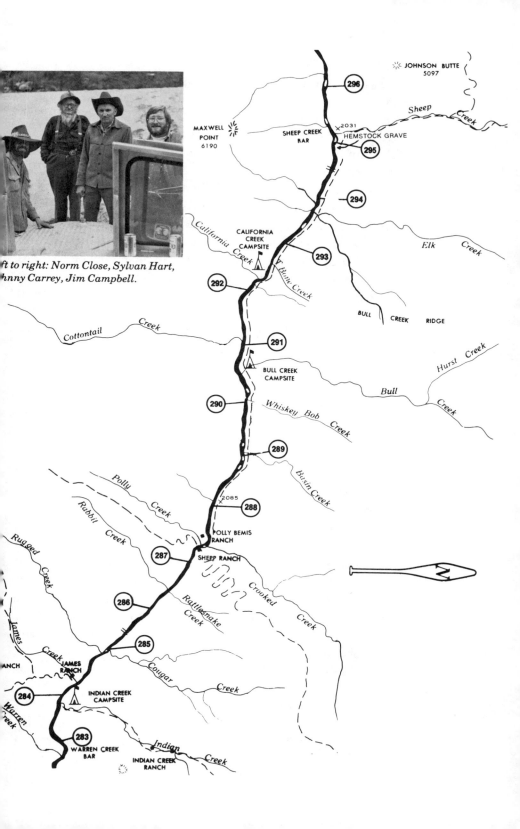

left to right: Norm Close, Sylvan Hart,
Johnny Carrey, Jim Campbell.

JOHNSON BUTTE
5097

Sheep   Creek

296

MAXWELL
POINT
6190

SHEEP CREEK
BAR

2031
HEMSTOCK GRAVE

295

294

California Creek

CALIFORNIA
CREEK
CAMPSITE

293

Elk   Creek

Bow Creek

292

BULL   CREEK   RIDGE

Cottontail   Creek

291

BULL CREEK
CAMPSITE

Hurst Creek

Bull

290

Whiskey Bob Creek

Creek

289

Basin Creek

2085

288

Polly   Creek

POLLY BEMIS
RANCH

Rabbit   Creek

287

SHEPP RANCH

Rugged   Creek

286

Rattlesnake   Creek

Crooked   Creek

N

285

James   Creek

JAMES
RANCH

Cougar   Creek

RANCH

284

INDIAN CREEK
CAMPSITE

Warren   Creek

283

WARREN CREEK
BAR

Indian   Creek

INDIAN CREEK
RANCH

Pete Klinkhammer: Aryan blue eyes, a German accent, and lean as a lizard. He was the sixth of 12 children born to German immigrant parents on a Minnesota farm in 1880. His father was a conservative Catholic disciplinarian, and Peter had left for a job in the Duluth shipyards by his twenty-second birthday. Coming west, he stopped to harvest grain on the plains of Montana. Before arriving in Hump-town, he worked at a brewery in Spokane.

About 1902, Klinkhammer met Shepp in the Buffalo Hump area. They got along like finger and thumb. The two of them formed the Hump Brewing Company and made two batches of beer, before they realized the ephemeral prosperity of the boom was already evaporating. They worked in mines at the Hump, Callender, and on Crooked Creek at the Blue Jay and War Eagle over the next few years. Shepp's journal from 1903-1905 portrays the monotony of mucking rounds on a drift face.

By 1909 he was dealing for the ranch site at the mouth of Crooked Creek.

Aug. 10, Tues.: "Saw Smith, got option on Ranch."
Sept. 22, Wed.: "Over river and had Smith shoe horses. Made bargain with Smith on ranch, pay him a hundred dollars down, $1000 as soon as we finish work on the Star contract, balance sometime next summer. Got 45 pounds vegetables from Bemis."

Shepp and Klinkhammer were in the ranching business for $500 apiece. They were aware of the 1909 railroad survey, and the fact that the Northern Pacific might run a line through the canyon.

When they settled on the ranch there was a barn, chicken house, and cabin. They chose to live in the barn rather than use the cabin that had been shared with pigs. The plan was to raise produce and sell it to mines in the Hump, and later to the War Eagle and Jumbo.

In the winters of 1909-10, the partners hauled logs with horse and go-devil to three different saw pits and whipsawed the 30-foot timbers for their two-story house. They cut joists and rafters as well. Charlie was the carpenter. He made tongue and groove flooring with a rabbet plane. He split roof shakes from fir blocks, and made the furniture for their rooms.

Shepp was the gardener, as well. Their first garden was on the downstream side of Crooked Creek. They made the mistake of planting too early (March). "Everything just came up and sat there," said Klinkhammer. "We got enough seed for 10 years."

Klinkhammer standing on the sawpit. Shepp would stand below and pull the saw down — the dirtier end of a rough job.

The original Shepp-Klinkhammer two-story house. Paul Filer added a 36-foot lodge across the right end, facing the river.

Charlie Shepp in 1912, feeding deer on the ranch.

Future gardens were as bountiful as they were attractive. They included: potatoes, corn, beans, beets, carrots, parsnips, turnips, asparagas, rootabagas, popcorn, watermelons, squash, tobacco, gooseberries, raspberries, blackberries, strawberries, currants, grapes, and hops. The orchard provided a dozen varieties of apples, six kinds of cherries, peaches, plums, pears, apricots, walnuts, and chestnuts. Produce sold for 3-5 cents a pound.

Peter, on the other hand, handled all the stock. He packed produce out and supplies in. He handled the team for plowing and haying. Once a year, he made the six-day round-trip to Grangeville via Concord and Adams Camp, to get the year's necessities. The trip was usually designed to coincide with Grangeville's "Border Days."

Two stories told by Pete Klinkhammer to Marybelle Filer convey a sense of that era and ought to be recorded here.

The first involves a trip Peter made in November, 1909, from Grangeville to Buffalo Hump. He and Jack Wilson caught the stage, which consisted of a four-horse team and an open sleigh. The first night out they stopped at Adams Camp, a way station.

Pete Klinkhammer snowshoeing to Dixie.

The next day they started at daylight. The snow was knee-high to a tall Indian, and the farther they went, the deeper it got. The driver traded the two lead horses for the pair behind. When those horses tired, he put saddles on them and had Pete and Jack ride ahead to break trail. It wasn't long before the powder was up to their saddle skirts, and Klinkhammer and Wilson walked, while the sled kept breaking through behind them. They made it to Moore's — a deserted cabin bereft of food, but shelter nonetheless.

The next day seemed endless, as men and animals moved like they were hobbled. Darkness came early, and they took refuge from the wind and snow under some large trees at Squaw Meadows, about three difficult miles from Humptown. They struggled with a small campfire in five feet of snow.

Suddenly, through the darkness, came flashes of light and voices — 20 men on snowshoes, with swinging lanterns, from Humptown. A sled, which preceded the storm and the stage by a day, carried word of their plight. The men of Humptown donned webs and packboards and were making their way to the stage by lantern light. No sight was ever more welcome.

Each man had a bottle of whiskey, some had two. They brought food, everything, even hay for the horses. Shovelling out a clearing, they built a massive bonfire, set coffee pots to boil, then sat around the fire and talked and sang all night. Three brothers sang wonderful harmonies. "I'll never forget that night," Peter reminisced, "and the sight of those 20 lights swinging single-file through the dark — they made a better trail coming to us than they did going back. They started straggling off toward daylight, one by one, and some didn't break very straight trail. We got through all right and got to town about noon the next day."

The second episode concerns an indomitable Swede. Peter was on his way to Humptown in June of 1911 when he passed a Swede who had come from Orogrande, over the Hump trail. The fellow had a tiny pack, no gun, and only one shoe. The other foot was wrapped in a gunny sack. He had traveled over a foot of snow on his way through the Hump country.

The Swede tried to by-pass Shepp Ranch by cutting up along the side of Jersey Mountain, but Shepp saw him from the garden and headed up to intercept him. Charlie offered the man breakfast and the hospitality of a rest at the ranch

"Naw, I tink dat I be on my way."

"Where to, man?"

He wanted to get to Long Valley, between Boise and McCall.

"Aw hell," Charlie offered, "come on down to the ranch and I'll take you across the river in my boat."

"Naw, I make it my way."

Charlie inquired how he planned to cross the river.

"I go 'till I get to bridge."

"Hell man," exclaimed Charlie, "there ain't no bridge from here to Salmon!"

"Den I schwim."

Shepp persuaded him to accept a boat ride. When they reached the other side of the river and started up to Polly's, the Swede saw some wild thimbleberries and reaching out, stripped the branch and popped them in his mouth. Polly fed him breakfast and Bemis found an old pair of shoes.

Marybelle asked Peter if he thought the Swede got where he was headed. "I tink so," smiled Peter.

Charlie Shepp's garden. The house is behind the trees on the right, the river is in the foreground.

In 1910-11 the composition of wildlife around Shepp Ranch was different than today. Grouse and rattlesnakes were plentiful. Peter said they killed 20 skunks the first year. Deer were thicker than feathers in a pillow. A doe even jumped up in the barn to rest in the hay. When Peter approached, she was startled and leapt out on the roof, sliding off the other side.

Charlie Shepp was interested in radio and made crystal sets. The diaries in the Thirties are filled with notes commenting on stations received. He was also intrigued by photography. The ranch was fortunate to be left with a fine pictorial history as the result of his efforts.

Peter's work was largely responsible for bringing in what cash was needed to keep the ranch functioning. He did assessment work on mines for companies and individuals who wanted to keep their claims valid. He worked at the Jumbo mine in Jumbo Canyon, which had a 24-stamp mill at one time, and operated until 1915. He also worked at the War Eagle, on a tributary to Crooked Creek. That mine was discovered by Bill Boyce in 1898, and several adits were driven to develop the vein. From 1928-1935 a hydro-power plant and mill were put into operation. The ore concentrates were hauled by mule to Dixie, then stored in Grangeville until a truck load was available for the smelter in Seattle.

Pete Klinkhammer cutting hay on the ranch in 1915.

Trapping was another source of income during the winter. Peter ran a line from the ranch to the Hump and down to Orogrande, with spur lines on the Clearwater drainage. He was primarily interested in marten, mink, and fox. Marten pelts would bring almost a hundred dollars at the time of World War I. They were nearly trapped to extinction in Idaho. Furs could be sold by mail to Sears-Roebuck.

Charlie Shepp, who had homesteaded the 136-acre ranch, died in 1936. Before his death, he signed everything over to his partner. Shepp is buried a few feet from the house.

During World War II, Klinkhammer went out to work in the Portland shipyards. Alec Blaine and Shorty Fleming stayed on the place while he was gone. When he returned, Peter worked trails out of Dixie for the Forest Service three seasons, but he feuded with them — the most lost of all causes.

Before 1934, Klinkhammer was getting supplies from Warren and bringing them down to Polly's place, then crossing them by boat. Peter began to deal with Paul and Marybelle Filer's store in Orogrande in 1935. Paul would drive the groceries to Dixie and meet Pete's pack string. They became friends, and Pete would stay with them when he was in town.

Paul was raised in Spokane. He quit the University of Idaho in 1933; times were tough. He took a job as a cook's helper in Orogrande and married the cook's daughter. Marybelle was a registered nurse, trained in San Francisco. The Filers were shivareed with a dynamite blast that broke the windows in their house.

Paul and Marybelle opened a cabin-store in Orogrande, and another in Elk City. Because of restrictions on gold mining, the second World War turned mining towns into ghost camps. The Filers enlisted: Paul as a Seabee, and Marybelle as a nurse in New Guinea, where he was stationed. They saw each other half a dozen times.

When the war ended, the Filers returned to their stores. The one in Elk City was used as a post office. The Filers had many friends; their place was the community magnet. But Paul had visited Shepp Ranch and dreamed of living there.

He tried to persuade Pete Klinkhammer to sell the ranch. It was like trying to talk a cow out of her calf. Peter wasn't interested. Eventually the two men arrived at a cooperative cattle raising agreement.

The Filers sold their store in 1950 and hauled a year's supplies down the Mackay Bar road to a scow Paul had built. They floated down to Shepp Ranch. During the winter, Paul succeeded in convincing Peter to sell. The price was $10,000, and Pete retained a lifetime right to live on the ranch.

Paul Filer motoring up-river.

Paul had grabbed the branding iron by the hot end. "I was pea green," he said. "I thought all I had to do was turn the bull in with the cows and wait for the money to roll in." There was a slump in the beef market in 1951, and 25 steers were scarcely worth taking to market. The Filers raised barley on the back meadow, and got two cuttings of alfalfa off the front ones. They built a herd of 49 cows, but the second winter they ran out of hay; the cattle ate pine needles and slinked their calves. The cattle business was worthless as change for a nickel.

Elk had moved into the area during the war. Friends asked to go hunting at the ranch and Paul soon discovered an alternative to the livestock business that might well support the ranch.

Paul Filer is living proof of the adage: "No man ever drowned in sweat." He built a bridge across Crooked Creek and installed a water system to the house by bringing a thousand gallon tank down the river and winching it uphill to a spring. He bought a 22-foot plywood boat with a 22-h.p. outboard from Don Smith, and began learning the river. He boated a third-hand tractor and a dozer blade down from Mackay Bar and over a 2-year period, scraped out a 1400 foot runway. After 50 hours of instruction and three perfect landings on the strip, he bought a plane.

Paul built a sawmill with salvaged parts, and over nearly five years, cut Doug fir timbers and planks to construct a four-foot by four, 900-foot flume to carry water to a hydro plant. A cement and gabion dam was built across Crooked Creek to furnish a 16-foot head for the power plant. The project cost nearly $50,000, but Shepp Ranch now had electricity.

As anyone who has lived at a back country ranch knows, there were problems, lots of them. But the Filers never let fate step on their sand castle. Paul cut, hauled, and peeled all the logs for the guest cabins which front the river. Then warm spring rains brought the river up so swiftly that it carried all their logs away. Filer went across to the Polly place for new logs and had the structure up within six months.

Marybelle canned 400 pounds of elk meat and preserved a ton of fruits and vegetables each summer. No one works longer hours than a cook during hunting and fishing seasons. Yet she found time to master the accordian by correspondence course, and went on to learn the piano when Paul boated one up the river.

Pete Klinkhammer lived with the Filers and added immeasurably to the fullness of their days. He was an avid reader, subscribed to half a dozen magazines: *National Geographic, Country Gentleman, Saturday Evening Post, Newsweek, Atlantic Monthly,* and *Kiplinger's*. He read newspapers two weeks at a time, and listened to the news on the radio.

Inside the house: Paul, Marybelle, and Peter.

Pete was an enthusiastic sports fan; even went to the World Series twice. He would go out to a motel in Seattle just to watch the series on television each year.

In financial matters, Klinkhammer was quite shrewd. He had invested in silver certificates, mining and transportation stock, and did well.

On Sundays, Peter, who was a tireless walker, would walk to Bull Creek. He enjoyed a drink if he'd earned one. He liked classical music, but packed the extensive record collection gathered at Shepp Ranch up to Dixie in 1943 when records were solicited for the war effort. He was a fine fisherman and an excellent skier.

Klinkhammer was a Republican on most issues, but he supported Debbs. At 82-years-of-age, he rode 18 miles to Dixie, through a snowstorm to vote in an off-year Congressional election.

He entered the hospital in 1970 for prostate surgery. From his bed, he asked Filer to get a lawyer in order that he might change his will. A suspicious attorney came to the hospital and asked Peter why he wanted to amend the document. Klinkhammer explained that he had left everything to his church, but now he'd decided to leave it all to his older sister, Mary. "She won't have it two days before she gives it to the church," he said, "and this way two people will have the enjoyment of giving." The lawyer made the change.

Pete Klinkhammer in his later years.

Pete died in the spring of 1970. At his sister's request, he was buried in Grangeville, rather than at Shepp Ranch. Those who knew him well will tell you: gold was plain dust beside Peter Klinkhammer. It is lamentable that no geophysical feature bears his name.

219

Paul and Marybelle built the Shepp Ranch into a successful sportsman's outfitting business. They had friends from one end of the river to the other. Paul built a lodge (across the front of Shepp and Klinkhammer's original house), two more houses, and another duplex. In 1969, they sold the place to a group of 10 persons from the Pacific Northwest. The Filers moved to Riggins, where they live at the time of this writing.

The ranch was managed by Glen and Mickey Schubert until an unfortunate accident. Glen was killed when his car went off the Salmon River road one snowy night as he was returning to his boat.

A nuclear physicist turned outfitter, Jim Campbell, bought Shepp Ranch in 1973. Originally from Illinois, Campbell had come to Idaho in 1961, and the Hells Canyon preservation movement involved him in the business of river-trips.

Jim integrated the river business with Shepp Ranch, running float trips to Shepp and pack trips to the high country. He and his wife, Anita Douglas, received their baptism by fire — literally. A 5000-acre fire the first summer burned their best hunting camp in Bull Creek. The following June, the worst flood in a hundred years swirled across the bar, putting four feet of water in the guest cabins, washing away a winter's wood, and disrupting plans for several weeks.

Shepp Ranch as it looked during the flood of 1974. The orchard was inundated, as were the cabins in the upper right hand corner, which overlook the river. Note the jet-boat tied up next to the lodge.

The Campbells put in a new septic system, remodeled and re-wired the buildings, and installed a diesel generator. Jim became a proficient jet boat pilot.

Anita supervised the ranch, ran the kitchen, cared for an extensive garden, and looked after horses, goats, and rabbits. She also became the first woman to qualify for a jet-boat operator's license on the Salmon.

Shepp Ranch remains an active and attractive center for outfitting and dude-ranch vacations. The country up Crooked Creek is even quieter than it was when Shepp and Klinkhammer first saw it: the mines are abandoned, elk, bear, and cougar tracks imprint the trails, and for 20 miles there's not even a fence to tangle the wind.

Mile 287.2: **Polly Creek,** on the left, across from Crooked Creek. One of the most engrossing tales on Salmon River attaches to the clearing by this creek.

It began in China, September 11, 1853, when Lalu Nathoy was born of impoverished parents. Starvation forced her father to sell Lalu into slavery in order to get seed for his crops. The daughter was brought to America as a slave, undoubtedly by the Six Companies of San Francisco, which ran an immoral but lucrative business dealing in Chinese indentured servants. She was brought to Portland, probably through San Francisco, where by her own account, she was acquired by a Chinese for $2500. He took her in a pack train to Warren in 1872.

Warren at the time had a sizeable Chinese population. The trans-continental railroad was completed and demand for coolie labor had subsided. The Chinese moved to goldfields where they bought used claims and industriously re-worked them. When Lalu arrived with the pack stock, someone helped her off her horse, saying "Here's Polly." The name stuck.

At this date, no one can be certain how Polly obtained her freedom from Hong King, the man who brought her to Warren. Sister Alfreda Elsensohn, in her book *Idaho Chinese Lore,* writes that Polly was working in a saloon owned by her master, and was lost in a poker game to Charles Bemis, another saloon keeper. Years later, Polly denied the story she was a "poker bride," but she may have been referring to the tale of how she eventually came to marry Bemis. If she was not freed as part of a gambling debt, then some other arrangement regarding her release was negotiated by Polly or Bemis, because Hong King would not have forgiven the indenture without payment. In any event, as A. W. Talkington, who knew her in Warren, said "Polly was a good woman and entitled to a great deal of consideration because of her upright conduct in rather difficult circumstances."

Charles A. Bemis was born in Connecticut, five years earlier than Polly, and came to Warren with his father, who was a miner. Charlie quickly decided the saloon business and gambling were a lot less demanding than rocking gold. Hard work and Bemis were antonyms. But C. A. was honest and he helped Polly if a situation at her boarding house got out of hand.

Charles Bemis, before the shooting.

On the morning of September 16, 1890, Johnny Cox, a half-Indian from Lewiston, was mad enough to eat the devil with his horns on. He had lost $250 in a card game to Bemis, the night before. He approached Charlie as he lay resting in a small bedroom at the rear of his saloon. "Give me back $150. You've got till I finish rolling this cigarette, then I'll shoot your eye out."

The men must have taken each other's measure. Cox fired into Charlie's face, shattering his cheek and narrowly missing his eye. Claiming it was self-defense, Johnny left town. On September 26, the Idaho County Free Press reported: "Dr. Bibby returned from Warren Tuesday night and informed us that Chas. Bemis's wound would probably be fatal, sooner or later, as the ball, on entering the head, struck the cheek bones and split, and he had only succeeded in finding and extracting one half of the ball and 14 pieces of bone. The other part of the bullet is still in the head and in all likelihood will induce blood poisoning, unless the system is strong enough to expell the remaining fraction of the ball."

Mr. Troll and Polly succeeded in extracting the rest of the bullet and began nursing Bemis back to health. A month later the wound hadn't healed, but Charlie could sit up and smoke. With Polly's attentions, he gradually recovered.

On learning the truth of the incident, Warren's camp raised $300 to pursue Johnny Cox. H. W. Cone tracked him to Pocatello and arrested him, nine days after the shooting. On October 31, 1891, John Cox was sentenced to five years for assault with a deadly weapon.

As an alien, Polly faced the threat of being deported to China, so Charlie Bemis married her August 13, 1894, at Warren. (The justice of the peace, A. D. "Pony" Smead, was married to an Indian woman and had passed an anti-miscegenation ordinance.) A short while later, Charlie and Polly moved down to the banks of Salmon River.

Polly was about as big as the small end of nothing, whittled to a fine point — she couldn't have weighed 100 pounds. She wore boy's shoes, because her feet had been bound as a child in China. This gave her walk a rolling motion.

She was a hard worker, growing a productive garden, cutting firewood, cooking for Bemis, and caring for ducks, chickens, and a cow. As she worked in the garden, she would often stoop for a worm, which she deposited in her apron pocket. With the precision of a chronometer, she would drop her hoe at 3 o'clock and go down to the river fishing.

Polly had a marvelous sense of humor. In Warren at her boarding house, she overhead some men complaining about her coffee. She came running out from behind the stove waving a cleaver and said, "Who no likee my coffee?" Once she caught Bemis watching the workings of an ant mound. "Bemis," she told him, "if you'd work'um like ants we no be poor folks." Another time she was gathering chestnuts with Pete Klinkhammer. Suddenly she burst out laughing. He looked at her, quizzically. "When you start picking up horsenuts instead of chestnuts it's time to quit," she said — and did.

The Chinese lady could not read or write. Charlie started to teach her, but she caught on so fast he discontinued the lessons. She could add and play cards. Once some prospectors camped at the mouth of Crooked Creek and got vegetables from the Bemises. Polly never charged them. Each trip one of the fellows would flash a hundred dollar bill, believing he was making a big impression. Finally getting tired of his game, Polly snatched his bill and changed it. That was the end of the matter.

By 1919, Bemis was an invalid. It didn't make much difference in regard to the chores, since Polly always did them anyway. In August, 1922, Charlie Shepp's diary reads: "Peter went to Dixie a.m. Bemis house burned. Got the old man out by the skin of my teeth. Lost Teddy (Polly's dog). He got burned. Polly and I got the old man over about 4. Had hard time. Didn't save a single thing. The whole place was on fire when I got over. Everybody's feet burned."

Two months later Charlie Bemis died. Shepp writes: "Bemis passed in at 3 a.m. I went up to War Eagle camp at 5 a.m. to get Schultz and Holmes. We buried the old man right after dinner. Fine day." (Bemis was buried at Shepp Ranch.)

A couple of days later, Klinkhammer took Polly on horseback to Warren to live. While she was there, it became necessary for her to be fitted with glasses. She was taken on her first automobile ride, all the way to Grangeville. It was the summer of 1923 and she was 70 years old.

In Grangeville Polly was treated like a celebrity. She saw her first motion-picture show, her first train, and was given a new wardrobe by friends. She sat with a handkerchief held tightly against her face and burst into a laughter of tears attempting to describe what she had seen.

Polly Bemis on her place.

The Bemis Ranch, looking up river. The two-story building was the original Bemis house which burned in 1922.

Their garden occupies the center of the picture.

It was in Grangeville that people became aware of Polly's phenomenal memory. She knew the name of every child born in Warren, its birthdate; she remembered every death, and the detail and date of any particular event with which she was familiar.

Polly made a trip to Boise the next year, to visit a dentist. She saw streetcars, rode in an elevator, saw another movie. Polly made an agreement with Shepp and Klinkhammer that year, too. She was homesick for the river and said she would leave them her place if they would put up another cabin. They readily consented.

There was a phone line across to Shepp Ranch, and Polly would call once a day, often just to compare the number of fish caught: "None! You no good! You fella come over Sunday. I cook a great big one I catch today."

The wonderful lady became ill in 1933. Klinkhammer and Shepp took her by horseback up to Dixie, where she was met by an ambulance, driven by Glen Ailor, which took her to Grangeville. When a nurse told her she would soon get well, Polly replied, "No, me too old to get well, me have to go to other world to get well."

Polly Bemis photographed in 1921 with the Countess Gizycka river trip. Left to right: man unknown, E. G., Cap Guleke,

Polly Bemis, R. E., Arthur, Ben Ludwig with dog, Cissy Patterson (the Countess).

Polly Nathoy Bemis died November 6, 1933. Though she had wanted to be buried alongside the River of No Return, neither Shepp nor Klinkhammer could be reached, so she was laid to rest in Grangeville. Pete Klinkhammer saw to it that a headstone was placed on her grave.

A number of Polly's personal effects are on display in St. Gertrude's Museum at Cottonwood, Idaho. Her second cabin still stands in the flat, by the creek that bears her name. The name was suggested by Shepp and Klinkhammer to the government survey party that boated down the river in 1911. They thought Polly might be remembered longer than Bemis. (However, there is a Bemis Creek and Bemis Mountain on the outskirts of Warren.)

Mile 298: **Basin Creek** runs in on the right. River elevation 2075 feet. Used by Bill Hart and Pick Ward as a winter horse range.

Mile 290: **Whiskey Bob Creek,** on the right. He was an old miner and his grave is under a pile of rocks and deerhorns way up on the head of the stream. Pete Klinkhammer tried to show Paul Filer where it was, but was unable to relocate it.

Mile 290.5: **Bull Creek** flows in from the right. Named for Alexander Bull, an early miner. Neal McMeekin and Charlie Shepp met on this creek to trade bulls. It represented quite a trip to make the exchange since there was no trail along the river at the time. The Forest Service acquired a compressor from the War Eagle mine and floated it alongside the bluff in order to drill rock for the trail.

Mile 291: **Cottontail Creek,** on the left, lies in a large basin burned by a forest fire in 1930. It was once a fine elk range.

Mile 292.2: **California Creek** comes in from the left, draining War Eagle and Marshall Mountain. War Eagle and Humboldt mines and California Lake are on the headwaters.

An old German, Andy Scroggs, built a nice cabin and ran a few milk cows on Ten Acre Flat, about five miles up the stream.

The crew at the Holte mine, later known as the Golden Anchor, in 1915. The mine was located on the head of Bear Creek.

Mile 292.5: **T-Bone Creek,** on the right. Shorty Fleming built a cabin a 150 yards up this creek. Shorty was a prospector and placer miner along the river for years, working from South Fork to French Creek. He had a few burros he acquired from Paul Filer.

While at French Creek, late in life, Fleming suddenly struck it rich — through an inheritance. It was quite a shock to him.

Shorty, and his pard, Slim Forrester, decided to jubilate. They bought a flashy convertible sports car, and with Slim at the wheel, hit town like eggbeaters in troubled water. Fleming's money went so fast

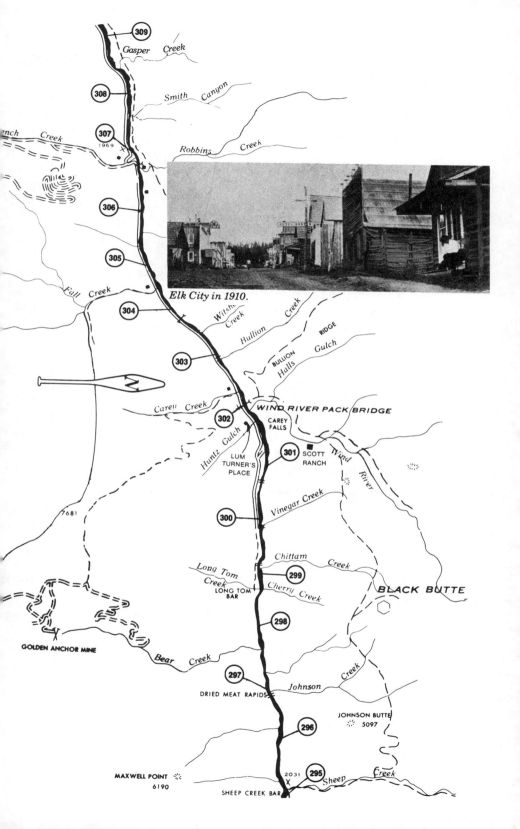

309

Gasper Creek

308

Smith Canyon

307
1969

Robbins Creek

Elk City in 1910.

306

305

Fall Creek

304

Witsh- Creek

Bullion Creek

303

BULLION Halls RIDGE Gulch

N

Carell Creek

WIND RIVER PACK BRIDGE

302

CAREY FALLS

Huntz Gulch

LUM TURNER'S PLACE

301 SCOTT RANCH

Wind River

7681

300

Vinegar Creek

Chittam Creek

Long Tom Creek

299

LONG TOM BAR

Cherry Creek

BLACK BUTTE

298

GOLDEN ANCHOR MINE

Bear Creek

297

DRIED MEAT RAPIDS

Johnson Creek

JOHNSON BUTTE
5097

296

MAXWELL POINT
6190

2031

295

Sheep Creek

SHEEP CREEK BAR

he must have had a hole in his pocket big as his pant's leg. He kept his burro pack string in the front yard of the Riggins Hotel.

The old prospector died in the summer, when the blowout was over.

Mile 293.8: **Elk Creek** comes down through the rocks on the right.

Mile 295.1: **Sheep Creek** is the substantial stream flowing out of the canyon on the right; it drains the Buffalo Hump country. Bruce Crofoot had a cabin and garden at the mouth of Sheep Creek in the early 1900's.

Jay Shuck's family started a cabin at Plummer Creek, four miles up Sheep Creek, in the spring of 1912.

Two hundred yards up river from the Sheep Creek corral, just below the trail, by a big yellow pine is a handmade gravestone: James Hemstock, 1840 - 2-27-09. by Rice 1-58. Hemstock was an elderly miner who lived at Elk Creek. Peter Klinkhammer heard he was seriously ill, so took the trail to the Hump, where he got two miners to come down the other side of Bull Creek with him.

When they arrived, they found the man had dropsy. He was an abnormally ample man to begin with, and it took the three of them with a stretcher to get him to a horse. They had no idea of how they would ever get him to Elk City. At that moment, Hemstock rolled over and died. Peter remarked, "You know, it was the nicest thing he could have done for us." The three buried him there. (Jay Shuck remembers the miners saying his name was Hempstead.)

Glen Rice, miner, packer and boater, made the grave marker. The Forest Service threw it in the river and replaced it with a wooden routed sign. Filer retreived the original, and placed it back on the grave.

The tents at Sheep Creek are part of a special-use permit outfitting headquarters for Shepp Ranch.

The trail up Sheep Creek goes down 13 miles to Wind River pack bridge, or 17 miles up to Oregon Butte.

Mr. and Mrs. Frank Ludwig lived in a cabin on the bar across from Sheep Creek. They had a garden and flowers. They went out to the ship-yards in World War II and their cabin was burned. Whitey Cox had packed in the materials for its cement floor from Wind River.

In the basin above the Ludwigs, lived a Mexican named Ray Perrie. He was a superb craftsman: made violins, and wove magnificent saddle blankets. Ray was killed by a car in Riggins, when he was there one fall for supplies. His cabin has returned to the earth.

Mile 296.9: **Dried Meat Rapid.** In 1962, five people drowned in a jet boat accident here. Lucky McKenna was an outfitter who ran the James Ranch. He was coming up-river in early July and experienced some engine problems. He had the shroud off his motor.

At the rapid, he stopped to put four people ashore who wanted movie footage of his run. He lost power in the rapid and a wave broke over the boat, washing it into the hole. Lucky, his three children, and his mother were drowned.

The rapid was an impediment to up-river travel, until Paul Filer and Glen Rice dynamited some of its boulders.

The rapid washes out over 25,000 c.f.s. At lower flows, the run is right of center.

Mile 297: **Johnson Creek,** on the right. Named for Graf Johnson, a Forest Service district ranger. Ike and Ellis Painter had a cow camp on the creek, two miles below Johnson Saddle. They ran cattle in the area for several years. Jim Remington, from White Bird, ran wethers for their wool in this drainage.

Mile 297.7: **Bear Creek** streams in from the left. It drains a rich mining area, three miles from the river. The Holte-Golden Anchor, and Goodenough mines were good producers.

Mile 298.8: **Long Tom Creek,** on the left. Named for the Long Tom mine on its headwaters, which operated from 1906-1910. Ed Heintz built a tight, handsome one-room cabin at the mouth of the creek in 1935, using winch, crosscut saw, and axe. He filed the Beaver-Placer mining claim and skim-dug and trapped off and on for nearly 20 years. The supervisor for the Payette National Forest ordered the cabin burned in 1975. This myopic action occurred while the river corridor was being evaluated for "wild and scenic" classification. It is a considerable irony that the governmental agency, which stresses Smoky the Bear's message of care with fire, incinerates buildings of historic and aesthetic interest. It is time and past that forest supervisors realized "we need old buildings in the sun to gauge our humanness against indifferent skies."

Mile 298.8: **Cherry Creek** on the right.

Mile 299.1: **Chittam Creek and Rapid.** Named for the cascara tree; whose bark is called chittam and was collected for use as a laxative.

231

On high water, Chittam becomes a difficult rapid. The water piles into the rock face on the left side of the river. It bears scouting on high flows. At any stage, the scout and run are on the right bank.

Mile 299.2: Cement boat ramp and Riggins road on the left. The road was built by C.C.C. crews.

cAlong the River:
Vinegar Creek to Riggins

Mile 299.9: **Vinegar Creek and Rapid.** This rapid has dumped a lot of boats. The run is obvious, but it's best to take a look. A boat flipped here in 1976, and while the guide got out of the river on the right bank, he was never seen again.

Mile 300.7: **Carey Falls.** "Sound and fury signifying nothing."

Mile 301.8: **Huntz Gulch,** on the left. Lester "Lum" Turner has lived in the cabin on the downstream side of the gulch for 40 years, at the time of this writing. Lum was born in Minnesota, and arrived at Burley, Idaho in 1908. He drove the mail stage to Grand View, Idaho, ran a service station, worked as a welder, Caterpillar mechanic, and a road builder for the Forest Service.

Pearl Turner, Lum's wife.

Lum Turner in 1927 on his way to Jackson Hole.

233

Turner worked a hydraulic placer claim across the river from his place; its location is marked by the ocher scar on the hillside.

The original Huntz cabin is probably about a hundred years old, and stands just below Turner's house.

In 1949 Lum observed a waterspout that washed out Huntz Gulch and temporarily dammed the river.

Turner's placer claim on the north side of the river with the hydraulic "giant" in action.

The slide coming out of Huntz Gulch, filmed shortly after the river had broken through the mud.

Mile 301.9: **Wind River** pours in on the right. This stream was called Meadow Creek on early maps. There was a trail from Florence Basin, past the Bullion mine and down to a wire bridge crossing at Carey Creek. It was naturally called the Meadow Creek Trail, and a ferry house next to the "new" bridge is mentioned in the *Lewiston Journal.*

The historic cabin at the mouth of Wind River which dated back to the time of the Florence boom. Photo taken in 1926, before the building was burned by the Forest Service.

Neal McMeekin was the first homesteader on the stream, locating about two miles up the creek, on a flat still known as the McMeekin Ranch. He built a cabin, made the usual improvements, and ran a few cattle.

In 1919, Neal bought out Charles White, who owned the mining claims at the mouth of Wind River. White decided to remain until he had finished placering. In addition, he tried to take some tools and the sourdough jug. McMeekin got sore as a sore-tailed bear, arguing that he'd paid for everything. White disagreed, and bang! it was "no sourdough forever" for Charlie White. He is buried in a grave by the mouth of the creek, on the downriver side.

A court case ensued. Neal turned the ranch over to his brother, Sam, who spent $6000 defending Neal.

Neal McMeekin died an old man, with the lonesome wind blowing in him, herding sheep for wages.

Charley and Wilma Warnock, from Snake River and Cougar Creek on the Middle Fork, settled at the mouth of Wind River, where they lived out their years.

Slim Forrester was found dead in a cabin a quarter of a mile up the creek, apparently the victim of a heart attack. Many people must live and die alone — especially on Salmon River.

The log cabin used and extended by most of these people had stood on the bar since the time of the Warren gold rush. With all the perception of a tree stump, the Forest Service burned it.

A cabin built by McMeekin still stands on his ranch upriver.

A second grave, that of Clarence Rowley, 22 years old, who died of exposure in 1898 on his way to the Marshall Mountain mines, lies next to White's grave at the mouth of Wind River. The crosses on the two graves were made and placed by Mrs. Joe Crozier, fashioned with cement from the Wind River bridge job.

E. A. Parisot, who died of pneumonia in 1920, is buried by the Bullion mine, which is three miles from the north end of the bridge.

Mile 302: **Wind River Pack Bridge.** The first modern bridge erected by the Forest Service collapsed into the river as it neared completion because the anchor bolts pulled out of stone on the south side, in the fall of 1961. One tower and half of the bridge was salvaged, and the present bridge was opened in the spring of 1962.

Mile 302.3: **Carey Creek** comes down on the left. The Meadow Creek Trail crossed here and climbed over Studebaker Saddle to Warren in the 1860's and to the Marshall Mountain mines in the 1890's. It was heavily used to haul mining supplies, and traces of the trail are still dimly discernable. For over 50 years there was a long log watering trough in the Saddle, where a pack string could drink in route.

Jim and John Carey, Englishmen, operated a ferry house at the crossing for many years. Johnny Woods followed their residency.

When the state bridge was completed five miles downriver at French Creek in 1892, wagon traffic there forced abandonment of the Carey Creek crossing.

The cabin which was situated at Carey Creek was built by Jake Wilson at Peterson Flat, a couple of miles above the road. He was selling milk to the Golden Anchor mine. The old Carey house burned, and mining activity tapered off, so Wilson moved the logs down to the mouth of the creek and reassembled them. He was killed in a tractor accident. The Forest Service ordered the 43-year-old cabin removed in 1978.

Halfway to Fall Creek, on the bank above the road, is Joe Roger's grave. Joe was on his way to the Goodenough mine at the head of Bear Creek when he sustained a leg wound from his own pistol. He was unable to get help, and died by the river. His grave was relocated by Lum Turner when the river road was pushed through.

Mile 303: **Bullion Creek** on the right.

Mile 303.3: **Witsher Creek** enters on the right.

Mile 304.4: **Fall Creek** rushes down on the left. This stream descends 4,500 feet in five miles. Curiously, rain which drops on the south side of the Fall Creek divide will flow to the South Fork by way of Lake Creek and Secesh River, and come down the Salmon to mingle with the waters of Fall Creek, after a circuitous route of almost a hundred miles.

Mile 305.8: **Scott Creek** draw on the left. Just a mile above the bench, not visible from the river, is the Scott Ranch. It was settled originally by Mr. Knott, who farmed and ran a ferry at the river near the mouth of the warm springs. Sam Large remembers Mr. Knott selling potatoes to the Florence miners at 75 cents a pound. That was with the clay on them and when they were washed, half was taken off in dirt. They were so small that they became famous to every old-timer as "Knott's Pills." Knott is buried in an unmarked grave alongside the trail to his ferry.

Sylvester Scott bought the place in 1894, and moved there with his family from Scott Valley, east of Cascade. The Scotts had 21 children.

The Scotts raised cattle and produce for the mines. With Chinese help, they put in an irrigation ditch to bring water from Robbins Creek. When Sylvester died, he was buried on the ranch. His son, Reuben, lived there until his death, and it now belongs to his niece, Beverley Eason, who ranches in Rome, Oregon.

Mile 306.8: **Robbins Creek** flows in on the right. This stream was known as Cow Creek, but the name was changed by the Forest Service mapmakers. The houses belong to Mrs. Standish, who moved there in the late Twenties, before the road was pushed up the river. She planned to raise poppies for their seeds.

An old German miner, by the name of Chris Arnold, stayed on the Standish place. He was at the hot springs before Fred Burgdorf. Arnold is buried below the rocky bluff, behind the Standish house.

Mile 306.9: **French Creek** pours out from the canyon on the left. This stream was named after eight French miners. The earliest locaters were the Shisslers, who built a house on the flat, just upriver from the mouth of the creek. Annie was born to Frank and Elizabeth Shissler, March 7, 1872 — perhaps the first white child born in the canyon. She died of typhoid fever during her eighteenth year. The Shisslers had come from Warren, where they ran a sawmill; they apparently moved on to Grangeville. Records indicate Frank died in Newsome.

A state bridge was completed across the river at the mouth of the creek in 1892. Construction had been delayed a year because the Salmon bridge iron was sent to Spokane and the steel for the Spokane bridge, which was 50 feet shorter, was sent mistakenly to Weiser, Idaho.

Aaron F. Parker, founder of the *Idaho County Free Press,* lobbied at the territorial legislature for appropriations which would allow construction of the bridge and road. The road allowed wagon traffic to travel from Meadows to Burgdorf or Warren, down French Creek, across the river and up through the Scott Ranch to Florence and Mount Idaho. By 1901, it was designated a state highway. In November of that year, the bridge blew down in a windstorm and the flow of traffic ceased.

There was a post office and school active in 1903-06 at the mouth of the creek. Jim and Alice Wiley ran the place and Etta Scott taught the Scott and Howard children. This site was homesteaded by Albert and Royston Soards after their father was murdered on the lower Salmon. Mrs. Soards lived with them until she was killed in 1919, by falling from a bluff while looking for the family cow.

The Waldon-Keys Ranch was located about a mile up the creek, on the eastern side. Charley Waldon had started a homestead there, with an irrigation ditch coming out of French Creek. He was an elderly man and turned the place over to Swanson Knudsen.

Knudsen was tough as a 1807 prune and touchy as a badger. He caused so many problems that if he'd fallen in the river it would have been considered a tragedy only if someone had pulled him out. He was shot on the road to the Scott Ranch in 1902; no one was convicted of the killing.

Stover's Mansion at French Creek. Mr. Knott lived in this house while he ran the ferry. It was located on the little flat across from the mouth of the creek, on the north side of the river. In 1910 it burned, while Jake Stover was using it.

Myrtle and Joe York at the Waldon-Keys Ranch on French Creek, packing hay Salmon-River-style.

Joe and Myrtle York worked the place from 1910 until the Thirties. They developed it as a stopping place for anyone traveling the road to mines or ranches. Joe left and Myrtle later married Slim Keys. They sold the ranch and moved to Riggins, but it is still known as the Keys' Ranch.

Edna Hinkley and her son Clifford ran a store, rooms, and post office at French Creek from 1937 to 1943. At that time the bench on the downriver side of the creek, above the road, was the location of a Civilian Conservation Corps camp. The camp buildings were dismantled by the Forest Service in 1943, and the materials were used for district construction.

Hinkley's lodge is the large log building on the west side of the creek, next to the road. Al and Mary Tice ran the lodge for a couple of years, serving meals, and catering to hunters and fishermen, before moving to Mackay Bar.

Art Francis, Tom Koskie, and George Anderson leading a pack string up the Salmon River past the Howard Ranch in the early Thirties, with supplies for the C.C.C. camp at French Creek.

Mile 308.5: **Gasper Creek** comes in on the right; it is sometimes incorrectly labeled Jaspar; Jim and John Gasper homesteaded and developed the flat. John had a wife and two children. All supplies and lumber for their house and building were packed up the old county trail from Riggins. They had an orchard and hay field.

Mile 310.5: **Shearer's Ferry-Howard Ranch-Elkhorn Creek.**

Elk Creek was altered to Elkhorn Creek by the Forest Service. Along the Salmon River, it is a historically significant site.

The creek was the location of the first ferry crossing established by Frederick and Susan Shearer during the mining boom in Florence.

Their son, George M. Shearer, was born in Winchester, Virginia, and was educated at Tuscorara Academy, Pennsylvania. He traveled to California in 1854 with his parents, returning home in 1859.

At the outbreak of the Civil War, George enlisted in General Bradley Johnston's regiment of Maryland volunteers and served the Confederate cause until captured and imprisoned in Fort Delaware.

Wounded several times in the war, he escaped from the Federal prison and made his way in 1865 to Idaho. He settled at Elk Creek and rowed the ferry there for his parents. The boat was eventually replaced with a wire ferry.

George volunteered for the Nez Perce War in 1877; was twice wounded in that conflict. He again volunteered for the Sheepeater Campaign, serving under Lieutenant Catley. In 1883, he married Carrie Vollmer and they had three children. Shearer served several terms in the Idaho legislature, snowshoeing from the ferry to Boise and back — 300 miles. He was district court clerk for Idaho County at the time of his death.

The ferry was acquired by Orvil and Flora Howard in August, 1889; they came by way of White Bird with their four children. In Flora's words:

At last about noon we reached the river and found the ferry boat tied up on the side away from us, but on the same side where the house was. The man we had sent up to take care of things till we got there was off visiting five miles up river so we sat around on blistering hot rocks till he came back and brought the boat over for us. After we had some dinner we began to look around, and found the house to be quite a large building made snug and warm of logs squared on all four sides. One large room had been a post office, store, and saloon, and the rest was a hotel and living quarters — all that while Florence was yielding its rich gold output, but that was mostly passed before we went there. The post office had been closed and it was sometimes three months we were without any mail at all and had no contact whatever with the outside world. But I never seemed to feel any loneliness, it was and is a place with much natural loveliness."

The Howards raised nine children on this ranch. They had stock and grew fruit and produce which could be sold in mining camps.

Jack Howard, the third son, lived on the ranch from the time he was old enough to hold an apple to a colt, until his death in 1966 — 74 years. He married Mattie Rowe and they raised their family there. Howard grazed cattle that were wild as a Riggins' wind, but he was cowboy enough to handle them.

After Jack's death, the ranch was purchased by John and June Cook, mentioned in the section on Allison Ranch. They make their home on the place with Everett Van Arsdale at the time of this writing.

The large Japanese walnut tree in the front yard was planted by Jack Howard as a boy, so it is over 80 years old.

Mattie Rowe and Jack Orvil Howard on their wedding day in 1908.

242

Mile 311.5: **Manning Bridge.** This bridge was built by the CCC men. Manning was working for the Corps and fell off the bluff, above the right end of the bridge, when he was returning from Riggins one evening. The old crossing was upriver, just behind the barn on the Howard place.

The area below the bridge is known as The Crevice. It is the site of a dam planned by the Army Corps of Engineers. The dam, if built, would have backed water 200 feet over Shepp Ranch.

Mile 312.2: **Partridge Creek** trails down to the river on the left. This stream drains Partridge Butte, and is named for an early miner who had a cabin on the creek.

Louis Howard first homesteaded the ranch at the mouth of the creek with his family. He was a son of the Howards at Shearer's Ferry. In 1920, his wife, Maude, drowned by the sand bar in front of the house. It was a Fourth of July celebration, and her niece, Lucille, got into difficulties while swimming in the river. Mrs. Howard went to her aid, and the girl got out, but Maude didn't. Her body was recovered downriver. She left three boys; one was only six months old. Mr. Howard continued to work the ranch for some time.

Ed Long, son of a Warren miner, homesteaded a site four miles up the creek. He built a cabin, and remained until tuberculosis caused his demise.

Frank Rogers and Mr. Thompson homesteaded a hundred acres on the ridge between Partridge Creek and Lake Creek.

The Partridge Creek bridge as it appeared when the June, 1974, flood waters were receding. The cement piers which support the bridge are 38 feet high. Seven people drowned in the river that week.

Mile 312.4: **Partridge Creek bridge:** built in 1956 by the Forest Service at a cost of $135,000, the road goes three miles south, to a dead end. At one time, plans called for linking the bridge with the Goose Lake-Hazard Lake road to the south, but lack of funds and a shift in thinking regarding the impact the road would have on the drainage terminated construction plans.

Mile 313.5: **Kelly Creek** enters on the right. Bill Kelly, known as Poker Kelly, came down from the Florence mines and settled by this stream. He was found dead in his house in 1898 and is buried about half a mile up river from the creek. The grave is marked. (Kelly was the Howards' nearest neighbor, and had been buried a week before they even knew he was dead.)

Frank Austin, an old-time miner, with a bay horse and a Jersey cow, lived between Kelly and Van Creek, until he died of asthma.

Mile 313.8: **Van Creek** runs out on the right.

Mile 314.4: **Spring Bar** boat landing on the right. A take-out point for boaters; the cement ramp can be seen on the edge of the river.

Mile 315: **Allison Creek** flows in from the right. William Allison settled on his claim in 1871, about a mile up the creek from the river. A trail ran by his place and he provided meals and lodging to miners. He died in 1890 and is buried across the creek from his house, alongside a sheriff who was killed when his horse fell from a bluff.

Mile 315.4: **Riggins Hot Springs,** on the left. The hot spring here was well-known to the Indians long before white men discovered it. The Nez Perce called it Weh-min-kesh, and scores of them gathered on the site to take advantage of the reputed medicinal properties of the spring waters. Miners, cowboys, and packers came to ease their aches and ills.

Fred and Clara Riggins bought the site in 1900 from two squatters, Frank Austin and Gus Veiro, for six $20 gold pieces. The squatters owed Berg for supplies, so they slipped down river past his place in an old boat.

Fred Riggins was 29 years old when he settled with his family on Warm Springs Flat, as it was then called. All of their possessions had to be packed in over a narrow and overhung trail along the river. They put in some grain, a garden and orchard. It was several years before a survey made it possible for the Riggins to file homestead papers.

They lived in a tent until lumber floated down from the Kelly bar flume allowed them to fashion a board shack. Fred ran cattle in the surrounding hills.

The continual stream of visitors seeking restoration of their health in the spring waters made Fred and Clara decide to build a more substantial cabin to care for the frequent guests. They skidded 30-foot timbers down the icy mountain slopes and hewed them with broadaxe. Rafters were obtained from a black pine stand a mile away. Timbers for inside partitions were salvaged from the old state bridge at French Creek, which had fallen into the river. The finished house had four bedrooms upstairs for visitors.

A sawmill was constructed back against the hill. Water was brought around the hill by ditch and flume from Warm Springs Creek to turn the eight-foot undershot wheel. It cut lumber for a barn, sheds, and a bridge.

Produce from the garden could be packed up the Allison Creek trail to Buffalo Hump (a five-day round trip) or up French Creek to Warren's diggings.

In 1917, Riggins borrowed money to buy 700 sheep which he brought across the mountains south of his place. The next spring he sold them for a $7000 profit, but had to deliver them on the north side of the river. He managed this by stringing a cable across the river from the gable of his barn, and sending the sheep over in a carrier, seven head at a time.

Fred ran a ferry at the mouth of Allison Creek in 1914-1915, but high water washed it out. He felt it was imperative to build an all-season bridge. He arranged for Cap Guleke to bring a cable down from Bear Creek that had been used at the Marshall Mountain mines. Guleke missed the landing at Bear Creek and thereby delayed delivery for months. He charged 25 cents a foot to transport 2000 feet of cable. Pieces of 24-foot steel and additional cable were packed from the settlement of Riggins.

The completed bridge was 316 feet long and 6½ feet wide. It opened in 1919 and 1500 sheep crossed immediately — without charge. In order to get a permit from the Forest Service to build the bridge, no charge could be made for the traffic. Fred did get $2000 from the owners for his hay and $500 for pasture.

245

The Riggins sold out to George Behean and Fred Dennison in June, 1919. They used the place as one of several cattle ranches they were operating, until they went belly-up a couple of years later. The cabin remained, as a haven for gamblers and moonshiners.

In April of 1935, the CCC men replaced the pack trail to the springs with a passable road. When Andy and Helen Casner took over the springs in the Thirties, it was largely a cattail swamp. They incorporated a business and sold shares to people in the area who supported their efforts to maintain the springs as a community asset. The Casners built a hotel, cottages, and a large bathhouse. The charge for bathing was a dollar a day.

In 1943-44 the Forest Service and the county rebuilt the bridge. A boulder fell and broke one of the cables in 1954. The Forest Service completed the present bridge three years later.

When Mrs. Casner sold the springs, the buyer called in the outstanding shares at a fraction of their par value. It was resold at a later date and is now a private residence. The bridge simply gives access to a trail which goes to the top of the ridge.

Mile 316.9: **Ruby Rapid** takes its name from the industrial-grade garnets that can be found in the bank above the road, alongside the rapid. In high water (65,000 c.f.s.) Ruby Rapid ranks among the half-dozen worst rapids on the river.

The first draw on the left side of the river at the tail end of the rapid is Devil's Slide. The draw immediately below the slide had a rock house which was home for James Clayton in the late Twenties. He herded sheep during the summer and trapped and mined through the winter. A boat allowed him to cross the river. Jim was a talented artist, doing superb renderings of wildlife and scenery on gun stocks and pack boxes. A flood washed away most of the house.

Mile 318: **Lake Creek and Rapid.**

A homestead up the creek was proved by Fred and Earl Hinkley, and Charley Komack located on the land at the mouth of the stream. Komack had a house, barn, and orchard.

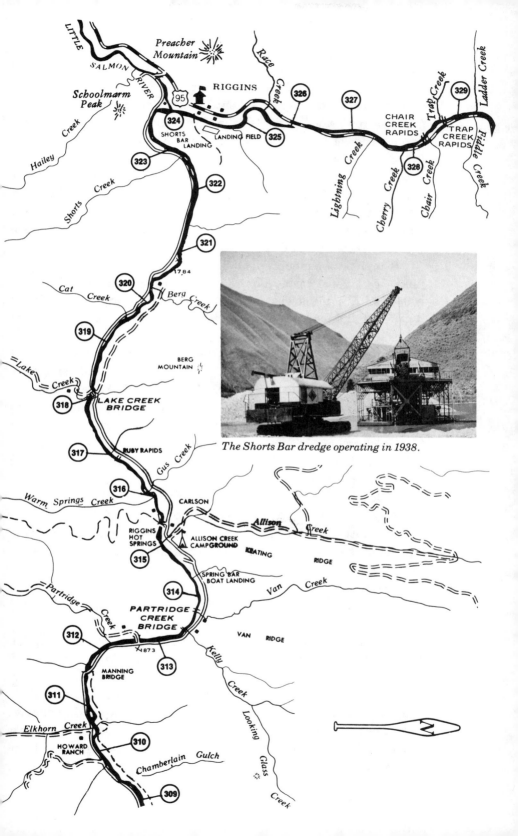

LITTLE

SALMON RIVER

Preacher Mountain

RIGGINS

95

Race Creek

326

327

Ladder Creek

329

CHAIR CREEK RAPIDS

Trap Creek

324

325

SHORTS BAR LANDING

LANDING FIELD

TRAP CREEK RAPIDS

Fiddle Creek

328

Schoolmarm Peak

Hailey Creek

323

322

Lightning Creek

Cherry Creek

Chair Creek

Shorts Creek

Cat Creek

320

321

1784

Berg Creek

319

BERG MOUNTAIN

Lake Creek

318

LAKE CREEK BRIDGE

317

RUBY RAPIDS

Gus Creek

The Shorts Bar dredge operating in 1938.

316

Warm Springs Creek

CARLSON

Allison Creek

RIGGINS HOT SPRINGS

ALLISON CREEK CAMPGROUND

KEATING

RIDGE

315

SPRING BAR BOAT LANDING

314

Van Creek

PARTRIDGE CREEK BRIDGE

Partridge Creek

312

VAN RIDGE

Kelly Creek

MANNING BRIDGE

1873

313

311

Elkhorn Creek

Looking Glass Creek

HOWARD RANCH

310

Chamberlain Gulch

309

N

Louis Howard floated a sawmill from French Creek to Lake Creek in order to cut timber for a five mile flume. The ditch was to carry water out of Lake Creek onto Shorts Bar, where it could wash gold bearing gravel deposits. The plan was financed by R.E. Lockwood, owner of the Weiser Signal, but it never worked because the flume grade was erroneously surveyed.

There are seven lakes about six miles up Lake Creek. Three are named for the Carreys: John, Gay, and Mary. They packed the first trout to the lakes for the Fish and Game Department. Piper Lake honors Ira Piper, a sheepherder. The road four miles up Lake Creek was constructed by CCC men.

The slope of a mountain on the edge of a lake up the west fork of Lake Creek came down into the lake during the summer of 1964. A wall of water came down the drainage ruining buildings and fields as it came. It dammed the river and washed out the north abutment of the bridge.

The present severity of Lake Creek Rapid is a memento.

Mile 316: **Gus Creek** on the right. Gus Keating lived here before he homesteaded on Keating Ridge, which parallels Allison Creek.

Fritz Music was a German miner who lived up Allison Creek for 15 years and then moved to the mouth of Gus Creek. He lived in a Chinese rock house and wore stove pipes on his legs when he walked to Riggins, in order the frustrate the numerous rattlesnakes. Music Bar wears his name.

Mile 320.4: **Berg Ranch and Creek** on the right.

August Berg was born in Germany, September 5, 1833 and came to this country with his parents when he was eighteen. He sought his fortune in the California gold rush, then the Florence boom, before drifting down to the shores of Salmon River in 1864.

Berg's place was on the downstream side of the creek. He ran a small store there, did some placer mining, and started a herd of beef cattle.

In the spring of 1871, Berg hired a Chinese cook as a helper. He dismissed the man when fall round-up was over. August may have kept considerable money on his place because the closest bank was in Lewiston. The Chinese returned while Berg was sitting at his desk and attacked him with a hatchet. Berg's dog drove the assailant away.

Severe lacerations on his head, hands and shoulders resulted in a two day delay before the storekeeper could make his way to William Allison's place up-river.

Word of the attack spread to Florence and a party was formed to pursue the Chinese. He was caught on the trail to Warren and hung from the French Creek bridge.

Berg married Margaret Kettmer-Gotzinger in 1884; she had four children by her prior marriage and two by August. In 1903 she passed away, and she may be buried on the ranch.

Margaret and August Berg on their wedding day.

Three years later, August scratched his hand while cutting meat and developed blood poisoning. His hand was amputated in White Bird, then his arm, but he didn't recover.

After his death, the several hundred cattle were sold, and Charley Clay bought the ranch for sheep range. The succeeding owner was Scott Brundage, for whom Brundage Mountain is named.

Gus Carlson acquired the ranch and has worked it for over 40 years.

Mile 322.1: On the left side of the road, just east of the cattle guard, is a small cross made from pipe. It marks the grave of two CCC boys who were killed when their truck went off into the river. Ben Turpin was the driver.

Mile 322.8: **Shorts Creek and Shorts Bar** on the left.

William H. Short left the snakeskin of place after place before settling along the River of No Return. Born in Massachusetts in 1833, he received a good education and learned the trade of ship carpenter. Between 1853 and 1879, he crossed the Isthmus of Panama to the California goldfields, mined in Oregon, Warren and Florence, British Columbia, Sitka, Victoria, Portland, and Santa Barbara.

In the fall of 1879, he came down to the Salmon from Florence and bought the mining claims on the bar that bears his name. Evidence of the hydraulic mining that occurred is still obvious.

The Curtis family worked for Bill Short at times, and in 1893 he married Samantha Curtis. They raised three girls. Short sold the 160 acres to R. E. Lockwood and moved to southern Oregon. After he died there, Samantha returned to Riggins and married Artie Hollenbeak, who pioneered on Little White Bird Ridge.

Lockwood took possession of Shorts Bar in 1906, but as mentioned earlier, his scheme to bring water from Lake Creek didn't pan out. He was killed as he was leaving the place, when he accidentally discharged a .45-caliber pistol.

Guy Kimbrough and Scott Brundage grazed the area with sheep. Guy drowned while fording the river on horseback. Brundage sold the land to Tom Carrey in 1925.

Tom resold it to J. Mason Kerr, grandson of the fruit jar manufacturer. A year later, Kerr was murdered in the barn on the bar by a drunken ranchhand.

The place reverted to the Carrey family. A dredge boat from Sacramento worked the bar from 1935 to 1938. The dredge operation was profitable at the time. It employed about 20 men on two shifts.

John and Pearl Carrey obtained the last homestead in Idaho in 1939, at Shorts Bar. The Carreys ran sheep on the claims until 1943, when they sold it to Bruce and Helen Walters. The Walters family has retained title.

Early days at Shorts Bar. Bill and Samantha Short and their two daughters, who were living in the house *at the time, can be seen in the center of the photograph.*

Mile 324: **Little Salmon River** joins the Salmon from the left. This river drains Meadows Valley (once known as Salmon Meadows) 40 miles to the south. The Indians called the river Mulpah. Salmon come up the tributary to the Rapid River hatchery.

The first house in Riggins, Idaho, 1893. Left to right: W. H. H. Palm, school teacher, the Irwin boys: Noah, Ike, and Dick, Issac and Mary Irwin, seated. When a better house was built, the inside partitions were removed and it served as a dance hall for a time. It was here that the epic Levander-Maull fight occurred, which caused the community to be known briefly as "Gouge-Eye."

On the Road Again: Riggins to White Bird

Mile 324.5: **Riggins.** The bar was used as a camping area by Nez Perce Indians: Yellow Bull, Little White Bird, Black Elk.

In 1863, Mike Deasy stopped on the bar long enough to find traces of gold on the north end. He went on to mine at Florence and Warren, but returned a few years later to placer, while he wintered his horses on the bar. Deasy's claim was traded in 1893 to Isaac and Mary Irwin for two horses and a gold watch. Irwin moved his family of five boys down from Meadows Valley, and they built the first house on the bar. Issac was a member of the initial state legislature in Boise.

Charley Clay and his brothers, John and Bud, moved to the bar from Palouse country. For three years they worked on a ditch that would bring water from Squaw Creek to the bar so they could mine and irrigate.

Noah, Dick, and Ike Irwin and Charley Clay took homesteads on the bar. Dick and Charley donated land for the second school in 1894. Classes were attended by 14 students taught by W.H. Palm from Meadows. The second school was located where the Idaho Bank and Trust building now stands.

The C.C.C. camp in 1934, which occupied the site where the Riggin's sawmill is now located.

253

The Riggins school in 1896 — Big Rock District #31. Far left, with book, Dick Irwin. Back row, left to right: Ernest Carothers, Homer Levander, Noah Irwin, Minnie Reeves, Maggie Clay, Ike Irwin. Front row, left to right: Frank Reeves, Virgil Levander, Pearl Gage, Leslie Levander, Carrabelle Clay, Frank Carothers, Harry Clay, George Irwin, W. H. Palm, teacher (standing), and Charley Clay (holding horse).

Riggins post office and store in 1925, with Johnny Clay at the door.

Gay, Mary and John Carrey on their way to the Riggins school in 1927, having crossed Charley Clay's bridge over the Salmon River. Shearing shed, barn and corrals can be seen in the background.

At that time, the trail to the bar came up the east bank as far as Lightning Creek, where John Riggins, a native of Missouri and a blacksmith by trade, ran a ferry. The trail on the west side of the river at the ferry dock went up along the shoulder of the mountain and then dropped down to the mouth of Race Creek at the north end of later Riggins.

John Riggins had the mail delivery contract in 1893 from Grangeville south to Meadows. He traveled with a three-seated buggy to Fiddle Creek, then proceeded on horseback.

John's son, Richard, moved to the bar in March, 1901, with his wife Ethel. Dick Riggins had spent two years at the University of Idaho studying civil engineering, then worked as a stage driver, farmer, and freighter before settling on the location that was to bear his name.

The wagon road was pushed up-river along the east bank, until in 1902 it was opposite the mouth of Race Creek. Edgar Levander had installed a new ferry at that point.

John Riggins then moved his blacksmith shop and ferry up-river to the bar. Charley Clay persuaded a railroad survey crew that came down the Salmon to survey a townsite on Noah Irwin's homestead. Dick Riggins served as the town's first postmaster. His name was suggested for the town by the Post Office Department because the names offered by local people were duplicated in almost every state. Until that time, Riggins had been known as Gouge-Eye, Clay and Irwin Bar.

Main Street, Riggins, 1904. There are six Clays and six Irwins in the photograph, explaining why the area was often called Clay or Irwin Bar.

Ed Otto built a saloon. George Curtis moved his mercantile business from Lucile. Dick Riggins built a hotel, blacksmith shop, and feed barn.

James Aitken bought squatters rights to the ranch at the mouth of Squaw Creek from Loren Gruell in 1903. He and his wife raised five children there. He served on the school board, edited the literary society's paper, and wrote poetry. His son, Stewart, has lived and worked at the ranch all his life.

In 1912, a steel bridge was built across the river at the north end of town. This meant the ferry could be moved to the site now occupied by Bruce Oake's boat shop. It facilitated the transfer of horses and supplies to Charley Clay's shearing shed on the bar across the river. Three years later, Clay built a cable bridge to the bar so that livestock could be crossed with ease.

Hotels, homes, stores, and churches gradually filled the bar. Riggins is still the center of a livestock industry; but it is also a modern community with accommodations and services for tourists interested in the river and its backcountry.

Schoolmarm Peak, on the east side of the river, by the confluence with the Little Salmon, takes its name from the traditional spring class outings which hiked to the top of the 3500 foot mountain. Preacher Mountain, 4645 feet, on the west side of the town, is named for Mr. and Mrs. Hess and their twin boys who homesteaded the peak.

Mile 325.5: **Race Creek** comes in on the left.

John Goff built a house at the mouth of Race Creek in 1871. The rock remnants of his cabin can still be seen to the right of the road, just after it starts up the creek. The stream is named for Patrick Race Hickey, who was a miner and packer in Florence, and settled on the creek at an early date, with his partner, McLee.

They brought their horses down for the winter, then built a log house and traded the string to Mr. Thorp for cattle. By 1880, Hickey and McLee had a sizeable operation. Then McLee went head over tin-cups off Salmon Point, 300 feet to the river. Though the fall didn't kill him, he was crippled for life.

Hickey held the business together despite their problems. His brand was 33 and some fellows on the adjoining range started borrowing his cows without asking and the brand became 88. The men were brought to trial in January, 1897, at Mount Idaho. Race was called as a witness, but during the trial he developed pneumonia, which proved fatal.

John and Sarah Levander moved to the mouth of Race Creek in 1894, from Meadows Valley. John was born in Sweden; Sarah Cox was from Missouri. Mr. Levander had worked as a bookkeeper, miner, freighter, and rancher. He built a hotel-store, blacksmith shop, and feed barn, planted hay and vegetables in the clearings up the creek, and began operating a way station on the route from Grangeville to Thunder Mountain, known as Goff. His son, Edgar, built a ferry and ferry house about a mile south of the station.

The Levander children at the Goff ferry house. The wagon in the right hand corner was left by a miner bound for the Florence gold rush, because there was no road.

The Levanders had four children. Goff became a post office and the turn-around point for mail stages coming from the north and south. As John and Sarah grew older, they moved farther up the creek, and continued to raise hay and a garden. They are buried behind their house, which is still in use.

The Levander hotel stands to the left of the road up Race Creek, just above the mouth. Tony Seyfried was working at the Keys Ranch on French Creek and met Bessie Soards there. They moved to the Levander's hotel about 1912 and the residence is still in the family. The range up Race Creek is where Hickey and McLee ran their cattle. Tom Pogue operated a productive sawmill a few miles up the stream, as did Dick Irwin and Julius Pipes.

The Goff ferry, just north of downtown Riggins. The men are tentatively identified as John Clay I and Scott Stone, father of western movie actor, Jack Hoxie.

Mile 326.7: If one looks at the slope on the left side of the river, he can see the traces of the old trail which came up-river from the ferry crossing at Lightning Creek.

Edith Ingram, granddaughter of John Levander, wrote her recollection of traveling that trail in 1898; they were going to Goff where her father built the ferry.

I must have been about six years old, at least I was old enough to recall the last part of the journey very well.

Mother rode her side-saddle, my brother Roy rode in front of her, on her lap. Roy was about two and mother was pregnant with my sister Hazel.

My sister Edna and I were buckled into alforjas — or saddle bags — one on each side hooked over a pack saddle which was on Old Beans, a horse with small spots on the pot-bellied portion of his anatomy. Following came a pack horse with the chickens, which were placed in coal oil boxes with slats nailed over the top. I do not remember how many pack horses there were in all, but at the end of the train was father and our brown water spaniel, Bryan.

On the last leg of our journey, we followed a trail that left the river's edge and climbed the mountain side to a section known as High Trail; outside was a sheer drop to the raging Salmon.

There was just enough room on the steep trail for a horse with a pack. As the animal carrying the cargo of chickens rounded a sharp turn, the slats on the inside box caught on the rocks and were torn off. The frightened hens flew out of the box, some clung to the mountainside and others flew off into space and landed in the waters far below.

Edna and I, being typical children, were very frightened, and began crying, which of course did not help the situation in the least. We were hot and tired, cramped in the saddle bags and seeing our hens, who were dear to us, falling helplessly into the river was a sad thing indeed!

Mother came to a wide place in the trail where it crossed a gully. Shaking, crying and completely exhausted, she climbed off her horse. I can imagine the fear she felt for her two little girls.

Papa made his way past the horses to where mama was and taking her in his arms, talked to her until she was finally able to once again climb on her horse and continue.

260

The remainder of the move is forgotten, but I remember father and I went back to the scene of the mishap the following morning and caught some of the hens who had made their way to a more level spot on the mountain side.

Mile 327.3: **Lightning Creek** runs in on the right. Until about 1902, this site was the end of the wagon road from Mount Idaho and Grangeville. The trail forked here, with one prong going to Florence, the other to John Riggin's ferry, about 300 yards up-river from the mouth of the creek.

Mile 328.4: **Chair Creek** flows down from the right. The stream is named for an old-timer who built himself a comfortable chair where he could sit and wait for the mail stage.

Chair Creek Rapid has a rock on the right and a hole on the left in lower flows.

Mile 328.8: **Trap Creek Rapid.** Worth scouting from the beach on the left.

Mile 329.3: **Fiddle Creek** enters on the right.

Fiddle Dick Martin raised thoroughbreds on his ranch just above the mouth of the stream, on the down-river side. Martin was in demand as a fiddler at all the dances in the area.

The ranch was acquired by Tom Pogue of White Bird, who put in a two-mile ditch and flume from the creek in order to raise excellent hay crops. He slid his hay downhill into a barn on the flat above the road.

Fiddle Creek Rapid is a difficult run on high or low flows — lots of boulders.

Mile 329.6: **Clarks Creek** on the left. Named for the Henry Clark family, early settlers with six children.

Mile 331: **Carver Creek** on the right. It is a spring, rather than a creek, and is overgrown with blackberries. Richard Devine's place was located on the flat above the river and below the road. He was the first victim of the Nez Perce War. Several competent books have been written about the events of that conflict and it is not the purpose of this guide to repeat them. Only the most concise explanation of actions which occurred on sites adjacent to the river will be attempted, and the reader should refer to the bibliography for a complete view of the war.

Richard Devine was a retired sailor and was not considered a friend of the Indians. The Nez Perce were moving to the reservation at Lapwai. Someone taunted a young Indian named Shore Crossing for never having avenged the murder of his father by a white man. He came to Devine's place on the afternoon of June 12th or 13th with two young relatives: Red Moccasin Tops and Swan Necklace. They murdered Devine, possibly with his own rifle. He is buried alongside the old pack trail, about a hundred yards up-river, at the edge of the clearing above the road.

After the war, Amos Carver, a miner in Warren for 15 years, took up Devine's place, mined and raised cattle. He lived there for 30 years. George Curtis ran a store on the south end of the bar and Carver Creek was a mail stop, as well. When Amos died, his estate was sold to Tom Pogue, who annexed the acreage to the Fiddle Creek ranch.

Charles Sullivan driving the Meadows Valley-Grangeville stage in 1914.

Mile 331.5: **Crawford Creek** on the right contains a small waterfall. An elderly German immigrant, Henry Ricke, lived at this location for three decades. His flat is above the river, but west of the road, and can be identified by the solitary weeping willow tree on the bank. Ricke worked mining claims and planted a large orchard of English walnuts. The trees provided him with an income until the new highway was built. It affected his water table and the trees died. Henry had to leave then, and he passed away in the Cottonwood hospital, a suicide.

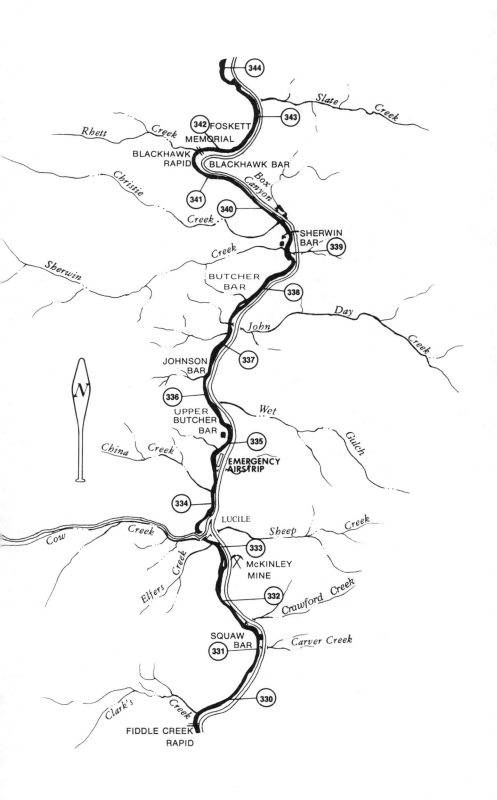

Bailey and Emma Rice homesteaded Crawford Creek and raised a family of eight children. Their place was on a bench above the highway.

Evidence of mining tunnels can be seen across the river. The placer ore was wheelbarrowed to ore chutes where it could be washed with river water. Tailing piles from placer mining activities can be detected on almost every bar on both sides of the river from this point to White Bird. The highway has obliterated a lot of the claims worked along the eastern side of the river. An item in the *Idaho County Free Press,* April, 1895, says over 100 men were rocking for gold along the river from John Day to White Bird.

Mile 331.5: **Elfers Creek** comes in from the left. The name honors the memory of Henry Elfers II and his wife, Capitala, who lived here. It was Henry's father who was killed at the start of the Nez Perce War on John Day Creek.

Mile 333.3: **Lucile Bridge.** Put in by the Forest Service in 1937. A rough road goes up Cow Creek and down to Kirkwood Bar on the Snake River.

The town of Lucile, on the east side of the river, was named for the daughter of Judge James Ailshie. His influence was helpful in getting a post office for the miners at Lucile in 1896. Lucile was a center of mining activity until 1939; it supplied the McKinley quartz-gold mine up Sheep Gulch, and the Blue Jacket and Crooks Corral mine on the Snake River side. The town was also the focus of some fierce early sheep versus cattle feuds.

Mile 333.4: **Cow Creek** pours out on the left. The Sewell, Elfer, Baker, and Callison families were early settlers on the creek.

Mile 334-335: **China Creek and Butcher Bar** on the left. Eben Butcher was a miner at Thunder Mountain who came to the bar in 1890, and bought up Mr. Crandall's claims at the mouth of China Creek. Eben married Anna and they raised five daughters and a son on the bar, which they homesteaded. The bar extends downstream almost a mile. The Butchers placered it with water diverted from China Creek and did well enough for their efforts.

Twilegar Bar is the flat on the right side of the river, below the road. Frank and Ruth Twilegar cared for their family of 12 children on this piece of ground. They mined and ran cattle. Frank was killed June 15, 1917, while riding for cattle in the high country up Fiddle Creek. He was dragged to death by his horse. He and his wife are buried in the John Day cemetery. Their place is now occupied by the state highway maintenance building.

Mile 335.7: **Wet Gulch,** on the right, is not visible from the river. Settlers came to the large boulder bar on the right side of the river to gather their winter wood from the drift piles left by high water.

Wet Gulch was the home of Ed and Laura Clark for 30 years. Mrs. Clark is one of the dozen Twilegar children, and at this time still lives up the gulch. She taught school in Riggins, as did her daughter.

Mile 335.9: The remains of a Chinese rock house can be seen on the bank a few feet above the road. The man living in this house operated the John Day ferry. The ferry was installed in February of 1889. In April of 1890, it capsized, drowning 25 cattle. Ferry Bar was the flat across the river.

Mile 337.3: **John Day Creek** is the sizeable stream which flows in on the right. John Day, a freighter and miner, camped at the mouth of the creek in 1862. Henry Elfers followed Day's residency on the stream in 1863, but he and his hired hands, Harry Beckroge and Robert Bland, were killed while working in the hay field by the same Indians who murdered Devine. They took a horse, rifles, and ammunition from Elfers' cabin, but didn't bother his wife and children.

Henry Elfers I.

265

Aerial view of the John Day Ranch, looking north, down river.

Mrs. Elfers later married Phil Cleary and they continued to raise cattle and horses on the ranch. The John Day Ranch became a stopping place for freighters, packers, and miners. There was a post office, as well as a school taught by Mrs. Walsh.

Kitty Elfers-Gordon lived in a house on the downstream side of the mouth of Day Creek all her life. For a hundred years, the ranch has descended through the Elfers' family. Many of the Elfers are buried in the John Day cemetery, on a knoll overlooking the creek.

A remarkable four-foot square redwood and tin flume carried water out of John Day Creek for several miles before irrigating row crops on the 160-acre flat above the creek's mouth. Herb Brown replaced the flume with a siphon pipeline.

The historic John Day hostelry burned in 1928.

About a mile up the creek was the site chosen by Henrietta Deasy, wife of the first locater on Riggins Bar, to settle and raise her family of five boys. Mike Deasy died in 1889; Mrs. Deasy married his cousin, who was also named Michael, and moved to Idaho in 1882. The next place above is known as the Loomis place, because Al Loomis raised sheep there for many years, until he was killed in a truck accident.

The Elbert Rhett Ranch was two and a half miles up the creek. He was one of the sons of William Rhett, mentioned at Rhett Creek. Elbert and Minerva Rhett ranched the site for years, raising cattle, and later sheep. They had three sons: Henry, Robert, and Homer.

They left their place to Homer, who, with his wife Mary, built a capacious home there, while ranging several hundred head of cattle, haying the John Day Ranch, and keeping an impressive garden. Homer also worked as a hunting and fishing outfitter and guide on the Salmon River at the Crofoot, Whitewater, and Shepp ranches. When the Homer Rhetts sold their place on John Day Creek, they moved to a new ranch on the Clearwater.

Mile 339: **Sherwin Bar-Gill Ranch.** The bar runs for almost a mile along the left side of the river. Ed Sherwin was among the first miners to arrive at the Warren boom. He promptly opened a blacksmith shop, sharpening picks and other tools for the 700 prospectors. He labored at his trade for seven years, saving his money so that he could bring his family over from Germany. When they arrived, he settled with them on the bar by the river. They mined the location with water from Sherwin Creek.

The Gill brothers, Clark and Robert, were next to take possession of the bar. They homesteaded the place, irrigated the arable ground, raised hay and cattle. They built a ferry boat which could carry a four-horse team and wagon. It operated at the lower end of the bar.

Clark was married to Dolly Cain. Her two brothers, Leonard and Charles, young men at the time, drowned in the river on Christmas, 1916, while crossing at the island to visit her.

Clark Gill lived to be 102, and was still heel roping calves from his horse at the age of 100. He died in 1975, and is remembered with affection by all who knew him.

Clark and Dolly Gill at their ranch.

Looking up-river toward the Gill Ranch from the head of Box Canyon. The road on the left became Highway 95 and was routed across the middle of the island.

Dick Carter's dog, Old Mack, at the Gill Ranch.

Black Hawk Bar view of Slate Creek as it looked in 1909.

Mile 339.5: **Christie Creek** on the left. Charlie Christie was a miner and store keeper at Slate Creek. He sold his business to Josh Fockler, and died in September, 1893, while walking down the street in Grangeville.

Mile 341: **Blackhawk Bar and Rapid.** This area is known as the Box Canyon. The bar on the left is named for the Blackhawk placer mine. The rapid is considered the most difficult for jet boats of all the whitewater below Riggins. It should be scouted.

Mile 341.7: **Rhett Creek** on the left. William Rhett — the only man on Salmon River to have *two* creeks named for him.

Mile 342: **The Foskett Memorial,** on the east side of the river, at the edge of the highway. Doctor Wilson A. Foskett was born in Warsaw, New York, in January of 1870. He graduated from Rush Medical College in Chicago and began a practice in 1897 at White Bird. There he met Loura Taylor, whom he married in 1903, and they had three children.

If ever any man was his brother's brother, it was Doc Foskett. For 27 years, he traveled over Camas Prairie and along Salmon River answering calls from the sick and injured, on foot, horseback, in horse and buggy, and finally car. The nearest hospital was in Lewiston, so he pulled teeth, set bones, delivered babies, and performed operations under conditions contemporary doctors would find intolerable.

Doc's courage, patience, and indefatigability earned the love and respect of everyone in Salmon River country. He made four 30-mile round trips from White Bird to Large Bar to treat Sam Large. When Sam asked Foskett what he owed, Doc said, "Well Sam, I just about have to charge you $20." Sam pulled two $20 gold pieces from his pocket and pressed them on the doctor, knowing it wasn't nearly enough.

April 13, 1924, Doc Foskett spent the day caring for his livestock. He went to bed tired and late. He was summoned from sleep with a call to help a rancher's wife in childbirth at Riggins. Doc was up all night. He headed home, and refused to rest in Lucile because he was concerned about a young, expectant mother. Coming around the last curve in the Box Canyon, he fell asleep at the wheel and went off into the Salmon River. He was found the next morning.

The whole country was stunned by his death. River and prairie people gathered to pay their last respects; they had lost more than a doctor, they'd lost a friend. A memorial was erected and when the highway was widened, a new monument was placed at the present location.

The time is over 50 years away, but Doc Foskett's memory shines like a famous poem. In the words of a pioneer western eulogy: *He did his damndest, angels could do no more.*

Volunteers pulling Doc Foskett's car back onto the road the morning after he was killed.

Mile 343.3: **Slate Creek** flows in on the right. The community of Slate Creek or Freedom was established in 1861 and owes its name to early miners who discovered that the creek had no placer gravel.

Pack trains and cattle were wintered at Slate Creek by men such as the Thorp brothers and Jack Splawn, waiting for spring so they could transport meat and supplies to Florence.

According to the *Illustrated History of North Idaho,* land at the mouth of Slate Creek was bought by Charles Silverman in 1861 from an Indian, Captain John.

Silverman's house is believed to have been one of the first on Salmon River. The *History* also reads that John Wood bought the place in the spring of 1862, paying a thousand dollars to Silverman and Captain John. While the sum exceeded the value to an inordinate degree, he thereby acquired the lasting friendship of the Indians.

Mr. and Mrs. Wood sold their land on the downstream side of Slate Creek to Charley Cone in 1874. Cone opened a way station. Until 1884, the Woods kept their station. Josh Fockler, a miner from Florence, opened a store at the creek with Charles Wood.

At the beginning of the Nez Perce War, Shore Crossing, Red Mocassin Tops, and Swan Necklace encountered Charley Cone, who spoke the Nez Perce language, near Slate Creek. He recognized Elfers' horse and asked about it. They informed him of the killings and told him to warn the Slate Creek people, who had always treated them fairly, to stay home so they wouldn't be shot by Wallowa Indians who didn't know them.

Cone gave the alarm and about 30 families gathered at the Slate Creek post office. A trench was dug around a stone structure, and logs were set on-end in it, forming a stockade. Because they were unable to spare any men and were short of arms, a Nez Perce woman, Tolo, made a night ride to solicit aid from the miners in Florence. A party of 25 came to the fort. Fockler and Woods distributed $2000 worth of goods from their store.

After the battle of White Bird, the Indians appeared in force at Slate Creek, but never attacked the stockade. Several times they came under a flag of truce to settle their accounts at the store and to tell how the war was going.

After the war, Fockler and Woods were years recovering from their loss of merchandise. Tolo was the only Indian given an allotment off the reservation. She lived about two miles north of Slate Creek.

Slate Creek was used as a C.C.C. camp in the Thirties. The Slate Creek Ranger District headquarters are located on what was William Rhett's ranch. There is a massive walnut tree on the property, said to have been planted by Rhett between 1862-69.

A ditch line can be seen about a third of the way up the hill beyond Slate Creek, east of the road. It was dug by Sam Large, Sam Small, and Harry Cone in 1877 to carry water four miles north to Large Bar.

Early photo of the horse corral at Slate Creek. Marcus Mose, son of Moses Blackeagle and Tolo's daughter on the

left, Moses Blackeagle in center, Ed Robie on the right. Identifications by Ben Large.

Slate Creek about 1900. The fort was on the south end of the bridge, below the road. The state highway building now occupies the site. Logs for the fort were

brought up from the Big Eddy. The house on the north bank of the creek was home at times for John Wood, Charles Cone, Josh Fockler, and John Baker.

273

Slate Creek post office about 1914; built by Josh Fockler — it later burned. Left to right: Josh Fockler, unknown, Bailey Rice, Henry Elfers II, unknown, Ed Robie, Harry Owens, unknown, Harry Suthered, Ben Aspaugh, Deafie Reeves, unknown, John Baker, unknown. Identifications by Ben Large and Elvia Rice Fisher.

Mile 344.8: **Large Bar,** east of the road, before the bridge that crosses the river. This property was mined by the Larges and Cones for many years. Sam Large was from Dublin and his wife, Mary Porcell, came from Tipperary. They began working the claim in 1875, and raised four boys and a girl (Mamie Robie) here. A considerable quantity of gold was removed from this ground.

Ben Large was born on the homestead, and at this writing is 88 years old and still lives on the place. He has been a valuable source of history concerning this area.

From the Large homestead, the river bends to form a horseshoe. The two highway bridges allow the road to cut across the base of the shoe; the old road followed the curve.

Mile 345.5: **Sleppy Creek** on the right. According to Ben Large, who knew him, Peter Sleppy was an old-time miner who loved children. His cabin was on the downstream side of the creek, and he is probably buried there.

Tolo, who was a friend of Mary Large, lived at the mouth of the creek for some time. Tolo's daughter married a bronc rider, Moses Blackeagle. Through an act of Congress, she was granted a 160-acre homestead at Sleppy Creek. She had ten children.

Commercial mining venture at Large Bar using water that was ditched and flumed from Slate Creek.

Mile 345.9: **McKinzie Creek** comes in from the right. There is reason to believe this stream is named for Donald McKenzie (1783-1851), trapper and shareholder in Astor's Pacific Fur Company. McKenzie passed this way with his men in November, 1811, on his way to the Clearwater, Snake, and Columbia. His commander, Wilson Price Hunt, encountered problems in Hells Canyon to the west, and arrived at the mouth of the Columbia a month later than McKenzie.

McKenzie Frank Taylor, a good hand with a rope, established a ranch here, which he worked with his wife and six children.

The last rodeo at Slippy Creek, held in the fall just before World War II.

Mile 346.5: **Robber's Gulch** on the right.

Ben Large indicated the mail trail came past the mouth of the gulch. A fellow tried to hold up Mr. Atkinson when he came through with the mail, but Atkinson galloped by him, and the would-be robber ran up the gulch. A posse was formed to chase him, but he wasn't apprehended — undoubtedly because he had joined the posse.

Mile 347: Second bridge coming off the Horseshoe.

Mile 347.4: **Joe Creek** on the left. Joe Amera was a California Indian married to Tolo's sister. They lived on the Horseshoe. Fine neighbors, they were loved by everyone. Mrs. Amera made moccasins for children who were out of shoes. As a child, Edith Levander remembered: "Indian Joe used to bring us big red apples and completely won my heart. I don't recall ever seeing him get off of his horse, he said very little, just gave us our presents, turned and rode down the trail and over the hill."

The Ameras sold their rights to the Conklins, a family of musicians. The Horseshoe was farmed by the Chaneys; now it is owned by the Jim Killigore family and they have made it the most productive orchard on Salmon River.

Mile 348.5: **Wolcott Creek** on the left. Larry Ott's cabin was up this stream. Ott was, in the words of Goldsmith, "an abridgement of all that is pleasant in man." His neighbors agreed it would have been better if his mother and father had never met.

Larry weighed over 200 pounds and had shoulder-length hair. He squatted on the land with the acquiescence of old Chief Eagle Robe. When Ott began plowing up Eagle Robe's garden and the chief protested, Ott shot him. Eagle Robe was the father of Shore Crossing, and it was his murderer the three young Indians were seeking the day they killed Richard Devine. Records show that Ott took refuge in the Slate Creek stockade — his name in his own handwriting was on the roster of volunteers made up on June 30th. He was probably welcome as a pole cat at a picnic. Ott died in 1912 at White Bird.

Larry Ott: he had as many friends as an alarm clock.

Mile 348.8: Near the end of the curve, the river shelves over a diagonal shallows, which is evident enough that it can be seen from the road. This was the ford used by the Nez Perce to cross the Salmon after the battle of White Bird. They proceeded down the river and waited for Howard's troops across from White Bird Creek.

The gravel flat on the right side of the river, just up-stream from the ford, is Russell Bar. This is where Ed Robie settled with Isabella Benedict after her husband, Sam, was killed during the first days of the Nez Perce War. The bar takes its name from Robie's son-in-law, Ralph Russell.

Mile 350.1: **Campbell Flat,** on the right bank below the road. Bill Campbell lived on this bar, using water from Skookumchuck Creek for hay which he fed to cattle. Campbell died in the early Twenties, and the ranch was purchased by the Taylor brothers, Everett and Mark Evan. It was later made part of the John Day holdings by Herb Brown.

Mile 350.8: **Skookumchuck Creek** flows in on the left. This name appears as Skookum on maps as early as 1867. Skookum chuck, according to the dictionary of Chinook jargon, means strong rapid.

The pioneer families on the site were the Carnes, followed by the Reeds. Some of the Doumecq brothers lived up the creek, as did the Fosketts. Bill Jackson lived on the Painter place about 8 miles up the creek at the time of his death.

A ditch carried water from the creek south to Russell Bar.

Mile 351.8: **Deer Creek,** a sizeable drainage coming in on the left. After the Indian war, Frank Wyatt was the first cattle king on Salmon River. His cognomen was "Bow" because his bow and arrow brand was so big it could be read at a considerable distance. His holdings at one time included the Johnson and Warnock ranches on the Oregon side of Snake River, the range from Pittsburg Landing to the mouth of the Salmon on the Idaho side, and the lower Allison Ranch. At his peak, Bow was grazing 2500 head of cattle. Deer Creek was his headquarters. The Wyatts had three children.

A ditch dug with Chinese labor can be seen along the shank of the hill — it carried water from Deer Creek to Sotin Creek behind a dam, and then on to Cooper Bar.

Mile 352.6: **Sotin Creek** on the left. This stream is named for Marieyves and Izora Sotin who were the first to locate here. They had six children, three of whom lived past childhood.

Barney Rogers, an early settler up Sotin Creek, spent two years snaking logs down the mountain for his house. He and his wife, Lodicy, were on White Bird Hill, then moved to the creek. Rogers packed supplies from Sotin Creek before 1900, to Lewiston, Buffalo Hump, Warren, and Edwardsburg.

Frank Sotin and Afton Rogers, sons of these pioneers, still live on the Salmon River at this writing.

Mile 353: **Cooper Bar** on the left, first settled by Bill Gess. A. Cooper had a saloon in White Bird; he died in California. Archie Hadorn, Tom Cone, and Afton Rogers hayed the bar at times.

French Bar is across the river, above the road. Harry Mason and his married sister, Helen Walsh, ran a store here and used Chinese rock houses to warehouse their goods. Harry's brother-in-law was William Osborne who lived and mined on the bar with him. Helen had two children, the Osbornes had four — the oldest was nine years.

At the outbreak of Nez Perce hostilities, Cone got warning to Harry Mason. Mason didn't take it seriously until he learned of additional killings. Then he and his sister, Mr. and Mrs. Osborne, William George, and the six children headed for Baker's place on White Bird Creek, downriver. They only had three horses, and at the Baker place, near evening, they encountered rifle fire from Indians. They hid in the brush until the moon went down, then headed back to Mason's store because they knew they couldn't get to Mount Idaho before dawn and they needed food for the children.

Back at the store, they found the Indians had plundered the place and gone up-river. The group hurriedly gathered some food and set out to cross the river at a ford, so they could hide until darkness would allow them to travel toward Mount Idaho.

Just as they got to Osborne's cabin, Indians came into view. In the shoot-out that followed all the men were killed, and the Indians sent the women and children to the stockade at Slate Creek.

After the war, Mrs. Osborne married Thomas Clay at Warren and raised three more children at Meadows Valley.

The site of Mason's store became the second John Doumecq ranch.

The gulch across from French Bar is designated Bracket, after Charles Bracket, who had a homestead in 1902 on Sotin Creek.

Mile 353.5: **Doumecq homestead and Remington ferry.** The large bench on the left side of the river was originally occupied by Henry Moon.

John Doumecq was on the place at the same time, married to a Nez Perce woman, and raising a family and livestock. Doumecq was born in 1845, in France, and educated there. When the Indians came through in June of 1877, his wife chose to go with her tribe, taking her daughter, and leaving her son, John. Both mother and daughter were killed at the battle of Big Hole, Montana, less than two months later.

Indians raided the place, and according to young Doumecq, he and his father fled to a ridge, where they hid by a spring. They managed to cross the river on a log and eventually made their way to Lewiston. Bachalerie, Glatigny, and Christian, without guns, escaped down-river in a boat. Henry Moon and Doumecq's partner, August Bacon were killed. All of Doumecq's possessions were stolen.

After the war, John Doumecq returned to the bar. He remarried, to Helen Colemant, from Missouri. They had five boys and a girl. When Helen's sister died, they raised her daughter as well. The family ran cattle on the mesa northwest of the original homestead and it was christened "Doumecq Plains."

Helen (Colemant) and John Doumecq photographed in 1936.

After John Doumecq's death in 1902, John II took over the task of raising his step-brothers and sister on the second ranch, across the river at French Bar. He had several hundred head of cattle and almost 300 acres of hay. The bar below the road was a vineyard. The second Doumecq house, two-storied and square, has been moved above the road.

To this day, no one has an unkind word concerning John Doumecq II.

M. Glatigny returned to the Doumecq bench on the west side of the river, and built a hewed log house on the north end, with the help of William Shuck. It is now the Jim Killgore home.

The Remington ferry operated just below the Doumecq homestead. Jim Remington was related to the Remington Firearms family and displayed remarkable mechanical ingenuity. Before establishing the ferry in 1894, Jim and Cornelia had done some saw-milling and stock raising on White Bird Creek. Jim ran a blacksmith shop, forging wagon wheels, and grazed sheep above the river. Barney Rogers packed the wool by wagon team to Lewiston. Mr. Remington died in 1916, the day after Christmas.

James Remington.

The Remingtons had two sons: Ike and Virgil. Ike ran the second ferry, which operated after the White Bird bridge collapsed in 1932. He is remembered as a marvelous fiddler. Virgil was a blacksmith, like his father.

On the hillside, above the old state highway, on the right side of the river, a pipe fence can be seen next to a hackberry tree. It surrounds the graves of William Osborne, Harry Mason, Francois Chodoze, August Bacon, and Henry Moon, killed at the outbreak of the Nez Perce War. They were buried by soldiers. Charley Burlinghoff is also buried on the site, in an unmarked grave. He was shot in White Bird in a dispute over the establishment of the Deer Creek road. Charley was killed in the early 1900's, his widow was left with seven children.

The first Remington ferry, pictured in 1885 from the west side of the river. The Remington ranch can be discerned in the background.

The second Remington ferry, built in 1908 by Remington and Barney Rogers. Dace Harriman on horse, Jim Remington in front.

Mile 355.2: **Gregory Creek and Shuck Creek** on the left. Gregory Creek is named for Bill Shuck's brother-in-law.

William A. Shuck was born in Iowa in 1866, and worked his way west on ranches and cattle drives. On Salmon River he worked for Bow Wyatt and M. Glatigny on the forks between the Salmon and Snake.

He homesteaded up Shuck Creek, and in 1894, married Elizabeth Obenland. Billie built a beautifully crafted home, cleared fields for barn and livestock, fenced orchard and garden, grew berries and grapes. The ranch was their sole support for a family of five children; they traded for the necessities they couldn't produce, such as flour and clothing.

The house was destroyed by fire in 1912, and four years later Billie built an impressive, two-story lumber house above the Glatigny-Killgore house, on what is, at this time, the Warren Brown ranch. The wood came from the Richey Mill on Deer Creek. The house is still a landmark.

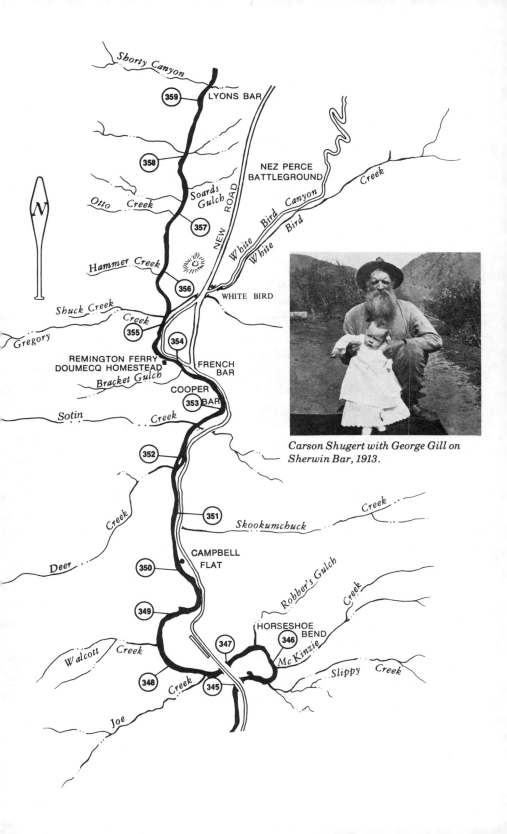

Shorty Canyon

(359) — LYONS BAR

(358)

NEZ PERCE
BATTLEGROUND

Otto   Creek

Soards
Gulch

(357)

NEW ROAD

White Bird Canyon

White Bird

Creek

Hammer Creek

(356)

WHITE BIRD

Shuck Creek

Creek

Gregory

(355)

(354)

REMINGTON FERRY
DOUMECQ HOMESTEAD

FRENCH
BAR

Bracket Gulch

COOPER
(353) BAR

Sotin

Creek

(352)

Carson Shugert with George Gill on
Sherwin Bar, 1913.

(351)

Skookumchuck

Creek

Creek

CAMPBELL
FLAT

Deer

(350)

Robber's Gulch

Creek

(349)

HORSESHOE
(346) BEND

Walcott   Creek

(347)

McKinzie

(348)

Creek

(345)

Slippy   Creek

Joe

Back in the Boat:
White Bird to Snake River

Mile 355.3: **White Bird and White Bird Creek** on the right, eponyms for a Nez Perce chief.

A.D. Chapman, with his Umatilla Indian wife, was the first settler at White Bird Creek. As early as 1863, he was offering a boat-ferry service at the river. A.D. sold a place to an elderly man, James Baker, and another, up the creek, to Jack Manuel. Samuel and Isabella Benedict had a store near the river, on the downstream side of the creek. H.C. Brown also had a store of sorts, down-river a short distance.

Fifty-seven residents of the Salmon River signed a petition to General Howard on May 7th, 1877, saying that the Nez Perce were stealing their livestock, destroying their property, frightening their families, and asked that they be restrained on a reservation. Baker and Benedict signed the request. The General read it to Chief White Bird on May 15, at the council in Lapwai. In this manner, the Indians learned who could be counted among their enemies.

To shorthand the events that occurred during the first week of the Indian war, it can be said that Sam Benedict and James Baker were killed, Jack Manuel was wounded, his wife and child were murdered, Pat Price, with Maggie Manuel, a baby, George Popham, and Isabella Benedict, with her children, were permitted to go to Mount Idaho. George Woodard and Peter Bertard may also have been killed at Baker's cabin. The Indians had obtained liquor at Benedict's and Brown's stores. Brown was wounded, but escaped with his wife in a boat across the river.

Sam and Isabella (Robie) Benedict.

The White Bird Battle Ground is located about three miles up the creek. At dawn, June 17th, 1877, "F" and "H" Companies of the First Cavalry, consisting of 99 cavalrymen, advanced down the canyon, where they were resisted by 60 Nez Perce warriors. The Indians routed Perry's soldiers, killing a third of his command. The Nez Perce suffered no losses. The site is now part of the Nez Perce National Historical Park.

Early-day White Bird. The first battle of the Nez Perce War took place in the canyon above the town.

The town of White Bird began to form in 1891, when S. S. Fenn established a stage station and hotel. The Fenn brothers opened the first post office. Within a few years there were three more hotels, a blacksmith shop, livery stable, grain warehouse, meat market, barbershop, and a two-room schoolhouse. A. Cooper ran a store-saloon that had a chalk line drawn across the floor — children were not allowed to cross it.

George W. Curtis established a ferry at the mouth of White Bird Creek in 1892. Six years later he sold it to his son, A. Fred Curtis, and moved his store to Riggins.

Main street of White Bird, early days.

Fourth of July horse race in White Bird.

Mile 355.6: Cement piers for the old White Bird bridge are visible on each side of the river. The pillar on the right shore still stands, while the left one has tumbled into the water. The steel bridge collapsed on the morning of August 11, 1932. R. H. Otto was crossing a dozen head of cattle and some of them suffered broken legs.

When C. Ben Ross was running for governor, he made a campaign speech in White Bird, promising to repair the bridge. Ross was elected, but a politician's promise isn't worth a Dixie dollar. The old State Highway 95 came past the broken span, and for years a sign faced the road with the message: "The Bridge That Ross Built."

The old White Bird bridge after it collapsed in 1932. Newt Otto was crossing George Lynch's cattle to White . Bird at the time. He and his daughter,   *Florence, who was on horseback, escaped without injury. Kilgore house is in the background.*

Mile 357: **Otto Creek** enters on the left. Named for Newt Otto, early cattle rancher.

This was the location of the Lyons ferry. It was operated by the Charley Lyons family for many years, serving the people of Doumecq and Joseph Plains.

Mile 357.4: **Soards Gulch** on the right. Henry Soards had a cabin on the bank, just up-stream from the gulch. He grazed a small band of sheep. The animals were as welcome on cattle range as a rattlesnake in a cowboy's boot. One night a can of black powder was placed on Soard's doorstep. Rifle bullets were used to set it off. Henry's body, with his two dogs, was found beneath the rubble. Nearly 150 cartridges were scattered around the area. There should have been numerous cattlemen with saddle-sore consciences over this incident — many of them were ranching with sheep only a few years later.

Soard's wife and three children moved to the mouth of French Creek, east of Riggins.

Mile 359.8: **McCulley Creek** on the left. Homer and Helen McCulley had a ranch on the head of the creek. They raised 12 children. Their 11 boys served in the first World War, which may well be a record.

Mile 360: **Big Foot Island.**

Mile 360.8: **Wildcat Creek** comes in on the left.

Mile 361.2: **Lee Creek** on the right.

Mile 362.2: **Sharkey Creek,** left side.

Mile 362.4: **Lightning Creek** enters on the right.

Mile 363: **Short's Bar II.** On the right is a small cabin. Green Canyon begins just below this campsite. Pealy Castle occupied the flat above the bar.

Mile 363.3: **Sheep Creek** flows in on the right.

Mile 365: **Hells Gate Creek** drainage on the left.

Mile 365.9: **Pine Bar and Pine Bar Rapids.** The large sand bar on the right marks the end of Green Canyon.

On the upper flat, between the road and the river, is a grave marked by the B.L.M. It is that of young Spedden, who drowned in 1906. He was helping Frank Wyatt and Burt Canfield swim cattle across the river. When they broke back, Spedden rode in to turn them. Somehow his horse failed him. His fiancee, Lottie Canfield, was watching from the shore.

The rapid can be scouted from the right bank.

Mile 367.6: **Gill Gulch** on the right bank. The land along this side of the river, from Gill Gulch back up to Pine Bar, was included in Joe Lamon Robert's 1923 520-acre homestead. He packed lumber from Rocky Canyon for his cabin, a quarter mile above the river.

His father, Alex Roberts, homesteaded the ground in 1910, from Gill Gulch down to Rock or Graves Creek and up the creek for half a nile, and extended it under the Taylor Grazing Act, to 640 acres.

Mile 369.4.8: **Graves Creek-Rock Creek-Rocky Canyon,** running in on the right.

The old Boise Trail, which passed east of the Seven Devils, forded the river at this point and went up Rocky Canyon to the Camas Prairie. It was used extensively in the 1800's. Mr. Glatigny, who later resided on the Doumecq place, kept a store in 1861 at the mouth of the canyon.

In 1911, Alex and Bertha Roberts' homestead encompassed the and along Salmon River from half a mile up Rocky Canyon over to Gill Gulch.

Earlier, the Roberts had filed a homestead on Captain John Creek, but a flash flood came down the canyon and carried off their house, barn, cow and calf, and their hay crop, along with all the topsoil. They were lucky to escape with their lives.

They relinquished that claim and filed a few years later on the Graves Creek site.

In the winter of 1908-'09, George Burgund, who had a placer claim at the mouth of the creek, and Ed Taylor, who owned Cooper Bar across the river from Burgund's claim, built a road with pick and shovel down Rocky Canyon to the river.

The Roberts raised cattle on their homestead. The county improved the road in 1921, and Alex bought a car to use in the canyon. In 1935, he granted the right of way for a W.P.A. project which would link the water grade road from Lewiston to the city of Salmon. A road camp was established at the Roberts' ranch in the canyon. The effort was abandoned when the road reached as far as Pine Bar. Roberts was given the camp buildings on his ranch. He and Bertha lived in the structures, and friends and visitors used the camp site for picnics.

But another flood visited their second ranch. In the spring of 1948, a wall of water came down the canyon like Grant through the Cumberland Gap. As the Roberts waded to the hillside through waist-deep water, their buildings and park were carried away. Alex was 84 and Bertha 70, at the time. They stayed at the ranch a while longer, before moving to Cottonwood.

The Army Corps of Engineers and the state of Idaho rebuilt the road and bridges in 1950, and installed flood control measures.

Cooper Bar is the bench on the left side of the river, across from the mouth of Grave Creek. Ed Taylor first ranched the flat, but left in 1909. Ben Cooper and his wife, Frances, settled there in 1908. Ben's first place was on the same side of the river, across from Pine Bar. He was born in California, and came to Idaho in 1880, with his father. Frances was from North Carolina. As early as 1903, the couple began running a band of sheep in the Buffalo Hump country. They moved to the bar and raised alfalfa, while running a ferry across the river, for four years.

Ben Cooper.

Frances Cooper.

When the Coopers bought Jimmy McBrady's homestead in 1908, up Graves Creek above Alex Roberts, Wallace and Doris Jarret took over the ferry at Cooper Bar. The Coopers developed the ranch into a sizeable cattle operation. Their daughter, Gladys McLaughlin, who was born on the river, still runs the cattle ranch at this writing.

The contour of a ditch line can be seen high on the hill down-river from Cooper Bar, on the west side. This is the Rice Creek ditch, which goes six miles up that stream to bring mining water around to Cooper Bar. It was constructed with Chinese labor.

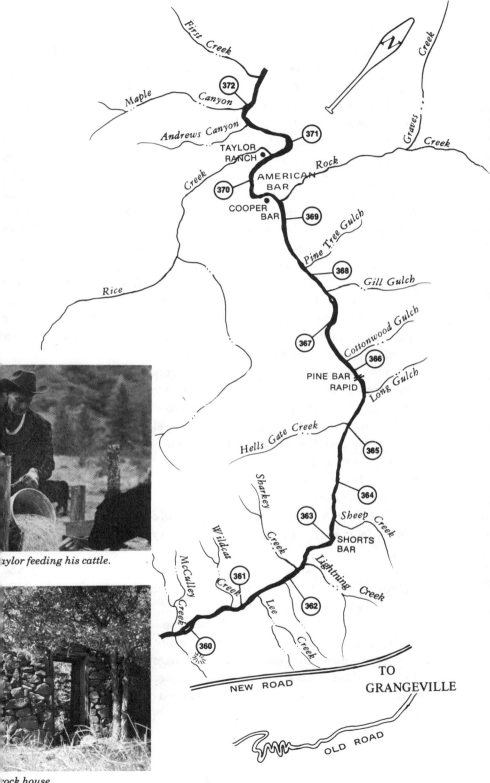

First Creek

372

Maple

Canyon

Andrews Canyon

371

Graves

Creek

Creek

TAYLOR
RANCH

AMERICAN
BAR

Rock

370

Creek

COOPER
BAR

369

Pine Tree Gulch

Rice

368

Gill Gulch

367

Cottonwood Gulch

366

PINE BAR
RAPID

Long Gulch

Hells Gate Creek

365

364

Sharkey

363

Sheep

Creek

SHORTS
BAR

Wildcat

Creek

Lightning

Creek

McCulley

361

Creek

Creek

362

Lee

Creek

360

NEW ROAD

TO
GRANGEVILLE

OLD ROAD

...aylor feeding his cattle.

...rock house.

Mile 370.6: **Rice Creek** flows out of the canyon on the right.

This stream, according to the late Elmer Taylor, received its appellation from the presence of Chinese working on the ditch.

The mouth of Rice Creek was an Indian camp site. It was homesteaded at an early date and the rights were purchased by Bill Eller. He sold the ranch in 1940 to Elmer and Eva Taylor.

From the time he was old enough to shave, Elmer Taylor lived on Salmon River. As far as can be learned, no rancher spent more time in the canyon. He was born in Amity, Oregon, (Wilamette Valley) in 1887. In 1908, he came to the river with Ben Reeves. Though under age, he filed a homestead at the mouth of lower Rock Creek near Flynn Creek. He later relinquished that claim.

Like a pony without a bridle, Elmer worked at different ranches along the river. He hired out to Bill and John Platt. He rode for Charley Beard. In 1914, he filed homestead papers on a place near Deer Creek, down-river. He called it "Smoky Hollow" because the winter fog would linger for days at a time. He married his wife, Eva Murdick of Lewiston, three years later.

They established title to the homestead, but feeling the isolation, sold to Pete Jensen and moved to Lewiston for three years. Then Elmer, and Eva's brother, Roy, decided to go into the cattle business at the lower Horse Shoe Bend on Billy Creek.

Elmer and Eva packed half-a-dozen hens, a rooster, and their personal belongings on a horse and came over four feet of snow through Forest and down to the river. Asa Jones crossed them in a boat at Billy Creek.

The Taylors began their cattle career with 36 head, acquired from Gilbert Wayne at Maloney Creek. They eventually had 450 head of stock.

Elmer worked ten years for the Fountain brothers: Billy and Volney. They had a large cow and horse business, headquartered at Cave Creek on the Snake River.

For 20 years they lived at Horse Shoe Bend, dependent on horse and trail for every necessity. Their land lay inside the south curve of the Horse Shoe. Supplies were boated across the river at Mahoney Creek to their pack string. Six seasons were spent herding sheep to provide needed revenue, while Roy worked on the ranch.

Elmer and Eva Taylor in the fall of 1930 on Glory and Spider. Eddie Lancaster, rear left, and Roy Murdick on the right. They had spent the day dehorning cattle.

They borrowed money to buy a hundred heifers, after obtaining a summer range near Boles. The Taylors broke cows to milk, using kicking hobbles and letting the calf suck until the milk came. They bought a Malotte cream separator on the installment plan, and took the cream to Boles, where it was put on the mail truck.

When the Taylors bought their ranch at Rice Creek, they were still busier than little dogs in tall oats. There was no bridge across the river, but a year's supply of grain and groceries could be trucked to the shore.

Their location was a stopping and crossing point for much of the area's cattle traffic. Eva and Elmer were always fair-weather side out, and so was their latch string. Theirs was an exceptional generosity, even in a country of traditional western hospitality. Visitors were frequent and welcome.

Death put the running iron on Elmer Taylor in November, 1977. He was still feeding cattle the last year of his life, and as long as there's a button on Job's coat, he'll be remembered as the archetypal Salmon River cowboy. At this writing, his wife, Eva, continues to maintain the renowned Taylor Ranch at Rice Creek.

The Taylor's pack stock moving out from Horse Shoe Bend in June of 1941.

Mile 371.2: **Ed and Lula Lancaster** were on the river in 1892, across from American Bar. They homesteaded the flat in 1904. Their ferry operated just below the bridge, where remnants of the cable can be observed. The Lancasters raised three children, one of whom drowned in the river.

The Lancaster ferry was in active service through most of the Twenties.

Elmer and Eva on their 60th wedding anniversary.

Mile 372.5: **First Creek** enters on the left. Roy Hunsacker had a homestead at the mouth of First Creek. The Hunsackers had another house at Second Creek.

Mile 372.8: **Second Creek** is on the left.

Mile 373.7: **Wickiup Creek** in the small draw on the left. Moughmer Point on the right, named for a cattle ranching family, one of whose members was killed in a quarrel with sheep men. Even in the Thirties, this ridge was leased with the stipulation no sheep would be grazed on it.

Mile 373.8: **Packers Creek** comes in on the right.

Mile 375.8: **Telcher Creek** flows down the drainage on the right from Keuterville Butte. It was named for a German immigrant, farmer, stockman and miner: Dedrick Telgher. He mined in Florence and Warren, then in 1866 took land on the Camas prairie. He was county commissioner, county assessor, and commissioner for the road from Grangeville to Meadows Valley.

The area at the mouth of the creek was homesteaded by Jack Martin and Eva Canfield. Eva was the widow of Sherm Canfield of the Doumecq Plains.

Mile 378.3: **Round Spring Creek** on the left.

Mile 379.6: **Mahoney Creek** runs in on the left.

Mile 380.1: **White House Bar,** the large sand bench on the right. The site has been heavily mined, with water provided by a reservoir above the cabin. The location is B.L.M. public land. It is the last sizeable campspot before Snow Hole Canyon.

Whitehouse Bar, looking downstream.

Mile 380.3: **Burnt Creek** comes in from the left. Clyde Ireland, an elderly miner, had a cabin next to the river here, and placered for gold.

Mile 380.8: **Home Sweet Home Creek** on the left.

Mile 382.5: **Rickman Creek** flows in on the left. The Rickman ranch extended along the river, above and below the creek, for almost a mile. Bobby Rickman was dragged to death by a horse and is buried on the flat above the river.

Soldier's Grave is three miles west of the ranch. When General Howard's soldiers were pursuing the Nez Perce, the volunteers from

Dayton, Washington Territory, caught up with the army there. During the night, a young lieutenant mistook one of his own blanket-wrapped guards for an Indian, and shot him.

Mile 384.5: **Snow Hole Rapid.** The run here is just right of center, but there is little room for error. It should be scouted from the left shore.

Jet-boat, center of photo, testing Snow Hole Rapid.

Mile 386.9: **Deep Creek** comes down on the right.

Mile 387.6: **Maloney Creek** is obvious on the right. The stream was baptized for an early Irish miner.

Bob Starrs and his wife homesteaded the property at the mouth of the creek. They sold their place in order to buy an upright steam engine and pump to sluice for gold. Mrs. Starrs had to gather the wood that furnished steam.

Lumber and supplies could be skidded down to the river on a drag road from the ridge above.

This area is fine Idaho winter range for cattle.

Maloney Creek represents the tip or front of the Oxbow. Carl Flynn and Elmer and Eva Taylor had holdings across the river, after Chance and Herschel Emmerick left.

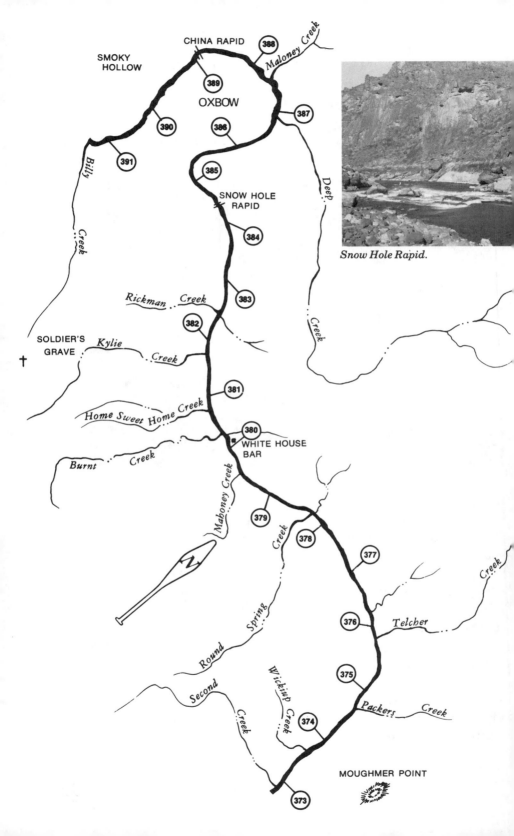

CHINA RAPID

SMOKY
HOLLOW

388

Maloney Creek

389

OXBOW

387

390

386

391

Billy

385

SNOW HOLE
RAPID

Creek

384

Deep

383

Rickman   Creek

382

Creek

SOLDIER'S
GRAVE

Kylie

†

Creek

381

Home Sweet Home Creek

380

WHITE HOUSE
BAR

Burnt   Creek

Mahoney Creek

379

378

377

N

Creek

376

Telcher

Round   Spring   Creek

375

Wickiup Creek

Second

374

Packers   Creek

Creek

373

MOUGHMER POINT

Snow Hole Rapid.

Mile 389: **China Creek Rapid.** The ledge causing this rapid is on the other side of a blind curve. While the run is clearly on the left, it may be a good idea to look at it the first time through.

Mile 390.8: **Everett Spaulding's** boat camp on the right.

Mile 391.6: **Billy Creek** enters from the left, at the foot of the Oxbow. Salmon River Billy, a Nez Perce Indian, lived on this site, where he planted apple trees long before the Nez Perce War. His son, Luke Billy, followed him to the location at a later date. Luke raised cattle until he sold out and moved to Lapwai.

There was a good ford at the eddy below the creek, which was used by Chief Joseph's tribe on their way to the reservation, and again following the White Bird battle, when being chased by Howard's soldiers. The ford has washed out.

Dan McPherson settled on the ranch; he was succeeded by Dave Gorman, an enormous Scotsman, who raised cattle here. When Dave died, his body was boated up to Mahoney Creek and sledded up the hill to Genesee for burial.

Bob and Asa Jones and Bill Platt all ran stock on the Billy Creek ranch, before it went to sheep men like Mr. Tolman and the Sloviaczek brothers.

The largest cattle operation on the lower Salmon was that of William T. Platt and his sons, John and Bill. At one time they ranged 1700 head on both sides of the river. The winter of 1919 was colder than an icicle's backbone, and cattle outfits like the Platts and the Wyatts never really recovered.

Elmer and Eva Taylor's "Smoky Hollow" was about a mile uphill, across the river from Billy Creek.

Mile 392.4: **Cottonwood Creek** comes in on the left bank. Indian George was the first man to farm this drainage. Mr. Goodnight and Bill Forgy started cattle ranching on the stream, and were followed by B. F. Taylor. Taylor packed mule strings to the area's mines and owned most of the creek.

Jim and Ed Wylie grazed sheep on the drainage until 1917, and were followed by the Van Pools and Bill Jones.

The cow camp settlement on the headwaters of the creek is known as "Flyblow," because of one camp cook's difficulties keeping any meat.

According to Frank McGrane's recollections recorded by Sister Alfreda Elsensohn, when Mrs. Asa Jones had a house there she tried to change the name by putting up an arch with the words "Willow Springs." She said she did "finally get one cowboy to call it 'Willow-Springs Flyblow.' " She also reported that on one occasion a stranger asked, "Is this the Fly-blowed Willows?"

Mile 393.7: **Deer Creek** enters the river on the right. Wes Dorchester developed the ranch on this bar and sold it in 1907 to John and Emma Platt. They put it under irrigation and raised four children here.

One spring the children, holding hands, crossed the foot-log bridge over turbulent Deer Creek and fell into the swollen stream. Elmer Taylor jumped in after them and succeeded in rescuing them.

The Platts sold out to sheep interests — Kemp and Bettison — shortly after the winter of 1919. They used the ranch as a lambing quarters.

Reed Glisby, a boy from Winchester, was hired as cook for the lambing crew, and was also paid to feed the orphan lambs. The lambs adopted Reed as their foster mother.

In the afternoon, when the Glisby boy finally had some spare time, he would wander down to Eagle Creek where he could visit with the young, and lovely Louise Rudolph.

The lambing crew would wait until he arrived at the Rudolph's, then they'd turn the 30 head of orphan lambs loose, and the animals would gambol down the trail after Reed, blatting and bleating. Louise was not impressed.

Three miles up Deer Creek, sheep man Andy Malam discovered the Deer Creek gold mine in 1899. With pick, shovel, and dynamite, he, George Horseman, and Ross Babcock worked it for several years.

Then the mine was taken over by the Lorang Family. Vince Lorang, who had placered between Deer and Maloney Creeks, interested W. J. and C. P. Orr in financing the lode. They incorporated the operation and bought out most of the shareholders.

Water was ditched from Deer Creek. A sawmill was established, cabins built, and a steam boiler was hauled down the drag trail from Winchester. There was a rock crusher, a Chilean ball mill, and Vanner belts to catch the concentrates.

The Orrs retained control until the early Twenties, when they went back east and sold their interests. Only the foundations marking the millsite are visible today.

The Deer Creek mine as it looked in 1915.

Mile 394: **Eagle Creek** drops in on the right. Mike Rudolph came to the river to mine in 1895, and stayed to raise his family. He planted an orchard below the creek and grew alfalfa for his stock. When neighbors needed help, Mike was always there before anyone had to ask.

The power line which can be seen on the ridge along the right side of the river, from Eagle Creek to Pot Creek, carries electricity from Hells Canyon Dam to Lewiston. The base of the poles is sheathed with metal to prevent them from burning in a grass fire.

The B.L.M. jeep road which begins near Lewiston comes down Eagle Creek and joins the river at this point.

Mile 396.3: **China Creek** enters from the right-hand canyon. The Cecil Rock family lived here, running their own band of sheep and working for Bettison and Kemp.

Len Kemp lost his life going up the creek to the community of Forest, for supplies. He was picking up mail from the neighbors as he went. Kemp was an experienced Salmon River trail rider, but he apparently made the pilgrim's error of dallying his lead rope around his saddle horn while he lit his pipe. He was found dead near the trail, with his boot sole torn off.

Mile 397.4: **Skeleton Creek** comes in on the left. The remains of a rock wall almost a hundred yards long can be seen on the right shore. This was the work of Seth "Sourdough" Jones and his son, Asa, assisted by some Chinese laborers.

Seth Jones was truly a pioneer on the Salmon River. Orphaned in New York at age ten, he came across the plains in 1853, to Oregon. He mined in California, lost 50 of his horses to Indians in Utah, returned to Illinois, where he married Jane Castle in 1858.

The two of them settled in California before moving to Florence over the Milner Trail. As Jane was the first white woman over the trail, Moses Milner refused to accept any payment from the wagon train.

The Jones settled on Camas Prairie in 1863, and built the first cabin there. They began general farming and stock raising. Their horse and cattle enterprise prospered — Jones shipped 650 head of cows to Montana. They had 10 children and 1300 acres of fine agricultural land.

Seth put the first cattle across the Salmon River the year after the Indian War. (He encountered two bands of Nez Perce warriors on June 13th, the year of the war, but they didn't bother him because he had refused to sign the reservation petition.) The rock wall was a means of getting the cattle to take to the river when he wanted to start them swimming across.

Sourdough had some hard luck with the first herd of cattle because they were new to the country. They encountered a hard winter and many of them starved — hence the name Skeleton Creek.

William Platt crossed cattle here in 1894, with a partner, Lew Barlow. They headquartered on the creek. Platt's sons, John and Bill, worked with him. Bill homesteaded here, and packed the flooring for his house down from the Doumecq Plains.

Mile 399.3: **Wapshilla Creek** flows in on the right. This stream was the home of the Nez Perce Wapshilla family for many years.

Ben and Julia Reeves developed a large ranch on the drainage. A drag road was cleared down the creek to the river in order to pack supplies to a mine on the west side.

Jackson Sundown was a Nez Perce Indian who married Cecilia Wapsheli, and worked on Ben Reeves' ranch.

Sundown was born in the Wallowa country of Oregon and was in the Nez Perce flight of 1877. He escaped from the Bear Paw battlefield into Canada, and reappeared in Culdesac, Idaho, a couple of years later.

Jackson was tall, of superb physique, and had the handsome features of his race. He entered local rodeos and his reputation grew rapidly. He competed in the Pendleton Round-up in 1915 and won second third place. In 1916, he tried again, and rode his way into the grand finals. On an outlaw bronc called Angel, he brought the capacity crowd to its feet yelling, "Sundown! Sundown! Ride 'em Sundown!" He had won the World Championship at the age of 53.

Blanket of the Sun, also called Jackson Sundown, photographed in 1908, age 42 years.

Mile 400: **Birch Creek** on the right.

Mile 401.7: **Flynn Creek** streams in on the left. This point marks the beginning of the Blue Canyon. The site on the left bank was settled by Charley Flynn, who used the creek water for mining purposes.

Charley Beard, who had run a harness shop in Lewiston, began a ranch on the location with his wife, Lizzie. They grew hay and raised cattle, finally selling in 1916, to Bill Platt. Burril Smith ran sheep in the area in 1921, then it reverted to cattle ranching and is so used by the Heckman brothers.

The Len Kemp family were sheep ranchers who occupied the land across the river from Flynn Creek. They trailed their bands clear to Buffalo Hump for summer forage, until they acquired the Deer Creek range. (Len was killed in the accident on China Creek.)

Mile 402: **Rock Creek** is on the left.

Mile 402.3: **Miller Creek** to the left.

Mile 403: **The Slide Rapid.** This whitewater can be anticipated by the obvious rock fall on the left side of the canyon and by observing the Idaho Power transmission lines which cross the river just upstream from the rapid.

The rapid was rougher than a stucco bathtub 30 years ago. It can be dangerously severe during the high flows of spring runoff.

Mile 403.7: **Pot Creek** on the left.

Mile 404: Another Army Corps of Engineers' dam site.

Mile 406: **Eye of the Needle Rapid.** Even a camel could make it.

Mile 406.6: **Pullman mine** on the left. The mine was more prospect hole than producer.

Mile 407: **Confluence** with the Snake River.

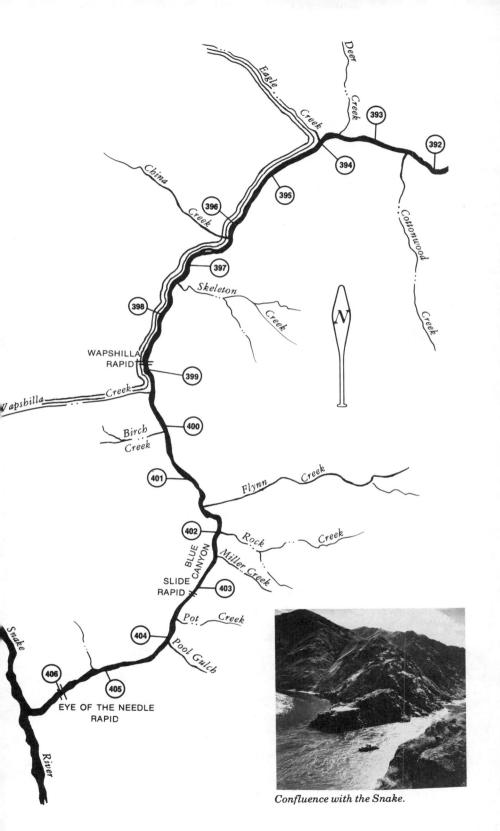

Eagle ... Creek

Deer ... Creek

393

392

394

395

Cottonwood ... Creek

China ... Creek

396

397

Skeleton ... Creek

398

N

WAPSHILLA
RAPID

399

Wapshilla ... Creek

Birch ... Creek

400

401

Flynn ... Creek

402

Rock ... Creek

BLUE
CANYON

Miller Creek

SLIDE
RAPID

403

Pot ... Creek

404

Pool Gulch

Snake

406

405

EYE OF THE NEEDLE
RAPID

River

Confluence with the Snake.

Epilogue

Loren Eiseley wrote, "It is the stream, and not the clashing boulders, that makes up life." After 400 miles along the River of No Return, patterns become apparent.

A man named Charley, and a woman, whose name has been lost in undeserved obscurity, arrive in the canyon and build a cabin. Together they raise a family, plant garden and orchard, mine and trap. Love and rancor touch their struggle and that of their neighbors. Aspirations are realized; hopes plowed under.

The children were drawn elsewhere, the cabins burned, yellow pines grow in their fields. None today would willingly endure their hardships, and in retrospect, their accomplishments seem extraordinary.

A water ditch, a fruit tree, a grave — remind us of their efforts. They were remarkable and magnanimous people, with lives rooted in split-rail values. Hopefully, the stories held here will contribute in some measure toward their rightful eulogy.

> "You passers by
> Who share my journey,
> You move and change,
> I move and am the same;
> You move and are gone,
> I move and remain."
> River God's Song,
> Anne Ridler

Bibliography

Bailey, Robert G., *The River of No Return*, revised edition. Lewiston: R. G. Bailey Printing Company, 1947.

Beal, Merrill D., *"I Will Fight No More Forever,"* Chief Joseph and the Nez Perce War. Seattle: University of Washington Press, 1963.

Brown, Mark H., *The Flight of the Nez Perce*. New York: Capricorn Books, 1971.

Elsensohn, Mary A., *Pioneer Days in Idaho County*. 2 vols. Caldwell: Caxton Printers, 1947-51.

Gizycka, Eleanor, *"Diary on the Salmon River,"* Field and Stream Magazine, XXVIII, No. 1 (May, 1923), 18-20, 113-15, and XXVIII No. 2 (June, 1923), 187-88, 276-80.

Illustrated History of North Idaho, San Francisco: Western Historical Publishing Co., 1903.

Irving, Washington, *Adventures of Captain Bonneville, U.S.A.* Norman: University of Oklahoma Press, 1961.

Josephy, Alvin M., *Nez Perce Indians and the Opening of the Northwest*. New Haven: Yale University Press, 1971.

Lockhart, Caroline, *"The Wildest Boat Ride in America,"* The Outing Magazine, LIX, No. 5 (February, 1912), 515-24.

McWhorter, Lucullus Virgil, *Hear Me, My Chiefs!* Caldwell: Caxton Printers, 1940.

——————————— *Yellow Wolf, His Own Story*. Caxton Printers, 1952.

Miller, Lee, *"The Sheep and the Sign,"* The Outing Magazine, LVIII, No. 4 (July, 1921), 166-67.

Mulkey, Selway L., *"Place Names of Lemhi County, Idaho,"* (thesis, University of Idaho, 1970).

Peebles, John J., *"Rugged Waters: Trails and Campsites of Lewis and Clark in the Salmon River Country,"* Idaho Yesterdays, VIII, No. 2 (Summer, 1964).

Shenon, P. J. and J. C. Reed, *"Down Idaho's River of No Return,"* National Geographic Magazine, LXX (July, 1936), 94-136.

Shoup, George Elmo, *History of Lemhi County.* Boise: Idaho State Library, 1969. (Published originally in the Salmon *Recorder Herald* May 8-October 23, 1940).

Smith, Elizabeth M., *A History of Salmon National Forest.* Ogden: U.S.D.A., Forest Service, 1971.

Work, John, *The Snake Country Expedition of 1830-31.* Norman: University of Oklahoma, 1971.

Yarber, Esther, *Land of the Yankee Fork.* Salt Lake City: Publishers Press, 1963.

——————*Stanley Sawtooth Country.* Publishers Press, 1976.

Index

314

315

THE AUTHORS

Johnny Carrey was born on the South Fork of the Salmon. He has been a cattle and sheep rancher all his life. John makes his home on Little White Bird Ridge, where he lives with his understanding and hospitable wife, Pearl. They started in the harness together in 1939 "For better or for worse" — "Mostly it's been for the better," laughs Johnny. Pearl can't help but smile.

Cort Conley is an Idaho river guide.

COLOPHON

Typeface: Century Schoolbook 10/14
            Century Schoolbook Italic 8/10
Paper: 70# Coated Shasta Gloss
Layout: Fletcher R. and Julie Sliker, Evergreen, Colorado
Front Cover: Boyd Norton
Rear Cover: David Sumner
Typography: B & J Typesetting
Printing: Joslyn/Morris, Inc., Boise, Idaho